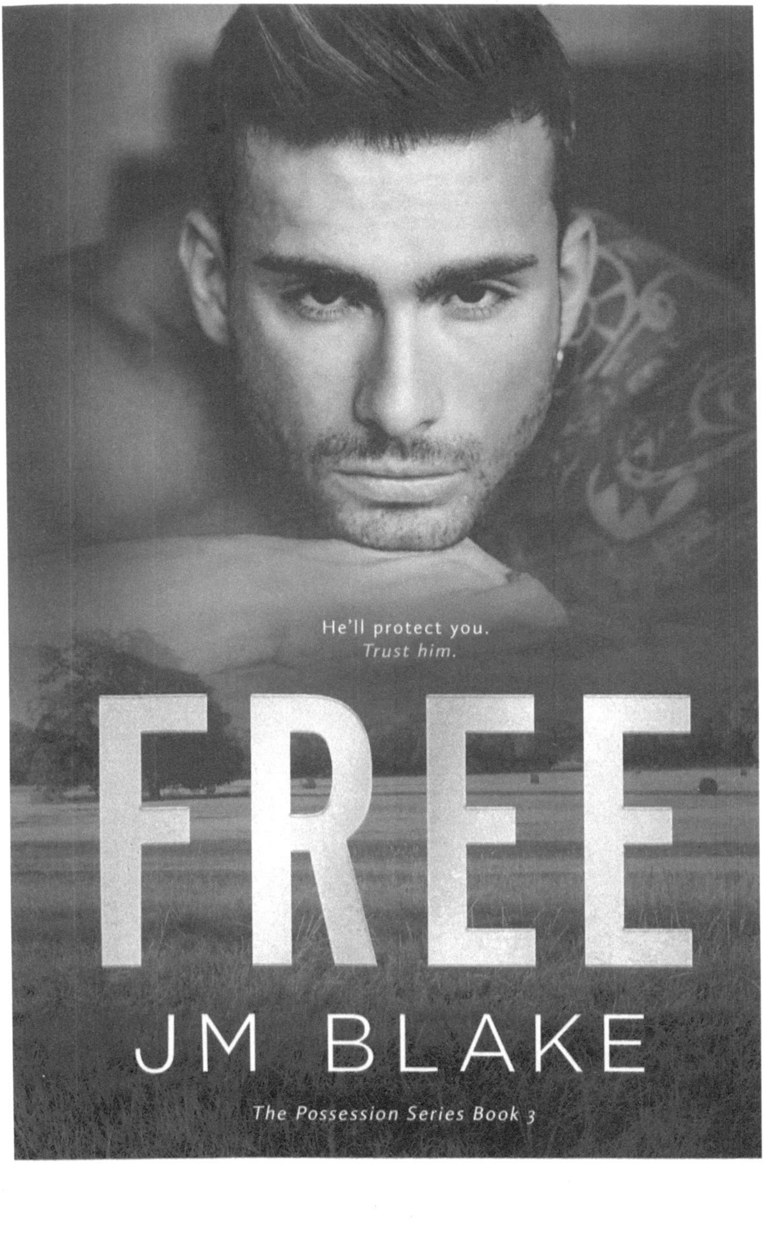
He'll protect you.
Trust him.
FREE
JM BLAKE
The Possession Series Book 3

FREE

THE POSSSESSION SERIES
BOOK THREE

JM BLAKE

COVER OKAY CREATIONS
SARAH HANSEN

JM BLAKE PUBLISHING

CONTENTS

STEM

A portion of the proceeds from "The Possession Series," will be going toward NGCP, The National Girls Collaborative Project (NGCP) 'which brings together organizations committed to informing and encouraging girls to pursue careers in science, technology, engineering, and mathematics (STEM).'

For more information on NGCP or to donate on your own, click here: NGCP or go directly to their website— https://ngcproject. org/about-ngcp.

Thank you for supporting our future. #girlsinstem

To my Sydney- for spending countless hours finding the artist from the Barnes and Noble bathroom artwork and buying me a replica. You remain my ride or die.

To our Texas family—M, K and Chicken. We love you! And K...are you happy now?

Hello Reader—

Thank you so much for jumping on the ride that is in front of you. This book is the **third** *in The Possession Series. If you haven't read the first two,* **don't freak out.** *This book operates on a parallel timeline, so you can go back and read the others when you are done. You won't be missing anything, though, because you are reading slightly out of order, you may pick up on clues in a very interesting way. I'd love to hear your feedback if this is your path—and where you think this saga is going.*

If you picked up this book hoping for a standalone, I have some news: I love a cliffhanger. Yeah, yeah, I know there are a huge swath of readers who HATE (with the stamp of a foot) HATE cliffhangers.

Personally, I love them.

Reading them and writing them.

It pisses my readers off in a big way, but I always deliver satisfying conclusions.

Eventually.

For those of you who are still mad at me because of how Book 2 ended, guess what—you aren't going to be any happier with me here. But, I SWEAR TO YOU— on the five pints of Chunky Monkey in my freezer— that you will be 100% satisfied by the end of Book 4. You know how much I love these characters, and my girls deserve their happiness.

Anyway, buckle up, buttercup. Not only is it an area I haven't

PART ONE

"I'm gonna run to you
Yeah I'm gonna run to you
'Cause when the feelin's right I'm gonna stay all night
I'm gonna run to you"
—Bryan Adams

CHAPTER 1
VIVI

You either love Las Vegas, or you don't.

Love, as in deep in your soul, craves all-you-can-eat buffets, lives for the unrelenting sun, jumps up to join drunk off their asses tourists in spontaneous sidewalk dance challenges, and enjoys super tight traffic jams—love.

Or. You hate it.

Once was enough for you. Your friends threw up all weekend, you lost your rent money in a dodgy casino, got groped in the club, and that buffet gave you food poisoning. Excessive cigarette smoke permanently damaged your voice, and an Elvis impersonator stole your cell phone. You never want to come back to this overbaked hell hole again.

Me? I'm in the middle (leaning toward the hate side though.)

There are things I like about Vegas, like the food, people-watching, and the pool scene. Give me an air-conditioned mall and a hot cabana boy, and I'm all set.

As for the things I hate—well, let's just say that some of the items on that list have happened to me.

So when my best friend, Riley (who incidentally loooooooves Vegas), invited me to tag along to a convention she was attending, I hesitated —big time.

"Come on, Vivi! Who turns down an all-expense-paid trip to Vegas? It's VEGAS, baby." She did some sort of weird hair flip and a finger snap. "We won't do anything crazy, I promise."

Sure we won't. I think we are still banned from that one place.

"Riley..." my voice sounded pitiful, a mix of horror and absolute terror. "The last time you said that, I wound up in a cast for a month." I held up my arm and twisted it at an odd angle. "And you still have that scar on your stomach."

"It's a quick few days—we will be home on Sunday night. Vivi, c'monnnnn," she moans in exasperation. "You used to be so much more adventurous than this!" Her pretty face roils in exasperation.

"Yeah, when? It's been a long time since I have wanted to do anything edgy, and you know it. I nearly fucked everything up, Riles."

"So maybe you got into some shit once or twice. We are young; we *should* be fucking things up." She shrugs in that adorable/annoying way that normally gets her out of everything.

"First of all, Riley Mansour, we ain't that young. And it's not once or twice, either. It's every freakin' time we go anywhere, and you know it."

"It's not *every* time..." She suddenly finds my recycled countertops fascinating.

"Yes, it is."

"We had a lovely time when we went to Costa Rica."

"We got on the wrong bus because you thought the driver was cute, and I got bit by that big fucking spider. My ass swelled up, and I could only sit sideways for a month."

"Well, ok, I forgot about that. New York was a grand adventure, though."

"Riley, we got stuck on the subway for six hours, and I had to pee into a cup in front of thirty-five strangers. And that weird man kept the cup."

"Oh. Yes, there was that. What about Los A...."

"Don't you even think about bringing up Los Angeles. Or New Orleans. Or Milan." Her mouth clamped into a thin line as she mean-mugged me. That look stopped affecting me years ago.

I've been friends with Riley since the fifth grade. We met when her family moved to Seattle from Miami in the middle of the school year. Her father is a big-time doctor who took over a high-profile spot at Virginia Mason and had to report immediately. Her mom wanted the kids to finish the school year, but Dr. Mansour wanted his family with him, regardless. So Riley and her two brothers barreled into our elementary school like rocks in an avalanche.

They were wild—all of them.

On Riley's first day, she exploded into the classroom, a wild dervish of tangled blonde braids, gleaming white teeth, and scraped-up knees. She plopped into the seat beside me, holding out a dirty hand. "Hi, I'm Riley Starla Mansour. I'm pleased to meet you." I tentatively held out my hand, and she pumped twice with a crooked smile. "I'm Vivienne."

"Cool. Let's be best friends, ok? I like your hair. There's a lot of it. And your shirt is cool, too." She scooted her chair a little closer and tugged on my sleeve. "Vivienne is a big name. You got a nickname or something?"

"My dad calls me Vivi, though my mom hates it." I stared at her pierced ears and rubbed on my naked lobes. My mom was very old school in many ways; pierced ears were akin to the devil to her.

"Really? Well, I like it. Imma call you Vivi from now on. Where are we sitting at lunch?" She prattled on and asked me a million questions, even after our teacher Mrs. Sullivan shushed us a dozen times. She strutted straight over to the popular kids' table at lunch and held court like she'd been doing it for years. She and her brothers were all a little over one year apart, so they were all in the same school for the time being. They sat with us too, both loud and funny, with a large swatch of mischievous. They started a spitball fight twenty minutes into the period, and I couldn't help but scream in horror and delight along with everyone else, which is why I got sent into detention with the Mansour kids two hours later. It wasn't the last time Riley and I got into trouble together.

"I swear to God, Riles, you better not pull me into any shit this weekend. I have a piece that I need to finish and sketches due to the university in a week." I gave her my sternest look, which she brushed off with an eye roll and grin. I'm curled up on the couch, waiting for her to finish the margaritas for our weekly Netflix night.

"Yeah, yeah, the artist must work and all that shit," she mocks with a terrible British accent. "It'll do you good to get out of that garage for a little bit. Your skin is starting to look like a pasty shade of dead." She prances over to the couch and scoots herself into an opposite spot, our feet touching in the middle. She hands me my drink, complete with a swirly straw.

I take a deep sip, the sweet tingle sliding down my throat. "I am not that pale, fool. And I get out all of the time."

I don't, but whatever.

Riley snorted so hard that she almost choked. "No, you don't. I don't know what to do when you have your next show. I'll have to find a new best friend for a few months."

It was my turn to snort. "Well, maybe you can start interviewing when we're in Vegas. Prostitution is legal there, isn't it?" Her loud screech makes me laugh, and I duck the pillow thrown at me. "It'll be fun, Viv. Innocent fun. I'll wow them at the convention, and you can park your pasty ass at the spa: a little dinner, a bit of the pool. Then we come back home, and life goes back to normal. No reason to worry," she winks at me and grabs the remote. I glared at her in suspicion, but she won't meet my eyes.

I should've known better.

There was no way Riley Starla Mansour would have a tame time. Ever.

Sure, the first day was great.

Riley is a medical rep who specializes in non-invasive heart surgery equipment. She is unsurprisingly the top producer in her company, and it's normal for her to attend conventions where she woos both the public and private sectors. She had meeting after meeting, including a late dinner with a military representative. I was on my own most of the day, so I took my sketch pad down to the grotto and finished some of my work. I soaked up some SPF one thousand sun, and when the pool got a little rowdy, I ordered room service up to our suite. Riley texted that she was meeting up with some other reps for a few drinks, and I fell asleep early on those high-thread-count sheets.

I woke up the following day, and she was already gone; day two of the convention is when the high-profile deals are made. So I went to the spa, where the masseuse clucked her teeth at the state of my back muscles. She worked out every kink and knot, and I won't deny that I fell asleep drooling. Riles texted me while I was getting dressed, telling me where to meet her for a late dinner. I ignored her plea to wear something "steamy" and slid on my favorite black jumpsuit. The restaurant was in a hotel further down the strip, so I hailed a rideshare, not sure I could make it in my high heels that far.

The driver was chatty, and we both laughed at a group of bridesmaids in thongs and sashes running across the boulevard. I thanked him for the ride and let Riley know I had arrived. She messaged back quickly to meet her at the bar, and I narrowed my eyes in thought. I crept into the restaurant, and sure enough, Riley was surrounded by about ten guys at the bar. Judging by their suits, they must be convention attendees too. I sigh deep in my soul and creep forward. Two of the guys turn as I walk up, and both do a double-take.

"Riley, you didn't tell us you had a beautiful sister." I give the biggest internal eye roll in history.

I can't count the number of times that people have said that. It's a testament to how unobservant humans are—Riley and I look nothing alike. She's tall and willowy- in heels, she is an absolute killer. Her skin has a natural tan that never fades, and her sparkling eyes are a rich hazel color.

I'm about seven inches shorter, curvier, and have blue eyes.

She is blonde by birth—I'm blonde by bottle.

Her chin is elegant and round—I have the dreaded butt chin, the middle dented with a giant dimple.

And yet people insist that we are related.

Ugh.

I slither through the crowd and plant myself next to her, signaling the bartender desperately. I'm not good in situations like this—and I'm really not good at what I can tell is coming next.

"So...," One of the suits maneuvers his way next to my side with a smirk. "What can I get you to drink?"

He's not a bad-looking guy in a cookie-cutter type of way, all tight pique polo and custom suit jacket. However, the over-confident film over his eyes sets my teeth on edge. "Nothing, thank you. I'm just going to have water."

The bartender overhears me and slides a sweating glass a

few inches from my elbow. Cookie-Suit smiles wider and leans in closer. "Sweet. I love a girl who can pace herself. We might have a long night ahead of us." His breath tells me that he is definitely not pacing himself. I fight the grimace I can feel growing and crowd closer to Riley. She turns her head and, seeing that I am imitating a third set of limbs, makes a deft move that effectively cuts me off from everyone else while still making me part of the group.

"Guys, this is my best friend, Vivi. Vivi, these are the guys." She gestures her hands at them dismissively while I wave awkwardly. The whole lot of them are staring at us like juicy seals surrounded by starving killer whales, and I gulp loudly. Riley snickers softly and grabs my hand. "Thanks for the drinks, guys. We have reservations to make." They all groan in disappointment, but she blows them kisses and sashays away, pulling me along like a downed kite.

"You can breathe now, weirdo. They weren't going to bite you, you know." She laughs as we walk through the casino to a swanky place on a mezzanine. The maitre'd shows us to our table, pushing our chairs and draping napkins over our laps.

"I know it, but I still hate that shit. I'm no good at that stuff, Riles. I never know what to say. I'm not clever like you are." I sip the wine slid in front of me and shrug.

"Vivi, you are the smartest, most talented woman I know. You have every man that meets you willing to eat out of the palm of your hand, and yet your instinct is to throw the food at them and run. I'll never understand it." She sits back in her chair, slim arms crossed over her chest in judgmental affection.

"It's not every man, fool. And I wouldn't run if I thought they were interested in me as a person and not a fuck doll. That guy back there had my bra size figured out in ten seconds flat. I felt like a cheap piece of meat. And his eyes weren't right." I shudder as she throws her hands up in exasperation.

"Vivi, what do you expect? You are a stupidly gorgeous woman with a banging body. No amount of baggy material can hide it, despite what you think. Any red-blooded man that spots you will want to know your bra size. And how are they going to get to know you if you won't talk to them? And don't get me started on the eye thing...." She ticks off her points by finger and ends with a finger snap.

"Have I ever been wrong about the eye thing?" I fling back. "Craig the psycho mailman, Rodney the Rat, that guy from Colombia City...." I tick off my own list as she bursts out laughing.

Ever since I was little, I have had this weird ability to read people's eyes. Not in a tarot card, tea leaves type of way, but a remarkable instinct. I can meet someone for the first time and tell if I can trust them or not, if they are good people, or if there is something dark inside of them. My dad always said it was the artist in me, a particular way of dissecting a face. Regardless, I never ignore the feelings I get—and ninety percent of the time, neither does Riley, though she loves to tease me.

"All I'm saying is that you've got to chop down those giant redwoods surrounding your vagina at some point. That poor girl is probably oxygen-deprived." Her voice carries over to the table next to us, luckily filled with women, who snicker loudly. I hiss at her and throw my napkin at her face. "Will you shut up? They probably think you mean my pubic hair, you ass."

She giggles uncontrollably, and I eventually join in. The girls at the following table introduce themselves; soon enough, Riley and I have been invited to a new club with them. They slip us two VIP passes, which Riley squeals at —me not so much—and promises to see them later. I open my mouth to object and am scowled right out of my shoes.

"Don't even think about it. We are going." Dammit.
God, I hate Vegas.

I sip my club soda and glare at the dance floor for the thousandth time.

After an excellent dinner (Riley knows me well enough to know that filling my belly is the way to my surrender), we rushed back to the hotel so that Riles could change out of her black business suit. She tried to get me to change into some scandalously small piece of fabric masquerading as a dress, but she gave up once my eye started twitching. My tried and true jumpsuit will be just fine, thank you. Somehow Riley yanked and pulled a piece of red elastic into an outfit (yes, I made her do the bend-over test. Besties and all that) and slipped on a pair of matching stilettos. Her naturally straight blonde hair was slick —shiny, delicate lips painted crimson like a siren. My one concession to her pleading was a quick dab of mascara and clear gloss, though she grumbled again about how pale I was. Once we hit the hotel lobby, a love-struck concierge hustled over, offering us the use of the VIP car service. Riley flicked a lock of hair over her shoulder with a giant smile and thanked the poor guy with a syrupy sweet voice. I rolled my eyes until I could see back to Seattle, shaking my head at the wink she gave me.

I'm not falling for it this time, sista.

The new club is at the north end of the Strip, where there are surprisingly large tracts of open land among the older, dustier hotels. The limo driver drops us off in front of a sleek white building where sunburned tourists are mixed with scantily clad club-goers, and even a few 'just married' couples. A topless male valet hands Riley out with a flourish and me with slightly less enthusiasm. There is a prominent metal figure in the center of the driveway, and before I can examine it further, Riley drags me inside.

"We are here to have fun, Vivi. If I let you near that statue, you'll be here until the morning." She keeps pulling at me until we reach a dark, pulsing hallway, lights already flashing from a distance. She hands over our gifted passes, and a shadowy bouncer directs us to *another* hallway where *another* bouncer awaits. He examines our passes with a flashlight while demanding our identification. He alternates the light between the cards and our faces before slipping glow-in-the-dark bracelets tightly onto our wrists.

"Sisters?" He raises a brow at us- Riley grinning like a loon and me shaking my head in disgust.

"Gee, what gave it away?" Riley snorts at my sweetly sarcastic response, though the guy looks confused. I stamp past him, with Riley on my heels.

"I'm sure in the dark we look alike, Viv," she shouts above the music. The whole floor is packed, with the oversized round bar dominating the space. Several booths are scattered and strategically placed so that while there is an illusion of privacy, you can still see other people. The DJ is suspended by a cabled stage directly over the balcony, red neon lights strobing with every movement he makes. There are dozens and dozens of bodies writhing and squirming, some on beat, some not.

"This place is hell on earth."

"What was that, Vivi?" Riley is already jiggling inside her shoes, hips twitching like an electric shock coursing through her system. The "Toxic/Pony" remix starts blasting through the speakers, and she looks at me pleadingly. I sigh deep in my soul and hold up my hand for her clutch. She squeals and practically throws it at me as she grinds her way to the dance floor. She glances back briefly, and I point at the bar while she nods happily. I find an empty seat and ask the central casting bartender for a club soda.

That was two hours ago.

Since then, Riley has made three brief appearances, one to slam back a series of shots with two guys, another to secrete her phone on her person, and another to take a sip of water. In between, I have had to fend off a whole of host men who either thought I needed company or thought I could give them an in with my best friend, who is the life of the party.

Two of the guys were pretty decent though, not batting a lash when I solemnly explained that I was allergic to liquids and the containers they came in. The third and fourth were comically opposite; one with shifty beady eyes and a wiry, nervous body. His hair was double-gelled, flakes flying off with every gesture of his head. I watched as one landed on the rim of my glass and barely held back my gasp of horror. I shook my head wildly and scooted my chair back as far as possible without toppling over.

"Say you wouldn't wanna put in a word with your friend, would ya?" He hiccups, HICCUPS- ambling off before I can even answer him.

I sigh some more.

The bartender babysits me with sympathy and doesn't blink when I ask him for a pen and a stack of napkins. I stare at him hard for a few seconds before quickly sketching out a drawing of him. I hand it to him, and he grins in delight. I smile slightly as he tapes it to the wall by the cash register. He slides me another club soda, and I spend another hour plucking out faces and bodies to draw.

Guy Four is giant all over; huge head, thick neck, big feet. Everything. His beefy arms are straining against his shirt as he does the worst fist pump dance I have ever seen. I must have said it out loud because he leans in close and whispers, "You wanna see where else I'm huge?"

I can feel my lips quivering and really try to hold it in but fail. A honking laugh pops out of my throat and won't stop coming. His face turns murderous for a moment before he scrapes me with a look that should shoot me into the sun. I'm still snickering as he stalks away, and I quickly draw him with his square face in a pout. I show it to the bartender, who also cracks up and tapes that one to the wall. I glance to my right and see a guy smiling at me—in that way. You know which way. The one that tells you that this guy is about to lay the creepiest vibe on you imaginable, all Ken doll harmless, while the hair on your arms stands up in warning.

"Your pretty talented and pretty, sweetie." (SWEETIE??) "Think you could make one for me?" I scowl at him while an evil smile stretches across my face. The pen moves quickly over the napkin before I toss the finished product to him. His smarmy face creases in disgust before he glares at me coldly. He stands up slowly before crumbling the napkin and throwing it to the floor.

"Bitch," he spits out before taking one last look at my face. I raise my eyebrows in question as he follows in Guy Fours' direction. My friend, the bartender (his name is Thorin. I asked him if his parents were Lord Of The Rings fans, and he just smiled at me mysteriously,) whisks away my empty glass, replacing it with a wink. I'm starting to get hungry, wondering how tacky it would be if I got pizza service delivered to the bar, when I see a movement out of the corner of my eye. A strong, tanned hand smoothes the crumpled napkin, a deep chuckle dancing across my skin.

"I can't decide what's worse— that you made him a worm with a widow's peak or that you made him a worm with horns *and* a widow's peak." There's an underlying teasing note to the voice, a hint of familiarity. I keep my eyes on my phone, but my mouth ticks a little in satisfaction.

"Probably the teeth. I made sure to add that chipped fang he's got in the front," I sip my fizzy water.

A loud laugh pops over the music, slightly hoarse but rich and natural. Against my better judgment, I take a peek and freeze in my seat.

So here's the thing. Remember how I'm not good with men? Oh, I have male friends and colleagues, and I'm super close with Riley's brothers, but actual hit-on-you men?

I suck.

The man sitting by my side is everything I panic over. He's tall—even sitting, he towers over me. His dark hair is thick and straight, cut short on the sides but long enough to tug on. His face—Jesus— his face is a chiseled combination of complex masculinity and boyish charm—with plenty of confidence sprinkled in. His eyes are liquid brown with abundant, plush eyelashes and brows, nose straight. His lips are thin yet shapely, and they quirk in amusement as I pick him apart. He's clean-shaven, skin smooth and unblemished. I'm sure my mouth is open like a flopping carp. I quickly take in the rest, a fitted jacket over a slim t-shirt, matching pants clinging to his muscular thighs. I gulp loudly and face forward again. There is no way a man this beautiful isn't either taken or up to no good.

"Maybe I can get you to autograph this? I'm sure it'll be worth something someday." He slightly waves the white-inked paper at me, "And since you never work in print, I can claim exclusivity."

My head snaps around, and I stare at him. "What do you mean I never work in print?"

His filthy gorgeous head tilts, and his smile spreads; damn, his teeth are perfect too. "You are V. Woods, aren't you? I was at your last showing in New York. And I would never forget a face like yours."

Though I try to brush it off, my whole head flames up like a Roman candle. "Um, yes?"

His eyes crinkle—dammit, he has the crinkle thing—and

he rests his head on a fist. "Sorry if I just made this awkward. I'm just a huge fan of your work, and I'm just shocked you manage to fly under the radar the way that you do. You didn't even have a headshot on your program."

"Yeah, I don't go to the showings for publicity; I just like to hear what people think. There are few enough women metal sculptors, and I want my work to speak for itself. I'm almost never recognized anywhere."

He nods solemnly, though his eyes are aggressively flitting across my face. "I understand that. I only figured out who you were when two critics from the *New York Times* were discussing a piece, and you looked murderously at one of them. Only the artist would look at someone like that," he chuckled. "I asked the curator if it was you, and he confirmed. You disappeared before I could meet you, and now here you are. Right in my clutches."

I remember those critics too. One of them asked me to get him a drink and then to meet him in the men's room. Grrrrrrr. We chat briefly about some of my past work, and I tell him about my current commission. He's funny as well as a heart-breaker. Ugh. Lethal combination.

After a few minutes, my phone vibrates insistently on the counter, and I swipe it open absently.

> Riley: WHO IS THAT????

> Riley: Whatever he wants u to do—DO IT. ALL OF IT!!!!

> Riley: OMG that body! Please tell me you aren't snarling at him???

> Riley: VIVI????? ANSWER ME!

I look toward the dance floor and see Riley gesturing at me like a crazy person. I snicker and type back:

Vivi: He knows who I am. We are just chatting

Riley: Girlllll. Chatting would be the last thing
on my mind. And he is looking at you like you
are a Snickers that satisfies.

Riley: I think he has an axe big enough to
chop down those trees you've got growing, u
know where…

Vivi: RILEY!!

Riley: Chop Chop Chop!!!!!!

I glare at her on the floor as she makes obnoxiously awkward chopping motions with both arms. I snort loudly and glance at him. He is watching me intently; for once, I'm not creeped out.

"Friend?" He nods at Riley.

Ohhhhh points, points, points he gets for not asking if she is my sister. "Best friend. She's here for a conference, and I tagged along, though I have weird feelings about Vegas."

"Sounds like a story I'd love to hear. Do you want to get out of here? I promise I'm harmless." His smile says he's full of crap, but I grin anyway.

"I don't even know your name. And we try not to leave each other if the other has been drinking," I shrug apologetically.

"I understand. My name is Trace, by the way. Trace Scanlan. I'm six foot two and weigh two hundred and ten pounds. I'm thirty-one years old, single, and my teeth are all my own. I work for a tech firm and split my time between the Bay and Seattle. I'm an only child, and I'm allergic to pineapple. I already know that you are an outstanding artist, and your first name starts with a V, hopefully not Veronica, as that was the first girl who broke my heart." His dark brows shoot up in expectation, waiting.

"What if I say that it is Veronica?" I tease him gently with a grin.

"That's my favorite name in the whole world."

I burst out laughing and shook my head. I grab my phone again and type.

> Vivi: He wants me to leave with him, and shit do I want to.

> Riley: WHAT? If you don't leave right now, I will KILL YOU. CHOP!!!

> Vivi: Sober sister, remember?

> Riley: I will leave right now. MEN LIKE THAT DO NOT EXIST.

> Riley: I am not even drunk. And I'm taking the limo. I'll be fine.

> Riley: Bye! Use condoms!

I feel a whirl of wind and see the fleeing back of my best friend as she waves her clutch over her head in triumph. Trace cracks up next to me; his smile widens in victory.

"Ready....?" He waits with his hand out for mine.

"Vivi. My name is Vivi."

CHAPTER 2
TRACE

Vivienne Micheline Duplantier to be precise.

The only child of Denis Duplantier and Suzanne Duplantier neé Barban.

She was raised in Seattle and only left when she attended RISD, while her best friend, Riley Starla Mansour, attended Brown University a mile away. Both girls went home after graduation, briefly moving into the same condo building.

Up-and-coming metal sculptor, very much growing in demand as her pieces become more prominent. Last year she netted over a quarter of a million dollars in sales and the promise of more to come with her latest project.

I spotted her at once, though I would have noticed her immediately without the benefit of studying her file. While Riley is a bright, flashing firecracker—all long limbs and slim figure—Vivienne is a slow-burning stick of dynamite. Though I was expecting it, she's petite with a bundle of abundant curves and hollows. She's probably one of the most beautiful women I have ever seen, objectively. Her eyes are an azure blue, tinted with the tiniest hint of green, high intense cheekbones, and that mouth.

That mouth.

A man could go insane dreaming of ways to use those plump, deep pink lips. Her skin is luminous and clear, though a trifle pale, and the unprofessional part of me wants to nibble on that dimpled chin. Her thick, unruly honey-blonde hair tumbles in a million directions, landing slightly above that delectable ass.

I watched her from only two seats away, her determination to stay in a self-imposed bubble working in my favor. A few of the assholes who approached her were indeed pigs- one even attempting to slip something in her drink. The others were of my doing—wanting her to be so repulsed that my smooth introduction would go over like a warm blanket. My men occupied her friend on the floor, though I knew enough about their relationship to know that Miss Mansour would favor my pursuit.

I've been ordered to use 'any means necessary' to get her to do what we desperately need from her. My boss told me that while dropping pictures of her one by one on the table. Some were regular action shots, though the last few were more intimate and candid.

I got the hint.

My name *is* Trace. But everything else is a dark, brutal, conniving lie. In my line of work, meeting people on a lie is an everyday occurrence. They roll off my tongue like slick, oily rain that permeates everything they touch. I memorized every inch and word of her file, studying it until I came up with the perfect plan. The rest was a given, of course. I'm always chosen for assignments like this because of my looks. I've weaponized them enough in the past, and little Miss Vivienne is no less susceptible.

I could see she was attracted to me and maybe even flustered by the attention. Her sweet uncertainty tweaked the guilt in my gut, but I buried it deep down and pushed on. I had about twenty tricks up my sleeve, but as expected, Miss Mansour swooped in and helped make her decision. Her vivid eyes searched mine for assurance, and I ensured that mine bled absolute sincerity. She took my hand with a giant smile, and I tightened my grip around her slim fingers, murmuring about how much I wanted to get to know her and how she could trust me.

Even if it isn't true.

Even though I already know everything about her.

Even though I'm about to ruin her life.

CHAPTER 3
VIVI

I'm trying not to freak out.

I've had a few one-night stands in my life—I'm not all *that* innocent. None of them have been terrible experiences, but I have a feeling that Trace is about to knock my block off.

His tight grip on my fingers doesn't lessen as we move swiftly through the club. His movement is like liquid, slipping us around the undulating bodies, barely touching anyone or anything. Though I am behind him, I feel oddly protected and safe. I refuse to continue that line of thought. This is one night and nothing more. Get it together, Vivi.

Our hands abruptly break apart as a giant presence slams into me from the side. I'm thrown back a step or two and glance up at a shadowy face—all I see is a shock of white-blonde hair. My arm is throbbing from the contact, and before I can react, Trace is between us, pushing me behind him. I hear a low hum of brief curt words between them before his arm wraps around my waist, and I'm hustled faster out of the club.

"Are you alright?" His voice is a whisper in the dark. I nod as the sudden blast of bright light from the hotel lobby causes me to squint. I glance at his face again and am again struck by his looks. I notice pretty much every woman with a pulse (and some men) taking second and third looks at his tall, lean perfection.

"Are you hungry at all?" His hand squeezes my hip as the other raises to hail a taxi. Immediately, a shiny sedan pulls out of the formation, and I am quickly deposited inside. "Vivi?"

I shrug and figure honesty is always best. "I was thinking about getting a pizza delivered to the bar."

He chuckles at that and gives an address to the driver. "Believe it or not, there is an amazing pizza place just off the strip. One of my co-workers took me a few years ago, and I never miss a chance to go whenever I'm in Vegas. So how do you take your pizza? Be careful. This could make or break this relationship."

I snort, which makes him grin broader. "Extra cheese, ham, black olives, and pepperoni. I'm not opposed to an occasional mushroom or two."

"I can work with that. Make it stuffed crust, and we might make it after all." He sticks his hand out to shake, and I grip it lightly. "Deal." His hand falls away and lands on my thigh. The warmth of his palm penetrates the thin material of my jump-suit, and I'm suddenly reminded of what tonight is all about. I squirm slightly at the contact out of a sudden rush of lust. I take a peek at his profile while his lips twitch knowingly. His thumb rubs back and forth in a lazy, casual fashion, and I squirm again. At no point did he ever really proposition me; he just offered easy conversation and blazingly smooth confidence. And I fell for it like a rock.

Yup. He's going to ruin me for all men.

The car pulls up to a small restaurant that unsurprisingly

has a line out front. Trace leans over and has a few words with the driver slipping him a bill.

"He'll wait for us to finish and then take us home." He ushers me past the line, and a cute young hostess in a navy blue polo shirt and shorts seats us at a table toward the back. I raise my eyebrows at him, but he smiles. "I texted them from the club. I've come here enough to have a good relationship with the owners."

Our conversation skips around easily, going from topic to topic as if we've known each other forever.

"How often are you in Vegas?" I ask him as frosty glasses of water and a bowl of garlic knots with sauce are placed on the table. We both dive in, and I moan loudly over the buttery, yeasty taste. His dark eyes widen slightly, and those perfect teeth bite his bottom lip. "Keep it up, and we won't make it to the pizza." I blush like a fire engine as he leans forward and wipes a few crumbs off my top lip with his thumb, licking it after slowly.

Sweet Jesus.

"I'm in Vegas a few times a year," he starts, and after giving the waiter our order, he keeps going. His tech job sounds complicated, and he lights up when I tell him I live in Seattle too. He has a corporate apartment across the city from where I live, ironically close to Riley's parents. He's in Seattle quite a bit though he is based in the Bay. I tell him about my friendship with Riley and have him in fits of laughter, recalling some of the scrapes that girl has gotten me into. Finally, the pizza arrives, and we both debate the glory/horror of being an only child. He reveled in it while I dreaded it.

"My mom was a true worrywart, which turned her into a control freak. She hovered over every second of my life, even when my dad tried to intervene and get her to loosen up. I think she's always been afraid that I was going to disappear or something. And she really started losing it when I became friends with Riles. That whole family is a circus. Even now, and three of them are doctors." I peruse the dessert menu and settle on a scoop of strawberry ice cream. "And when I started working with metals and welding a little, she basically fell out. She was terrified I would burn my house down with me in it. So she won't set foot in my workshop, though my dad likes to come over and play."

"My parents were different," he says with a killer quirk of his lips. "Free-spirited and all that. They let me run wild. So it totally shocked them when I settled into a white-collar job. Secretly I think they are disappointed, though I know they are proud of me." He also orders a single scoop of ice cream but in vanilla.

"You don't seem like the vanilla type," I tease him with a smile.

He sits back in his chair and contemplates me for a moment. I can feel his eyes caressing me from a distance, and I force myself not to fall off my chair in nervousness.

"I absolutely am not, Vivi. Are you prepared for that?" He takes a small sip of water while I freeze like a popsicle.

"Um. Yes?" Crap on a peanut butter stick, I probably sound like a squeaky fool. Of course, it doesn't help when he grins at me like a panther about to pounce down from a tree. "I mean, I think so?" I open my mouth to keep rambling and then snap it shut.

"Good. So you don't mind a little fire game or strapping? Maybe some age play?"

I can feel my eyes growing to the size of Jupiter as my shoulders inch toward my ears. What the fuck have I gotten into? I stare at him in horror until his perfect face creases with the biggest grin. His chuckle increases to outright laughter when my face switches to a black scowl.

"Not funny, dude," I scold while his laughter gets louder. "I don't even know what those things are— age play? Strapping? Sounds out of my league," I huff and fold my arms across my chest.

His laughter dies down, but his dark eyes still hold a deep spark. "I promise you, Vivi, that whatever I do to you tonight, you will enjoy— I don't need to add anything extra to satisfy you. But if you ever want to explore something...different, I will be more than happy to indulge you. Deal?"

I have no idea what to say to that because I think the vanilla one here is *me*. I can hear Riley in my head shouting at me, "SAY YES, Bitch!!!" I study his face for a moment before nodding a little. He stares at me a bit longer before leaning back, satisfied.

"Are you ready?" He pushes his chair back and holds out his hand to me. His lips quirk again, and I roll my eyes before slipping my fingers between his. He laughs lightly but doesn't let my hand go as he guides me out of the restaurant. Our driver is right where we left him, and Trace places me into the car with care before sliding in next to me.

"Where are you...." I start to ask, but his long fingers grip my chin, and he suddenly leans over to slide his supple lips across mine. In surprise, I take a short breath, and his tongue melts into mine. It strokes inside my mouth slowly and sweetly, and my nervousness flees into the night. He deepens the kiss, the hand holding my chin moving to my neck, rubbing and caressing his way to my collarbone.

I feel faint. I don't think I've ever been kissed like this in my life. My eyes feel as heavy as wet velvet, and my heart is galloping. He pulls away slowly, and I'm almost positive that my mouth is still making empty kissing motions. His thumb brushes restlessly across my chin and cheeks.

"This dimple..," he pinches my chin lightly in a husky

whisper. "These lips…" he leans in again and bites my mouth. I inhale sharply and move closer. "Vivi, Vivi, you have no idea how much I will enjoy this. Enjoy you." He nibbles on me again as my thighs rub together in anticipation. A light throat clearing breaks me out of my haze, and I remember in acute embarrassment that our driver is two feet away. I try to straighten up, but he holds me fast in place, his eyes boring into mine.

"I'm sure he has seen worse, Vivi. Come back here." His voice has a slight edge of command, and distantly I feel a drop of rebellion. However, it's quickly overruled by the feel of his hot breath whispering in my ear. "We are almost at my hotel, and I want to keep you close to me." I melt back into his arms as he nibbles on my lobe.

The Strip is a long/short road whose length is dictated by traffic and your alcohol intake for the night. I haven't had one drink, so this ride seems endless, though it's probably less than two miles. Weird doubts are having a battle with my libido—and with each stroke of his tongue, you can guess who's winning. I'm in a haze of lust and heat when I feel the car come to an abrupt stop. "Here we are, sweetheart." I snap to and peek at the driver, who has a giant smirk on his face. Grimacing, I take Trace's hand and slide out of the backseat. He is staying at one of the glitziest hotels on the Strip, and though I want to stop and stare, he whisks me along the casino floor and straight to the elevator bank. There is a crowd of girls in their short sparkly dresses waiting as well, and they all stare at Trace with their mouths open.

"Christ," one of them mutters, and they all begin whispering in awe. I look at his handsome profile and see that he is staring at *me* with a wicked grin. "Shall we give them something to whisper about?" He leans close to my face, rubbing his nose with mine. Before I can answer, the doors open, and Trace gently pushes me in, while holding his hand up to the girls.

"Sorry, ladies. We need some privacy." And with a move that I will remember for the rest of my life, he hitches my leg up to his waist with one hand while diving into my mouth with so much heat, I'm shocked we don't go up in flames. The gaggle of women gasps in unison, and I can hear their fading exclamations as we ascend to a high floor. He doesn't let up until the bell chimes that we have arrived, and I barely have my breath.

"Here we are, sweetheart." He snaps on a light, and the spacious room is revealed. I stand stock still in the middle of the room, mute with nerves. "Look at me, Vivi."

I look up at his face and stare into his warm dark eyes. I feel a slight sense of ease trickle down my spine. "What's worrying you?" He cups my face in his hands and kisses me with a light smack.

"Ummmmm, I don't know? I'm just awkward in these situations, I guess." He steps back to remove his suit jacket, his lean, tight muscles bunching with the movement. His slim shirt caresses his chest and arms, and I watch as he pulls it free from the tuck of his pants. I gulp at the prominent bulge of his desire, the length of him crowding down his thigh. My eyes are glued to it, and to my flaming embarrassment, it twitches back in interest.

"He likes the look of you, too."

My head falls back, and I cover my face with my hands. He chuckles loudly, and I can hear him move closer. "How such a gorgeously sexy woman could be so bashful is a mystery." I'm not about to tell him about the more than mediocre one-nighters I've had in the past. Instead, I cringe inwardly, thinking about one guy who barked loudly as he came. The next day, his apartment neighbors reported his apartment as having an illegal dog, and I never spoke to him again.

He pulls my hands away and tilts my face toward him. I see that he has removed his shirt, his bare chest winking at me. I lift my hand and stroke a finger down the middle, the warm smoothness of his skin begging for more attention. "I'm just a man, Vivi. And right now, I want you so much that it hurts." My hand continues its exploration, and I pluck at the button of his pants. His breath inhales sharply, and I gaze at him with what I hope is confident mischief. "What are you waiting for then?"

His fingers quickly seek out the fasteners to my jumpsuit, deftly unsnapping both shoulders. It immediately falls to my waist, and he goes silent as my bare nipples pucker in the warm air. His stare is so intense that I'm a moment away from covering myself before he suddenly reaches down and sweeps me into his arms.

"You don't have to ask me twice, sweetheart."

CHAPTER 4
TRACE

There are aspects of my job that are harder than others. Fucking a woman as gorgeous as Vivienne Duplantier is not one of them.

A low light emanates from the lamp on the nightstand, giving the room a warm, dim glow. The king-sized bed is off to the side, while a group of chairs is situated in front of the floor-to-ceiling windows. I chose this room because it would project comfortable wealth and illusionary intimacy.

I set her on her feet and let her jumpsuit fall to the floor, leaving her in plain black underwear and strappy black heels. Kneeling at her feet, I lift first one shapely, smooth leg and then the other, untangling her from the drapey fabric. My hands sweep restlessly up and down her body, her skin a feast of smooth cream. She is a petite woman in height, but the curves of her body are wondrous.

I've had to sleep with other women during my assignments, some decent-looking, some not. I have a tried and true mental image that helps me get hard enough to flatter these women's egos, but I do not need to conjure it now. I pull myself to my full height, immediately gripping her thick blonde hair and tugging her head back. Her deep blue eyes close, missing the satisfied and smug expression I let leak onto my face. I school my features back and take a nip out of her smooth neck, licking it slowly after. Her skin tastes like tart, sweet strawberries. I suck and lick my way to her ear, watching closely for signs of sensitivity. Her body shudders when I reach the patch between her neck and shoulder, and I take my time making a meal out of it. Her breath is coming in gentle pants, and more than anything, I want to flip her over and pound into her like an animal.

But all of my research showed that her past lovers were either horribly inept or inexperienced. So, I decided on a softer approach with sugary, dirty words and easy movement.

Trace Scanlan would be a good lover—not so good to make her wonder where he got the experience, but good enough to satisfy her fully. He wouldn't leave any marks on her body, and while she would crave more, crave something she didn't understand, she would never be left wanting. Trace Scanlan would understand all of this.

If he existed.

Her body is starting to sway, so I sweep her onto the bed, bracing myself above her. Her arms are flung over her head, eyes heavy-lidded, and moist lips slightly open and inviting. "You are an absolute feast, Vivi. I almost don't know where to begin." I lean down and sweep my tongue into her mouth slowly. A moan erupts from her throat, and I pull away with a smile. "What was that?"

"I said I can offer a few suggestions," her slightly raspy voice comes with a laugh. "I can even make a list for you."

"Maybe for round two. Right now, I have twin objectives to accomplish. I'll get back to you," I smirk at her. I see her full lips repeat "round two" with no sound. I smother a chuckle and move down until I am face to face with her pink mocha nipples. "Ah, here we are." I take one in my mouth with a light bite and hold the other between my thumb and forefinger. I alternate between licks and light pulls, watching her beautiful face strain with the sensations. Her legs restlessly move back and forth on the bed, back arching unconsciously. I bite back some of my instinct and smooth a hand slowly down her stomach, stopping to tickle her belly button and rest my hand on top of her warm pussy. I can feel the moisture through the thin material of her panties; wait a beat before sliding one finger underneath.

"Oh, sweetheart, I want you too," I coo at her as I rub her little clit lightly in a circular motion. She lets out a ragged cry, and I pause the movement to once again suck on her nipples. I keep up my easy, light motions, backing off when I think she's getting too close, then pushing her faster and deeper. Her whole being is limp and tense, her body entirely at my mercy. I push down the urge to dominate her, using teeth and anger. I focus on a distant point in the room, taking deep breaths until I am back in the moment. I can feel her muscles tighten with her impending orgasm and increase my efforts between her legs. The slick sugar pouring from her makes my dick harden like steel, and suddenly her back launches off the bed, her surprised cry echoing throughout the room. I slide two fingers inside her, flicking them lightly, watching the spasms shake her body in unrelenting waves. Her voice begs in slight protest before I take pity on her and stop my torture. I carefully remove my fingers, resisting the urge to suck her juices off. I rest my weight on her lower half while still hovering over her. Her skin is slightly damp, accentuating the scent of her tangy perfume.

"You doing ok?" Her eyes are squinched tightly, teeth tugging at her top lip. By the subtle twisting of her body, I can tell she wants to curl up in an embarrassed ball. "Vivi?"

One eye pops open, and she grins at me. One hand swings up and gives me an "ok" sign. "Peachy keen jelly bean." I burst out laughing, kissing her tempting mouth soundly. She giggles as she kisses me back. I pull away

"Are you ready for me?" I undulate slowly, letting her feel my length. Her eyes widen, and she gulps loudly. "Ummm, yes?"

My face falls serious. "Good, Vivi. Because I am more than ready for you." I slip my mouth over hers and continue my slow motions. His legs fall open of their own accord, and I settle between them, feeling the sticky silk of her panties slide roughly over the head of my dick. I groan loudly and push back onto my heels, hooking both sides around my hands and pulling them swiftly down her legs. I push her knees apart and stare between them. "You are ridiculously gorgeous all over, Vivi." The scent of her arousal reaches my nose, and I give myself leave for one taste. I lean forward and run my tongue from the bottom of her pussy to the pulsing bud of her clit. Her cry echoes through the room, and her flavor shakes me to my core. I finish with one deep suck and reach for the condoms I hid beneath the pillow earlier in the day.

I slowly slide it down my length and see that she is watching me raptly, her face a mix of concern and hunger. "I'll fit you, sweetheart, don't worry." She blushes in the gloom, and I grin as I lean over her supine form. I grasp one leg and press forward simultaneously, my thick head piercing her tight passage, the dampness and heat surrounding me immediately. I groan and push further, hoisting her leg over my arm and pulling out while pushing in without pause. My eyes struggle to stay open as her body mimics my rhythm, her hips meeting mine stroke for stroke. Her fingers dig into my ass as she pulls me deeper, and my eyes almost cross at her feel.

Fuck. This woman is a goddamn paradise.

I change my angle, coming at her slightly from the side, and her body seizes. I'm hitting that spot inside her, sending her into a begging spasm. I don't want her to come yet, so I move back and slow my movement, lifting her hips and pressing until I reach the end of her and stop altogether. I press hard against her and feel her shakes returning.

"Vivi, you are so beautifully responsive. I need to slow us down, or it will be over too fast, ok sweetheart?" She is pulled as tight as a string, fists grasping the duvet and twisting it, back arched in agony.

"No, please, Trace, I'm so close. Please, please, please..." Her vivid blue eyes beg me, and the surge of triumph I feel threatens my composure. I slide back and forth slowly, watching as her breath hitches in frustration. I hide a smile and continue until I instinctively know when she has reached her limit.

"Alright, I've got you now." I increase my speed and hit a little firmer, waiting until I feel the first deep shakes before I push my thumb onto her clit and rub. She goes off like a rocket, one loud, long wail erupting from her throat. I feel the familiar zip up my spine and groan louder than necessary as I come harder than anticipated. She flings an arm over her eyes, and I grip the end of the condom and pull out with a grimace. I would have happily spent more time inside of her, but that's not part of my objective. I crawl off the bed, kissing her cheek heartily, and sure enough, she turns over and curls up in the comforter. I head to the bathroom, flush the condom, and wet a washcloth with warm water. I look at the digital clock on the wall and am pleased with my time. Her petite frame is a tiny lump in the giant bed, and I sit next to her, pushing her tangled golden tresses off her face.

"Sweetheart, can I clean you up a little?" I lean over and see one embarrassed orb that meets my eyes with a nod. I smile and pull back the covers, pushing her onto her back. She plops a pillow over her face as I clean her gently, a lover's caress. I toss the washcloth onto the floor and climb in beside her, tugging the pillow away in amusement. She turns her face away, and I grasp her dimpled chin and pull it back. I study her flushed cheeks and decide humor is the way to go.

"So, was that vanilla enough for you?"

She bursts out laughing and flips onto her side, biting my bicep and pinching my arm. "Am I supposed to call you Daddy, now?" Her eyes are shining in the dark.

"Should I call you Mommy instead?"

Her mouth widens in horror as she chokes on her giggles. "Oh God, no. I will run out of here so fast." She laughs harder. I slip an arm around her supple waist and pull her closer.

"Well, I can't have you running away, so I guess I'll have to devise something else to keep you busy. I might have an idea or two."

CHAPTER 5
VIVI

My back is itching.

It steals me from my dreamless, deep sleep, an irritating needling feeling. I shift around to try to alleviate the itch on the sheets, but it worsens. I frown, trying to figure out a way to not move, but also reach around and scratch it. My limbs feel like heavy cups of jello, gelatinous and wiggly. I want to stay in this bed forever. I squint one eye open; all I can see is the shadowy shape of some chairs and the weak light of the early morning sun. I can't hear Riley banging around the room, so it must be too early for even that hellraiser.

Now it's itching in two spots. Damn it all.

"What's the matter?" A deep voice grumbles from behind me, and no lie, I yelp like a scalded rabbit. I scramble up, banging my elbow on the nightstand, and come online in one big rush.

Last night.

The Club.

Pizza.
Trace.
A lobby kiss.
His big di—well, you know.
And I'm naked.
I'M NAKED!

I try to rub my elbow, pull the sheets up to my chest, and not fall off the bed simultaneously. A large, firm hand grasps me around the waist and steadies me. My hair is in a wild mess, and I shove it aside, the sheets slipping down as I meet Trace's amused dark eyes. They dip down briefly, crinkling in appreciation, before squinting at me. "Why are you flailing about at," he looks over at the nightstand, "six-thirty am?" I grab a pillow and cover up my nipples, which went tight at his notice.

"My back was itching, and I kinda forgot where I was." I stare at him, my awe of his perfect features creeping forward. In the daylight, his thick hair sticking up in a million directions, with some sheet wrinkles crossing his face, he is even more beautiful than I thought.

Shit, and I probably look like something the Loch Ness monster threw up.

"You are perfectly stunning in the morning, Miss Vivi. Now, where does your back itch? I am a champion scratcher." He sits up and makes a twirl motion with his finger. I do not know how he knew what I was thinking, but I've never been accused of having a poker face. I turn around awkwardly, and he starts scratching in the middle of my back as I start directing him, higher or lower, finally hitting the spot. I practically thump my leg like a dog and sigh in happiness.

"Thank you. It woke me up out of sleep." His hands rub up and down my back, suddenly hitting a sore spot. "You have a bruise here." He pokes the area gently, and I frown. "This is where that guy bumped into you last night, remember?" I try to peer over and see it, but it's just out of my vision. I think back and recall a big dude with crazy white hair. Was there a flash of pale blue eyes?

"Not really. It was dark, and it happened so fast. I'll live, though. In case you haven't noticed, I'm all scarred up anyway— it's par for the course for a metal sculptor. I also have burn scars and calluses." I hold up a hand, and he grasps it, kissing the ridged tips of my fingers. My awkwardness returns, and I sneak a peek around the room, cataloging where my clothes are—neatly stacked on a nearby chaise, along with my shoes—phone, and purse lined up on the nightstand. I don't want the weird 'when are you leaving?-do I have to kick you out?- you are still here?-' to rear up and be unprepared. Generally, by this time, I am rushing out and praying I never see the guy again. Remember the barker? Ugh.

"I would have charged your phone, but I don't think any hotels have chargers for phones that old. How do you even have coverage for that thing?" I glare at him behind me, his white teeth gleaming at me. My lips twitch, and I roll my eyes. "It works just fine, thank you. It makes and receives calls; people can leave me a message and even text messages. And my coverage is excellent. I'll bet I have more battery left than you." I lean over and flip my phone open, which causes him to snicker and check. "See, I still have seventy percent battery left." I smugly show him the screen and then text Riley, letting her know I'm alive. True to form, she answers back right away.

> Riley: OMG! I woke up, and you weren't there!
> You spent the night??? EEEEKKK!! I need
> details!

Vivi: He's right here, fool! I can't go into
details!!!

Riley: Did he chop down those redwoods? Is
his axe BIG???

Vivi: BYE

I flip my phone back and see Trace staring at me. "Do you have any games on there? Music?" His chest is bare, and his perfectly sculpted abs are on display. Jesus. His body is a work of art. No pun intended. "Vivi?" I snap out of my drooling.

"Nope, no internet at all. Just a phone." I waggle it at him. "I'm a simple girl. So, where's the bathroom in this joint?" I look around the suite and notice how luxurious it is. Dang.

"The bathroom is over there," he points to the left of the bed, "Your clothes are over there," he points again, "and my company pays for this room for all of us. We keep it for anyone traveling to Vegas. Now I'm about to order room service. What do you want for breakfast?" He stands up, and yup, he's fully naked too. He is on display all -however- many- inches- over - six feet, and parts of him are more awake than others. I would give my left arm to be able to sculpt Trace. And maybe take a few pics. For research, of course. (And maybe show Riley. You would, too, if you could see what I am looking at.) I'm trying so hard not to stare at his dick, but it's staring at ME.

"You have about two minutes to decide what you will do. Once the two minutes are up, you get breakfast or my dick. Your choice."

My mouth drops open, and I squeal when he steps toward me. I jump up and race to the bathroom, heedless of my clothesless state, and slam the bathroom door behind me. I hear him laughing as I hurry up and pee, washing my hands with the thick soap. I look at the shower with its dozen jets and decide to enjoy myself. "I'm going to take a shower," I call out and turn the hot water on, messing with the dials and temperature before stepping in, the quick massaging pulses easing the aching muscles I just realized I have. I use all the fancy soaps and shampoo, scrubbing myself up and down, enjoying the heat.

A knock on the door precipitated his arrival, "I have some pancakes and fruit coming up. It should be about 15 minutes."

"Ok, I'll be done soon." I wait a minute as he closes the door before shutting off the water. I see that he dropped my clothes off and sigh gratefully. I grab a warm (!) towel and wrap it around myself, contemplating what's on the shelves. There are four different kinds of body lotion, and I settle on a silky one that smells like lilacs and honey. There is some expensive leave-in conditioner, and I snoop enough to find a comb. I braid my hair quickly and pull on my bra and jumpsuit. (Though my underwear is...nope.) I shove them in my deep pocket, hoping to slip them into my little purse when he's not looking. I peek out the bathroom door and see breakfast has arrived and is set up in front of the windows.

"Feel better?"

I whirl around, my heart in my throat. "You scared me!" Thankfully, he's only a few inches behind me and covered up. His tight grey t-shirt and low-slung lounge pants are doing wonders for him.

"Come on, little rabbit. Let's eat." He guides me to the table and pulls out my chair, the beautiful smells of coffee and syrup teasing me. I waste no time piling stuff on my plate and yipping happily when I see the giant bacon tower. I'm halfway through two pieces and working on a pancake when I notice Trace sitting back, sipping coffee, and watching me. I stare back before shrugging and continuing to eat. I like my food.

"I want to see you again, Vivi. I'll be in Seattle next week, and I'd love to spend more time with you," he sips his coffee, peering at me over the rim. I freeze mid-chew and stare at him. I'm almost certain I have grease on my face. And I'm also positive I can hear Riles hollering and doing a drum routine from our hotel.

"Uhh, ok?" I commence my eating and avoid eye contact. Should I be more grateful? More aloof?

"Good. Let me have your phone number. Is it only seven digits, or does your phone allow you to use an area code?"

"Haha. Someone's got jokes, I see." I rattle off my number as he types it in and hear the dull tone of my phone's text sound. I polish off the rest of my plate and sit back, patting my tummy happily. "Are you not going to eat?" I point at the rest of the bacon and fruit. I ate all the pancakes, though.

"I've got a breakfast meeting in two hours—it will be rude if I'm not eating with them. I got all of this for you, anyway. I'm going to get dressed while you finish, then I'll take you to your hotel. When do you and Riley leave?" I tell him we leave tomorrow morning, and he looks disappointed. "I have meetings all day, a late dinner, then a club opening with clients. I doubt I will have time to see you before you leave. I'll text you, though, ok?" I nod and swallow some apple. His need to reassure me is actually freaking me out. He stands, heads to the bathroom, and I dive for my phone.

Vivi: OMG HELP!!!!!!

Riley: OMG WHAAAAT? WHAT'S HAPPENING?

Vivi: He wants to see me again! We exchanged numbers, and he wanted to text me!

Riley: ....

Riley.......

Vivi: Can you say something besides "......."

Riley: ************

Vivi: RILES!!!!

Riley: You just about gave me a heart attack, beeyotch! Ugh. I'll see your silly butt when you get back here. **frown face**

I throw my head back and grunt. It's not that big of a deal, right? Right?

CHAPTER 6
TRACE

"Is this line clean? " I roll my eyes though he can't see them.

"Of course, it's clean. Did you forget who I am?" I huff in annoyance.

"Is it done?" I can hear by his inhalation that he's smoking. Probably something filterless and Turkish.

"Literally and figuratively. Everything is on track," I cross my feet at my ankles, and munch on the one piece of cold bacon Vivienne left hours ago. I need to order some lunch. "I told her I would be in Seattle next week and wanted to see her again. She fell for it."

He snorts. "Of course she did. What are your thoughts so far? We gonna get what we need?"

It's my turn to show disdain. We go back and forth like this all time. It's a game to see who can be more cynical. More often than not, I win.

"I foresee no problems at all. This should be a piece of cake." I snap my fingers and grin.

"Good. You've got one month to do this the nice way,

Trace." I hear him inhale deeply, his lungs protesting with a heavy cough.

"I probably won't even need a month." I'm not being cocky (much).

"That's good to hear. Because, Romeo, we either get what we need, or your little artist is not going to like what happens. We will be doing things my way."

CHAPTER 7
VIVI

"Okay, tell me one more time about the elevator kiss."

The flight attendant just dropped off our snacks and drinks (juice for me, a vodka and OJ for Riley), and I am telling Riles all the details for the third time. I fight the urge to roll my eyes, but I know if I don't let her get all of her inquiries and nosiness out of the way, I will never hear the end of it. I already had to give her every itty bitty morsel when I returned to the hotel yesterday morning. I barely got a foot in the door before she was on me—I swear she should work for the CIA or something because no one can get information like Riley can. Then, over dinner last night, she got me to repeat the story, and now again on the plane. I'm whispering because we are in the business class seats, and part of me is terrified that one of these rich suits knows Trace.

"It was so hot—like out of a movie. And you should have heard all of those girls freak out. I swear, Riles, I have never been kissed like that in my life," I munch on the tasteless chips.

"We could've ended the night there, and I would've been satisfied."

Riley snorts while sipping on her cocktail. "Girl, based on everything you told me, I would've been pissed if the date ended there, and I missed out on all those orgasms. Kissing is great, but nothing beats some good dicking down." She whispers the last few words, but not low enough because the guy across from us coughs/chuckles and winks at me. I sink in my seat and pinch her on her toned thigh.

"Will you hush it!" She cracks up and pinches me back. The guy chuckles again and then goes back to whatever he is looking at on his phone. "You know I'm right, Vivi. You've had a perma-smile all day, and your skin is actually glowing. Ain't no kiss gonna do that for you." She snatches the last few chips, waving the empty bag in the air. "I'm proud of you, ya know. My normally safe and boring little Vivi stepped out of her comfort zone for once." She places a manicured hand over her heart and bats her eyelashes like a fool. "Maybe we need to go to Vegas more often."

I stare at her in disgust, and she laughs so hard she chokes on her drink. I pound her on her back until she is under control, and the friendly flight attendant brings her a water bottle. "Anyway, we need to talk about what's gonna happen when I see him again. What am I supposed to do?" I nibble on the callus on my thumb.

Riley looks at me closely, smacking away my munching. "What do you mean what are you supposed to do? You are going to let that fine-ass man wine and dine you. You are going to let him charm and romance you. And you are going to let him fuck you ten ways till Tuesday. Anything extra, we will deal with as it comes. I won't let you go into this with those same old fears; hear me? Trace gives me the impression that he can handle anything that comes his way, including pretty little sculptors with…interesting pasts. Ok? We are going to take deep breaths," she pauses and takes a breath, motioning for me to do the same. "And then we will do this one day at a time. *Capice?*"

"*Capice.*" I grab her face and smoosh it while kissing her as the pilot says we must hand over our trash and prepare for landing. I look out the window and see the typical grey skies of Seattle, the city coming through the clouds. The wheels touch down smoothly, prompting several passengers to applaud, something I thought only my mother did. Riley turns her airplane mode off, and her phone beeps with tons of incoming messages.

"I'll text Marshall when we get to baggage claim and tell him where to pick us up." Marshall is Riley's oldest brother and the most protective. He's an emergency room doctor and usually works on the weekends, but he had canceled plans that led to him offering to pick us up. "I'm sure he wants to make sure his love muffin gets home safely." I roll my eyes and don't even respond. Riley has claimed for years that her brother has a crush on me, and no matter what I say, she won't give it up.

"Let me text my mom and let her know that we made it home safe," I change the subject quickly. My phone doesn't have airplane mode—I have to shut it off. I power it on and wait the long minutes it takes to come online. We are walking down the concourse when the first few dull tones sound. They are followed by more, and I stop and stare at my phone with a frown.

"Who is it?" Riley asks nosily. I flip my phone open and stop in my tracks.

Trace: Hey, sweetheart, I just left my last meeting; let me know when you girls land.

> Trace: Back at my hotel for a minute, and I
> swear I can still smell your perfume

> Trace: Distracted. I can't stop thinking
> about you.

> Trace: Vivi, don't be mad at me. Call you later.

"UHHH," I show Riley my phone, and she grins like a bandit. "Gurrrlll. You put a spell on that man. What would you be mad at him about?"

"I have no idea. I'll call him when I get home." I snap my phone shut, and we crowd onto the escalator to baggage claim. I'm looking at the weird statue in the middle of Sea-Tac when Riley inhales sharply and shakes my arm like a crazy person.

"What is it?" I ask her and follow her pointed finger. At the bottom of the escalator is a group of professional chauffeurs and private drivers holding up signs for their charges. One tall, handsome man is standing front and center, holding a bright red sign that reads "VIVI AND RILEY." My mouth drops open, and Riley practically drags me over to him when we disembark.

"Miss Vivi?" The guy has to be at least six foot six and has a face like an Abercrombie model. He looks straight at me with the tip of his shiny hat. "Mr. Scanlan asked that I escort you and Miss Riley home. My name is Stephen." He waves us in front of him and follows us to baggage claim, where our bags are already on the belt. He quickly grabs them and directs us out of a smaller door at the end of the row. A sleek Mercedes sedan is parked, and he swiftly loads our luggage and us inside before smoothly pulling off. I give him both of our addresses, and he nods discreetly. Riley nudges me and hands me her phone. She has Trace's professional profile pulled up, and my eyebrows raise when I see his fancy executive title.

"Explains a lot," she murmurs, tapping her phone rapidly. She finds his other social media profile, flipping through it rapidly. "Not a girl in sight," she whispers, showing me some generic pictures as well as a few of Trace with his group of friends. There aren't many, but with his busy schedule, I'm not surprised. She continues digging, making pleased noises as she CIAs her way into Trace's life.

"No dating profiles either, by the way," she swipes her phone off in satisfaction."Jackpot," she says with a smile. "Oh, I forgot to text Marshie." She fires off a message to her brother, and they go back and forth for a minute. My phone pings, and I flip it open.

Trace: Mad at me?

Vivi: No, not at all. It was very sweet of you

Trace: I want to spoil you

Vivi: Ummm, I don't know what to say to that. Thanks?

Trace: LOL. You can thank me when I see you on Thursday. I'm cutting my week short and coming to Seattle.

Vivi: ….Ok

Trace: Walking into another meeting. Talk later?

Vivi: Ok

Trace: Vivi…I can still taste you

I GULP and throw my phone at Riley. She snatches it up and reads the messages, a slow smile spreading on her face. "Damn. The boy has game." She re-reads them and then hands me back my phone. "You don't, but he surely does."

I hiss at her and yank on her ponytail. "What am I supposed to say? You know I'm not good at this stuff." She just laughs and wiggles in her seat.

The car turns, and I see we are close to my house. I live on a quasi cul de sac at the end of a quiet street in Hillman City. My neighbor, the Lesters, home sits on a weird peninsula of land that hides half of my house from the street. They have a canopy carport where Mr. Lester works on his old rusty Mustang, directly across from my back door. My garage and their backyard share a fence, though I have an extra fence inside my property line to protect them from any debris. I pull straight to the back most of the time, but Stephen stops the car at my little-used front door, popping the trunk as he gets out. He straightens his jacket, pulls my door open, and holds his hand out for mine. I let him pull me gently out of the car, careful not to stumble, and turned to see Riley hanging out of the window like a wayward puppy.

"Call me later, ma'am." I salute her, Stephen waiting for me at my front door. I hurry and unlock it, shutting my alarm off while he wheels my bags into the foyer. He tips his hat at me again and then strides off. I wave at Riles, who is grinning like a jackal, and close my door with an eye roll. My stomach rumbles, and I contemplate what could be in my fridge when my doorbell rings behind me. I open it without thinking, expecting it to be Riley forgetting something, but I am faced with another handsome man holding a pizza box.

"Miss Vivi? Dinner." He hands me the box and a black shopping bag before bowing slightly and disappearing up the driveway. I peek inside the bag and see a fancy to-go cup and a small bottle of red wine. Next to it is a pint of strawberry ice cream, all from Lupo's in Fremont. My stomach is churning, and I set everything down before peeking in the box. Yup. Extra cheese, ham, black olives, and pepperoni. And precisely three mushrooms. I grab a slice and plop down on my ancient sofa, taking a vicious bite. I don't care what Riley says; I'm freaking out.

WHAT HAVE I gotten myself into??

CHAPTER 8
VIVI

This week is flying by.

I turned in my sketches to the university, and they were thrilled with my initial proposal. Their medical school wanted something dramatic for their quad center. Instead of doing the expected (a double helix or a skeleton), I went with a modern interpretation of a caduceus. I'll do the wings in bronze and then strip-dye wrought iron for the snakes. The final sculpture will be about twelve feet tall—one of my most extensive to date. The final say will rest with the alum board for the school—not just on design but pricing. I'm not anticipating any pushback; they came after me.

But now I'm in that weird lull where I am anticipating a project but not ready to start. I take inventory in my studio, ensuring all storage bins are organized to the teeth. I have all types of scrap metals: carbide, steel, brass, copper, aluminum, and copper. My dad was out last week making sure my industrial fans were in top shape; without them, my studio would be almost stifling. My chemicals are all tightly sealed and labeled, and I double-check my arc welder and other tools for wear and tear. I have several in-progress personal pieces, but my creativity doesn't work like that. Once I dial into something, I have to see it through and look forward to it.

Of course, it doesn't help my nerves that every day that goes by is one day closer to Trace coming to town. He's been texting and calling me nonstop, and I've tried to keep up with the tone of his flirting, but I think I'm failing spectacularly. Thankfully most of them are relatively tame—if they turned sexual or racy at any point, I probably would have thrown my phone and buried my head under a pillow. He pleaded with me to have dinner at my house since he wanted to see my studio, and I reluctantly agreed. He promised to bring dinner over with him; all I needed to do "was provide utensils and that face."

"So Meg will be there at nine am. Don't forget and get lost in your studio," Riley reminds me, chewing over the line. "She will get the whole house done in no time." At some point this week, Riley told her mother all about Trace and the whole escapade. Her mother was thrilled to say the least, and insisted on sending their beloved housekeeper, Meg, over to my house to get it in shape. I know you think I should be offended, but when I tell you I am a terrible homeowner, that would be an understatement. My obsessive neatness does not extend to my house's living part. Mrs. Mansour, knowing this, gently offered Meg up, and I grabbed it like a chocolate-covered life preserver.

"Is Trace still saying six o'clock for dinner?"

"Yeah, he's got meetings all day, but he said he's cleared for the rest of the week. I guess that means he plans on seeing me the whole weekend."

"Condoms, lube?" She asks as she types something in the background. Riley suffers from a severe lack of indoor voice. I hope no one in her office is listening in.

"Yes, I got all of that yesterday. I don't think I'll need the lube, but as you said, better be safe than sorry." I choked in horror when she gave me a shopping list that included 'cute underwear from *Honey Birdette*, flavored and non-flavored lube' and more. I swear the pimply teenage cashier at the pharmacy smirked at me when he saw my haul.

"Girl, you never know what that man will try and talk you into. Nothing worse than being in the moment and him trying to use spit to pave the way."

"Why would he use spi...you know what, never mind. I don't know where your head is, but if you think I am letting him do a little uphill gardening—you are smoking something, my friend." She sputters and cracks up, which causes me to laugh as well.

"Where the hell did you get that from? You've been listening to BBC radio again?"

"I'll never tell." I've totally been listening to BBC radio again. "Anyway, I don't think he's into anything like that." Riley snorts.

"Girl, all men are into that. Trust me." I wrinkle my nose and change the subject. "My mom has already called four times today. I'm terrified that she will show up for dinner too."

I made the mistake of telling my mom about meeting someone in Las Vegas, leaving out all of the sex stuff. I thought she would be happy about it since she's been on a holy crusade for grandchildren since I turned twenty-one. But of course, instead of being excited, she went on a tirade for over an hour, warning me about everything from sex traffickers to exotic diseases to men who prey on wealthy women. I tried to interrupt several times but couldn't get a word in. My dad finally had to take the phone from her, but I could still hear her chattering in the background. My dad asked a few questions and then sighed with a tinge of laughter.

"You know your mother just worries about you, darling

girl. If you trust this guy, then that's all that matters." He wished me luck with my date and told me to call him in the morning before hanging up.

"Is it me, or has she gotten worse as you've gotten older? She was crazy protective when we were kids, but I thought she'd loosen up after a while."

I sigh this time, kicking my feet onto my old leather ottoman. "I think what my mom wants most of all is for me to marry someone from her circle of friends, move into a house two blocks from her, give up my career to raise some kids, and just live a safe, boring, insulated life. She and my dad are so....normal. It kills her to have a creative, weird kid. And after everything that happened, let's just say she expects the worst all time." I know part of my mom's hysteria is my fault; constantly reassuring her about my every move can be exhausting. It hurts because I know, in the end, it's because she doesn't trust me to make good decisions. "I just wish she was more like your mom." Mrs. Mansour has always been the best backup mom known to man. She filled in all the gaps my mom's worry couldn't fill.

"Well, don't wish too hard. My mom is hoping you marry Trace too. She's been going on about how handsome he is for days now. Marshall is devastated, as you can imagine." It's my turn to snort. "Quit it already, fool. Your brother isn't interested in me. He's like an extended bestie."

"If you say so, chica. Anyway, I gotta go. I have back-to-back Zoom calls in a few. I'll be over after work. Do me a favor and do something outside of the house today. I can only imagine you pacing the halls looking like a pasty ass dustmop in overalls."

"I am not in overalls, you jerk!"

I'm totally in overalls.

"Girl, guess who I saw yesterday? Looking as creepy as

ever? Pat." I wrinkle my nose. Pat and his brother Miles were a few years ahead of Madden, but played in the same rec soccer league. They used to haunt the Mansour's house, but Pat singled me out every time. He always made me uncomfortable, though Riley thought he was kind of cute.

"Ewww. I hope you told him I moved to Antarctica." Somehow, he got my phone number last year and called me for two weeks straight. Riley thinks my mother was involved.

"Nah, I told him that you were currently getting pole-tented by a hottie you met on the internet."

"RILEY MANSOUR!"

"Love you—get out of the house!"

She snickers as she hangs up, and I give the middle finger to my phone. I flip it shut with emphasis and then laugh. She's right. Though I have a few phone calls to return, if I don't leave the house, I will go crazy with nerves. I grab my trusty iPod (yes, iPod, you know, I'm old school), my sketch pad, and a snack.

Anything to take my mind off of tomorrow night, right?

"So this is where the great artist works? It looks exactly like I thought it would, and also nothing I imagined." Traces trails his hands over an unfinished piece and smiles.

"In what way?" I ask, watching him slowly walk around, inspecting everything with the closest attention.

"It's very organized, but also...I don't know, crowded? You have so many sculptures here that I almost don't know where to start. What's this one?" He stops at one I made for my dad, slipping the cover off. It's an aggressive turn of steel, its body serpentine, amid a deep fall.

"My dad is a huge fan of rollercoasters, like obsessed.

We've been all over the country going to as many amusement parks as possible since I was a kid. Last year, his doctor diagnosed him with high blood pressure, so my mom put the kibosh on him riding them. Though the doctor said they were safe for him, and it was more diet-related...well if you knew my mom, you'd understand. I made this for him to help make up for it. It's for his birthday next month." He smiles and takes a sip of the excellent wine he brought over. I gulp as I watch him lick a drop off of his shapely bottom lip.

As promised, Meg came this morning, and like a human cyclone, she whipped my house into a Trace-worthy shape. She came armed with two caddies of cleaning supplies and bags of stuff from Mrs. Mansour—new freshly laundered sheets, flowers, a few throw pillows, and a small set of matching dinnerware. When she was done, it looked terrific, with candles (???) and even soft music playing. (Riley sent over one of her fancy portable speakers.)

Trace showed up at precisely six o'clock, his handsome face split with the biggest grin, toting three bags with dinner. Somehow, he picked my absolute favorite restaurant, The Pink Door, and ordered a feast including the *tortelloni in bordo*, which is BOMB. I managed to plate everything, and we ate at the newly sparkling dining table, laughing and demolishing the fantastic food. I catch him staring at me a few times during dinner, and he doesn't even look away when I do. He's pretty casual tonight, wearing a pristine open-necked white button-down with jeans that hug him in all the right places. I tried to trick myself into believing he wasn't as hot as I remembered—but nope. He's even hotter. I honestly don't know how he goes about his life without being kidnapped on the daily. I'm glad Riley convinced me to borrow a silk off-the-shoulder blouse from her vast closet—though I'm wearing jeans of my own—so I don't feel over or under-dressed. My hair is somewhat tamed, though the curls and waves slowly take control of the mountain of product Riley put in it. We put dessert on hold, Trace wanting a tour of my studio first.

"And this big empty area? What's this for?" He's standing in the middle of my workspace, adding unexpected life and color to the industrial zone. "That's what I call the 'landing.' All of my bigger pieces start there." I turn in a circle and point. "If you notice, the whole studio is built around it. I move a lot when working, so how I access stuff is important. My dad is an engineer, so he helped me design it so I could meander around safely. There are extra outlets and vents, see?" I show him my dad's handiwork. I'm leaning on a barrel of scraps and watching him examine everything before he turns to me, perching on a nearby stool. "What made you decide to pursue art full-time? You are ridiculously talented, but it can be a hard road, especially in your genre. Did you ever want to be anything else?"

Danger! Danger! I try to control my panic, turning around and pretending that I heard something. I give myself a beat before turning back.

"A long time ago, I met a guy at an art class my dad signed me up for. It was supposed to be for adults only, but my art teacher at school told my parents that the instructor was the only one in Seattle who dealt with prodigy kids, so my mom allowed it. Anyway, I was waiting to get picked up, and this nice man started telling me this story: His best friend, an artist, was big enough to get a secondary commission whenever his pieces were sold or resold. His specialty was photography/photo realism. One day, a gallery in Marfa contacted him about a piece that had been sold within a day of them obtaining it. An older gentleman seemed to be selling off his artwork as he downsized houses. The gallery published a catalog of his collection, and within a few minutes, another older man came in inquiring about a particular photo. It depicted a town in Alabama on a summer day. Nothing extraordinary, just a snapshot of Main Street on a normal day in the nineteen eighties. It turns out that photo was of the guy's hometown, and in that photo was the guy's wife, driving a brand new convertible that he had just bought her. In the background, you could see a blurry version of him, arms crossed and smiling at his happy wife. He had no idea that photo existed. His wife had died one month earlier, and he wanted the photo badly. He bought it immediately and left with tears on his face. I don't want to be cheesy and talk about how art brings people together, blah blah blah, but that story stuck with me in a way I can't explain. So after that, I decided this is what I wanted to do." During my speech, he's moved closer and now stands one inch from my legs, staring intently at my face.

"That's extraordinary. Do you think it's true?" He reaches out, running a slim finger under my chin and across my neck.

"I know it is. My dad looked up the sale, and it made the local paper there," I gulp a little as his fingers continue to stroke my skin lightly. It feels like a burn from the sweetest match.

"And you never wanted to be a doctor or anything else?"

I snort. "Riley's whole family, except for her, are doctors. Her dad is a world-renowned cardiologist, her brother Marshall is an ER doctor, and her other brother Madden is a pediatrician. I've seen enough of the medical field to last a lifetime. I'm sure I had little dreams here and there, but art is where I belong." He says nothing, sweeping his hand across my shoulders and down my arm before twining his fingers with mine. "I agree; art is where you should be. Do you want to watch a movie and eat our dessert?" The Pink Door makes a ridiculous basil cake I can't wait to sink my teeth into.

I shrug in slight embarrassment. "We can, but I don't have Netflix or anything. Riley brings her little tech box over when we have movie nights."

His thick eyebrows raise. "Well, maybe we can just watch something on your laptop." He watches my face turn red and then cringe. "I don't have a laptop either."

"No laptop? No Netflix and a flip phone? Vivi Duplantier, are you a doomsdayer? Do I need to look for a bunker under your house?" I burst out laughing, shaking my head.

"No, I'm just low-tech. My agent sends all my emails and scans all my designs. I prefer good old-fashioned paper and pen to a keyboard."

Liar. Liar. Liar.

"Ok then, tell you what. We will get our dessert and find another way to keep ourselves entertained. I have a few suggestions." His warm brown eyes sparkle with mischief and not a little heat. My legs clench in needy anticipation, and I swear my whole body lights up like the sun. "I like suggestions," my voice sounds breathy and hoarse.

"Good. Suggestion number one...."

CHAPTER 9

VIVI

Riley's hazel eyes are popping out of her head, and for once, Señorita Chatterbox is speechless. She is sitting on my couch with an abandoned beer in one hand, her other one covering her mouth. I am in the midst of telling her about my weekend with Trace—an unbelievable string of nights that I am still trying to convince myself really happened.

"Ok, back up. Trace brings you dinner from your favorite restaurant—not my doing, by the way—and then challenges you to a CARD game?" The beer sloshes as she emphasizes her disbelief with a wrist snap.

I nod with a goofy grin. "Yup. He wanted to 'Netflix and chill,' but of course, I don't have cable, so he said he had other ideas. He went out to his car and came back with an overnight bag. Riles, no lie, I thought he had a bag of sex toys, but instead, he pulled out a deck of cards. "

Two things—I was so relieved that it was just a deck of cards that I let out an enormous breath, but I was also massively disappointed that it was just a deck of cards.

"Was it at least strip poker?" Her poor beer is abandoned as she clasps her hands together in prayer. I crack up and shake my head.

"Nope. We played Go Fish, Spit, and War," I answer, wiping the tears from my face. Her pretty face is contorted in horror but then suddenly brightens.

"Go Fish? Was it some sort of oral game?"

"Riley! No!" I am practically falling off my chair in hilarity. I might pass out from laughing so hard.

"Ok then, Spit—did you have to spit on his di-"

"Riley Starla Mansour, do not finish that sentence! I swear your sweet mama would croak if she knew how perverted you were," I scold her while sipping some water to get myself back under control. She sniffs with a dismissive hand wave.

"Girl, where do you think I get it from? Anyway, so then what happened? When did the fun stuff start?" She shifts on the couch, sitting cross-legged in skintight white leggings and picking up her drink again. I can only imagine what her reaction is going to be when I tell her how the night ended. I sip my water and study the new callus-looking blister on my forefinger.

"Nothing happened. We played until super late and fell asleep on the couch listening to music."

Dead silence.

I peek at her through my lashes and barely hold it in. She looks like a volcano about to explode.

"ARE YOU KIDDING ME?" Her voice bounces around the house, her beer officially all over the floor. "That prime piece of ass was in your house looking all kinds of sexy, and you just..fell ASLEEP?" She yells the last word, and I lose it again.

"Have I taught you nothing in all these years? I know you still have these good-girl tendencies that rear their head occasionally, but Vivi, seriously?" She's flung herself off the couch and is pacing around erratically, her blonde ponytail coming loose in disappointment. She yanks on it, and I take several ragged deep breaths.

"Riles, I swear it gets better." I scrub the tears off my face, patting the sofa to get her to sit again. She sits with a huff, then squeals when she realizes she is sitting on a wet spot. She jogs to the kitchen for some paper towels and then gives me an impatient swirl of hands. I chuckle and continue.

"We were listening to a playlist on his phone and discussing our childhoods. He was an only child too, and he went into detail about his parents and how hands-off they were with him. It somehow made him even more responsible and determined to be successful. I told him about my mom and how strict she is and how instead of falling in line, I...rebelled." Riley's eyebrows shoot up in surprise.

"How much did you tell him?"

I shrug and pick at a loose hem in my overalls. "Nothing really. I told him I didn't listen to my mom, which drove her crazy. I think he knew that it was a sensitive subject because he grabbed me into a hug." He also picked me onto his lap and started playing with my hair, but I will leave that part out because Riley's manic romantic heart would gallop around the room. And I barely want to acknowledge it myself. "Anyway, the talking just stopped at some point, and we fell asleep. We woke up at around five and then went to bed. We woke up late, and of course, it was raining, so we stayed in the rest of the day."

"Annnnd?" She props one hand on a curved hip and glares at me. Part of me wants to mess with her, but I think she is at her limit. Riley is *always* Team Vivi, and I can only imagine how disgusted she will be if she thinks I blew it with Trace.

"He made me breakfast, and then wehadsexfortherestoftheday." I rush it all out, and she leans forward with a giant grin.

"Did you say you had sex for the rest of the day? Vivi!" She rolls on her back and kicks her sock-clad feet in the air. She sits up quickly and pumps her arms in the air running around in a circle. I crack up some more as she flops beside me, releasing an exhausted breath. "I gotta get my cardio up. Anyway, how was it? And don't tell me it was 'good.' I need details. Wait!" She scrambles off again. She comes back with a bottle of wine and no glass. She takes a swig and waits for me excitedly. I love this girl so much.

"We sat on the swing in the back and watched the rain, and he leaned over and kissed me. Riley, he is the best kisser of my life. He's kinda dominant, but not, you know? He definitely knows what he's doing, but he doesn't make me feel like I don't. You know my history. I could be crowned 'the queen of the mediocre sex.' And he acts like everything I do, is the best thing he's ever had." I scratch at my head and frown. "I can't believe I feel so comfortable with him so fast. You don't think it's too fast, do you? I've only known him for a week, and I'm already about to give him the keys to the castle." Riley hands me the wine bottle, and I take a long swig.

"Vivi, you know how my parents met? My mom fell when she was roller-skating with my Aunt Des and had to go to the ER. My dad happened to be walking by and took one look at her, and that was it. He proposed after a month, and nine months later, Madden was born. They are still all over each other—ew— and my dad worships the ground she walks on. There is no set time-table standard for love or relationships. Shit just happens sometimes. And just because Trace is a fucking god among men doesn't mean you aren't the best he's ever had because you are *you*. He's no fool—he knows you are a fucking catch. Remember what I said? One day at a time, right?"

"Right," I sigh, taking another sip before passing it back over. "The kissing led to some other stuff, and then he carried me back to bed. And we never left unless it was for food or water. He finally let me sleep for a few hours, and we were at it again. Next thing I knew, it was Saturday night, and he had to leave this morning. He said he's coming back on Friday for the weekend again."

Riley's leaning forward, hanging on every word. "Has he texted you since he left?" I hand her my phone, and she flips it open quickly.

Trace: I'm on the plane, and all I want to do is turn back around to you.

Trace: Landed in The Bay. Is it Friday yet?

Trace: Just told my mom about you. She thinks you aren't real. Are you real, Vivi?

"Wow. Girl, you put a spell on this man." She leans forward, peeking at my waist. "Riley, what are you doing?"

"I'm looking to see what brand of magic your vagina is. I'm shopping in the wrong department." I snort and throw a pillow at her head. She chuckles, contemplating me for a moment.

"So, just how big are we talking about here?"

I gulp and grin. "As big as you'd think he would be."

"Stamina?"

"Outpaces me three to one." Her eyes go huge. "Three? Like three whole orgasms?"

"Yup." I can't help the smug expression I can feel stretch across my lips.

"Oral skills?" I hesitate. For all his ridiculous talent, Trace isn't that big on oral sex. I've tried a few times, and he just grins and pins me down. "Good."

"Just good? Have we found a flaw in his otherwise otherworldly perfection?" Those perfectly plucked eyebrows raise again.

"No, it's more like he's impatient. He gets so intense; he wants to be...inside." My face flames a little as I recall him flipping me over and muttering about needing to 'feel this heat' before plunging ahead.

"Damn," Riley fans her warm face too. "He's just straight dicking down. I'm not mad at it, though."

"Not mad at all." She picks up her phone and starts flipping and clicking rapidly.

"Now what are you doing?" She looks up with a purse of lips and eye roll.

"Ordering you some more lube. And an ice pack. Don't think I didn't notice that limp you have going on. Your poor forest has been plundered."

"Riley!"

CHAPTER 10

TRACE

Yup. He wanted to 'Netflix and chill,' but of course, I don't have cable, so he said he had other ideas. He went out to his car and came back with an overnight bag. Riles, no lie, I thought he had a bag of sex toys, but instead, he pulled out a deck of cards." "Was it at least strip poker?"*

I laugh out loud at the girl's antics, the sound echoing throughout the mostly empty room. I lean back in my chair, twisting dials and typing commands, recording their conversation and rewinding certain parts.

While Vivienne was asleep, I planted several bugs around her house, including one camera in the bedroom. I tried to wire her studio, but the interference from the industrial fans her father installed prevented me from getting a decent signal. Luckily she admitted that once she 'goes to work,' she rarely answers her phone, so the chances of me missing any information are small.

I was *thisclose* to getting her right where I wanted her this weekend. I thought she would go all the way, but she stopped herself suddenly. I could've pushed a little, but instinctively, I knew that would have shut her down. She's slightly more reticent than anticipated, but I know I will still get what we need. I always do.

"That prime piece of ass was in your house looking all kinds of sexy, and you just...fell ASLEEP?"

I snort at Riley's exclamation with a smug grin. Part of me wishes that she was the one I had to seduce, though I'm not complaining about having to fuck Vivi. She is an intoxicating mix of pent-up passion, shyness, and spice. Out of all the women I've had to use, she is the one I will remember the most.

"Oral skills?" "Good."

I roll my eyes with a smile. I'm saving that for the grand finale. I glance at the clock as my stomach rumbles. I left Vivi's house this morning and headed to the apartment we've been keeping in the city. It's about five miles from her house, close enough to monitor but far enough not to run into her. Stephen, for all his height and chiseled face, has been following Vivi for weeks without her having a clue. She never ventures down this way, staying in her little neighborhood bubble, oblivious to her surroundings.

"Ordering you some more lube. And an ice pack. Don't think I didn't notice that limp you have going on. Your poor forest has been plundered." "Riley!"

"Were they talking about your lack of skills, boss?" Stephen asks, chewing a slice of pizza, leaning in the doorway. A smirk creases his face, and I throw a pen at him. It hits the cardboard box he sets on a folding chair.

"You missed her talking about how big my dick is, you ass. Is there any left for me, or are you giving me an empty box and crumbs?" He flips up the lid, and I snatch two pieces, biting with a groan. "All of the bugs are working just fine. Any problems with Riley's place?"

"None. Got everything set up, including her Jeep."

"Fuck!" I throw down my pizza. "I forgot to get Vivi's car. Fucking hell! I've got to go back tonight" I can't believe I slipped like this. I punch down on the desk, making the expensive equipment jerk.

"No problem, boss. I'll go over in a few and do it myself," Stephen shrugs, still chewing his pepperoni. "They just said they were leaving for dinner. It'll take me three minutes tops. Her car is still parked in that little grove next to her house. Piece of cake, in and out." I frown and rewind for a few minutes.

"I'm craving Thai. Let's go to Bua 9. My treat." "Oh yes. Hey, where is that black Burberry slicker my mom got you last year? I want to borrow it. I have a date with Chris tomorrow. I'm driving, by the way. I hate your car." "Whatever"

Their voices move around as they leave, and I switch over to the lines that Stephen hooked up, their voices coming in loud and clear from Riley's Jeep. They've moved on to discussing the date Riley is going on and whether he will be as skilled as me.

"I'll leave now. Be back in a few." Stephen stops in the doorway and turns to me. "I never envy you having to get these women in line, but this may be the one time I do. That girl…" He whistles low, and I hear the front door close behind him.

I tune back to their conversation, plotting my next move. I might push my timeline to Thursday, claiming I'm pining over her and need to be with her.

I've got twenty-four days. And then Miss Vivi is off my hands for good.

CHAPTER II
VIVI

"*B*on jour, Maman. Ça va?

"*Bon jour, mon bijou. Tu vas bien aujourd'hui?* Are you ok today?

"*Oui. Je vais bien.*" Yes I'm good.

"You haven't been by to see your father and me in weeks. Are we not important anymore?" My mother's French accent always deepens with her disappointment. Right now, we are about halfway down the Mariana's Trench deep.

"Of course you are, Maman. I've just been so busy. It's been hectic between the trip with Riley and my new commission."

The silence is short and sharp. "*Oui.* And with that...man you met in Las Vegas, no? You have made time for him?"

And here it comes. My mom usually calls me daily, but I don't always pick up the phone. If too many days go by without me answering or calling back, she has my dad call since I usually pick up for him. He will lecture me about how I'm hurting my mom's feelings, and I will tell him that every conversation is an exercise in judgment— her questioning mine at every turn.

"I'm dating him, Mom. And it's new. So yes, I am making time for him. I'm sorry I haven't been by to see you guys, but I'll make time soon."

"Dating him? *Ah, vraiment?* When we last spoke, he was just a man you met. And now, a mere week later, you are 'dating?' What kind of sense does that make? You do not know this man at all, Vivienne Micheline." Oh boy, she broke out the middle name. "A respectable man does not meet a woman in that godforsaken town and then press himself upon her after seven days. What kind of a person is he?" She is starting to pant with coldness and is working her way into a real snit. "This is not how your father and I raised you. Please tell me, at least, that you did not let him in your bed?"

Cringe. "Mom…"

"*Mère Marie aidez moi!*" Now she is calling on the saints? I'm really in for it.

"You have! Is there no sense in you? No decent man wants a woman who will sleep with him after a week. Where do you think this could possibly go? A long-term relationship? Marriage?" I would bet money that she is pacing around the kitchen, her blonde hair in a tight chignon, polished as a new nickel in a cardigan and crisply tailored pants. Suzanne Barban has not lived in France in nearly thirty years, but she's never lost her style.

"Mom, we just met. It's way too soon even to bring up marriage. We are getting to know each other, and it's casual right now, ok? I know what I'm doing." Wrong choice of words. I wish I could snatch them out of the air and shove them back down my throat.

"Oh? Do you? And I am supposed to believe that?" Her sniff of sarcastic disbelief is like a string of barbed wire dragging through my soul. I take a deep breath and let the quiet speak for itself. This is precisely why I don't answer the phone when she calls—the cutting edge of her eternal disappointment. I'm sure deep down she has to realize that her constant overbearing worrying and stifling examinations have driven a wedge between us.

"Vivienne, mon bijou," *my jewel* , "I just want you to be safe and happy. That is not much for a mother to ask, is it?"

I'm still silent.

"I can see that you have nothing to say for yourself. I only hope that this little infatuation ends quickly and with no damage. When you are done behaving so poorly, Mrs. Rusthman's son is back from law school. You remember him, don't you? Astor?"

Yeah, I remember him. He's got bad breath and eats with his mouth open.

"Well, Astor has a lovely job with a firm in the city. What was its name? I don't remember— it's a string of American names—regardless, it's a large firm, very who's who. He asked about you, and I told him you were still doing your little art thing and that you were surprisingly making a living. He was impressed, needless to say. Astor hoped you would be at church this past Sunday, but you were not. Maybe this week, no?" She continues chattering, heedless of the fact that I haven't said a word in about ten minutes. But that is probably what she wants—for me to be bombarded by her plans for my life, hoping I will cave in one day. Comply. Give up my art, my heart. Let my past be buried underneath a pile of placid, safe goodness.

I tune back in and realize she has finally stopped for a breath. "Maman, I have to go. Tell Dad I will call him later." I hurry off the phone before she can start up again. I lay back on the couch and try to rub out the sting of tears in my eyes violently. I pick up my phone and text Riles a quick message asking her to come over and bring alcohol.

Riley: What's wrong???

Vivi: One word. Mom.

Riley: On my way

My phone rings again; this time, my dad calls. I'm sure my mother told him what a horrible child they raised, and now he's trying to mediate and gently lecture. He's always tried to balance being on my side and mitigating Mom's giant Gallic temper. I let it go to voicemail, silently apologizing for avoiding him. My phone dings again, and I want to bury my face in the sand. I unthinkingly reach for it.

Trace: I can't wait to see you.

Vivi: Me too

Trace: I'm moving things around and coming early. Is that ok?

Vivi: Yes. It's more than ok.

~

"Do you ever think your parents are disappointed in how you live your life? You know, since you were raised a different way?"

It's after midnight, and we are tangled in sheets and each other. Trace made magic happen at his office and was able to come out on Wednesday, even earlier than he initially thought. I guess the tone of my voice when he called me after my argument with my mother spurred him into action because he showed up right around dinnertime, taking the last commuter flight into Sea-Tac. I barely got a word out before he kissed me with sweet desperation and backed me straight into my bedroom. My shirt was off, his mouth latched onto my nipples, his fingers swiping through my wetness before I could breathe. I came with a blinding force, my head falling forward in exhaustion. He laughed lightly, biting my neck and flipping me onto my knees. I heard the snap of a condom before he plunged inside me, his hardness stretching me with a sugared sting. I could feel another orgasm creeping up my legs, everything in me getting tighter and tighter before it consumed me like a storm. Trace was behind me on a roar, fingers holding onto my ass like a life preserver, digging deep. We collapsed into a heap, dozing intermittently and chatting in between. My head is on his pillow, his warm breath puffing against my forehead.

"Sometimes I did when I was younger. They were so free-spirited and open; I just wanted structure and guidelines. The good news was they recognized it early on and adjusted accordingly. They allowed me to find my way, and as long as I was happy and safe, they let me find my path. Now I think they find it amusing that I'm a boring "suit." I snort softly. Nothing is boring about Trace whatsoever.

"Do you feel like your parents are disappointed in you, Vivi? You are a world-famous artist with years to come in your career; you are stunningly gorgeous, brilliant, and a good person. What more could they possibly want?" His voice is shocked.

I'm quiet for a moment, debating how deep I should go.

"Did you know that I'm French? My parents go generations back in France, though I was born here. We lived in Paris until I was two, and my then Dad transferred back here. I don't remember a time that my mom wasn't—intense. She was always after me about my manners, language, hair, everything. She wanted me to be a perfect little lady, seen and not heard, neat and clean, graceful and precious, close to her at all times. And I'm just not capable of being any of those things. I was always loud and messy, wild-haired and clumsy. Climbing, exploring, curious, independent. And she hated every bit of it. She lived in terror every morning that I woke up that I was going to 'be the death of her' from some scrape I got myself into. She could barely let me out of sight, usually only when my Dad could watch me. She put me in all kinds of classes: ballet, elocution, etiquette, and Latin—anything to turn me around and into the kid she wanted me to be. Of course, I failed every single one, and she was at her wits end. One night I heard her telling my Dad that maybe she needed to send me to her mother in Aix, which was terrifying because my grandmother was twenty times worse and used to pinch me." He chuckled here but kept rubbing my back in soothing motions. I took a breath and continued.

"Most kids would have heard that and started trying to act right. I didn't. I got mad instead and stopped speaking to my parents for about two weeks. I stayed in my room and refused to have anything to do with them." I stop here, struggling with how far to go. The silence stretches, and Trace tips my chin with his finger.

"What happened, Vivi?"

The words get stuck in my chest, my breath caught in a pretzel. "I, um, got into trouble. I did something horrible and almost ruined everything for my family. It scared me so bad that I straightened up pretty quickly. I met Riley and her family that same year, and she helped me stay out of trouble. Well, some kinds, because Riles and her brothers are a hot mess, but it was innocent stuff—kid stuff. At first, my mom didn't even want me to have friends, but my Dad convinced her it would help keep me occupied. And then, a teacher recommended art classes, and I calmed all the way down. I've worked so hard to be perfect since then. But my mom has never loosened up: she still despairs over everything that I do and has never, ever forgotten how close I came to fucking up my life." My throat spasms with long-prisoned tears. I sit up and wrap my arms around my knees, resting my chin on top.

"What about your dad?"

"He's always been more lenient than my mom, but only up to a point. Maybe if I were a boy, he would have had more say, but because I'm a girl, he let my mom pretty much run the show. I think he was secretly amused by most of my antics, but when the...incident occurred, he was devastated. I think he finally realized that my mom's way of parenting was not working well, so he got more involved. He was the one who put his foot down and let me be friends with the Mansour sand who signed me up for art classes. He drove me to the studio every week and has always supported my career. He brags to everyone about his 'talented daughter,' but my mom still maintains that old-fashioned French way of grudging praise. She has never been to any of my showings, and if you ask her what her daughter does for a living, she'll say artist, but in a way that sounds like an indulgence. Her one wish is that I give up my art and marry some boring ass guy from her group of friends. Preferably a rich one, and bonus points if he is French. I guess that's more than one wish." I turn around and look at him. His arms are bent behind his head, his handsome face grave and sympathetic.

"What could you do that was so bad? You were a kid, for chrissakes." I grin a little at his anger on my behalf and lay back down on his chest. I want to tell him so badly, but I also don't want to risk scaring him off. Riley's mom has encouraged me to come clean with Trace, stating that if he were worth his weight, he wouldn't let a twenty-year-old mistake affect our possible future. I want to take her advice because I have less than zero experience in relationships or men. Still, the words brick themselves into a wall every time I try. Part of me rebels against the vulnerability of it, but I squash that bitch down.

"I'll tell you one day soon. Just not now." I lean down and kiss his mouth, then chin, then neck. I take a tiny nip of his Adam's apple, and he groans, wrapping my hair around his hand and wrist. I keep up my assault, teeth then tongue, making my way down his hard stomach, stopping at his navel. It's cute—perfectly round with a little pouch and folds on one side. I rub my lips around it as his hips jerk in response.

"You know French kissing has different meanings?" I lick from one hipbone to the other. "Some people say it means with tongue." I take his hard cock, which has been standing up and begging into my mouth, grinning at his sharp intake of breath. I pull off with a loud, wet pop. "Some say it just means with a particular passion," I murmur at him, lapsing into French, which makes him groan louder.

"I don't know what you just said, but I will agree to anything you want if you do that again." He pulls at the hair in his grip, his voice hoarse and commanding.

"*Ver désirs sont des orders.*" Your wish is my command.

CHAPTER 12

HARLAND

"Yo."

"Go secure?"

"How many times do I need to tell you that I am always clean?" Trace's voice is annoyed, as usual. This kid has been a pain in my ass since I brought him into my employ. I met him when he was a snot-faced seventeen-year-old, teeming with rebellion and resentment. I twisted and molded him until he was the ruthless weapon he is today.

"I don't give a fuck, kid. What have I always told you— you may be good, but there is always someone better. Now give me a fucking update." I inhale deeply, the clove flavor from the *kretek* filling my lungs, making me cough slightly.

"Still smoking that illegal bullshit, huh? Anyway, I've made progress. I should be able to get her where we want her, maybe within the week, definitely in two." His smug overconfidence has always gotten on my nerves, but ten times out of ten, he usually comes through. He has zero conscience, using and manipulating women with his good-looking face and charm. He has an uncanny way of morphing into any woman's most fantastic fantasy. He doesn't always have to fuck them, but he doesn't care about using his cock to get whatever we need. I admire that about him.

"Two weeks ain't gonna cut it. We have to move up the timeline. I'm hearing some shit I don't like around the streets. We may need to pull you out and do this the old-fashioned way." I know his ego is going to take a bruise, but I don't give a fuck, as long as it keeps him alive.

"What are you hearing? Because Stephen has his ear to the ground, and he hasn't heard shit. She is still completely off the radar." I can hear some clicking and tapping as he adjusts his surveillance of Vivienne Duplantier. I knew it was a gamble looking for this girl to work with us. From everything we learned, she is one hundred percent done with that part of her life and would be hugely resistant to revisiting it. It's why we decided to send in Trace—seduction being a better tactic than threats. But it seems that our time is running out.

"Not anymore, she isn't. There are whispers you are haunting around Seattle, and inquiring minds want to know why. It's very high level, but it's escalating. If they find out you are there and do any digging into Duplantier, they will figure it out, and we will be fucked." I take another puff and chuckle at his colorful responses.

"I still think that I can get her to do it. You heard those tapes. She's got it bad for Trace Scanlan, and we can make it work." Yeah, I heard the girl and her best friend swooning over Trace and his skills in the bed. If it were any other job, I'd let him keep screwing the girl senseless, but shit doesn't always work out as planned.

"Ok, if I pull out, then what? What's the plan." I hear Stephen in the background laughing about something before he fades away—another kid I picked up as a teen, less ruthless but oddly more deadly.

"The plan is I show up at Miss Duplantier's house, tell her what we need, and that if she doesn't give it to us, I will find a way to imprison her father, deport her mother and ruin her best friend's family. Simple." I don't give a fuck about this girl and her life—I care about results.

"She's stubborn, you know. And smart as hell. Sometimes I forget who I am dealing with, and then she pops off with some shit, and I'm like, "damn." You could hit all the right buttons, and she will probably cave in, but she will make your life hell in the meantime." He chuckles in reluctant admiration. I sit up from my leaning chair and narrow my eyes. I'm hearing some shit I don't like. "You haven't developed feelings for this girl, have you?"

"Of course not. She's just another mark, Harland. I'm just warning you that she's got some fucking layers. She might not be as easy as you think."

I cough some more, spitting into the wastebasket next to my desk. "Look, Trace. Collateral damage is part of the game. That's all this girl is. Collateral fucking damage. First rule of the game—don't get attached. Once this job ends, you forget about her, you understand?"

"I told you I'm not attached or anything like that, alright? I'm seeing her this weekend—If I can't close the deal, you can move in. Also, next time can I go someplace warm? Seattle weather sucks."

"Ha! You go where the job goes, kid. Good luck this weekend."

"Thanks, chief. But I don't need it."

CHAPTER 13

TRACE

Fuck.

"Stephen, get in here!" I press a few buttons and transmit some of Vivi's conversation to a secure server. She was on the phone with her agent, Phineas, and once they hung up, she went back into her studio, probably for the rest of the night.

"What's up, boss?" He flips a folding chair backward and straddles it.

"We got a problem. I just spoke to Harland, and he wants us to either get what I need this week, or he will move in on Vivi." I run my hands through my hair and grimace.

"Why? We got her right where we want her. What's the rush?" His Abercrombie face creases in annoyance, a replica of my thoughts.

"He claims that there are some rumblings about me and Vivi. I need you to get on your contacts right now and figure out what the fuck is going on. I'd feel like shit if something happened to her." Stephen's eyebrows raise.

"Really? You normally don't care about any of the women

we use. Why is she any different?" His frown deepens. We've worked for Harland so long that our ability to feel compassion for anyone has practically been erased. It makes our jobs much more accessible and enables us to get results. So why is Vivi striking a chord within me?

"I can't explain it. She's cool, I guess? Just figure it out, alright?" He stares at me briefly before swinging his leg around and standing up. As usual, he is dressed all in black—like me, he has several weapons on his body, though you'd be hard-pressed to find them just by looking. He's lethal in the streets, but his biggest asset is his underground connections—he's got a whole army of snitches and informants who can get him information in seconds. "I'll get right on it."

He pauses in the doorway but doesn't face me. "Trace. If she is in danger, there's nothing you can do. You can't warn her and put everything we've worked for at risk. We have a job that comes before anyone and anything else. We took an oath, remember?" I stare at the back of his head, my loyalty at war with the tiny shred of decency I have left.

"I fucking know it, Steph. Just get me the information, ok?"

I'M COMPOSING my following texts to Vivi, who is finally asleep after holing herself up in her studio all day when Stephen returns. His eyes are dark and cold, but there is a hint of concern.

"Report?"

"Harland was on the money. I heard back from three guys I use. Somehow, it's out there that we are in Seattle and that a woman is involved. One of them even heard that she's an artist. They don't know her name yet, but it's only a matter of time. Maybe even by tomorrow."

"Fuck!" I push back from the desk and pace the room. "That means we have even less time than Harland thought. Shit. Fuck. I'll have to play the lovesick asshole and "fly in" to see her sooner. Shit, she isn't ready yet." I brace my hands against the wall. *Come on T, think, think, think.* "At this point, he may not even be able to use her, and I can't tell her anything. Harland will have my ass.

Steph sighs and sits at the desk, the chair creaking under his weight. "No, you can't. Trace, there is nothing you can do. I don't even think you should go over there tomorrow. Just text her that it's not working out, and let's go home. She'll be hurt for a while but will get over it." I shake my head, that teeny bit of humanity knocking in my head.

"I've gotta try, Steph. Harland is about to lay the hammer on her if he can. If he can't, he will just leave her to the wolves. I gotta give it at least one more shot."

My mind is clicking and whirling. *Think T. Think.*

CHAPTER 14
VIVI

"Vivi, your phone is pinging," Riley calls from the kitchen.

It's our weekly Netflix night, which we've missed the last few weeks with Trace spending so much time here. She called me this morning, demanded her 'Vivi' time, and said, 'Good penis does not trump your bestie.' She bought over her little internet stick and two bottles of tequila. I ordered tacos and fajitas from *Fonda La Catrina*. There's some new historical sexy drama show she wants to get me wrapped up in, and she also promised to watch at least two ghost stories, which are my favorite.

"Who is it?" I'm mixing the drinks while Riles plates the food. The recipe calls for one jigger full—I go for two.

"It's loverboy. Want me to open it?" She laughs, making smooching noises.

"Go ahead, fool," I grin at her antics.

"Is it terrible that I'm hoping he sends you some horny, sexy message? I need a little excitement in my life after that dud of a date. Let's see...Ohhhhhhh. He's coming tomorrow.

Says he has a big project and needs to see you before he gets wrapped up in it." She pokes her head out of the kitchen, blonde waves swinging. "Maybe this time you can stay at his house." She comes out with my newly matched plate set, each piled with food. We sit at my little dining table, and she sips the margarita with a grimacing smack. "Girl. How much tequila is in here?" She takes another sip while I dive into the food.

"All of it," I laugh with my mouth full. I'm starving, and no one can resist Fonda's tacos.

"I'll allow it," she says primly. She tugs at her Alo off-the-shoulder sweatshirt while regarding me thoughtfully. "How are you really doing, Vivi? This whole Trace situation is waaaaay more than you're used to dealing with. I'm all for it, but you guys have gone zero to sixty." Riley knows me better than anyone. Not only do I have an aversion to relationships, but normally a guy being all up in my business would be driving me crazy. I hate the thought of checking in with someone; it is probably a holdover tic leftover from my childhood. My mom would open every door I tried to close, even the bathroom and would make me tell her when I was leaving the room and for how long. Babies had more space in the womb.

I chew and swallow a few times before answering. "I feel ok, I guess? I mean, he's pretty much taken over my time in a way, but I don't necessarily feel suffocated if that makes sense. The sex is great, of course, but I like who he is, too. He's really funny and a great listener. Anyway, it's good that he has this project coming up because the university committee has approved my design, and I have to get started ASAP." She pumps her fist over her head and grunts happy noises while devouring her fajita. "You know what that means—lockdown time." Riley grimaces and gives a thumbs down. She hates it when I get wrapped in a project because I *really* get wrapped—

like no phones, no visitors, no leaving the house, almost no sleep. I go balls out and pour everything I've got into it. Maybe some people would think it's unhealthy, but that's how my brain works—I can't stop once I've started.

"Does he know what that looks like? Maybe he and I can start a support group with your parents—*The Abandoned By The Art Genius, Formerly Known As Vivienne Club.* Trace can be president— poor guy goes from having a girlfriend to having Thelma and The Four Sisters." She wags her free hand at me with a saucy grin. I snort into my drink, coughing for all I'm worth. She laughs harder, and I flip her off, controlling my breathing.

"Are you sure you weren't dropped on your head as a baby?" She shakes her head while shimmying her shoulders like a fool. "My dad did say I came flying out, and he had to catch me." She shrugs while I stare at her in amazement. "Back to what I was saying—maybe you can stay at his house this time. Doesn't his company pay for an apartment here?" She frowns a little, her CIA antennas going up.

"They do; it's near your parents, remember? But since he spends all his time here, he told them they could let another guy have it. He offered to take me, but I don't want one of his co-workers listening to us have sex." I shudder at the thought. One guy I dated purposely left his window open so his dudebro neighbors could ear-hustle on our activities. Pissed doesn't cover it; Riley told her brothers, who may or may not have roughed him up a little. They have alibis if anyone asks.

"That makes sense, I guess. Unless the guy is hot. Then I say go for it." She's back to her antics immediately, and I crack up. "So tell me about this date with Chris. What happened? I thought we liked him."

Chris is a guy Riley met while she was dining out with clients. He stared at her throughout her meal, and before he left, he not only paid their bill, but left her a letter with the hostess, declaring he would 'surely die if she didn't call him.' We debated for a whole week whether he was over the top or cute and decided she should give him a chance. He's super handsome—tall with dusky skin and green eyes, right up Riley's alley. They have gone out a few times, but timing is always an issue. He's an executive with an international hotel chain, and Riley is constantly traveling for work.

"Nothing happened. That's the problem. We had an amazing dinner and went back to his penthouse. It was a whole mood: dim lighting, candles, the works. And he didn't make a single move on me. I practically threw the pussy at him, but instead, he gave me a little kiss—no tongue, mind you —and then called his driver to take me home. Then he texted me about how much he missed me when I left. Like what? You basically threw me out of your house, but you miss me? Girl, I can't. I'm not going to see him anymore; he's given me blue balls for the last time," she makes a snipping motion with her fingers. "Unless he shows up with a bow wrapped around his dick and a year's supply of condoms, I'm done with him." I snicker quietly, cheering for Chris in my heart. My gorgeous best friend can pretty much have any man she wants, and Chris knows it. I think he's playing the long game, but Riles doesn't see it yet.

"Well, don't give up on him. I know he really likes you." Chris was Riley's date for one of my shows, and he told me repeatedly how much he liked her. "He can't help it if he's Mansour-Struck." She stops gulping the dregs of her margarita to glare at me. 'Don't you start that, DuPlantier."

In high school, a bunch of girls coined that phrase because of Madden and Marshall. They tore through the female popu-lation with only their smiles and charm. Once Riley arrived, they extended it to her, which became a joke in the family. I made the mistake of bringing it up years later in college when three boys simultaneously showed up at our apartment, all armed with flowers and candy. "Looks like y'all are Mansour-struck," I told them while grabbing the candy from one guy and eating it, while Riley somehow wiggled her way out of it with pretty smiles and promises. It spread around Brown's campus, and I'm pretty sure you could go there today, and it would still be part of the university lexicon.

"Enough about Chris. We need to get to the real question here." She sits up straight, hazel eyes locked on me. I frown at her. "What are you talking about, Riles?"

"The real question, Vivi. Are you in love with Trace?"

"Huh? Girl, I don't even know what that means. I think it's a meal I'm allergic to. Like Tofu. Or snails." She cracks up and I smile, leaning back and enjoying my drink.

CHAPTER 15
TRACE

I listened to Riley's interrogation of Vivienne, expecting her to admit to her feelings for me, but to my surprise (and huge ego blow, I can admit it,) she brushed the question off with a joke, and the girls went on with their night. Damn, this woman is tough. Generally, at this point in the situation, I got the woman so sprung that she is ready to do whatever I ask. I've pretty much pulled out every trick in the book with Vivi, and I still can't get her to open up. Maybe we shouldn't try to use her—she would give us hell the entire time.

"Fuck that was brutal." I don't turn around, instead shooting a finger up at Stephen over my shoulder. I hear a chorus of chuckles behind me. I glance at the mirror to my right and see Cash leaning in the doorway next to him. I haven't seen him since Vegas—him being the creep who hit on

Vivi before I approached her. His widow's peak and plain appearance often get him compared to Dracula, though Vivi's drawing of him as a worm is still my favorite.

"I think this is the first time that one of these bitches hasn't fallen for you, ain't it, boss? You must be losing your touch." His tongue snakes out to caress the slight chip he has in his front tooth—a nasty habit we have repeatedly tried to break.

"You sound like a jealous bitch yourself, Cash. Maybe if you stopped licking at those chompers, a woman would give you the time of day." I make an exaggerated clicking noise with my teeth, and he laughs. For all his mannerisms and slimy appearance, he still pulls pussy. Go figure. "What are you doing here, anyway? I thought you were on the advance team for Florida?"

"Harland wants me here as a backup. He doesn't like the shit Stephen is hearing, so I'm here to protect your pretty ass. Can't have Miss America in danger or something." His voice is sneering, but I can hear the genuine concern underneath. Cash, Stephen, and I all came up together, our backgrounds as similar as they were different. We were separated for training for a few years, but we became a team once we were the ruthless machines that Harland built. Where my specialty was human tradecraft, and Stephen's was surveillance, Cash was an expert set-up and shutdown man. He could create whole lives out of thin air, complete with documents, social media, and history. He could just as quickly erase them, which meant his appearance in Seattle ended my time with Vivi.

"Ol' Harland is turning into an old woman—I can take of myself, for fucks sake," I grumble at him while Stephen frowns at me.

"That may be, Trace, but I don't like how loud the whispers are getting. If you can't get what we want tonight, then I think that must end this. I swear I saw one of Koslov's men when I followed Riley to the supermarket."

I sit up and glare at him. "Why am I just now hearing about this??" Fuck if this is true, then the danger is already here.

"Because it just happened an hour ago. He didn't see me, and it was swift. I'm not even sure it was him." He says this, but I know Stephen, and he is never wrong about shit like this. His face is relaxed, but a slight crease is at the corner of his eyes. He's worried.

"Just fuck this girl, see if you can break her, and that's it. I know that pussy is good, but it ain't worth the trouble headed toward us. I've got a nice exit strategy for you all lined up; I can put it into action starting the morning after. We get on a plane and boom. End of Seattle." Cash makes an explosion with his hand, and Stephen nods in agreement. I look at each of them, and my eyes narrow.

"Why are both of you acting like I don't want to leave or something?" They glance at each other, and I see Cash subtly nod at Stephen.

"Harland doesn't like how you are acting with this girl, and neither do we. I don't think you've fallen for her or anything—I know you aren't capable of that—but something is going on with you. You would normally never worry about what happens to a mark once we leave, but it's getting to you that DuPlantier might be in danger. Emotions like that get us killed, Trace. We are just trying to get you back on track, is all." I school my face into an annoyed sneer and shake my head.

"I don't care what happens to her. What I care about is my perfect track record being fucked up. This is the first chick that I couldn't break—I'm pissed. Sue me." I shrug my shoulder and mutter under my breath. Cash laughs loudly, and even Stephen snickers. "One of you assholes get us some dinner. And not fucking pizza, either. We ain't a frat house." Cash pushes off the wall and grabs his phone, shouting recommendations as he scrolls Yelp. I roll my eyes and turn back to the equipment.

"Trace?" Stephen moves to my left, adjusting a few dials and switches before crossing his arms over his chest.

I lean back in my chair and raise a brow. "What?"

He looks at me intently before leaning in and lowering his voice. "I don't know what you have planned," I open my mouth to protest, but he puts a hand up to stop me. "Don't bullshit me, I've known you too long. Whatever it is, it better not put any of us in danger. That's all I'm saying." He sits back with a warning nod.

"I'm not planning anything, Steph. Swear it." I hold up two fingers, and he snorts. "Again, I know you, Trace. And you were never a fucking Boy Scout."

He's right. I was never a Boy Scout. I have been other things.

A liar.

A seducer.

A killer.

"So what would you do if you went into your backyard and there was a bear just calmly lying on your porch?"

Vivi's blue-green eyes widen, and she shudders dramatically. "Um, I would scream? And maybe throw something at it?" I chuckle at her expression and shake my head. "No, you are supposed to lay on your stomach and play dead. You're also supposed to spread your legs out really wide so the bear has difficulty turning you over. Like this." I turn over on the bed and show her, giggles flitting in the air.

"I'm telling you, I would scream first. Maybe the bear would leave." I flop back over and bite the thigh that is closest to me. She squeals and squirms away, but I grab her around to me.

"Ok, what about a zombie apocalypse? What would you do?" She cracks up at this one while I grin but then scowl in fake seriousness. "It could happen, Vivi. So what would you do?"

"I would....barricade myself in my house or studio. I've got chemicals and metal tools in there to fight them off." She sits back in pride, and I give her a slight nod. "Not a bad idea. But the real secret is to get to the water. Zombies can't swim." I lean over her nude body and bury my face in her neck, making growly noises and nibbling on her skin. She screams in laughter, trying again to wiggle away. The sheet that was giving her slight modesty slips down, her perfect mocha nipple making an appearance. I lick it lightly, and she stops trying to get away.

"How do you know zombies can't swim?" Her breath hitches as I continue licking, adding a soft suck. I pull off with a pop. "I read it somewhere." I return to her nipple, pulling it further into my mouth with my thumb and forefinger—her back arches off the bed, thick honey hair a wild mess.

I arrived at her house this afternoon "early," catching her slightly off guard. She was in the process of continuing her new project, something I heard her say on audio was intense. I searched her eyes for any hint of annoyance but only saw surprised happiness. I told her to finish what she was doing and that I would cook her dinner while waiting. Her face lit up, and she hurried back to her studio, showing up two hours later to a clean kitchen and homemade lasagna. (Not really homemade, though. Cash found an Italian place that lets you buy dishes to bake at home, and I transferred it to a plate I bought this morning.) She changed out of her ever-present overalls, and we ate on the chairs on her back porch. She was chattering on about Riley and that idiot Chris, and I made all the appropriate noises while the ghost of a ticking clock sounded in my head.

I stared at her beautiful face and realized bitterly that I would never reach my objective. Maybe with more time, I could have gotten her to open up and brought her to confide her transgressions. But this girl has had years to build up that concrete armor. And not even my expert charms could break it down that easily. I consoled myself that I've probably ruined her for all men, especially with the fucking losers she picks—that soothed my ego immensely.

I aggressively pulled her off her chair, pressing my mouth to hers. She squeaked but softened immediately, sucking my tongue into her mouth. I swung her into my arms, striding into her bedroom and stripping her quickly. I get my fill of her perfect body, before leaning over and giving her sweet, wet pussy a hard lick. Her wild shout eases down my frustration, and I zero in on her clit, flicking it relentlessly, growling when her tense body shakes with her release. I gave her no time for recovery, flipping her onto her knees, slapping on a condom, and plunging forward with force. I fucked her like the real Trace would, all teeth and anger. Her orgasm squeezes me like a fist, mine chasing behind hers like a freight train. She fell immediately asleep, and I shot Stephen a quick text. He came in through the back door and removed all the bugs we'd placed in her house, including her car. I eased off the bed, plucked the camera from the shelf in her room, and passed it to him swiftly. I glanced back at the bed, her snuffling noises ensuring she was still asleep. Steph quickly passed me a cloth, and I wiped down every surface I touched, erasing any fingerprints possibly left behind. I had already bleached the kitchen while I cooked, and this was the last bit to do. Steph nodded at me silently, and I returned to bed, waking her up with sweet kisses. I fucked her slower, giving her another orgasm, and now I'm setting her up to be ghosted. Fun times.

I stop my torture and pull her into my body, spooning her. I bury my face in her hair and breathe in the sweet floral scent. "What would you do if you ever got into some trouble? Like real trouble, not Riley type of trouble." I grin at her despite some weird tightness happening around my eyes. What's that all about?

"I would go to my parent's house, of course. No one wants a piece of my mama. She's a dragon." She smiles back, but I shake my head slowly.

"A bad guy would take about two minutes to find you there. You need a better plan than that, babe," I tap her nose with a slim finger.

"Well, what should I do, then? Put on a mustache and a trench coat? Get a fake passport? Get a backpack and hitchhike out of town?" She waggles her brows as I snort.

"I'm serious, Vivi."

She tries to turn over, but I grip her tightly. I can feel the fear swirling on her skin and how desperately she tries to tamp it down. I'm not surprised to hear a nervous laugh. "Or I would go to the Mansour's. Their house is a fortress."

"So you would bring the danger to your family? To your best friend's family?" I'm being harsh, but I need to get through to her. Our time is short. "That's the wrong answer, Vivi."

"Well, what is the right answer then, Mr. Tech Exec?" Her annoyance is clear and also amusing. I bite back my laughter.

"You run, Vivi."

"Run?"

"Yes. If anything ever happened to me or anyone else and you were in danger, you run. You don't go to your parents, or Riley's. You get in your car and leave."

"That's crazy, Trace. I would maybe run to the police. That's good, right?" She's trying to lighten the mood, but I won't let her. I lean over the bed, pick up my pants, and dig into my wallet. I pull out the plain black metal card and snuggle into her back again. "Here." I hand it to her— she squints in the dim light. "Is this card blank, Trace?"

I don't answer her, folding my hand over hers and squeezing lightly. "I want you to keep this with you at all times. Don't give it or show it to anyone. And remember what I said. You run. Not to the cops, either. Got it?"

"I got it." Her voice is quiet. She stretches to slip the card onto her nightstand before squirming her way back into my embrace. "What time do you have to leave in the morning?" I told her that my "boss" wanted me to start a critical project immediately and that I needed to fly out sooner. She seemed disappointed but was understanding.

"At eight am. So we better get some sleep. I need to look pretty for my clients." She snorts in the dark, and I massage her skin until I feel her relax.

I did what I could. I can only hope everything I think will happen... doesn't.

"HOW DID IT GO?" Stephen climbs into the driver's seat while Vivi waves from her doorway. I wave back, and we pull off. "Fine. I'll be glad to put this failure behind me." He glances at me in the rearview mirror and hums as an answer.

We drive about three miles before we pull over and meet Cash at the rendezvous point. We switch out cars, one of my guys ready to take this Mercedes to a junkyard where it will be broken down into parts. Stephen changes his chauffeur's clothes, handing them over to be burned. We are back on the road and headed to a no-name airstrip in less than five minutes.

"So, do you wanna know how Trace Scanlan will disappear?" Cash twists around to me from the front seat. I usually would be interested, but for some reason, I don't want to hear it this time.

"Nah. I'd rather not dwell on this one. When do you want to prep me for Florida?" He stares at me for a second before turning back around. "We can start on the plane. I took your suggestion and planted the bugs and cameras at the mark's house so that we will be ahead this time." He drones on as I stare out of the window. I should be paying attention and peeling off this persona to prep for the next one, but I can't seem to shake it like I normally would. A frisson of worry is pulsing in my head, worming its way into my corroded conscience.

"...And since it's Florida, it should be easier anyway..."

I hope I got through to Vivienne last night. For all of her suppressed instincts, she is ridiculously innocent. There are glimmers of toughness there, but she slaps them down unconsciously every time. The only thing she won't let go of is that weird eye-reading thing she does—and even that is faulty because I lied to her fifty thousand times, and she never caught on.

"...Harland sent over the files. I think this one may actually work..." God, Cash won't shut up.

"WHAT THE FUCK?" Stephen screams out as he pulls the wheel to the left. There is no time to think as we are hit from the right; the force of a battering ram spins us around as we are hit again from behind. Stephen tries to gain purchase, as Cash screams into a phone. I catch a glimpse of something familiar, something I need to warn them about before a loud gun snap pushes me into a deep, dark bliss.

CHAPTER 16
VIVI

Eleven days have gone by.

I haven't heard from Trace. At all.

At first, I chalked up his absence to the work his boss wanted him to work on. He warned me that he would probably be in and out of contact, and honestly? I dove into my next sculpture head first and immediately lost track of time. I was up at dawn and in bed a few hours before sunrise every day. The hum of my fans and the rhythmic banging of my mallets haunted my dreams, my adrenals firing with creativity. I finally came up for air and wasn't entirely shocked to see that so much time had elapsed. I checked my phone and browsed through my messages, seeing complaining whines from Riley and lectures from my mother. A few were random, and there was even one from my agent, though he just wished me luck and suggested food and water. But there were none from Trace. I frowned and quickly shot off a message to him.

Vivi: Hi! I came up for some air and seemed to be missing you. Are you ok :))

I waited a few minutes, and when I got no response, I tried again.

Vivi: I hope your project is going well. Call me
later when you have a sec?

I returned to my studio, pulled my goggles down, and fell back into work. The base of this sculpture is coming along better than expected, and I want to finish it this week. I woke up the next day and grabbed my phone while sipping a large mug of jet-black coffee. No response. I leaned back on the kitchen counter, my head hurting a bit. I text Riley, and she calls me back before the message finishes sending.

"What do you mean you haven't heard from Trace?" She doesn't even start with a hello, instead diving straight into conversation.

"I mean, he hasn't texted or called me at all. Nada. I've texted him, and when I call, it goes straight to a weird mailbox." I try to hold the worry from my voice but fail miserably. Every unspoken apprehension I had was screaming into the void.

"What's his number?" I rattle it off to her and hear the dial tone from her office phone. The line rings halfway before a robotic voice asks you to leave a message. She hangs up and tries three more times. She hums in frustration, and I hear the clicking of her computer.

"All of his social media is stale and not updated. Professional profile, everything. Vivi, I'm coming over later. I've got to stop by Madden's and drop off some stuff my mom bought him first. His apartment was broken into, and someone sliced up his sheets."

"Wait, what? When did that happen? Is he okay?"

"It was two days ago, and he's fine. He's positive it was this nurse he was seeing—bad breakup. The big baby needs his seven hundred thread count sheets, and Mommy bought him several sets. I'll drop them off and be right over after. Try not to worry, okay?"

I worried anyway.

We went down every avenue we could but were hampered by an odd lack of information. I couldn't remember the name of the building his company apartment was in—or if he ever told me. We tried all close-sounding corporate offices, but none of them had ever heard of him. I knew he lived in San Francisco, but not the neighborhood or his address. We were coming up on two weeks and hit every dead end possible. My work slowed down, my appetite fell off, and my headaches were daily. What could have gone wrong?

"Riley, do you think something happened to him? Like he's hurt somewhere?" I'm pacing around my living room a few days after we burned down the internet. Riley is still tapping away on her computer, twisting every combination she could think of, using Trace's first and last name, the little we knew of his job—everything. But nothing matches the man that we know.

She stops her searching for a moment and stares at me pensively. "I hope not, Vivi, but I think it's more likely..." She's biting her bottom lip, a sign she is trying to hold back something. I stop pacing and gesture at her, winding my hands. "You think it's more likely what?" My voice is snappy, but I'm tired, hungry, and scared. Luckily, my best friend doesn't bat an eyelash at my bad attitude. She snaps her computer closed, throws it on the sofa beside her, and turns to face me. She is silent for about a minute, but it's closer to an hour for my frayed nerves.

"I think he ghosted you. Full on love-bombed you and then peaced out."

I sink onto the cushion next to her and bury my face in my hands. This was the one thing I didn't want to say aloud—trust Riley to zoom in on my fear.

"You thought the same, didn't you?"

I nod my head silently. "He was kind of acting weird his last night here," I start, then stop. Something deep inside me, a long-buried instinct, prevents me from going too far. I never keep anything from Riley, but I can't fight past the need to keep that last conversation with Trace to myself.

"What do you mean?" She frowns, reaching out to hold my cold hand.

"I mean...he was more...assertive than usual. Sex-wise. But when he kissed me goodbye, it was oddly, I don't know, distant?" I think back to his face when he waved goodbye. Was there a finality that I failed to recognize?

Riley is nodding. "He probably was mentally already gone." She squeezes the hand she is holding. "I'm so sorry, Vivi. I know you liked him."

I pull my hand away and start pacing again. "I did. I mean, I really did. I didn't love him, but I could've maybe someday? I feel weird about this. Like, am I mad? Sad? I'm definitely confused." I'm rambling, but I feel disjointed inside. I've never been good with feelings like this, and it's throwing me for a huge ass loop. Do I want to cry? Scream? I just don't know. I can decide if I am pulling emotions out that don't really exist. Are they genuine, or are they something I feel like I should be feeling? Fuck, this is hard.

"Everything you are feeling is valid, Vivi. Remember when RR promised me all that romantic stuff, and we found out he got arrested? I cried for a week."

RR, as we call Rodney the Rat Mancini, is a guy Riley picked up at one of my shows. He pursued her hardcore before disappearing. We found out later he was arrested for illegally transporting rodents for medical research. Hence, "The Rat" was born. Also, she only cried for two days. Then she made his mugshot a dartboard.

"Is it bad that I'm still keeping my hopes up?" I'm sure I sound like a pitiful little fool.

She tilts her head at me and pushes her lips out in sympathy. "No, of course not. There may still be a super reasonable explanation. You will know when you are ready to let it go."

I stare at her a moment and sigh. "Thanks, Riley. I don't know what I would do without you."

Her braces-perfect teeth flash at me. "You will never have to know that. Now, we need to get you cleaned up and back to work. You look like hell, babe. "

I groan and pull at my ratty hair. "Yeah, I've got to get it together before my dad comes over tomorrow. One of the kids in their neighborhood apparently popped all four of my mom's tires and spray-painted some gang signs on her windshield. He's getting her car towed, and I've got to give him a ride."

"Excuse me? In that snitchy-ass neighborhood?" My parents live in a pretty affluent suburb; the whole community is like a giant slam book. You can't sneeze without it being reported that you are dying. Which is one of the reasons my mom is always after me. They have a private app, and everything that happens winds up there.

I nod and grimace. "Yeah, it's a huge scandal because only my mom's car was targeted. All the whispers and innuendos mortify her. They'll have her leading a cartel before the end of the day." Riley snorts and grins.

"I could see it. Your mom is something else. Get your smelly butt in the shower, and I'll order some dinner. Make sure you shave, too. I can see hair poking through those sweatpants." She starts howling in laughter before she even finishes her sentence. I pull off one of my dirty socks and fling it at her, which causes her to scream louder. For the first time in two weeks, I feel somewhat human.

CHAPTER 17

TROUBLE

I click the recording off and contemplate if I have a next move. I knew Trace had some shit he was doing behind the scenes, and finding out that there was one last bug monitoring Vivienne's house pisses me the fuck off. This tape was at least two weeks old, and things were in motion that I couldn't stop. The escalation was in effect, though we did everything possible to throw them off her path. I thought about listening to the rest but decided against it. My loyalty to Trace warred with my oath; sadly, Miss Duplantier will always lose in that battle. I picture her beautiful face, framed by that wild honey hair, and sigh. Picking up a hammer, I violently smash the equipment, silently wishing her luck.

She will need it.

CHAPTER 18
VIVI

I slam the car door and plant my head on the steering wheel, banging it a few times. I take a deep breath, pushing the tears down, down, down. I reach blindly for the keys and start the car, still not moving my head.

After those punks vandalized my mom's car, someone threw a brick through their living room window, and my dad's office had a break-in. My parents were frantic, and the police had no leads. I came over with my dad's birthday sculpture, hoping to ease some of their tension. My mom was scared and demanding that my dad not go to the office; meanwhile, my dad wanted to take a trip away while the cops investigated. I thought surprising them with the gift and a box of *Tarteau Citron Meringuee* from Mom's favorite French bakery would make for a pleasant visit. Instead, I spent the next two hours listening to my mother scold me for all my life choices. When she brought up Trace, I abruptly cut her off and told her we no longer were seeing each other.

Wrong move, Vivi. Wrong fucking move.

She jumped on the news like a cheetah on fresh meat, pushing and insulting me until I couldn't take it anymore.

"What more do you want from ME?" I screamed at her, feeling something almost pop in my throat. "I am not seeing him anymore; I'm not seeing anyone. Was he a mistake? Maybe. But it was my mistake to make. I'm over thirty years old, Maman. How long are you going to hold this over my head? Let it go. I was a fucking KID!" My breath is panting in the silent room. She sat on a floral settee, her hands folded neatly in her lap, while I paced like a wounded tiger.

"When, Vivienne? *Je ne suis pas sûr.* Perhaps when you realize the damage you almost cost this family? When will you stop your reckless behavior? When you give up on this ridiculous career with your little metals and welding. Settle down with a good man and become a productive member of our community. Maybe then I can 'let it go.'" Her voice was cold and exacting- the unbending steel of her disapproval a quiet hum against my fiery rage.

"You are behaving like the child you claim to have left behind. You will lower your voice and never disrespect me like that again. You are being irrational and terribly American." She never raised her voice; instead, it lowered to a decibel only a mother can reach.

"I can't do this with you. It's been a hard couple of months, and I thought I could come here and spend some time with you without all this...bullshit." Her eyebrows raise slightly at the curse word, but she makes no movement or sound otherwise. "I'll never understand why you even had a child that you were primed to hate." The words pop out of my mouth before I can stop them. I have always suspected that my mother never loved me, and her tactic of silence drives the thought home. When I was a teenager, I kept a tally of her insults vs. any compliments for a whole month. I don't need to tell you which one won.

"Vivienne Micheline!" My father's voice thunders into the room. "You will apologize to your Maman at once!" I turned around to his horror, but I was immune to the guilt.

"I will not! You are always refusing to take a side, Dad. Did it ever occur to you that this stupid Switzerland routine would backfire? I can't spend the rest of my life killing myself not to live up to her endless disappointment. And I can't wait for you to take my side anymore. I want a normal relationship with my parents. And I don't see how it's possible." His face is a mask of conflict, while my mother, who briefly went pale, now has bright red spots on her cheeks.

"Leave my house." She points at the door, still having not moved from her perch. I open my mouth to retort but instead, lift my chin and slam my way out. My emotions are at an all-time high, and I feel out of control. The headache that has been plaguing me for weeks is back with a vengeance. I just want to lie down and sleep for a millennium. I start toward my house but hit the brakes. I'd bet good money that my father will show up at my home; frankly, I don't want to see him any time soon. I snatch my phone and text Riley.

Vivi: World's biggest blow up with the 'rents.
Can I crash at your place?

Riley: Of course! I'm not home until tomorrow
morning. Use your key.

I forgot that she was in San Diego for a quick trip. Dammit.

Riley: There is no food, FYI. Grab something
and take a bath in my tub. We'll go to
breakfast in the morning, and you can tell me
everything.

Vivi: Okay. Thanks, Riles.

Riley: Love you.

Vivi: Back at you.

I decided to pick up some Chinese from a place near Riley's condo. They make seafood fried rice that sounds amazing. The restaurant is in a super busy area, and I pray there will be parking. When I turn on the street, I groan out loud. There are groups of people everywhere, and the gridlock is ridiculous. I toy with the idea of just getting it delivered, but since I'm already here, I decide just to head inside. There is a parking garage a few blocks away and down a side street that most tourists don't know about. I get lucky that the lot is open and snag a spot on the bottom floor. I leave my purse and grab some cash. I walk swiftly and am assaulted by loud cheers and the rancid smell of beer. I realize that the crowds are for a sporting event and walk faster. I ignore the catcalls and whistles from drunk college kids (and adults), wishing I hadn't worn this dress to impress my mother. My stomach twists with residual emotions, and I shove them down. The restaurant is packed, but I quickly order at the bar. I spend the wait time, studiously avoiding eye contact with a group of guys to my right, and breathe a sigh of relief when the cute bartender gestures to me with my bag. I smiled, thanked her, and hurried out of the door. The crowd's roar chases me—I guess someone scored or something. The smell of the food has my stomach growling, and I stop to grab an egg roll. The greasy saltiness coats my tongue, and I groan. I munch on it as I walk back to the car, dreaming of Riley's custom spa tub, two aspirin, and the foam mattress in her guest room.

A whisper sounds from behind me, and I turn around and

peer into the darkness. There is nothing there, just the lonely night. I shrug and take another bite. I'm a few feet from the garage when the whisper comes again. The intermittent cheering breaks the eerie silence, and I stop. I've seen enough horror movies to know that this usually is where someone yells a greeting into the dark before a monster jumps out to get them.

Nope. I'm outta here.

I hurry inside and click my key fob. The reassuring snick of the door opening eases the rapid beating of my heart. I'm reaching for the door handle when suddenly, that sound is right behind me. Before I can react, the bag is slapped from my hands, and a meaty thunk meets a sharp pain exploding in my head.

I fall to my knees and look at the amount of shadowy forms surrounding me. Were there really that many? The pain is almost unbearable. The shadows are saying something, but I can't make it out. I shake my head and am met with a fist to my cheek. I collapse further down and try to raise my arm in protection. It's swiftly grabbed and twisted, and the audible pop of bone echoes in my ears. There is shouting and pulling, the blows raining down upon me. My leg is on fire, and I feel blood pooling in my mouth. I choke on it as I try to scream, but all that comes out is a sick, gurgling sound. There is muted laughter at my efforts as I try to crawl away. I am quickly dragged back, and what feels like a two-ton brick kicks my side. I curl up in a ball, tears burning my quickly swelling eyes. Hot, smoky breath coats my face as an unfamiliar voice says something in a low harsh voice. Cold thick fingers surround my throat and squeeze, squeeze, squeeze. Dark lights flash in front of my eyes.

"*Ty ne pomozhesh' im seychas, ne tak li?*"

I can only make out a few other words and nod to what he is saying, hoping he will tell them to stop. He chuckles low, and I feel the cool air of his absence. The shadows are fading back, pain filling the silence. I lay on the cold concrete, willing my body to listen to my need to move. There is suddenly a fast squeak of a shoe before one last blow knocks me into oblivion.

CHAPTER 19
VÍVI

Beep

Beep

Beep

There is a chemical smell tickling my nose. My brain tries to identify it—tricked into thinking I may be in my studio. I can't put my finger on what it may be. My nose involuntarily wrinkles, and a weird sensation pulls at my face. What's on me?

"Vivi?"

Is Riley outside of my studio? Maybe I've fallen asleep with my goggles on my face? That must be it. I try to pull them off, but I can't find them. What the hell is going on?

"Vivi, honey, don't pull on your tube. You need it to breathe." Her voice sounds odd, like it's close but also miles away. I turn toward it, and a sharp pain sucks at my neck, the intensity instantly making me cry.

"Oh, sweetie, don't cry. I know it hurts, but try not to move, okay? Marshall..," her voice fades away, and I hear the deep rumble of her brother's voice. A warm hand gently covers my arm, and soon, a calm river flows over the pain as I sink under its weight.

Beep

Beep

Beep

THIS TIME, my eyes try to fly open, but they are stuck. Why are my eyelids glued?

"They aren't glued. They are swollen shut, more on the right side." Riley's voice comes from my left. I try to see if I can peek at her, and all I can see is a watery phantom. The phantom moves (I think), and I attempt a snort.

"H..urt?" Is that my voice?

"Yes, sweetie, you are hurt. But Marshall and my dad say that you will be just fine. You need some time to heal." Her voice is clogged, like she has been crying. How bad is it?

"..BBad?"

"Well, it ain't good, sista. Try to rest, okay?" The cool river is back, and I fade back into oblivion.

WHEN I WAKE NEXT, the room is dark. There are no shadows or phantoms in the gloom. I now realize the smell I couldn't identify is the cleaning products they use in hospitals. My body slowly returns online, and I wince at the pain storming at me from all directions. I swallow back a groan and discover the discomfort extends to my throat, which feels like a thousand needles piercing it. I take a deep breath and feel the mask helping me with oxygen. Alright. I need to figure out what is happening to me. I decided to start with my feet.

Right Foot. Check.
Left Foot. Ouch. Wrapped in something. A cast? Not good. The left leg also feels like it's not right. But I can at least move my toes.
Hips. The left one feels weird but not wrapped.
Right one, sore.
Torso. It hurts when I inhale too deeply. Also, what is that creaking noise?
Left arm. YIKES! Wrapped up. Deep throbbing pain. A break? Sprain? This is going to piss me off. I need both arms for work.
Right arm: Sore. Workable
Face: ...

It's going to be bad. I can see perhaps one centimeter out of my left eye and nothing on the right, and what I can see looks like I'm seeing out of a funhouse fish tank. My whole face feels like an elephant is sitting on it, and I wonder if my brain is okay. I think even my earlobes hurt. I hear a whispered shuffle and the sound of clothes rustling. My heart begins to gallop as blurry memories rush back to me. I can hear the beeping of a machine picking up its rhythm.

"Vivi? What's wrong?" Marshall's sleepy voice lilts into the dark. I struggle to control my breathing as my terror eases down. I'm okay. I'm safe.

"Ri-ley?"

"I sent her home to sleep and shower. She's been here since you were brought in. And she was starting to stink." His voice is amused as only an older brother would be. My brain slowly processes his words.

"How long?"

"You've been here for three days, Vivi. Riley hasn't left once. My parents have been here on and off, too, and Madden and I have been taking turns sleeping in here with you, in case you woke up."

Three days? Jesus.

"Vivi..when you were brought in, you told the ER team not to call your parents, so we haven't. My mom is about to break and call them. Do you want me to do it? I'm sure you want your mom with you." His handsome face is hovering over mine, and I can see a tiny bit of his messy blonde hair.

Even in my highly broken state, I know I definitely don't want my mother here. Somehow, she will find a way to blame me for this happening. And I don't need that shit right now.

"No. No call." I am firm—parts of our last argument filter into my head. Yeah, I definitely don't need her here.

"Vivi, are you sure? He grips my hand lightly, and I feel a few twinges of pain. "Riley has been pretending to be you via text. Sooner or later, they are going to figure it out." I snort as my throat hurts too much to laugh. I can only imagine what kind of stuff she has been sending them.

"Sure. Yes." I think I nod.

"Okay. Whatever you want, okay? Are you in any pain? I can hit your pain pump if you want." He's leaning closer, and I can smell the slight tang of hospital mixed with his spicy cologne. "Yes."

"Alright. You should feel some relief soon. Try not to worry. I'll be here to take care of you." I feel a light sweep over my hair, and then...nothing.

$\sim$

"A‌lright, let's hear it."

I'm finally sitting up in bed after dozing in and out of sleep for a week. I can see out of my left eye enough to see Riley's red face. Her eyes flit over to her brothers, both standing, arms crossed at the foot of my bed. If this was any other time, I might admire how hot they both look with their white coats and lean builds. But I have been trying to get them to tell me what happened for the past two days, and they just keep skirting around it. So I know there is something they are not telling me. I one-eye glare at all of them, searching for the weak one. I zero in on Madden, who shifts slightly.

"Madden? What's going on? Someone tell me something here."

He sighs and then sits beside me, ensuring I can see him. He picks up my mangled fingers, looking like he'd rather eat nails than talk.

"What's the last thing you remember?" He still won't meet my eyes. Eye.

"Ummm, I was at my parent's house. We fought. I was going to stay with Riley for a few days. I was hungry..." This was where things got hazy. I frown, though he taps my hand to remind me not to. It will pull my stitches.

"You were brought into the ER seven days ago. Someone found you on the ground inside of a parking lot. The police retraced your steps. You picked up some Chinese food and were attacked approximately sixteen minutes later. There is no video of your assault; the cameras in the parking lot were out. You were not robbed; your phone and purse were found at the scene. You were not sexually assaulted. A group of college kids found you and called the police. When you were brought in, you were in and out of consciousness. Marshall happened to be on duty; he took over your care, and you explicitly told him not to call your parents. Then you passed out." Riley comes over and brushes my hair back from my forehead soothingly. I'm in shock, but Madden's brisk bedside manner is strangely comforting.

"You have a broken ankle, we think from someone stomping on it. Both of your legs show signs of kicking and beating. You have three broken ribs, one severely. You have a bruised spleen; luckily, it didn't need to be removed. Your kidneys are also bruised. Your left arm is broken, and the same shoulder is dislocated. Two of your fingers, too. Your right orbital bone is fractured, and you lost a tooth. You have a Grade Three concussion, and we had to give you a total of forty-seven stitches." He stops for a breath as I stare at him. A horrible sound echoes through the room, and I realize it is coming from me. My damaged eyes burn like fire from the tears trying to find space to escape. "Why would someone do this to me?"

"The police think it was a random attack. They will want to talk to you when you are up to it. Vivi..." He stops and looks at Riley, who is still petting me.

"What is it?" I look at all three, and only Marshall will meet my eyes. He seems pained but resolute.

"You're pregnant, Vivi. Around eight weeks, give or take. The baby is healthy, and you will both be fine. I'm assuming the father is the guy you were seeing from Vegas?" He waits while I process about eighty different emotions.

A baby?

A fucking baby?

I don't even like kids. I've never really been around them, except for some of Riley's little cousins, and I wasn't too fond of those little gremlins. They were noisy and dirty. One of them peed on me.

How did this happen? I'm on birth control, and He Who Shall Not Be Named consistently wore a condom.

"Condoms are not one hundred percent, Vivi." Had I said that out loud?

"Yes, you did." Madden's amused voice comes from a tunnel. I look over at Riley, who, for all of her sympathetic noises, looks thrilled.

"Oh my god, are you excited? Riley! This is a disaster. I don't know anything about babies! Holy shit, my mother is about to have a stroke. Seriously, I may move out of the country." I push the button to lay my bed flat, my heart monitor going berserk. I grab the blanket and pull it over my face. It's tugged down, and I'm met with my best friend's shining eyes.

"Vivi, I know this is a shock, but I can't wait to be an aunt! Oh my gosh, the amount of shopping I can do! We can convert that room you use for storage into a nursery. My mother can help. I hope it's a girl..."

"Riley..."

"...but imagine if it's a boy? Holy smokes! Your looks mixed with Trace's? That kid would be a lady killer..."

"RILEY!" I yell as loud as my damaged throat will let me. She stops mid-planning and smiles at me sheepishly. "Can you please give me a little bit to process this? I'm not ready for nurseries or any of that shit, okay?" She nods and stands up. Madden throws his arm around her and pulls her toward the door. "We will give you a few minutes alone, Vivi." She grumbles but follows her brother. Marshall stays behind momentarily, a look of concern creasing his smooth brow. His face is covered in light blonde stubble, and I notice the dark circles under his eyes for the first time. Riley has been saying that he has barely left the hospital in the last week. I hope it's not because of me.

"I know this is a lot to take in, Vivienne. And I will not even pretend to know what you are feeling. But I can promise you that you and that little one will want for nothing. I don't want you to worry about anything. Just rest for now. Alright?" He lightly touches my good foot, and I gulp, nodding. He leaves with that charming grin, and I again cover my face.

A baby.

Damn you, Trace.

CHAPTER 20

VIVI

"Okay, Riley has all of your antibiotics and prescriptions for painkillers and prenatal vitamins. Your wheelchair has already been delivered to my parent's house, and either Madden or I will be over to check on you tonight. Promise me you won't overdo it?"

I'm finally being released from the hospital after ten long days. Dr. Mansour (the big one) cleared me, though if Marshall had his way, I'd be in here another month. I wanted to return to my house, but Mrs. Mansour put her foot down. If I were refusing help from my parents, I would be resting at hers— end of.

"I won't. Your mother won't let me anyway." Riley has already told me that her mother has thrown the household into a frenzy, completely re-decorating their downstairs bedroom and Vivi-proofing everything. I drew the line at them paying for a private home care nurse. Meg has gotten in on the action and has been cooking up a storm, all with a pregnant lady-approved menu. I feel bad about all the trouble they are going through for me, but Riley gave me a stank look when I told her that.

"You are my sister, Vivi. And that little baby is my niece or nephew. If we want to spoil you rotten, you will let us because we love you. So can it, okay?"

I canned it.

"The nurse will be by with your discharge paperwork, and then you can leave, alright?" Marshall smiles at me and pats my leg. I still have to wear this cast on my arm for a few more weeks, and my ankle is still in a soft one. My left eye is fully open, but my right is still crusted shut. I'm at about thirty-five percent, but at least I'm alive.

"Don't you have some patients to go see or something? Like, isn't the ER calling you?" Riley sasses Marshall with a hand on her hip. He's been hovering over me for days, and his sister has finally had enough.

His hazel eyes narrow in annoyance. "I'm going now, brat. Take her straight home, you hear me? No stops. I'm calling Mom as soon as you leave the hospital." He holds up his phone in a threatening gesture, which causes Riley to roll her eyes. She shoos him away with a huff, and he leaves while squinting evilly at her.

"Thank god! I know he's totally in love with you, but seriously?" She grabs the tote bag she brought and begins pulling out some clothes. "Okay, I had to be creative with what to bring you because—well...anyway," she waves at my injuries. "So I cut the seam out on a few sweatpants so they will go right over your cast. Plus, the waist is elastic since, you know," she curves her hand into a big belly pantomime. I glare at her and shake my head. I'm still in denial.

"I also cut off the seam of a few of Madden's flannel shirts so that you can stay covered. There's more at my mom's house. And I brought those horrid Birkenstocks that you love so much." She shudders as I laugh. Riley is a heel for every occasion girl. "Let's get you dressed."

My wonderful night nurse, Amy, helped me with a thorough but careful shower last night, so I am finally starting to feel human. Riley brushed out my hair, then French braided it to help it stay neat. She was slathering some foul-smelling arnica cream on my face when the nurse came to discharge me. Riley cheers when I sign out, the nurse laughing as she pushes me into the elevator. I can see the rain pouring down outside, hearing the distant thunder. Riley's Jeep is running, Madden outside of it with an umbrella covering him. I give him a big kiss on the cheek as a thank you. He pats me on the head and lifts me, carefully buckling me into my seat.

"Marshall has already called Mom. She expecting you right away, Riley," He shouts through the storm. "Please drive carefully—three pieces of precious cargo are onboard." She waves him away, blowing a raspberry as she exits the parking lot.

"The boys brought your car over; it's at Mom and Dad's. I have your purse and stuff here," she points at my regular backpack that's at my feet. "I packed up some of your things —undies and stuff. Is there anything else you need?" I pull my bag up with one hand and dig through it, finding my wallet, phone, and other essentials. One thing I don't see is my iPod.

"You didn't happen to grab my iPod, did you?"

"Shit! I knew I had forgotten something. We will swing by your house and grab it. It'll only take a minute." She takes a sudden right toward the highway to my house.

"Um, do you want to let Marshall and your mom know? They were pretty insistent about us going straight home."

She scoffs and speeds up the windshield wipers. The rain is really coming down. Typical Seattle weather. "It will only take me an additional fifteen minutes. We will be fine."

We ride along in silence, the low hum of the radio the only sound. I see Riley glance over at me before sighing deeply.

"Okay, elephant in the room. When are you going to tell your parents?" I wince and look out of the window.

"What have you been telling them?" Riley has kept up the charade of being me this whole time. Part of me feels bad, but I know she probably enjoyed the heck out of it.

"Well, at first, your dad was pretty mean and saying all kinds of shit. I didn't respond to any of that. Then he apologized and said he wanted to see you. So I told him you left town for some work stuff and would text him when you were home. He's texted you daily, just checking in and asking when you were planning on returning. No word from your *Maman*, though. Wanna tell me what happened?" I start telling her everything I can remember, with more coming back to me as I speak. She grimaces in places, snarling in others.

"I think this pregnancy might be the last straw for my mom. I'm pretty much living up to her every nightmare. I hope your mom is ready to be a surrogate grandma."

Riley snickers and nods. "Oh, honey. She is trying hard to be cool about it but has already started shopping. I think she called her interior decorator when I left the house today. She is more than ready." I smile at my reflection in the window, trying hard to ignore the black and purple bruises that mar my face. I've done a pretty good job of not freaking out, though Madden told me they would take weeks to heal. I recognize my neighborhood and direct Riley the back way.

"I don't want the Lesters to see us. Mrs. Lester is liable to faint if she sees my face." She slips the Jeep around the spit of land between us and pulls into the grove by my back door.

"Anything else while I'm in there?" She grabs my long-forgotten black slicker out of the back seat and shrugs it on.

"My sketchbook?"

"Gotcha, give me two minutes." I hand her the keys out of my bag, and she winks. "Be right back." She pulls the hood over her head and darts out of the car with a squeal. She unlocks the outer door before slamming it behind her and opening the inner door of my studio. The light flickers on in the sliver of window I can see.

Suddenly, there is a bright flash of light, and the earth shakes around me. The Jeep shudders, and my head hits the dashboard from the impact. I'm slow to comprehend what has happened, the flames from my studio shooting straight into the sky.

Riley.

"Noooooooooooooooooooooo! Riley!" I struggle to free myself from the car before a secondary blast hits the Jeep again. Loud pops like firecrackers sound and the acrid scent of burning chemicals fills the air. A final quake from a third rumble, and my whole house crumbles in smoke and ruin.

"No, no, nooooooo." I hear sirens in the distance, and a deep sob grabs my throat. I hobble around the car and painfully pull myself into the driver's seat—hands shaking, head throbbing from the blast. I slowly shift the gears and pull out of the grove.

Run, Vivi.

The sirens are getting louder, and my tears are pouring with the rain. I slam my foot onto the gas, whipping the car around and speeding down the street. Mud kicks up behind me, and I dodge in and out of an alley, hoping to avoid detection. My phone starts ringing, but I have no time to pull over and answer it. I weave in and out of traffic, ignoring the outraged horns following behind me. The shaking is getting worse, a cold wave sweeping up my legs. I know I've got to pull over before I cause an accident. I spot a sign for a giant superstore and cut across three lanes, pulling sharply between two semi-trucks. My breath is labored, my whole body jerking with sobs and shock. My phone rings again, and I reach to answer it, but my brain freezes.

A swirl of information battles my sorrow. I could've waited for the authorities, giving them the little information I had. I could've called the Mansours and shared their grief. I could've gone to my parent's house and laid in my dad's arms. I could have run into the chaos, and futilely looked for my friend.

But I didn't.

"If anything ever happened to me or anyone else and you were in danger, you run."

My mind flashes to all the incidents over the past few months. My mom's car, the brick through my parent's window, Madden's break-in, and the Mansour's house graffiti. My attack

Trace disappearing.

It all surrounded me. Every single dangerous tentacle connects to me.

"You don't go to your parents or Riley's. You get in your car and leave."

Somehow, he knew. He knew I would be in this situation and tried to warn me.

My arm is clenched around my middle, and I remember I am not alone. Not ever again.

A long-dead version of me swirls back to life. I scrub the tears off my face violently, ignoring the sting of my snapped snitches. I look at the time and see that about an hour has elapsed. I don't have much time. My mind hums with old instincts. I snatch my wallet from the ground, groaning at the pain stretching across my ribs. I dig out Trace's card, peering at the blank square in the fading light. It has weight to it. I examine it closer and see that while the front is stainless steel, the back is aluminum. I think for a minute before pushing the cigarette lighter on the console. It pops out, and I grab it and hold it to the back of the card. I watch as a faint script surfaces before the lighter cools off and the script fades. I curse and push it back in. I pull open the glove compartment and pull everything out. As neat as Riley is, she keeps the most random shit in here ever.

As Riley was.

I push down the scream in my heart and shout when I find an old Zippo lighter. I close my eyes and pray, and it clicks to life with one flick. I sob in relief and hold the lighter to the card. The writing appears again, and I keep heating it until the whole message appears:

Free.

30.7501° N, 104.0838° W

I know what I have to do.

TROUBLE

Run, Vivienne.

Run.

PART TWO

'I ask of the watchman the seasoned
question: What of the night? From what
will he protect me?'
—*Josephine Jacobsen, The Nightwatchman*

CHAPTER 22

FREE

"Hey boss, you may want to come look at this," Daze's voice comes over the intercom in my office. "There's a situation at the South Gate."

I ignore his annoying ass and go back to work. I'm hoping if I don't answer, he will go away.

"Like... it isn't good, boss. You need to get out here." There's a tinge of amusement staining the concern in his tone. I slam my hand on the desk and glare at the console.

I am in the middle of negotiations for an asset that I am desperate to have. The photos from the catalog don't do her justice—her silky dark mane and large expressive eyes are much more enticing in person.

"What the fuck, Daze? I'm trying to get shit done here. What kinda bullshit could be so urgent that *you*, of all people, can't handle it." Daze could handle an army of tanks with one hand. Blindfolded.

"There's a crazy chick out here. She looks—rough. And she is screaming your name, sort of. Anyway, we can't get near her. So you need to get your ass down here." I can hear some sort of ruckus in the background and then a feminine screech. I frown and think back. I've fucked three women over the past two weeks. One was a tourist passing through town, one was a one-nighter I met at a bar, and the other was Jolene, a waitress I sometimes hook up with when I'm bored. Come to think of it; she was annoyed when I left in the middle of the night.

"She a redhead? Big tits, bit hard in the face?" I've been fucking Jolene for a few months on and off, and she's seemed fine. But you can never tell with women nowadays. They could go crazy at the snap of a finger. Also, how would she know about the South Gate? Only me and the boys use it. It's not even on any schematics.

"It's not Jo if that's what you're thinking. She's blonde. Will you just get moving? This is getting dangerous."

Dangerous? I sigh and look longingly at the lovely girl on my screen. I quickly type out a message to the facilitator and pray he won't sell her out from under me. The gate is about half a mile from the main house, so I start a brisk jog past some of the guys working on constructing the new outbuildings and throw a middle finger up to Riggs, who laughs but starts walking behind my run. I am only a few feet from the wall when I hear the commotion. The scorching Texas sun beats down on me, and even Riggs is grumbling about the heat.

"So help me, if one of you assholes don't answer me, I'm going to start swinging, and I don't care which of you I hit first." I stop and try to place the voice, but I don't recognize it. There was a strange accent, thoroughly American but with a touch of something else.

"Now, darlin', why don't you answer us first? Who sent you here? What do you want?" Daze's lazy drawl normally has hearts breaking left and right, but I guess this one is immune.

"Don't you 'darlin' me, you ass. I'm not telling you a thing until you answer me. Is this place Free or not?" The last few words are screamed, but it sounds hoarse. Why would she be asking about Free like that? "And like I said ten times, I was told to come here. Your turn, turdface."

I ease the gate open and take in the spectacle before me. A dusty Jeep with Utah plates is parked at an odd angle as if it had narrowly avoided hitting the call box. Six of my men, Daze, Fallen, Nox, Devin, Cage, and Pallas, surround it, and smack dab in the middle is a petite woman with messy and gnarled dark blonde hair. I crane my neck and see that she is dressed in weirdly baggy black clothes and is wielding a hammer in her right hand. What the fuck?

I step out and to the right, avoiding her attention. I now see that her left arm is wrapped in a cast, and her left foot is also. Jesus, was she driving like this? I make eye contact with Daze and shake my head. I don't know this woman at all.

"Okay, but who told you to come here?" This from Riggs, who saunters to her left, letting me observe undetected.

"Oh good, another one. What's that seven of you all now? For one five-foot-tall woman? Why are there so many of you anyway? Is this some sort of asshole commune?" Her stubborn voice is fading, with what I assume is an injury. "Is this Free or not?"

"Where are you from?" Riggs again. She turns her head and, I assume, glares at him since he grins at the face I've yet to see.

Silence.

"Are you from Utah?"

"What happened to your face?" Her face?

"Who did that to you?"

More silence. I admire her tenacity. Most women faced with this crew would have blubbering in fear. Or dropping their drawers.

Riggs takes a step forward, and to my surprise, the little

vixen expertly twirls her wrist before re-gripping the hammer. Riggs' eyes widen, and he quickly backs up, hands in the air. He looks at me with a shoulder shrug, and I sigh, walking further around her side. I immediately see that her right eye is swollen shut, with inflamed stitches marching across her forehead. There are bruises all over her face, and the ones on her neck are clearly fingerprints. She is wearing a giant flannel shirt and baggy sweatpants. Her blonde hair is a wild halo, partly in a braid, partly straggling down her back. She is leaning heavily on her right side, hobbling in a circle, waving the hammer threateningly.

"Darlin, why don't you put down the hammer and let's be real civil-like. I don't want you to hurt yourself any more than you already are." Daze is laying the country boy charm on thick as mud, and I roll my eyes. He darts his eyes to me and gives a quick signal. They will keep her distracted.

"Are you always full of shit, or is it just today?" She rasps out insultingly, causing Riggs to burst out laughing. She turns her head toward him and taps the hammer against her leg. I quickly move forward and snatch the tool out of her hand, and she whips around in surprise. I get a complete look at her battered face and wince. It's worse than I thought, and I've seen some fucked up shit. Her mouth drops open, and her one good eye, which doesn't look that great either, widens. Choking sounds come from her throat, and I see her legs buckle. Daze and I shoot forward to catch her, but I reach her first.

"Trace?"

Fuck.

～

"Did she say Trace?' Riggs asks as we walk quickly back to the house. I've got an iron grip on the passed-out woman in my arms, who doesn't stir once.

"Fuck yeah, she did," Daze says from behind us. He had already called Kaz, our medic, to meet us at the house. "You think he sent her here?"

I grimace when I think about it. I haven't seen Trace in about five years—we speak next to never. If he did direct her here, then shit has hit the fan.

"We will find out more when she wakes up. In the meantime, have Cage bring her Jeep inside. I want him to scour it from top to bottom—everything out. Check it for bugs and cameras and get the VIN. Fallen, get her wallet out—I want to know everything about her by tonight. Check her phone, too. I want someone on her twenty-four-seven until she wakes up. Pallas, you take the first shift." I bark out the orders and head around the house to the cabins in the back. Kaz set up a full makeshift hospital out here years ago and keeps it stocked and ready. I see him inside, already readying a tray with shit.

"Put her down here, boss," he gestures to a bed with fresh linens and a flat pillow. I place her down gently, and Kaz winces at the sight.

"Jesus. What sick fuck does this to a woman?" He grabs a penlight, shining it in her eyes, "She is unconscious. Pupils reactive." He folds a hand across her forehead and grimaces, holding a digital thermometer. "One hundred three fever. Probably from an infection of some sort." He tilts her head to the side and nods. "Yup. Her stitches are infected. She'll need antibiotics. Daze, hand me my stethoscope." He listens for a bit, nodding approvingly. He moves it all over her chest and abdomen before pausing longer.

"What is it?" Kaz is frowning, listening to something.

"Probably nothing. I'm going to cut off her clothes and get

a closer look. I'll come to the house and give a full report when I'm done." He shoos us out the door, everyone leaving except me. He pauses when he sees me still standing in the doorway. "You have more directions?"

"She called out Trace's name before she collapsed," I bite out. Ten thousand things are going through my head.

"Damn," Kaz frowns, one hand gently touching her head. "Do you think he did this to her?"

I shake my head. Trace is a lot of things: a shady motherfucker, an arrogant asshole, a cheat. But beating a woman has never been his thing. "Nah. But I have a lot of questions that need answering. As soon as you have anything, ring me." He nods, turning back to his patient, entirely in doctor mode.

Pallas is already stationed outside the door, his stoic face betraying nothing. I chose him specifically— I knew with his past, he would protect this woman and Kaz with his life. "You got this?"

He nods once, hands braced before him, back ramrod straight. Eyes already looking for danger and ready to kill.

"Nox will relieve you tonight. Call if you need anything. I'll send food down with Evonne." He nods again, and I head back to the house, cursing Trace out. What the hell did he drop on my doorstep?

CHAPTER 23
FREE

"Well, shit is already weird," Cage throws himself into the worn brown leather chair in front of my desk. He's rubbing his hand over his spiky short hair, a sign he is frustrated. His long legs are splayed out, jeans and boots dusty.

"What do you mean, weird? Hold that thought." I text the other guys to come to my office, except Pallas, who is still on guard duty. I finished a quick email to the facilitator I was working with earlier, relieved that he still had possession of my current obsession. Nox is the last to arrive, and I gesture at Cage to continue.

"For starters, the VINs on the car have been completely removed. It looks like they were scratched off, then maybe melted. And, whoever did it was an expert." A VIN or Vehicle Identification Number is a seventeen-digit number assigned to every car, truck, or motorcycle at manufacturing. It was illegal as shit to remove one, jail and fines involved. We've gotten rid of many VINs in our time, so this shouldn't surprise me, but it does anyway. "How many are on that model of Jeep?"

"Three. And all three were removed the same way," Cage tells the room. "Then there is the GPS. That particular car has a top-of-the-line system, the kind that can dismantle the car remotely," he makes a motion with his hand like he is pushing a button.

"So, can we download the info or something?" Daze is to my right, elbows braced on his thighs. Cage looks at Fallen, who takes over.

"Normally, yes. But the system in this car has been completely dismantled. I've never seen anything like it. It not only disconnected the Jeep from the manufacturer's satellite, but it also wiped all data off of the hardware. It's like this car just fell from the sky."

"Also, I took everything out of the car. There was a handheld GPS, a bag with some clothes, a tool kit, and a few water bottles, girl stuff etc, but nothing else. She has some cash but no wallet — no personal items whatsoever. The history on the GPS, originating from Las Cruces, New Mexico, is erased. Her plates are from Provo, Utah, but are registered to a Cadillac Escalade. They haven't been reported stolen yet. I asked some of our contacts to check some things out discreetly, hoping that the plates were switched with another and we can search back further. There was some kind of sticker on the windshield, probably from an oil change place—it had been removed, too. All the tags on the clothes have been cut out. I can tell you they are men's clothing, probably a size large. They were altered, probably to accommodate her casts. This is the work of a pro, one of the best I've seen." He sounds impressed, which is hard to do because Fallen is a cynical bastard. Women love his blonde angelic looks until they get to know him—then they run.

"Fuck. So we are at less than square one," Nox pulls his hair out of its braid and yanks on it. "Who is this chick?"

Devin clears his throat, adjusting the thick glasses on his face. "The way I see it, we have three roads to go down. One, we can run her prints. But judging from what everyone is saying, I can safely assume this girl is in some sort of danger, and we risk the inquiry flagging the wrong folks. So let's think about that. Two, well, it's obvious. We can call Trace."

The room goes silent as we contemplate what Dev said. Neither of the options appeals to me. I've spent a lot of energy dragging us out of the darkness; going back isn't an option. And Trace...well...

"What's the third?"

"We can wait for her to wake up, go from there," Devin shrugs, standing up. "I've got to get back to work. Call me if you come up with anything." He strides out of the room, leaving the rest of us to contemplate his words.

"I vote four; we drop this chick off at the local hospital and let her fend for herself," Nox whips his hair back into its Viking bun and stands up. "We don't know her from shit, we don't owe her shit, and we don't need this shit. We are right where we want to be—we can't let some mess Trace started get us off track. In my opinion, let's wash our hands of her. I'm going to relieve Pallas." His walk is agitated, and he slams the front door behind him. Nox has always been the most hotheaded out of all of us.

"He's an emotional bitch, as usual. But he's got a point. All of this is spelling trouble that we don't need. I'll follow whatever you say, but that's my two cents. Fallen, let's go comb that car one more time. Maybe we overlooked something." Cage salutes me as they head out, too.

The old me would one hundred percent agree with Nox. We aren't some haven for runaways—nor are we a group of heroes. Any heart I had died years ago, and one chaotic mess of a woman isn't going to bring it back. The new me sighs in annoyance.

"You thinking we should just drop her off?" I forgot that Daze was still in the room with me. "I mean, that's the easiest thing to do. Let the sheriff deal with her." I roll my eyes at the thought of Crickets, our local sheriff. A more incompetent man I have never met. He's a grade-A pussy, too—that girl would have had him by the balls in ten minutes.

"Crickets couldn't keep a houseplant safe, let alone a beat-up woman. I think we do what Devin said and wait till she wakes up. Then, go from there. There is a reason Trace sent her here—all the women he has seduced? And this is the only one that has shown up on my doorstep—that means something."

A knock on the door reveals Evonne with a large tray of food. "I saw the other boys leave and figured you two would be ready to eat. I already sent some stuff down to Kaz and Nox." She sets it down on a side table, and the smell of her famous Salisbury steak tickles my nose. We both thank her, Daze digging in first, chewing slowly. "You're right. We will wait for her to tell us everything."

I nod, wondering why my instinct is trying to warn me that changes are ahead.

A KNOCK on my door the following day interrupts my thoughts. The price for this lovely creature has gone up overnight, and I'm fighting the urge to eradicate the facilitator. He knows how desperate I am, and the slick ass thinks he can take me to the cleaners. The desire to introduce him to my fists is strong, but I am different now. I let the businessman I am becoming take over and instead write him a short email accepting the new price and asking for the contract to be sent to me. I'll punch stuff later.

"Can I come in and give you my report?" Kaz pokes his head into the doorway, and I gesture for him to enter. I stopped by last night to see how the patient was doing, but she was still deeply asleep, and Kaz was waiting for some test results. Daze is right behind him, munching on a bagel.

"How is she?" I nod toward the remnants of breakfast Evonne dropped off, but he shakes his head.

"Well, she will live, obviously, but that poor thing has been through it. Her ankle is broken, her arm is broken, her orbital bone is broken, and she's got some broken ribs. Bruises everywhere, and the stitches on her face and head are infected. I managed to get her fever down a bit and started her on antibiotics. There is a healing hematoma on her head, where she was hit with something. Whoever did this to her worked her over good. She is skin and bones, so I'm hoping she wakes up soon and starts eating," he ticks off her injuries on his fingers. "The bruising looks old, at least two weeks, but the healing isn't going as fast as I think it should. Probably because of some trauma."

"When will she wake up?" Daze asks.

Kaz looks uncomfortable for a moment. "I have her on some light painkillers, and combined with her obvious exhaustion, she should be out another day or so. Look, boss," he looks contemplative, then continues. "Nox came in last night, steaming and griping about us leaving this woman alone. And I have to say, I am totally against that."

I sit back and stare at my longtime friend. "Is that Kaz talkin', or is it the doctor in you talkin'? Because you know that this can potentially throw us in some real shit." Kaz nods, staring at me.

"And this may sound far-fetched, but she could be a plant

—anyone could have sent her here. Did you consider that, Kaz?" Daze spits out.

"Well, aside from the fact that she is gravely injured, I think she is wonderfully brave. Fallen said her last GPS location was Las Cruces—over two hundred miles from here. Provo is over a thousand. For her to have driven that distance, that hurt, is remarkable. Anything could have gone wrong, and yet she made it here. We need to give her a chance," he folds his hands together like a prayer before he blows up the room.

"And before you say anything else, you should know — she's pregnant. So I think that blows your whole super spy theory out of the water."

CHAPTER 24

VIVI

There's that smell again. It's a chemical-y tang, but it's mixed with something else this time. A strong earthy scent mixed with something savory. Bacon?

My eyes peek open. I definitely don't recognize where I am. It's clearly some sort of medical facility, though makeshift. I can see the pine tongue-and-groove walls beyond the obvious paraphernalia. A cabin? My arm is connected to an IV pole, and I can hear the steady beat of a heart monitor.

"Hello there, sleepyhead. How are you feeling?" A pleasantly deep voice comes from somewhere in the room, and I turn my head toward it. Everything is dimly lit, and I can't tell if it's morning or night. I take inventory of the aches and pains, realizing that though I feel like crap, I feel better than I have the last few weeks.

"Um, okay, I guess. Where am I?" I don't remember much from my hellish drive to Texas, but arriving at the destination Trace left me and being confronted by a group of rugged-looking guys who wouldn't tell me anything. "Is this Free?"

"No, little one, this is the Konabos Ranch. This was the end of your journey. And Free isn't a place; it's a person." The voice becomes a face, and I squint. The face is a nice one. Young-ish, mid to late thirties, dark brown hair parted to the side and clean-shaven. He's got true-blue, kind eyes that put me at ease. "I'm Doctor Kazimir, but you can call me Kaz."

"Konabos? Like the horses?" I remember this from an obscure Greek painting I saw years ago. "This is a horse ranch?" I'm beyond confused. Why would Trace send me here?

He nods."Yes, it is. I'm sure you have questions, but so do we. Do you think you're up to answering some things? I assure you, you are safe. The baby is safe, too." I smile a little. I told the baby the whole torturous drive here that I would take care of it no matter what happened. Kaz sees my smile and returns it. He sits next to me and picks up my hand. "What's your name, sweetheart?"

"Its Vi-"

"So, you're awake?" A gruff question charges its way into the space behind me. It sounds like rich smoke, the roughest sandpaper, the deepest choppy ocean. I feel a bolt of energy before a very tall form makes its way beside Kaz. My eye meets a muscular torso covered in a tight black t-shirt. I make my way up, up, up past the thick, tanned neck covered in tattoos to a strong square chin covered in thick dark scruff. Full lips, slightly scarred on the top left, a slim nose— clearly broken several times, glass-cut cheekbones, and dark, ruthless eyes. Rich, straight brows arch arrogantly, the left one pierced with a small bar, a headful of messy beautiful black curls sticking out every which way. He's Trace—but not. This man is a soul breaker, an enslaver of hearts. His beauty is only matched by the danger he emanates.

"You—um—you look like...Trace." My voice comes out small, and I'm embarrassed by the tear that stings my one good eye.

"I should— he's my brother."

What? The tear dries up automatically. This lying motherfu—

"You can't be. Trace is an only child. His mom wanted more kids but couldn't have any." I recite the exact words that Trace told me. This giant man snorts.

"That's the story he told you? Let me guess—you're an only child, too?" His sneer makes the scar on his lip jump. The look he gives me is a combination of disbelief, suspicion, and distaste.

"I am an only child, but what of it? There is no way you are Trace's brother—so who are you?" I narrow my eyes and snarl back. This guy is a jerk. I didn't drive all this way to be doubted by an asshole. I don't care gorgeous he is, I'm not taking his shit.

"I assure you, darlin', I am his brother. My name is Free. And I assume some bad shit happened if he dropped you on my doorstep."

He's Free? I assumed it was a place, not this destruction of a man. And how could he be Trace's brother? The resemblance is there—though it's distorted in a rough way. Maybe he's a cousin. "You were saying your name—what is it?"

I narrow my eyes and pinch my lips together. I'm not too fond of the way he is asking me. I've never been good with commands. Ask my mother.

"Okay, how about an easier question—where did you come from? New Mexico? Utah?" I blink at the question and realize they probably checked the GPS and ran the plates. Good luck with that. I stole them off of a car in airport long-term parking. "How long have I been asleep?"

"You've been unconscious for two days," the doctor tells me gently. "You had a fever and some infection. I'm glad we got to you in time." He smiles again and gives the black cloud hovering over me a look. "Did someone do this to you? Or were you in an accident?" I glare at Free and turn my body so I am only facing Kaz. Free snorts behind me, and I grit my teeth. This guy may be hot as fuck, but he's also a bitch. Ew.

"A couple of weeks ago, I was attacked in a parking lot. I didn't see anything, but someone found me a bit later. The police think they left me for dead. I, um, had to leave suddenly…" A giant sob erupts from my chest. "My friend, um…" No other words can come, but a flood of anguish for Riley almost flows out. I'm pulled into a gentle embrace, but I push down my grief. I can do that later.

"Bad stuff, really bad happened. Trace told me to run if I ever got into trouble. So I did." The soothing motion on my back stops, and I'm handed a box of tissues. I have no tears, but I smile in gratitude.

"The kid, is it Trace's or someone else?" I scowl at the question. Relative or not, this dude can go to hell. Every word out of his mouth is coated in misplaced malice and skepticism. Not. Cool.

"I'm not a floozy. Trace is the only man I'd been with in a long time." I fight the urge to throw my box of tissues at his perfect face.

"So he doesn't he know about the kid?" I shake my head slowly, and he gives me that skeptical look again. I don't know why, but he seriously gets under my skin.

"Why didn't you just go to Trace?" Free moves to stand in front of me again, and I huff in annoyance. His fully inked, muscular arms are crossed over his broad chest. A tiny part of me wants to ogle him, but the rest of me wants to throttle him. Maybe I can find my hammer somewhere.

"I would have, but he left and never came back. He was working on some project for his company and said he would be busy. But he stopped answering the phone and pretty much disappeared. We tried everything to find him but couldn't."

"Who is we?"

"My...friend and I." My bottom lip trembles, and I bite it. "You're his 'brother', right? Why don't you tell me where he is?" Maybe Trace can pick me up and get me away from here.

"Because I haven't seen Trace in over five years. We, uh, live very different lifestyles. And those lifestyles don't mesh. Where did you say he was working?"

The abrupt questioning is giving me whiplash. "I didn't. He works for a tech company. He's an executive now." I don't tell him where or with whom. I don't trust him.

"I think that's enough for now," Kaz cuts him off. "These two need to eat and rest. Are you hungry?"

I smile at him and nod. "I thought I smelled bacon. Was I dreaming?" He laughs and shakes his head. "Daze was in here earlier watching over you; he had some. I'll tell Evonne to make you something." I wonder who Evonne is. Maybe she is married to Free. I look at his hands, also swirled with designs, and see he only has rings on each middle finger. But then again, a guy like him probably wouldn't even wear a wedding band.

Free takes that as a clue and stands up. "I'll be back later to talk more." He stalks out of the room, taking all the darkness with him.

I let out the breath I didn't realize I was holding. "He's pretty intense, isn't he?"

Kaz lets out a genuine belly laugh. "Oh, darlin, you have no idea."

CHAPTER 25

FREE

It's about what I figured. Trace was using this girl for something. And he either got what he wanted, or he didn't and left her out to dry. That is typical asshole behavior for my brother. What I can't figure out is why he sent her to me. I hear a sharp whistle and see Devin waving at me. He's been working with an almost two-year-old colt named Harley, who we hope will be ready to race next season.

"How's he doing?" One of the hands is taking Harley through some slow work, and he looks good. Really good.

"He's doing great. He is a little impatient, but he gets in line when needed. He's got that hum under his skin. Once we let him loose on the track, he'll blow everyone else away. Nox said he's been getting calls from the TXRC about him entering some local stuff," Devin grins while scratching under his hat. When he was coming up as a kid, his family had horses. Aside from the rest, it was one of the many reasons he agreed to our lifestyle change.

"I just spoke to the girl. Got a minute to download?" Out of all of my guys, I confide in Devin the most. Daze is my best friend, but like me, he tends to run on jagged instinct and anger. Dev is level-headed and strategic. He never loses his cool, but that doesn't mean he's soft. He's more deadly than two men combined.

"Yeah, let me just give some instructions." He calls over the trainer and hands over a clipboard that he was using to track Harley's drills. The colt has some stubbornness to him, which Dev is trying to work through without breaking his spirit. They speak for a minute before Devin jerks his head at me to walk.

"So what's up?" I told him everything the mystery girl told me, which wasn't much. He nods in a few places and frowns in others. "So Trace did his usual, but this time, he put his target in danger and sent her here for what? Protection?"

"Seems so. According to her, he didn't know about the kid, which makes this even stranger." We wind up at the construction site for the new stables. The frame is in place, and soon, they will lay the floors. Riggs and Cage salute in the distance before going to back to work.

"The big questions are who is she, and who is after her? What's her name? Has Fallen started a background yet?" I grimace and shake my head. "She wouldn't tell me her name." The little brat basically gave me the cold shoulder, and I swear once or twice, she rolled her eyes at me. She sure was cozy with Kaz, though.

"Well, how did you ask her?" I look at him, frowning. He's got a goofy ass smile on his face.

"What do you mean how did I ask her? I walked in when she was all gushy with Kaz—she clammed up when I started questioning her." Dev snorts loudly, scratching the back of his neck with reluctance.

"Free, this girl has been through hell and back—we don't even know the whole story yet. She's injured, pregnant, and probably scared as shit. You can't go in there acting like—well, like yourself."

"What the fuck is that supposed to mean?"

"It means that you are not easy with women. You don't have to do much to get one; the face alone drops every panty in a fifty-mile radius. Combine that with the rest of the package, and you've never had to be...nice. I'll bet anything you went into the cabin, blew hot air and evil at her, and then demanded information, right?" He removes his glasses, polishing them on his sweaty shirt, peeking at me from under his lashes.

"I wasn't that bad," I grunt. It's not my fault that women fall at my feet. I haven't had to ask for shit from a woman since I was thirteen. Charm ain't my thing—that's always been Trace's forte. He's a smooth motherfucker and always has been.

"Bullshit. I think you need to let Daze and Kaz handle the communication. We don't need her re-traumatized with your mean ass." He elbows me in the side and grins.

"Fine. I'll tell Daze to visit her and see what he can get out of her. She already seems comfortable with Kaz, so she will confide in him, too. Someone must have helped her with erasing all traces of her trip. I'll tell them to start with that."

"Good. Now, when is the new filly going to be here?" I finally got the invoice for the gorgeous two-year-old Quarter Horse, Lily, who I'd been fighting to buy for two months. Her lineage is impeccable, and she will hopefully be an excellent breeder, just like her mother was.

"That fucking broker ran me through the wringer, but she will be here in two weeks. I hate to house her in the old stable, but Riggs says we need at least another month. Some materials he ordered are running late." I kick at a rock, squinting at the relentless Texas sun. I wonder if I can call up the supplier and lay some hell into him.

"It'll only be for a little while. I'll make sure that her stall is nice and clean. What stable is she coming from?"

"Princeton Lake"

"Fuck. They are elite, so she is probably a spoiled little miss. I'll start working on her stall today." He turns on his heel, calling over his shoulder. "Make sure Daze knows that it's time for his best work. And to be nice to her. My woman is chomping at the bit to visit with her, so I don't want her mad at the world, because we were mean." I swear I hear him mutter something slick under his breath.

"What was that?"

"Nothing, boss. Absolutely nothing."

CHAPTER 26

VIVI

I'm staring at the fool in front of me, his toothy white grin a mile wide. I take in his shaggy brown hair, liberally streaked with blonde strands, light brown eyes, his hollow cheeks creased with dimples. He's tall, not as tall as Free, but he towers over my bed similarly. He's lean but extremely muscled, wearing a grey Captain America t-shirt and tight jeans. He swept his black cowboy hat off his head and bowed when he walked in. In another life, I would think he was cute as hell, but in this one, I remember him being the first jerk I encountered when I pulled up to the gate, half delirious. He's the fifth or sixth guy that has "visited" me since I woke up. At least a week has gone by, and it's been a literal revolving door. All of them handsome in their own way, strong, but wary. It's like a hot rancher factory is pumping them out from an assembly line. Tall? Check. Tan? Check. Rough in some way? Check. Muscles upon muscles? Check, check and check again.

"Why are you bringing me breakfast? Where is Evonne?" Once I was able to not stare at Evonne's huge, um, assets and actually speak, we became fast friends. Look, I am kinda blessed in the boobs department, but hers are on another level. She's super friendly, though and doesn't ask me any questions. She helped me take a shower and wound my hair into a top knot, chatting the whole time about an apple pie she was going to make me for dessert. I like her. She's here every morning right at nine am, rain or shine. I squint at this interloper to our routine. He's still grinning, and if anything, it gets bigger.

"Darlin', I came to apologize and make nice with you. We got off on the wrong foot, and I wanna be friends." He places the tray on the table next to me and sits on the edge of my bed, without my permission, I might add. "Now, Ev tells me you love her pecan waffles, so I brought you some. And since you got a little one baking in that oven, there's some fresh orange juice and strawberries. You eat up now." He places a plate on my lap and holds out a fork. I stare at him, suspicion creeping down my spine. My stomach suddenly growls, and his grin widens. I snatch the fork and dig in. So maybe I'm hungry. I'm pregnant, you know.

"I have to say you are looking much better than the little dustmop who tried to storm the castle. Kaz is a great doctor." He leans forward and stares at my face. "Your eyes are bluish-green. Very pretty. I imagine they are stunning when they are both fully open." I shovel food in my mouth and stay quiet, eyeing him. What is he up to? Most of the hot boy gang have been silent—standing guard in some way but not much conversation. One guy—Nox, I think?? He pretty much growls at me and rolls his eyes like a high schooler. Out of all of them, he gets on my nerves the most. Luckily, I only see him right before I go to sleep. I do enjoy seeing the different ways he braids his hair, though.

"My name is Daze, by the way. I help Free run the ranch—

I'm in charge of security. It's why I was the first one out when you arrived." I wanted to ask him what kind of name Daze was, but I'm sure it's a nickname. And I don't want to give him any of my curiosity. And why would an out-of-the-way ranch need security? What kind of horses do they have here? Unicorns? I snicker at myself.

"I like what Ev did to your hair. Blonde, huh? But bought. Your roots are showing, badly. I imagine you'll be fully brunette in a few months. Can't dye it while you're preggers." He ticks his tongue, grinning at the murderous look I am giving him. I unconsciously reach up to tug on my hair, which makes him smile harder. "All that dark hair and those eyes. Mmm. I imagine you are quite beautiful. Pale though. We are coming out of summer, yet you have no tan. From up north some-where. Not Canada, though. You don't have an accent, no 'eh' in your speech. But there is something there; I just haven't figured it out yet." I still say nothing but squirm a bit at his observations. He hands me my glass, and I take a huge sip. I don't know if the Texas heat or this weird interrogation is making my throat dry.

"You've got some interesting scars on your hands. Lots of calluses, too. With that and the pale skin, you must work exclusively indoors. Can't figure out what. You are really tiny, not more than what, five one, five two? Hmmm. A mystery." He snatches a piece of bacon off my plate, and I screech in outrage. "Hey!"

"Not good at sharing, huh? You really are an only child. Me? I'm one of five. I've had to share everything under the sun. Clothes, food, a bed, you name it, I've shared it." He munches on the bacon, crunching through the whole strip.

"You mean there are more versions of you running around? Are they annoying, too?" I snipe at him against my better judgment. He laughs out loud, his Adam's apple jerking attractively. Riley would love this jerk.

Riley.

My appetite disappears, and tears rampage toward my throat. I've been good at holding everything in, but for some reason, this guy, who I know my best friend would have taken for a few rides, is breaking me down. Somehow, I've managed to avoid thinking about her, focusing on every micro-interaction I've had instead of the big picture. I throw down my fork and sob. My greasy hands grasp the tender skin of my face, and I cry and cry. The tears are burning my stitches, but I only feel it from a distance. The pain I feel is in my heart.

"Whoa. What's wrong, honey? I won't steal any more of your food, promise." He pulls me into his arms, and I grip his shirt tightly. "Tell me what's going on." I want to more than anything. There is a well of angst and grief drilling a hole in my soul that every day gets bigger. I've been able to sleep or snark my way through the pain, but even I have limits.

"My, my friend died. And it's all my fault," I wail out, ragged breaths tearing up my chest. "I don't know how I will do this without her. She was my everything."

I cry it out, finally grieving for my friend, my sister, my heart. Grieving for the life she wouldn't get a chance to live, for the future she would never have. Daze rubs my back, making shushing noises, but at no time does he tell me to stop. I keep crying until I am an empty husk, a dry barrel of sorrow. I think of the Mansour's and how they must be devastated. I think about my parents, wondering if they even care. What do they think happened to me? Do they think I'm dead? Are they mourning?

"How was it your fault?" His big hand is in my hair, massaging my tender scalp. I take a shuddering breath but don't move from his arms.

"We were leaving the hospital, and I wanted something from my house. We were supposed to go straight to her parents but made a detour. She was only inside for a few seconds until..." I stop here. I don't want to give too much information if they decide to look it up.

"Until what? A fire? Explosion? She get shot?" I shake my head. "Okay, are you sure she is gone? Maybe she made it out." I shake again.

"I looked while I was on my way here. It, um, the news said, no survivors. She would still be here if I hadn't wanted that stupid iPod." I don't think I will ever get past the guilt. "They said it was an accident, but I know that's not true. It was meant to happen to me. But she got caught instead."

"What was her name?" Daze asks, and I bite my lip. "I don't want to say. I don't want you to look it up and be in danger, too. All kinds of bad things happened to my family and friends, and I didn't see the pattern until it was too late. I don't know why I was targeted, but I won't let anyone else get hurt because of me." I sit back and wipe my eyes, wincing when I see the state of his shirt. "Sorry about that," I gesture to the giant tear/snot spot.

"It's not the first time a beautiful woman has cried in my arms; it probably won't be the last. Why do you think Trace sent you here?" His caramel-colored eyes are severe but kind.

"I don't know. Maybe he wanted you guys to help me disappear or to hide me until it was safe. I'm not sure why he thought a horse farm would be a good place, but I guess no one would think to look here. I haven't been on a horse in years." When Riley and I were twelve, she had a serious horse phase; I'm talking full-on jodhpurs and riding boots every day. She must have read every horse novel in the library, and the Mansour's got us both lessons. I had a good time but was more interested in how they shoed the horses than in riding. It didn't last long, anyway. The minute Riley stepped in horse shit, that was the end of the phase.

"What kind of bad things?"

"Lots of things: car vandalizations, break-ins at my dad's office, and my friend's brother's house, graffiti. Someone threw a brick through my parent's front window. All kinds of stuff. And I just didn't put two and two together until it was too late." On the long drive here, I rapidly cataloged all of the weird things that happened to everyone I knew. Even my agent, Phineas, had his dog hit by a car. How could I have been so blind?

"And your assault?"

"It happened after all of that. I was walking back to my car and got jumped in the parking garage. I didn't see anything; they hit me too fast." I scratch at a scab on my face. Daze pulls my hand away.

"They? I thought you didn't see anything."

"I didn't. Not really, anyway. I just saw a bunch of shadows. It had to be at least five people. Maybe more. They were all around me. I couldn't tell you what they looked like, but I remembered that one of them whispered something to me while I was on the way here." I shudder at the memory of his hot, pungent breath while his fingers squeezed my throat.

"What did he say?" He grabs my hand and tugs gently.

"*"Ty ne pomozhesh' im seychas, ne tak li?"*

"What does that mean? Do you know?" His dimples appear with his frown.

"I have no idea. I meant to check, but I only remembered it when I crossed into Texas. Will you look it up for me?"

"Yeah, I will. I want you to finish your food if you can. You need to eat for the baby. I'll be back later, and we will talk more, okay?" I nod, though all I want to do is sleep. He kisses my forehead lightly and tucks the covers around my legs like a burrito.

"Daze? I'm sorry for calling you annoying. And a turdface. I'm not normally so mean." He smiles and winks.

"Oh darlin', don't you worry about it. I was an annoying turdface. It's what I do. Now lay down and rest. One last thing, honey. Who erased all the data from the Jeep's computer?"

I squirm down in the blanket. "I did."

He nods thoughtfully. "And the VINs? You do those too?" I shrug but give him a reluctant thumbs up. He salutes and strides out the door, leaving me alone with my thoughts.

CHAPTER 27

DAZE

"She's from up north, Washington, Oregon, Idaho. Someplace like that." I walk into Free's office and plop down on the battered couch, slinging my legs over the arm. I munch on an apple I grabbed from the fruit bowl Ev keeps stocked in the foyer. With all the food she has to cook to keep us fed, she insists that we at least have healthy snacks. Free leans back in his chair, listening closely. I am always amused by the professional demeanor he's tried to adopt. It's like putting a black panther in an Armani suit.

"What else?"

"She's not as young as I thought. I put her in her late twenties. She is not a natural blonde at all; she's brunette. She has probably been dyeing it for years. She's a little thing, but whatever she does for a living has made her strong. Her muscle tone is excellent. Lots of scars and calluses. Also, she's a fucking genius."

"A genius? How so?" Fallen sits down next to me, also eating an apple. Ev would be so proud.

"She's the one who erased the data from the Jeep. And the

VINs." Fallen's eyes pop out of his head. "She did? And you believe her?"

"I sure do. She's also at least bi-lingual. College educated, probably raised in a wealthy household. Got a kind of innocence about her, but she's not naive. I can see how Trace could get to her." Free's dark eyes narrow, and I make a note of it. I'm sensing something. He's been a fucking grizzly since this girl showed up, but there's more to it.

"So that tiny woman somehow hot-wired a satellite alarm system, a GPS, and got rid of all the evidence?" Fallen is a natural skeptic, so I know this is killing him. It's what makes him such a great hacker— he has to see the evidence with his own eyes. It's been bugging him that he can't find anything on our mystery guest.

"Yup."

"Daze, I always trust your interrogation tactics, but I think this may be the one time you are getting snowed." He pulls on the legs of his black sweatpants rhythmically, a tic of his. My job as 'security' isn't just to keep things out and figure out what's 'in.' I've got a mental file on everyone at this ranch, my brothers included. "You're just pissed that you haven't been able to dig anything up on her. I'm telling you, she's smart as fuck. Even smarter than you and Devin." He growls in annoyance, taking a vicious last bit of apple. I bet he got some core in there. Ew.

"Another thing. She's in trouble. Big trouble."

Free gets up from his chair and snarls. "Lead with that next time. What's she into?" He runs his hand through his already crazy hair. At some point this girl is going to drive him bald.

"It's not her; I'd bet my life Trace got her into this. She'd been experiencing all kinds of shit—parents getting jacked up, friends getting jacked up. Break-ins, brick throwing, graffiti. Sound familiar?" Free halts and then starts pacing. "Gang shit. Cartel, maybe," he scratches at his suddenly appearing beard.

"Correct. Send warnings through the family. If that doesn't work, go after the principal. She didn't figure it out until after she was here. That attack on her was supposed to kill her, I bet. Then, they tried to finish the job when they found out she was still alive, but her best friend got caught instead. She's devastated." Free winces. Once upon a time, I was on the unfortunate side of an enemy's gun. They held me for a few weeks, and Free went absolutely insane. Let's just say I lived, and they didn't. But that's a story for another time.

"Is Kaz around? I wanna run something by him." I chin nod as Fallen pulls out his phone and mutters a few words into it. He's still in a snit. "He'll be here in a few."

"Did you get anything else? Her name or her friend's name? How did the friend die? Fallen can at least work with that." Free goes back to his manic pacing. When he asked me to be the one who got close to the girl, I could tell it bothered him to trust that to someone else, even me, and I'm his best friend. The Trace element of all of this is probably driving his intensity. Probably.

"She doesn't want to tell us too much; she's afraid something will happen to us. That if we start digging, someone will notice, and we will be in danger." Free snorts.

"We are the danger," Fallen says with a smirk.

"Yes, but she doesn't know that. She is alone and pregnant. Everyone in her life was put in the line of fire, and she blames herself. She's trying to protect us. As far as she knows, this is a horse farm, and we are a bunch of ranchers." Free snorts louder this time but nods thoughtfully. A quick knock on the door admits Kaz, and I give him a dap and handshake.

"Kaz, I was talking to your patient, and she told me something I need your help with. When she was attacked, one of the assholes whispered something to her. I think it's Russian. Can you translate?"

"Russian?" Free and Kaz say at the same time. I nod, pulling out my phone and rewinding the recording of my interview.

"What did he say?"

""Ty ne pomozhesh' im seychas, ne tak li?"

"What does that mean? Do you know?"

"I have no idea. I meant to check, but I only remembered it when I crossed into Texas. Will you look it up for me?"

I touch the screen to pause it and look at Kaz, who looks more constipated than usual, if possible. "What does it mean?"

"You won't help them now, will you?"

"Fuck. Dialect?" Free has resumed pacing. He's about to lose it, I can tell. We have worked too hard to leave our old life behind, and one (I'm positive) gorgeous little chick is about to upend it. Free is the coldest man I know. He's never ruffled and executes (literally and figuratively) with no hesitation. This past week has shown me a side of him I never dreamed existed. And I am enjoying it immensely.

"Kyzyl, maybe. Sakha Republic. Bad news all around." Kaz winces. His mother and father emigrated from Moscow years ago, thrilled that their only son became an 'American Doctor.' His winding road to get there is *another* story for another time. If he's making a face like that, shit is bad. Really bad.

"So Trace somehow put this girl on the Russian Mafia's radar, took off, and sent her to me for protection. And she's carrying my niece or nephew. That fucking..." He goes off on a colorful rant that has even my eyebrows singed. I know there is no love lost between Free and his brother, but damn.

"We need her name. If we can't get it, I can always make a damn phone call... Fuck, this shit is too complicated already. Fallen, run a query: cross reference parking lot attacks with young women's deaths. Concentrate on the locations that Daze gave. We've got to find something." He exits the room, calling Fallen to follow him like a puppy.

"I've seen him in many moods, but never like this. Have you?" Kaz's voice whispers through the room, probably afraid Free will cuss him out, too. I shake my head slowly, grinning.

"No, I haven't. I think things are about to get really interesting around here. I have a tingle."

Kaz groans. "The last time you had a tingle, I got a broken leg. Keep your tingles to yourself," he stomps out of the room, flipping me off in the process, and I laugh in the empty space.

My tingles are never wrong, aiming straight at Free and our little houseguest.

Awesome.

CHAPTER 28

FREE

Fallen texted me about an hour ago, letting me know that he was getting nowhere with the search he's been running for the last few days. He is ridiculously suspicious that such a brutal attack would not pop up in any of the police databases he broke into. I can feel his frustration seeping through the brief words on the phone. There is almost no information that Fallen can't find, and this whole situation is driving him fucking nuts. Evonne said he barely eats, surviving on coffee and Doritos. I know he wants to barge into the medical cabin and demand answers from our guest, but Daze is adamant that she tells us things when she is ready. I'm running on both strategies, waiting for one to bear fruit.

I glance at my phone and see it's after one in the morning. Ranching has its own time clock; twenty-four hours can feel like a third of the time, or it can feel like the longest day of your life. I've been getting four hours of sleep a night for as long as I can remember. In our former life, we needed to be alert for danger around every corner, focused ten steps ahead. In this life, animals must be fed, buildings completed, and endless emails I never thought I'd be shackled to need to be answered. The exhaustion is the same, yet different. Your life constantly being threatened drains you in a way that cannot be explained, but good old physical labor tires you in the best way. I swear Daze is reverse aging, and even Pallas' grouchy ass has fewer lines around his eyes.

I twirl back and forth in my office chair, the full moon illuminating half the space and the other half in shadow. Earlier, I met with Riggs about Lily's arrival and spotted the girl hobbling outside the cabin. Kaz was hovering over her like a mother hen, jerking worriedly whenever he thought she might fall. Daze was leaning on the wall, calling out encouragement- at some point, something he said caused her to pause and flip him the finger. His roars could be heard for miles, and her light laughter floated on the hot wind. My stomach tightened, and I swung back to Riggs, who was watching me with a smug grin. I glowered at him, redirecting the conversation. I haven't been back to speak to her after Dev basically told me I was too much of an asshole to talk to her. Once or twice, I peeked in while she was asleep- her injuries were slowly healing, though her face was a mess of bruises and angry stitches. Still.. it's been interesting watching the swelling fade into some semblance of normalcy. Daze has announced to everyone who will listen that she is probably "fucking gorgeous," and I wouldn't be surprised. Trace may screw any woman he is told to, but this is the only one he has ever given a fuck about. He's incapable of going deep enough to appreciate a woman's intellect or anything else— it would stand to reason that he would fall for a pretty face. My phone beeps, and I see Jo's name flash on the screen.

Jolene: Tonight?

I tap my fingers on the desk and contemplate.

Free: Be there in thirty.

Jo works part-time at the only diner in town and is also a server at Clucks Bar. Her hours are sporadic, but when she's got a morning off, she usually hits me up. After I'm done with her, Jo normally needs the extra recovery time. She's not shy about asking for my dick, and I admire her bluntness. There is no future for us, and she knows it—someday soon, her pussy will bore me, and I will move on. She won't cry over it, and we will be friends at the end. I gather my keys and reset the house alarm. My truck is parked behind the house, and I can see the dim lights in the distance and Nox leaning back on the porch chair. He waves, and I nod, glancing at the dark back bedroom where the cause of our troubles rests her bratty head.

"Good...god!" Jo's voice is hoarse, her back bending at an unnatural angle. I've got her bent over a small chair in her bedroom, one leg over my arm, the other bracing against the floor. When she opened the door, she was in just a bathrobe, her nipples already hard and begging. I slammed it behind me and threw her over my shoulder, dumping her on the bed. Her robe came loose, and I could see the wetness already on her thighs. I leaned over, roughly sucking a strawberry nub while shoving two fingers into her greedy pussy. Her first orgasm came shortly after, and before she could recover, I was already gloved up and inside of her. I'm not small, but Jo takes me like a champ. Not into soft and easy—I take her hard, with no quarter given, my strokes relentless and deep. She screams with every thrust, alternately begging for mercy and more punishment. I get her off two more times, but my own release runs away as fast as it approaches. I flip her over, her somewhat flat ass propped up, legs trembling. She is almost at her breaking point, but I can't seem to stop.

"Fucking bitch. Beg me," I whisper in her ear. The sound of her wetness fills the room as she gets crazier with my words. I smack her ass, gliding my fingers between her legs until I trap her clit between two fingers, tugging hard.

"Please, Free. Fuck me harder. Please. I'll do whatever you want; please make me come again," she mumbles incoherently. I can feel her walls shaking and know she is gearing up for another wave. Her mumbles turn into shouts as her orgasm slams into her, and finally, I feel the lightening zip of my own come filling the condom. I shove my thumb in her ass, and she screams as a final shock hits her body. I slow down my thrusts, her prone body finally collapsing onto the mattress, pulling my still-hard dick out. Her harsh breathing fills the room, and I climb off and dispose of the condom, flushing it decisively. I walk back to the bed and see she is in the same position, but her eyes are open, and she's smiling.

"What got into you tonight?" she whispers in the dim light. I shrug and grab the water bottle she always keeps by the bed.

"Got a lot goin' on. Sorry if I was too rough." I don't mean it, but it sounds good, I think. At the end of the day, she was a willing hole, and I needed to clear my head. Jo is a good girl, though.

"Ha! You ain't sorry in the least," she quips, sitting up and tugging the sheets over her tits. She sits up, leaning against the headboard. She eyes me up and down, stopping on my dick before resting on my face. "You wanna talk about it?"

What? No, I don't want to talk about it. This isn't something we do—we fuck, and then I leave. There isn't any conversation or any of that shit.

"Nah." I finish the bottle and crush it before tossing it in the trash. She's staring at me, one finger tracing a circle around one of those giant pink nipples. Her legs part, and even though I just rode her hard, I can see she wants more. The sheets fall, and her legs spread wider. Her pussy is puffy, the faint lines of fingerprint marking the inside her thighs. Usually, this would make my dick stand up and jump in the game, but nope. I guess the day has finally come.

"Imma head out," I tell her, grabbing my jeans from the floor. I tug them on while she petulantly covers herself. "Already? I feel like you just got here."

I eye her dispassionately, schooling my features to the mask everyone fears. "We both got off, Jo. No reason to stick around." I pull my t-shirt over my head, then bend over to tie my boots. "You need anything?" She studies me, shaking her head slowly, with a slight look of wariness.

"You coming back?" I know she means in the future, not just tonight. I wander over and give her a brief kiss on the head. The roots of her red hair are dark brown, which makes me think of my unwanted house guest. I straighten while shaking my head.

"It's been good, Jolene. But I think we should start looking elsewhere. I'll be seeing you." I pull the covers over her, flipping off the light. She says nothing, but I can see the sheen of her eyes in the dark.

"Free?"

I don't turn as I grip the doorknob. "Yeah?"

"Whoever she is, she's a lucky girl," I say nothing as I push the button on the lock and close the door quietly.

CHAPTER 29

VIVI

A knock on the cabin door startles me out of staring at the wall in boredom. I have never been this idle in my life and it's slowly killing me.

Once a day, Kaz and Daze take me on a short walk around the cabin, never venturing too far. Kaz said I need to keep my muscles from atrophying, while Daze said I'm pasty and need the sun. Of course, I got sunburn the first day, so now both of them make me slather SPF two thousand on before I step foot outside. I've been at the ranch for three weeks or so, and I'll admit I feel good. My ribs are pretty much healed; Kaz said I can get my casts off in another two. My face is still a mottled jigsaw of bruises, but the swelling is down, and both eyes are open. My energy levels are almost back to normal, though I take way more naps than I ever have. Kaz says it is the baby and that it is all to be expected.

The door opens, and Daze peeks his messy head in. "You up for some company?"

Am I up for some company? At this point, I would welcome

the devil himself. Except for that jerk Free who hasn't cursed me with his presence since the first time. Jerk. Face.

They've brought me every fashion magazine (yuck) in the South and some wicked-looking romance novels (Of course, I skipped to the good parts. Sue me.) they could find. At one point, Fallen (what is with these names?) dropped off a laptop that I looked at like it was a pair of dirty underwear. I'm pretty sure the minute I open it, there will be a whole bunch of traps and tracking programs. He tried to sweet talk me with promises of movies and social media, even shopping for the baby.

Amateurs. Only an idiot would fall for that.

"Yeah, I can finally stop my twenty-four-hour binge-watching." He chuckles. I haven't watched more than one minute of television since they rolled it here. Fallen hooked it up to the ranch satellite, and there were so many channels and exploding colors that I immediately shut it off.

"Good, I've got someone who has been waiting to meet you," he smiles while pulling a girl behind him. I straighten up and stare at her, my curiosity matching hers. She has light brown pigtails with chunky red highlights, starry hazel eyes, and creamy skin. She's way above my height and is in full Texas gear: a pink plaid shirt, jean shorts, and boots. She's cute.

"Scoot, this is Dulcie—Dulcie, this is Scoot," he waves a hand between us a few times. I roll my eyes to the moon at his nickname. I still haven't felt comfortable giving them even the tiniest bit of information, especially not my name. Daze has taken to calling me that vile name because he says since I can't walk normally, I'm 'scooting.' Fucker. I know, I know, I could end all of my own misery by telling them my name, but I'm still worried about bringing trouble their way.

Dulcie rolls her eyes, too, elbowing Daze sharply while

pushing into the room. "Move out of the way, cretin," she pulls a large bag behind her and flops into the chair next to my bed. "I don't know how you have been putting up with having all of these fools hovering over you, but it's got to be driving you crazy. I mean, sure, they're pretty hot—except this fool," she waves behind her, causing Daze to scowl, "but a girl needs a girl, ya know? Anyway, I told them I was going to rescue you, but they made me wait until you were healed up a bit, and Kaz said you are much more mobile, so here I am! I brought you some stuff too—ya know, clothes, lotion, etc. Anyway, how are you?" All of this comes out in a rush; I don't think she took one breath. I stare at her, feeling an involuntary smile tug at my mouth.

"I'm ok, I guess?" I glance at Daze, who is staring at Dulcie with a lot of love and annoyance. Are they dating? Daze doesn't seem like the dating type. He's more the sneak into your bedroom at night after ordering you to leave the window open, type.

"The guys have told me everything, even about the little honeybun you've got baking in there. I bet you'd love to get out of here for a bit. OH! I haven't seen this one yet." She snatches one of the fashion magazines Fallen dropped off and rapidly flips through it. "I'll help you put on some clothes and then take you for a ride. Show you around the ranch." She rotates a finger in the air, shimmying to music only she can hear. She suddenly whips around and glares at Daze. "Why are you still here? I got this. Shoo," she kicks a foot out in his direction.

"I'm leaving, I'm leaving. Scoot, I apologize in advance for my genetically mandated connection here. If you feel like she's too much at any time, scream. We've all screamed to get away from her at one point." Dulcie screeches while I stare at them. I can see it now. The eyes and dimples are identical.

"Stop calling her that horrible name, idjit! And don't make

me call Mama and have her tell you again why I'm her favorite." She pulls her cell phone out threateningly. It's covered in pink rhinestones and has a gold tassel hanging from it. I squelch a chuckle.

"Mama lies."

Another screech comes out, and she launches out of the chair in his direction. "Imma tell her you said that! You're gonna get it!" Daze chuckles while backing out of the room, hands up. He winks at me, and I hear the door close behind him. Their interaction reminds me of how Riley and her brothers used to act when we were kids.

"How much older?" I ask her, planting my fists and pushing myself up further on the bed. She plops into the chair again, the light scent of cotton candy wafting around the room.

"Daze? Ten years. I'm the baby," she proclaims proudly. "And I really am my Mama's favorite. Don't believe anything he says." She stares at me for a minute, leaning closer by about a foot. "Daze said that you are really a stunner, and I can see it when you smile. Those bruises and scars are gnarly, but once they fade, whew! You got your eye on any of the boys? I can give you all the dirt on 'em."

"Uhhhh no. Maybe Daze didn't tell you, but I've got some issues. Bad stuff happened to my friends and family, and I had to run here," I gesture to my face. "And I'm pregnant. I don't think I'm a prize on the wall of stuffed animals."

"Girlllll. Nothin', and I mean nothing is going to happen to you anymore. In case you haven't noticed, you live on a ranch with a bunch of badasses. They aren't gonna let a single thing near you. Free could take on an army by himself. Plus, that baby's gonna be spoiled. Mark my words." She winks just like her brother. "Now, let's get you dressed and out of here. I got a surprise for you."

CHAPTER 30
VIVI

"I can't believe it's pink. Wait, maybe I can believe it." Dulcie laughs, and we zip along. When she told me she was taking me for a ride, part of me was worried it was on a horse or something, but it turned out that Dulcie had a tricked-out, solar-powered golf cart complete with gold seats and trim. The ranch is thousands of acres big (Dulcie said no one except Free knows exactly how big), though the living portion is over five hundred acres alone, and Daze and "her man" thought this would be the best way for her to get around. Thankfully, it has an awning that shields us from the sun and even a cooler filled with treats in the back.

"I don't suppose pink is one of your favorites?" I snort and shake my head. When I was growing up, my *Maman* would dress me in all manners of pastel laces and ruffles; the more European the label, the better. That lasted until I figured out that the dirtier I got, the more likely she was to dress me in more American jeans and shirts. When I started art classes, I pretty much only wore black or dark colors from then on. Once in a while, Riley would get me into some color, but I never wore pink again. "No, my *Maman* tried when I was a kid, but that girly stuff never stuck with me. I'm a plain girl. I'll leave the rest for you." Dulcie gives me a droll look but smiles.

"Girl, there is not a thing plain about you. You've got that je nay say kwoh going on."

I laugh out loud as she grins. "*Je ne sais quoi*? Thank you, I think." I laugh more. "Anyway, they will be able to see you from space in this thing," I quip, and Dulcie giggles—a true girly sound.

"That's the idea, peaches. Now, we are at our first stop—the stables. We won't get out because my man is working, and I don't want to disturb them, but you can see Devin over there with Harley, his new favorite. Ohhh, look how hot he looks. Hi honey!!!"

She yells at the top of her lungs. So much for not disturbing anyone. Devin pushes his hat back on his head and waves with a giant grin. Dulcie blows him a kiss, and to my amusement, he grabs it out of the air. "Dev takes care of the horses—he's like a whisperer or something. He's got a whole team of trainers that work under him and everything. He works with the jockeys, too." We watch him make some hand gestures, and the golden-colored colt tosses his head while obeying. I take a deep breath, and the smell of sunshine, hay, and animals fills my nose. I can feel my shoulders drop an inch. "It's wonderful out here."

"Sure is. If you look over there, you can see where they are building the new stables. We almost have no room for new horses." She pulls the brake, and we cruise past a group of men toiling in the hot sun. One of them raises his hand, and I stiffen when I recognize him from my arrival. He seems older than I remember. Dulcie waves back. "That's Riggs. He used to be super close to Free's daddy when he was alive. He's known all the boys since they were tadpoles."

Free's dad died? Was he Trace's dad, too? I frowned and

dialed back into what she was saying. "...anyway, we will all be glad when it's all done. All the guys are super cranky about it. There's Nox! Hey Noxxie!" She jumps out of the cart, waving wildly to the gorgeous giant Viking, shirtless and wielding a nail gun. He stares at her, shaking his head. His eyes drift to me and he gives me a head nod. I try not to stare at his tattooed chest, which is covered in sweat,--bulky muscles bunching with use. His blonde locks are braided into an intricate crown around his head. He might be the only man I've ever met who could pull off that look.

"Noxxie is my favorite, next to Daze, of course. He seems mean, but sometimes he braids my hair for me. Don't let him intimidate you. He's got a heart bigger than those muscles. Anyway, he is in charge of all of the buildings and works with Devin on getting the horses into races. The track ladies love him."

I bet they do.

"Are you hungry or anything? Kaz made Evonne pack us some healthy snacks, though I snuck in a bag of candy. You want something to drink, at least?" She pops open the trunk and pulls out one of the variety bags of candy you get at Halloween. My stomach starts making greedy noises, and I can barely stop myself from snatching the bag out of her hands. I rip it open and pull out a Charleston Chew, shoving it into my mouth. I haven't had one of these in years; the rough yet chewy texture satisfies something I didn't know I was craving. I tore through them before Dulcie handed me a bottle of water with a laugh. "I'll take that as a yes?" I shrug apologetically and slow my chewing. "I had breakfast, but my appetite is annoying right now. I want to eat all the time. And I already want to eat all the time, if that makes sense." She nods and starts to drive again. "Yeah, it's that little nugget you've got in there. Making all kinds of trouble already." We drive a ways, the hot wind blowing hair into my face. I glance at Dulcie's hair and scratch my head self-consciously. I feel stupid caring about how long my roots are when so much else in my life is up in the air, but when I looked in the mirror this morning, I almost cried.

We zoom past other buildings and even some barracks-type structures that Dulcie says house all the hands and workers when they don't want to drive back into town. Most live off-ranch, but some stay here full-time. She points out some paths that lead to Fallen and Cage's houses. They are behind privacy fences and trees, so I can't see much.

"Wait, do you live here too?" I realized I hadn't heard her say anything about her residence.

"Yup, all of the guys do too. When Free bought this place, he gave all the broth- guys a percentage of the ranch and about seventy-five acres each. Devin and I have a place pretty close to the stables, though it's still far. I was living in town, but when we finally got together, Dev had me packed and into his house in one weekend," she laughs. "Of course, Free has the biggest house on the property. I don't know what he needs all that space for, but when you and the baby move in with him, it won't seem so empty."

Record fucking scratch.

"Move in? With Free? No, we aren't?!" My mouth is opening and closing in shock. I have barely had a conversation with him, and I didn't like him within three words he uttered. Hell no, I'm not moving in with him! "I, um, don't really care for him. I'd rather not."

"Well, you can't stay in that hospital room. I know you can't be getting that much rest with all the workers coming in and out for bandaids and all that. Plus, you need a nursery for the baby and a room for yourself. Y'all are basically family, right? He's responsible for you now." She keeps her eyes forward and continues driving. "I know you don't have anything anymore, hell I don't know anything about you, and we've been driving for hours. But I do know that you want to keep that baby safe. Dev said you drove umpteen hours and miles to get here by yourself. That you somehow erased all evidence or something. Anyway, Free ain't gonna be cool with you being alone-- why do you think you have a guard every night? It's not because you will walk off with the family silver or something. He's taking care of you. So you are gonna have to suck it up, peaches. I already know the rooms y'all should have and everything. And why don't you like him? I know he's rough around the edges, but he's the best."

The best? "He's been to see me one time since I got here. And he was rude to me. There is no way he will want me and a newborn to live with him."

She snorts. "Girl, he knows everything there is to know about you being here. He knows when you eat, sleep, and are happy and sad. He knows we are out today and even knows exactly where we are right now. One thing about Free is he is INFORMED. It's his job to take care of all of us, you especially. But it's not cool that he hasn't been by to see you. I'll tell Devin." She steers down another path, and a giant building looms before us.

"You don't need to say anything about it. I'm okay without another visitor." I hurry and tell her, hoping that she drops it. She gives me a side eye and keeps driving. "This is the equipment warehouse and the boys' garage. This is Cage's domain. He is a crazy person about it, too." She stops, and we get out to stretch our legs. "That building is where he does all his doctoring—pretty much a giant garage. The one to the left is the toy factory. At least, that's what I call it. The boys have all of their stuff in there. It's why there's a keypad on it. I think it's even got a thumbprint sensor, too." I look at the windowless building painted a surprising red with state-of-the-art doors. I spot at least four cameras and would bet there are motion sensors, too. I see a smaller building in the back, obscured by some succulent plants. "What's back there?"

"I have no idea. There's a bunch of stuff around Cage's setup that I mind my business on. Like I said, he's a crazy person about it. Anyway, the only person who doesn't really have a spot is Fallen. He keeps all of his computer stuff at his place. And Dev says no one likes to go there because he never has food. Evonne has to drive dinner by there; otherwise, the fool would only eat chips and energy drinks. And, of course, Pallas doesn't either. But he does his own thing." She hurries and changes the subject, telling me about her stable admin job — filing and computer work. I'm not surprised to hear that she has a degree in business finance—her encyclopedic knowledge of everything ranch-related is impressive.

We wind our way back to my temporary home, and I'm shocked to see that Free's house is only a few hundred yards behind it. I never noticed the proximity until now, which makes his neglect even more annoying. A giant blacked-out pickup truck is parked in front of it, wheels, spokes, and trim all a glaring midnight. That could only belong to one person. I'd make a joke about the size of cars and men, but I have a feeling it doesn't apply to Free. At all. My yawn catches me off guard, and a deep, sinking feeling fills my bones.

"I think that means you need a nap, peaches." She pulls up shortly and I slide out of the cart. My legs are a little wobbly, and I do need a nap, annoying as it may be.

"Thanks for letting me spend time with you. It was a lot of fun," I tell her sincerely. "Promise me you won't say anything about Free, okay?" I really don't need the aggravation. And I'm not moving into his house, despite what my new friend thinks.

"No problem, girl. I'll stop by and see you tomorrow after I get back from town. Is there anything you want me to get you?

Besides some vegan dye for those roots?" Her eyes twinkle, and I laugh out loud.

"Some overalls? I left mine behind when I ran. I can pay you back—I've got cash." I point my thumb over my shoulder.

"Girl, I'm going to make Free pay for everything. He's loaded. See ya tomorrow, Scoot." She salutes me, her shiny braids swinging over her shoulders. I wait for a beat and then call out.

"Dulcie? Call me Vee, okay? Your brother's days are numbered if he keeps calling me that." She grins, and those dimples pop out.

"You got it, Vee. See ya."

CHAPTER 31
FREE

"Sooo, we got a little more out of your girl today." Daze slides into the leather chair in front of my desk without notice. He has a mouth full of chocolate and tosses a few empty wrappers and a file onto the pile already in front of me. When we spoke yesterday, he felt that the time was right to bring Dulcie in for a visit, though I doubt it was his decision as much as she was about to barge her way in anyway. I've known that girl since she was knee-high to a grasshopper, and despite her sugar-sweet appearance and demeanor, she is a force to be reckoned with. Daze felt that the girl's isolation was about at a breaking point and that if we didn't do something to ease it, she would start some trouble. And I have no doubt she could—it's written all over her.

"First of all, she's not my girl. And don't you knock?" I hate that I want to grab that file and read every word.

Daze snorts and gives me a look. This motherfucker hasn't knocked a day in his life. Even when it could have gotten him killed, he just burst forward with no fear. It's one of the many reasons he's my best friend.

"*ANY*way, it's not much, but we are getting somewhere. And she and Dulcie hit it off, so I'm sure it's just a matter of time before she gets everything out of Vee."

I pounce like a sucker. "Vee?" I curse under my breath at the smug look on Daze's face. "That's her name?"

"I doubt it's her whole name, probably just an initial or a nickname. I knew she would get tired of me calling her Scoot—I swear once or twice she grabbed a butter knife on me. Anyway, Dulcie calling her that sent her over the edge. I've got their whole conversation on tape. I already sent it to your email. She doesn't say much, as you can imagine," he grins. No I doubt she got a word in with Dulcie on an excited kick. A few other women are on the ranch, like Ev and a few of the hand's wives. But someone closer to Dulcie's age with a massive swath of mystery hanging over her? I should've sent along an oxygen tank.

"I was right about her being bi or multi-lingual. On the tape, you can hear her pronouncing a few words with a very French accent. I bet she's fluent. We might need to have Fallen expand his search to Montreal or thereabouts. But I bet she lives here. You can hear it for yourself. Here are the time-stamps," he peels a Post-it off the inside of the folder. "Also, Dulcie pretty much volunteered your house for her to live in."

Maybe there's have been a few times in my life I have been genuinely speechless? In fact, no, I doubt there has ever been a time. Not when Riggs told me my dad died, not when my brother told me who he was going to work for, not even when I bought my first horse and they quoted me the price. But this? My mouth is open, and no sound comes out for a full minute. Daze is staring at me, a weird look on his face. I can't tell if he wants to laugh or cry. I might do both.

"What!? She did what?"

"Well, I mean, she has a point. You've got your pregnant

sister-in-law living in a medical barrack. Where is the baby supposed to sleep when it comes? Plus, she's a girl—she needs space for all of her stuff. Were you planning on building her a house of her own or something? How are we supposed to keep her safe if she's alone?"

Every question is like a bullet to my resolve. Somewhere in my head, I knew that she would eventually have to move out of Kaz's cabin, but I kept pushing it away. Last week, Nox told me that one of the stablehands got a little too curious and tried to get a peek at Vee. Nox had to knock some sense into him. I almost raged out but trusted that Nox got his point across.

"I figured she would stay with Dulcie and Devin." Daze rolls his eyes and glares at me. "I hate to say it because she's my baby sister, but their house is like one giant honeymoon suite. I made the mistake of walking in there unannounced and almost had to acid-wash my eyes out of my head. I don't think Vee will want to be around all of that." He shudders dramatically, and I grin. I know that when Devin manned up and claimed Dulcie, Daze made him promise not to 'do any mushy shit' in front of him. If he only caught them once, he's lucky because I know they've screwed all over this ranch. "She can't stay here."

"Yes, she can. You have the biggest place on the property. You could avoid her altogether with all the room you have if you want to, though I doubt you do. Plus, Ev is here, and I know she would love to help care for the baby. And this way, we wouldn't have to have guards on her all day and night. No one in their right mind is going to break into your house. She needs to be safe, and you can provide all of that. It's a no-brainer." He ticks his points off on his fingers, and I glare at him.

"I don't want her here. Isn't that enough of a reason? It's my fucking house, " I seethe.

"Why not? She's your responsibility." Daze seems confused. Fake motherfucker.

"I don't trust her. She's hiding things. We might have this all wrong, and she was sent here as a plant." I cross my arms over my chest and lean back.

"Are you still on that shit? There hasn't been a peep anywhere about any trouble headed our way. No one is even thinking about us—we made sure of that. *I am* telling you, she is legit. That should count for something. Is this about Trace?" I shrug and spin my chair toward the window.

"Brother, you cannot hold that against her. You know that this is what Trace does. It's who *he is*. The fact that he left her with no warning but made sure she had options should mean something to you. He has never done that with any other woman, and you know it. It means she's special." I stay silent. "What did you think we were going to do with her? Ship her off somewhere unguarded and alone? This is her new home. She's one of us now. She's got nothing. A stolen car, a few clothes on her back, some cash, and your fucking niece or nephew. That's it. The least you could do is offer her your home." I still say nothing.

"Hello? Are you going to say anything? Are you just going to sit there in that stupid chair and pretend you don't care? We both know that's bullshit." I swing back around and pick up a report on a proposal from another ranch. We are both silent, and I can feel the heat from his stare boiling into my head.

"Fine. If that's what you want. She doesn't want to stay with you if it makes you feel better. She's pissed that you haven't been by to see her and isn't a fan of yours at all—you can hear it on the recording. Kaz offered for her to stay with him, and that's probably a better idea anyway. He'll be more than happy to have her in his house." My anger spikes, and I push the images of her and Kaz out of my head with a brutal vengeance.

"Here. These are apparently her favorite candy. When you go and tell her she is not welcome in your home, maybe you can soften the blow by throwing these on her hospital bed." He tosses a few Charleston Chews onto my desk.

"Why don't you tell her? You guys are friends, aren't you?" I sneer without meaning to, fighting to smooth out my face. I click my tongue ring behind my teeth, which makes Daze bare his teeth at me. Him and his stupid 'files' can go to hell.

"No can do, brother. I've done enough of your dirty work. Time for you to pull up your big boy pants and talk to her yourself. Keep in mind that she is grieving and pregnant—try not to be too big of an asshole." He pushes out of his seat and heads for the door, stomping his work boots the whole time. "Oh, and I gave Dulcie your credit card to do some shopping for Vee. I hope she spends every dime on your limit." He slams the door on his way out, and I wait a beat for the front door to slam, too. The sound shakes my desk, and I grab the candies and throw them across the room.

"Of course, Free has the biggest house on the property. I don't know what he needs all that space for, but when you and the baby move in with him, it won't seem so empty."

"Move in? With Free? No we aren't?!"

"I, um, don't really care for him. I'd rather not."

"Well, you can't stay in that hospital room. I know you can't be getting that much rest with all the workers coming in and out for bandaids and all that. Plus, you need a nursery for the baby and a room for yourself. Y'all are basically family, right? He's responsible for you now."

"Anyway, Free isn't gonna be cool with you being alone; why do you think you have a guard every night? It's not because you are gonna walk off with the family silver or something. He's taking care of you. So you are gonna have to suck it up, peaches. I already know the rooms y'all should have and everything."

"And why don't you like him? I know he's rough around the edges, but he's the best."

"The best? "He's been to see me one time since I got here. And he was rude to me. There is no way he will want me and a newborn to live with him."

I hit the rewind button and listen to her husky voice reject me for the tenth time.

CHAPTER 32
FREE

I can hear laughter coming from the cabin and pause. I recognize Dulcie's tinkling laugh but pay closer attention to her partner. The raspy giggle is unfamiliar, though I know who it is. I push the door open a little more, not one bit ashamed that I'm fucking eavesdropping like a teenager in trouble.

"...and then his tongue spun like a tornado, whipping my clit with force..." More laughter and even a snort. What the fuck are they talking about? Whose tongue whipped whose clit? I remember who was on guard last night and realize that Nox had the night shift. I don't want to have to kill my brother.

"...His fingers are sausage-like..." What the hell? The laughing is getting harder, and Dulcie is almost choking. "Ewwww. I don't want sausages near my vag." And I don't want to think about Dulcie's vag. I don't know who would chop me up faster, Dev or Daze.

"...His member throbbed with sticky rhythm..."

Okay, that's it.

I push the door open a crack and find Dulcie and Vee

leaning back on the pillows on her bed, a giant bag of Doritos and a plate of cookies between them, a beer on Dulcie's side, a giant glass of milk on Vee's. My ward is holding a book with a shirtless man grabbing a naked chick on the cover, and the girls have matching overalls and socks. Pink socks.

"Why is it sticky, though? Wait, never mind," Vee says, her face bright red. A smile threatens to break through my perma-scowl, and I wipe it away. Her mouth opens and I notice that her hair is deep, midnight black. It makes her eyes pop, and makes her bruises look almost nonexistent. I push the door all the way, and they both look up at me. Dulcie smiles big, but the brat scowls. Her face turns even redder.

"Free! How long have you been standing there?" Both of them look like they want to run away and I smirk.

"Long enough to hear about sticky sausages or something. Wanna tell me what that's all about?" Dulcie pulls a blanket over her face and giggles. Of course, the brat is still scowling and crosses her arms over her chest in defiance.

"Pallas brought Vee some books to read and, ummmm, we are having a book club. No boys allowed." The blanket muffles Dulcie's voice, and I snort, yanking it away. "Don't worry, I think I'm okay without all the action. Is that your dinner?" I motion to the junk food between them.

"Nope, Ev already brought us pot roast, mashed potatoes and gravy. This is just a snack."

Pot roast? Mashed potatoes? That's my favorite meal, but all I got was a sandwich for dinner. Come to think of it, I haven't had a decent meal since I told Daze that Vee wasn't moving in. Fuck. Evonne must have overheard. No one wonder I'm eating like a stepchild. Now I have to suck up to her to get some food in my own house. This is a whole mess. I sigh deeply in annoyance.

"I hope so. A baby needs more nutrition than cookies. At

least you're drinking milk," I watch her face as her lips tighten in anger. She still doesn't say anything. I push a little more.

"Wow, seeing your hair fixed and one color is nice. Dulcie, you did a great job. You're a great influence on See. It is See, isn't it?" I draw the name, watch the color drain from her face, and then storm back in splotches. Her plush lips are one grim line, and I see her fingers grip her overalls till her fingertips are white.

"It's Vee, Free. Ya know.." Dulcie holds her her fingers up in a V-shape. The devil in me rears its head, and I struggle with my face.

"Vee? Like Vagina?"

That does it.

"No, it's Vee, like FUCK YOU VERY MUCH!" Her voice whips out, and she pounds her little fist into her thighs. She starts looking around wildly, before grabbing the bag of cookies and throwing them at my head. Thank God my reflexes are on point because I barely have time to duck before she nails me in the face. She screeches in frustration and starts awkwardly lurching around for something else to toss. Dulcie has long since run to the other side of the room, and I stride forward to pull her up, pinning her arms against her sides. She struggles hard, and I squeeze her a bit. Her milk and cookie breath pants into my face, curly hair wildly covering her eyes. I absently push it away and gaze into her blue-green eyes. "Settle down now, girl."

"I am not one of your farm animals. I will NOT settle down on command. Let me go." She jiggles a little more, her tits pushing deeper into my chest. I move a bit suggestively, and her face flames when she realizes how close we are. Her teeth grip her bottom lip, brows gathering in a storm.

"You'll hurt yourself if you don't calm down." I push a finger into the knot between her eyes, which loosens slightly.

"Then you'll never get out of here." She swallows a retort and glares at me. Even with all of the faded bruising and faint scars, she's...

"Stop staring at me like that. I don't like it." How long have I been staring? Shit.

"I'm just wondering what my brother saw in you," I sneer at her face turning pale. "It can't be your personality, that's for sure. No wonder he left you." Her mouth opens wide and then shuts with a snap. I swear I see a glimmer of tears before she does a pretzel-like twist and slips from my arms. She struggles off the bed and hobbles to the bathroom, slamming it behind her.

Fuck. This girl brings out the worst in me. I sigh and drop my head back onto my shoulders. This is not how I pictured today going.

"That was seriously mean, Free. I'm ashamed of you." I turn at Dulcie's voice, who I completely forgot was in the room. Her hands are propped up on her slim hips—she is her mother's replica with a deep frown of disappointment. I give her a half-smile that normally gets me out of female trouble but does nothing to budge her anger. Have I ever sighed this much? "I'm glad she's not moving in with you anymore. Kaz will treat her so much better."

Oh. Fuck. No.

"Sorry to burst your hero worship, but yes, Vee is moving in with me. I came over to tell her to get ready. I have a bed and some other shit arriving in the morning. She'll sleep at the house starting tomorrow night. You can pick up whatever else she needs after, and then y'all can do all the baby crap." Dulcie's face contorts, struggling to contain her emotions.

"She doesn't want to stay with you, Free, and I don't blame her. She and Kaz already talked about it. He's clearing out the room that overlooks the stables for her, and it has a little nook for the baby. It's all settled," she states primly, her Daze-like nose lifting in the air.

"I don't give a shit what she and Kazimir talked about. This is my ranch, and Kaz works for me. She is staying at my house, and that's fucking final." I snarl the last two words, and a screech comes from behind the bathroom door. The door flings open, and Vee stumbles out. I reach out to steady her, and she snatches her arms away. Her eyes have darkened to an angry sapphire, and her candy-pink lips are quivering.

"I am not going to move in with you EVER," she stamps her bad foot and teeters again with a grimace. "I am not your responsibility, and I can take care of myself. Kaz is going to let me stay with him until I can figure out where I am going, and then I am leaving here. I don't need anything from you. And I don't LIKE you."

"I don't give a shit if you like me or not, girl. What I care about is that my long-lost brother somehow sussed out an entrance that no one on earth knows about except a few people and gave you directions to get to it. What I care about is that you've got a kid that's related to me growing in there. What I care about is protecting everyone on this ranch." I point at the floor in emphasis, taking a threatening step closer. This damn girl doesn't even move. Instead, she tosses her head and bares her teeth at me.

"This is exactly why I'm trying to keep you from looking..." I slash my hand in the air and cut her off.

"That is fucking stupid strategy. You'd prefer for us to be kept in the dark? So we won't have any idea what's headed for us?" She scoffs.

"No, what I would prefer is to get out of here as soon as I can. I just need to get this cast off my foot and my Jeep back. And you can't stop me. If I got here on my own, I can make it on my own." Her wild hair slips over her shoulders and tumbles down her back. I gaze at her for a moment and then go for the kill.

"You aren't going anywhere. Unless shit has changed in the last day or so, you are still in some sort of danger— You haven't told us anything about who you are, where you are from, or even how you met Trace. You are one big blank page. Do you think Kaz can protect you better than I can? Do you think you are safe on your own? With a fucking baby? You think the people after you will give a shit that you've got a little kid?"

Her dimpled chin quivers, but I don't let up. She's got to know what could happen to her. "You think they won't take your baby? Look at what they did to you. They tried to kill you twice. They got your friend. You think they won't take that kid and sell it? Or worse? I've heard of some of the most fucked up shit happening to kids as young as one year old; who is going to stop them? You? Alone?" Her skin is flushed, and her throat is spasming with emotion and fright.

"Daze seems to think you're pretty smart, so I will tell you this: Trace would only send you here if you were in some deep trouble. Do you understand that? Whatever it was, it was bad enough that he risked *himself* to send you here. So this is how it's going to go: you will move into my house. You will tell me everything that I need to know, and I am going to get your bratty ass out of the line of fire. We will figure out the rest later, but for now, getting you off the radar is the priority. Is that clear?" She stares at me for a minute but finally nods once.

"Good. Let's start with the obvious. What's your goddamn name?"

Her eyes glaze up again, and this time, the tears start streaking down her face. Her fear is tangible, but she swallows it, chin lifting in surrender.

"Vivi, my name is Vivi."

CHAPTER 33

DULCIE

Yay! I can't wait to tell Daze! Oh! And I gotta warn Kaz cuz you know Free looked really mad and I don't want him to get in trouble and I wonder what kind of furniture he ordered for Vee, I mean Vivi's, room and who picked it out, and from where and.....

CHAPTER 34
VIVI

"**S**tart from the beginning."

I look over a Daze sitting to my right, leaning forward, elbows resting on the knees of his light ripped jeans. The rest of the room is filled with all of the men I've gotten to know over the past month. Fallen and Nox are on the long brown leather couch against the wall, while Pallas is standing near the doorway, half-hidden in the shadows. Cage and Devin each have a chair opposite me, Dulcie sitting at Devins's feet on a thick floor pillow. The room is large, a living space with tons of seating and dark wood beams on the whitewashed ceiling. It should feel intimate, comforting even. But filled with these men, who I just realized are all one step away from an explosion, it instead feels like a barrel with a lit stick of dynamite attached to a string. The only one missing is Kaz, who is running late from his hospital shift.

"Ummmm, okay," I struggle. How far do I go? How much do I say? The deep need to protect myself rears its head. Okay. I can do this. I think.

"Vivi, you are thinking too hard. Start with where you are from and go from there."

The order comes from over my shoulder, where Free is standing. I glance over at him and grimace. After we agreed that I would move into his house, it took him less than twenty-four hours to make good on his threat. Nox showed up with Cage, and they had all my little belongings and I transferred over in no time. When Cage put me down in the foyer, Evonne ran in and led me upstairs to my room. The furniture was all a light mango wood, with dark grey linens. There was a large window seat that overlooked the pastures, where I saw several horses grazing and faintly heard them calling to each other. It's a good size, and I spied a few doors. I opened the first one and saw a gorgeous en suite with a clawfoot tub. I raised my eyebrows and opened the next, which led to the room next to mine. It's empty, but I can see a few decor magazines on the floor. This would be the nursery. The last door is a large closet, where someone hung up my pitiful wardrobe. It was a lovely room, and I should have felt grateful, but instead, I was annoyed. It's got to be hormones because instead of gratitude, I felt homicidal. I was still pissed at how Free spoke to me, and I'm chafing at my lack of choices. Luckily, I only see him briefly twice daily, once in the morning and once at night, until he knocked on my door to tell me he would call this very meeting.

"Vivi?" It's still weird hearing my name after over a month of being called everything but. Daze grinned about a mile wide when he walked in and called me it for the first time.

"Okay, um, I'm from Seattle. Washington, you know. I'm thirty, uhhh, thirty one. My parents are Denis and Suzanne."

"Are you French? Canadian? I can't help but hear the accent now," Daze interrupts. I nod. "Yes, both of my parents are French. I was born in the States, but we lived in France until my dad got a job here. I grew up in Seattle. I only left when I went to college."

"Where did you go to college?" This is from Fallen, who I'm pretty sure is recording everything I am saying.

"I went to RISD. Um, Rhode Island School of Design. My dad was, and still is, an industrial engineer. Plus, Riley was going to Brown, so it was a no-brainer," I swallow hard.

"Was Riley your friend?" Daze asks quietly, and I nod jerkily, tears welling up and stealing down my face. I feel a hot presence, and a tissue appears from behind me. I look up at Free, who nods and steps back, but only slightly. I can feel him like the sun on my neck.

"She moved to Seattle when we were in fifth grade. We hit it off right away. She's got two brothers, older— we all were best friends. They are both doctors in Seattle. I didn't have a lot of friends— it's always just been Riley and me. When we finished school, we moved home and started working. Riley was a pharmaceutical rep for Pharmtec. She was their top producer. She had a conference in Las Vegas and dragged me with her. I didn't want to go, I hate Vegas and now I wish I never did." I press the tissue to my eyes and take a shuddered breath. "We got invited to a club opening while there, and Riley never could pass up a good party. She was out dancing, and I was at the bar."

"Were you drinking? Did anyone approach you?" Devin asks, frowning when I shake my head. "No, I'm not the club type. I get bored. And Riley and I had a pact that if one was going to party, we had to have a sober sister. She and I had a few adventures when we were younger, so..." I shrug before continuing. "A few guys approached me, but they were either trying to get an in with Riley, or I scared them off. Anyway, I was drawing on a napkin when a really creepy guy approached me. I drew a picture of him, and he was kinda pissed."

"Why was he pissed?" Daze.

"I drew him as a worm with a widow's peak and a chipped tooth. He kept licking that tooth—it was really gross. Anyway, he threw the napkin at me, and someone picked it up. And it was Trace." I see Daze look at Free, and they have a weird, silent moment. I file it away and continue. "He was nice. Normal. Handsome. We had a great conversation, and he asked me to dinner. I didn't want to leave Riley, but she threw me at him and returned to the hotel. We went for pizza and then, um, back to his hotel. I, uh, spent the night. It wasn't something I normally did, but..." Ugh, I probably sound like the biggest hoe in the world. But then, judging by these guys, maybe not. None of them look like saints.

"Anyway, Trace had meetings with some clients, so we didn't see each other again that trip. When Riley and I got home, he sent his driver to pick us up at the airport. Stephen."

"Stephen?" Free asks behind me. I see Daze glance at him again, and Pallas makes a weird noise.

"Yes. Do you know him?"

There's a long silence before Pallas himself answers. "Yes, we know him." That's all he says, and I feel the tension in the room ratchet up a bit. It's weird that they would know Stephen, right?

"Anyway, Trace texted me right away that he was going to come visit. Luckily, his company had offices in San Francisco and Seattle, so he had legitimate business reasons for being there. He spent the next few weeks shuttling back and forth to spend time with me. We were getting along great..." My voice fades as I think back. "Trace had a big project he was getting ready to be tied up in, and so did I, so we spent one last night together. We knew it would be a while before we would see each other. I think...I think he knew something bad was going to happen. He was asking me all kinds of weird questions, and at the end, he gave me a blank card. It was metal. He told me that if I ever got in trouble, not to go to the police or my parents. He told me to run. To just run. I thought it was strange," I realize that vocalizing it. "But I didn't give it much thought at the moment. We got, uhhh, distracted, and he left the next morning. I never saw or heard from him again."

"Riley and I tried to contact him, find out something about him, but we couldn't. It's like he never existed in a way. His socials were all stale, and I couldn't even remember the name of his company. He just...disappeared."

"How long after were you attacked?"

"A few weeks. I'd fought with my Maman and went downtown to get dinner to take to Riley's house. I'd just left the restaurant when I was jumped in the parking lot. I woke up in the hospital a few days later."

"And then?" Free moves closer, his legs pressing into the back of my chair.

"And then, the day I got released, Riley was driving me to her parents' house, but I wanted my iPod and a few other things. We, um, pulled up at my house. It was raining, so she put on a raincoat. My raincoat. That's why they thought it was me. Everyone always thought we were sisters, you know. She was taller and prettier, and it used to drive me crazy. She opened the door, and then it...." I stop here, crying harder. Free pushes closer, and the room silently lets me sob. "It was instant, you know. Like my house just went up in flames. I got in the driver's seat and drove off. It was like all I could hear was Trace's voice telling me to run. So I did. Now I'm here." The room stays quiet as I sniffle and try to stop crying.

"Did you really erase the VINs and GPS on your own?" Fallen asks. I nod, staring at the floor. "How?"

I pause, using my tears to stall. "I looked it up on the internet."

"On the internet? Oh, okay?" I can hear the sarcasm in his voice. It's partially true—it's not my fault he doesn't believe me. "The card that Trace gave you. Do you still have that, at least?"

"Yes. I left in the Riley's Jeep. It's wedged between the window and the doorframe. Drivers side." Cage stands up and strides out of the room.

"I think that's enough for now, don't you, Free?" I see Kaz leaning near Pallas in the doorway. "Vivi needs her rest. You guys can pick up from here later." Dulcie leaps up and wraps an arm around me, leading me out of the room. I turn around to see Free giving Kazimir an evil look and frown.

"One last thing, Vivi. What was the club name you and Riley went to?" I frown deeper. "It was new, um, The Golden Lick." Fallen nods, and I feel that peculiar exhaustion wash over me.

"Let's get you a nap, Peaches. The boys will figure everything out." Dulcie croons with her soft twang. She tucks me into my bed and pulls the curtains shut. "Don't worry about when you wake up. I'll be downstairs if you need anything." I nod sleepily and snuggle deeper into the soft sheets.

"Vivi? I'm sorry about your Riley. I can't replace her, but I can be a good friend to you too." Dulcie whispers as she closes the door softly behind her.

CHAPTER 35
FREE

"I still have about ten thousand questions."

"Yeah, she is full of shit. I mean, I think what she says happened, but she's hiding something. It's all over her face."

"She is definitely leaving shit out. Notice she didn't tell us where she worked. I bet it's what Trace wanted from her. And it's clear she doesn't know who he really works for."

The comments were flying around the room. I had Devin send Dulcie home after she went upstairs with Vivi. Cage returned a few minutes ago, tossing a black square onto the table. Fallen snatched it up and then passed it around the room. My first thought was that there could potentially be a tracker inside, but Cage checked. I could see the faint numbers-coordinates etched into the front with my name above it. Fallen whipped his computer out of nowhere and plugged in the numbers, and sure enough, they precisely led to the South Gate. Trace never set foot on the ranch, so for him to know the existence of that entrance was a problem.

"You had to heat the card to get the numbers to show up. I

wonder how she knew to do that?" Cage asks with his arms twitching at his sides. "Also, that card was soldered into the window frame. I had to take the whole door off and pry it loose. You tryin' to tell me that five-foot termite did that on her own? She had help." His normally tight buzz cut has grown out some, the natural side part taking over. He looks like a choir boy—if the choir boy had piercings and a ripped tank top.

"Fallen, where do you want to start? She's given us enough information to get fucking going. What're you thinking?" Everyone is sitting, but my energy is ruthless. Part of me wants to find Trace and beat the living shit out of him, and part of me wants to go upstairs and make sure Vivi is okay. Yeah, I could smell bullshit a mile away, but her grief and confusion are real. I wanna know what she is hiding, though.

"I think I'll start with Vivi herself. Make sure that everything she told us about her life was real. Then I'll spread out to Vegas. I want to see their first meeting for myself. I'll also look into the friend, though she was clearly collateral damage. If Trace needed her for anything, he would have just targeted her instead. Vivi was clearly his endgame."

I nod and turn to Daze. "So we know that bitch Stephen was there, posing as a chauffeur. And Cash is definitely the guy at the bar who was licking his tooth. Who else from Trace's crew?" Daze goes through anyone we ran into across the years, and Fallen makes a list. "You still have that file on Trace?" Fallen looks at me with *that* face.

"Hell yeah. I don't throw away shit. You know that." He taps a few keys and then sends the file to the printer in my office. I separate the pictures from the generic information and pass them around the room. Everyone in the room was present when Trace and I had our last run-in. His crew was hanging back, letting us fight, but my brothers were right behind me.

"Ugh, I forgot how ugly Cash is. Vivi described him perfectly," Nox makes a sour face. "So he was the set-up man? Insult or scare her, and then Trace swoops in to save her. Sounds textbook." I frown.

"Vivi doesn't strike me as the type, though. Trace had an in. We need to find out what it was," I click my tongue ring in thought. "Daze, has she said anything to Dulcie at all?" The girls have become thick as thieves, Dulcie spending more time in my house than her own. Devin has to come look for her every night.

"Not really, but she gets the impression that Vivi didn't date much. She's got a strange innocence about her. I don't know how to explain it. I don't think she's naive, but she's got walls up too. I agree; Trace didn't approach her blind. He knew exactly what to say." Nox nods, as does Cage.

"Alright, let's start with what we've got. Fallen, I'd like an update on the hour. You can text it to us—I know you are gonna want to work out of your cave. Cage, I'd like more information on that card. Everyone else can go back to work. Daze and Devin, you stay a minute."

My men amble out of the room, Cage shoving Nox and Nox screeching like a girl. Kazimir laughs behind them, and the front door closes. I face the windows in thought, hearing Daze settle in behind me. Devin is perched on a stool, one jean-clad leg braced on the floor.

"How do I tell Vivi the truth about Trace? Should I wait?" Daze, of course, surges straight ahead.

"I say you tell her as soon as possible. She's having his kid —she should know who he really is. All of the bad shit." I look at Daze, who never liked Trace, and know he means it. Hell, I never liked Trace either.

"Dev? What do you think?"

Devin pulls at his lip with one hand while the other taps his thigh. "I agree that you need to tell her. She's been here a month. I don't know if you noticed, but she's got a little belly now. Dulcie was screaming about it this morning. Kazimir wants to sneak her into town and do her ultrasound immediately. They want to pick out baby furniture. We can't let her plan the future if she hasn't closed out the past--Plus, to your point, she's smart. A lot smarter than I think we know." I scowl. This is the first time I've heard about a fucking ultrasound. I think Kazimir and I need to have a chat. "Now that we have movement on her background, we can prepare." I nod again.

"Tell her, Free. Do you want me to be there? I know y'all don't get along." Daze smirks at me, and though I wanna smash his face in, I know he's right. We've spent the last few days circling each other like lions in a cage.

"Let's give it a few days. Let Fallen get more information, and then talk to her about it. Then I agree that Daze needs to be there. Free, we all know that you can't ease into it." I glare at him, too, but agree.

Daze offers to work with Kaz on a plan to sneak her into the hospital for a checkup. He and Devin chat about it while my mind wanders. The girl already hates me. This is going to make it so much worse.

Fuck you, Trace. Seriously.

~

SHE DIDN'T COME BACK DOWNSTAIRS the rest of the day. Dulcie stopped by to check on her, but I sent her home. Evonne made her a plate but wrapped it up in the microwave. The house is silent, more silent than when I lived here alone. She's only been here a few days, but everything already feels different. My normal rhythm is disrupted, my peace gone. I find myself listening to her movements, her footsteps shaking my concentration. It doesn't help that she and Dulcie cackle like hens every five minutes. Even with my office door closed, I can hear them carrying on. I don't know what I will do when the baby comes. I may have to move to the stable barracks.

I shut my computer and rub my eyes. So many things are going on at the ranch, and the specter of danger taints all the changes. It was an aspect of our lives that we thought we had left in the past, though the saying about it catching up to you because it's part of you, comes to mind. The remaining bunch of us made our pact and stuck to it. But all it took was for one tiny vixen to hurl us backward. I stand and stretch, switching off the lamp and closing my office door. I check the locks, making the rounds to the windows too. Old habits die hard.

I step lightly up the stairs, pausing at the top. My room is to the right, but Vivi's is right off the staircase, the nursery further down. I turn the other way, but my feet take me to her anyway. The door is ajar, and I push it further open. The room is pitch black, the only light from the full moon streaming through the window. I step closer, listening to her deep breaths. Every other intake, there is a tiny whistle from her nose. I snicker quietly, knowing I would win zero points if I ever told her that. She's still wearing her overalls from earlier, and I unconsciously smooth her hair away from her face. She moves slightly toward my hand, and I back away quietly.

Fuck you again, Trace. Seriously.

"Oh. My. God. Yes, right there, don't stop. Harder, good god, yes." The litany of words pouring from the woman's lips does nothing to drive me to come. I went to Clucks to get a few drinks and clear my head. Maybe get my dick wet. I knew it was Jo's day off, so I didn't have to worry about hurting her feelings if I snatched some willing pussy. I wasn't seated at the bar for more than five minutes before I spotted the chick in the last chair. She didn't look familiar, like she was from town, which was confirmed when she asked for a menu. Everyone in a fifty-mile radius knows that Clucks only serves wings and fries: one way and only one size. I chuckled when they handed her a Post-it note instead of a full menu. Fred, the owner, was nothing if not a son of a bitch. Her facial expression said every-thing, and I laughed out loud, which made her look in my direction. She was a cute little thing, blonde and skinny with a slight overbite. Her eyes got big in her face when she spotted me, and I knew what she saw. The bad boy that every girl's mama warns her about but that she can't resist. I wag my fingers for her to come to me, and that's all it took. Now I'm in her hotel room, fucking her like she owes me money.

"Oh, oh, oh.." She groans as I bend her legs further back, her knees touching her ears. She's slick, her come practically dripping down to her ass. She's already gotten off twice, and I'm pushing her toward another orgasm if she has it in her. She looks like she might pass out. I tunnel deeper, my dick at war with my brain. She's tight and pretty, but I can't seem to find relief. The same thing happened with Jo, which is pissing me off. I've never had a problem enjoying pussy, and I refuse to examine why I'm struggling. I feel the walls of her cunt wavering as another wave bears down on her, her breath stop-ping in her chest as she wails out her pleasure. Fuck it. I pull out of her and strip off the condom, rubbing my dick in her wetness and jerking myself off hard. I push three fingers into her throbbing hole and stroke myself mercilessly. I can finally feel the heat of relief boiling before I groan and shoot it into her stomach. I rapidly fuck her with my fingers and give her one final orgasm, which indeed causes her to pass out. My head drops back onto my shoulders, and I stand up and head to the bathroom. I throw the condom out and brace my arms against the sink, staring at myself in the mirror. Sex has always been something I enjoyed, but lately, it's just been a means to an end. An itch I scratch. Maybe I'm just getting old. I grab a wet washcloth and wipe off her juices, then walk back to the bed and clean her up. She doesn't move. I quickly jumped on my clothes and covered her with the thin hotel blanket, snapping off the lamplight. She'll feel me tomorrow, that's for sure.

I've already forgotten her name.

CHAPTER 36

VIVI

"I hate you for this." Dulcie snickers and even Kazimir laughs.

Free was adamant that if the doctor wanted to take me to town for my ultrasound, I had to be fully in disguise. My hair being its naturally dark color was a bonus, but he wanted me to look as far from myself as possible. Dulcie pulled some stuff from her closet, and I almost walked out of the room when she pulled three dresses from the garment bag. All of them, every single one, was pink.

Bright, awful pink. One had flowers. Kill me.

"I think this one fits the best. What do you think?" I don't even look in the mirror; I just glare at her. "It's too tight." I tug at the bust and squirm.

"Well, I can't help that you have giant boobs, and I don't. Stop pulling; you're just making it worse," she slaps at my hand, frowning. "Now all we need to do is put one of these boots on, and you will look like a little Texas expecting mama." She points down at a pair of badass black and white cowboy boots, and I feel a little interested. "We don't wear the same size, though."

"I know. These are your boots. They came this morning. Come on, pull it on." I'm still in my cast, though Kaz said I can probably take it off in a few days if I promise not to overdo it. I sit and yank the boot on, feeling the buttery soft leather mold about my foot. Ohhhhh, I like these.

"Those are really cool. There are two more pairs in your closet. This hat might be a little big, but it'll cover your face a little." She plops a white cowboy hat on my head, and it covers my eyes. I push it back so I can see and grin. "Do I look like you?" Dulcie laughs. "No, you look like a biker chick pretending to be a cowgirl. Let's get going."

Because I can't go to the doctor's office like a normal pregnant person, Kaz has to sneak me in the back way. We had to wait until nighttime, so we had less chance of running into someone. We are taking one of the ranch trucks that Cage fixed to look anonymous. The last step was to make me not look like me. So now here we are.

"Don't you want to look at all?" Dulcie sounds disappointed, and I swallow the groan that threatens to pop out of my mouth and turn around in a huff. I gasp in horror and then laugh.

The dress is long—on Dulcie, it probably hangs just below her knees. But on me, it's just above the floor. The dress itself is light pink with blue and yellow flowers. The sleeves are short, and it gathers in the front into a deep vee. Every bit of boob I have is hanging out. Seriously, if a cricket sneezes near me, a whole nipple is going to make an appearance. The dress flows straight down before it gathers weirdly on the left with a slit. She slipped a ton of red bangles over my right arm that jingle when I move. The hat is large and keeps slipping down my forehead. My boot is the only cute thing; you can't even see it under the dress. I blow a curl out of my face and grimace.

"I look like an idiot."

"You do not! You look adorable. Doesn't she Daze?" I look up to see her brother lounging in the doorway, a look of comic horror on his face. His eyebrows shoot up when they linger on my boobs, then frown down again.

"The middle looks good." I scratch my collarbone with a middle finger and glare at him. He laughs and takes another look before Dulcie shoves him out of the way. I walk past him, covering my chest with both hands, making him laugh again.

Kazimir is next to the truck, and his face goes through fifty things before focusing on my face. "You look different," is all he gets out before lifting me into the truck. Dulcie hops into the backseat, and I fasten my seatbelt. I look over to where Free typically has his big black truck parked and see that it's gone. I want to ask where he is, but I also don't want to look interested. He stopped by my bedroom this morning and told me arrangements had been made for my doctor's appointment, and that was it. I said nothing, just nodded, and then he left. I didn't see him for the rest of the day.

Dulcie is already chattering, and I watch the ranch buildings slip by. We make a few turns and then are through a plain white gate and onto a main road. There is a steep incline, and then we twist and turn down.

"Wait, Konabos is on a mountain?" How did I not realize it on my way here? I have delirious memories of my last bit of driving, but I think I would know if I was driving up?

"Yup. The way you came, the secret way, is stretched so long that you don't even realize you are going up. The whole mountain is private; I think Free owns most of it. The other part is government-owned, but I don't know which part. It's one of the only privately owned mountains in Texas."

Wow. "How did he come to own it then?" Silence fills the truck, and I look over at Kaz, who has a perfectly blank expression on his handsome face. He says nothing as Dulcie answers.

"You'll have to ask Free that, Peaches. It's not my business to tell." I grunt and stare back out of the window. I don't want to ask Free anything.

We make it down the mountain in no time and then drive through some more dusty roads. Before I know it, houses dot the landscape, a barn or two. A sign proclaims the town limits, and there is a small burst of civilization. The town isn't as small as I thought—I see several fast food restaurants and even a Buc-ees.

"Why is it called Blue Falls City?"

"I have no idea. Devin probably knows. We'll ask him." I smile at Dulcie's worship of her boyfriend. I have never heard so many variations of lovey nicknames in my life. This morning, she called him her "chipmunk sugar cube honey bun," and I almost cried laughing at the look on his face. I can tell he loves it, though.

Kazimir takes a few more turns and then makes a right onto a quiet office-driven street. He pulls into the back of a building and parks, helping me out of the truck while Dulcie jumps out on her own. The backdoor is shadowed, and Kaz goes to enter a code into a discreet keypad on the doorframe. He pauses and then pushes the two of us behind him abruptly.

"What's wrong?" I whisper while my heart pounds out of my chest; Dulcie breathes hard behind me.

"The alarm is already shut off. There shouldn't be anyone here. And the parking lot is empty. Go back to the car right now." I turn to run when the door swings open, and a large shadow fills the doorway. Dulcie and I scream before the figure moves into the meager light, and I see Free's stupid face come into view.

"Free you, you, you buttface! You scared the hell out of us! Vivi, are you alright?" I bent over at the waist, my slight belly preventing me from going too far. I feel lightheaded and seriously think I may pass out. I manage to nod when the smell of sandalwood and mint fills my nose, and I'm hoisted into a pair of steel arms. I want to struggle, but truthfully, I'm too shaken up.

"Sorry," his voice comes in a still whisper. "Didn't mean to scare you." He strides through the silent office and carries me to a back room. Dulcie is still grumbling behind me, and Kazimir hasn't said anything. I put down on a paper-lined bed and look up to see Free staring at me. "I'm okay." He nods and then leaves the room.

"So weird that he's here," Dulcie whispers and Kaz hushes her.

"Vivi, put this on, and we will get started. Do you want some water?" I nod, and he places a blue gown at the foot of the bed and leaves the room. I struggle out of the tight dress, and Dulcie comes over to help me. My heart is still struggling, and I take a few deep breaths. Kaz comes back, super professional, with a doctor's coat on, which I think is cute, and a clipboard. His face looks a little disturbed, and I can only imagine why when Free opens the door and steps in. I frown and look at Kaz, who is busy cleaning his stethoscope and won't look at me.

"Why are you in here?"

He says nothing at first, his perfect face impassive. His jaw works and then I hear the faint click of his tongue ring against the back of his teeth. "Because I want to be," his rough voice lightly touched with humor. I frown deeper and look at my two companions, but they might as well be whistling Dixie because they are both staring at everything but us.

"What if he wants to do inside stuff? I don't want you in here for that." His full lips twist into a slight grin.

"I'm sure I have seen everything you've got and more. Won't be news to me."

Ew. "Well, I don't care how many...things you've seen. I don't want you seeing mine. You need to leave if he does anything like that. Got it?" I point a finger at him, and he looks at it briefly before staring at my face.

"Vivi, we won't be doing anything transvaginal today. We are going to go with a traditional ultrasound, okay?" He asks, but I feel like he's really asking Free. I roll my eyes and turn my back, legs swinging to the end of the bed. Kazimir sighs, starts with my blood pressure, and we go from there. He's super gentle and thorough, and I forget that Free is in the room until Kazimir lays me back for a breast exam.

"Okay, I want to make sure everything looks good here. Any tenderness or redness?" He gently palpates around my nipple, and I look up to see Free staring at him with a murderous look on his face. It's not that his expression changed that much; it was all in his eyes. They looked arctic cold, the areas around them desolate as a frozen sea. Those eyes swung to me, and the look was gone with a blink. I knew he couldn't see anything with the way my gown was situated, but I still felt stripped bare. He unwraps his tightly crossed arms, the fabric of his jet-black t-shirt stretched over his biceps like a lover's caress. I briefly take in his dusty black jeans that grip his thighs and flit down his tall frame to the tips of his old work boots. There really was a run on perfect genetics in that family.

"Okay, Vivi, everything looks good. I'm going to grab the ultrasound machine. Try and relax, okay?" He gives Free a look and then leaves the room.

"I'm so excited! What do you think you want to have? Of

course, we want it to be healthy, right? But, oohhhhh how cute would a little boy with a cowboy hat be? We could get him little boots and everything." Dulcie bounces around the room with too much energy, and I smile.

"I never really thought about it. To be honest, I never really liked kids. Riley had some little terrors who were cousin's kids, and I ran from them every chance I got. I hope the kid won't be as bad as I was. I put my parents through it," I laugh. Kaz comes back, pushing a large machine. He fiddles with it for a moment before he's satisfied.

"This will be cold," he tells me with a smile, squirting some gel onto my belly. He places the wand just under my small bump and moves it around, clicking buttons on the machine. Everything looks like blobby images until a distinctive form pops onto the screen, a fast whirring sound filling the room. "There we are. Hello, little one." Dulcie starts sobbing behind me while I go completely speechless. There is a little person inside of me. Holy. Shit. I mean, I knew it in abstract, but looking at it on one screen is a whole other matter.

"She's sucking her thumb, see?" Kaz points at something, and I freeze. "She?"

'Yup, it's clear as a bell. You're having a girl. And she looks beautiful and perfect." Dulcie is sobbing harder and muttering about barrettes and boyfriends, and I still can't move. Tears pool in my eyes.

Riley. My sister. I wish you were here.

CHAPTER 37
FREE

"Vivienne, pronounced *Viv-yenn*, Micheline DuPlantier." Fallen throws a few-inch-thick file onto the table, startling me from my reverie. "What?"

"You alright, boss? Anyway, that's your girl's name. Her whole name. Vivi is a nickname, though it looks like only her friends used it. Her parents called her by her full name, but they look like tightwad snotbags." He braces his hands on the back of the deck chair, grinning in triumph.

I haven't seen Fallen in over a week now. His promise of hourly texts went to the wayside, which I figured they would. Once he gets his teeth into something, he doesn't let go until it's chewed all the way up. Truthfully, I've been too distracted to notice the passage of time. Once Kazimir said that Vivi was having a girl, my whole concentration was upended.

What the hell do I know about little girls?

She seemed emotional about the announcement, but I didn't ask. In fact, I left right after that, and we returned to our regular routine of ignoring each other. Evonne has joined the baby train, and Dulcie is over every day after work—the three of them aggressively planning the nursery. Vivi got her cast off a few days ago, and she has taken to roaming around the ranch, poking her nose about. Pallas makes sure she stays safe, following her at a discreet distance. She seems to like feeding the horses snacks, which is stressing Devin out, but I tell him to let her do it anyway. A few extra apples and carrots won't kill them.

"Boss? Do you want the full report?" I hear Fallen from a distance and frown. "Of course I do. Send for the rest of the men." He gives me a funny look. "I already did. Remember? I told you that."

Fuck, I'm losing it. Is this ranch even a safe place for a girl? How do you girl-proof thousands of acres? Maybe I'll have Fallen google it.

I hear the troop of boots and a lot of low laughter—I'm sitting on the back deck of my house, the open space matching my thoughts.

"Let's move this into my office. I don't want anyone wandering by and overhearing some shit they shouldn't," I say, standing. Fallen is still staring at me, and I have a feeling he already suggested it. Fuck again. I push the double doors that lead to my office and wait for everyone else to file in. I count heads and take a seat, then decide to stand up. Devin watches me closely, and even Daze raises his eyebrows at my restlessness. Once everyone takes their spots, I give the floor to Fallen.

"Ok so Vivi's, full name is Vivienne Micheline DuPlantier. Her parents were born in France, and she still has a few grandparents living there. Her mom is old nobility, like a few generations of that shit. There are a few Viscounts in there or something. Her dad *is* an engineer, but she left out that his family was one of the founders of the *École D'ingénieur et de Sciences Appliquées*— the top nerd school in France. Her great great someone someone started it. So this girl is like French royalty in her own way. The dad got a tech company job and moved to Seattle when she was a kid. All of that she said was true.

"Her friend Riley was Riley Starla Mansour, the only daughter of Dr. And Mrs. Mansour. The Mansours are Algerian-American, and Dr. Mansour is one of the country's top cardiologists. Both of his sons followed him into medicine, and there is some evidence that Vivi dated one of them. Riley was a hellion. Her social media showed her all over the place, and although there are next to no pictures of Vivi, she was with her every step. She dated a lot, the last guy a CEO for a tech company in Seattle." He handed out little packets of pictures, and I saw a very pretty girl in a bikini, raising her margarita glass at the cameraman. Off to the side and almost out of frame is Vivi. You can't see much of her except one startling blue-green eye and her slim nose, blonde hair obscuring the rest. Cage whistles as he flips through the rest—the girls in several exotic locations, on boats and beaches. The same is true in all of them. Riley is front and center, having the time of her life, but Vivi is almost invisible. I read the caption: *Me and My Sissy Vivi Killing It in #costarica.*

"They were close?" I state the obvious.

"Yeah. They were literally like sisters. What a fucking waste." Fallen is silent for a moment before continuing. "Vivi has no social media. Like at all."

"What? How is that possible?" Nox sits up. Devin frowns.

"I don't know. She has nothing at all. It's why she wasn't tagged in any of her friend's photos—there was no one to tag. And if you notice, you barely see her face in any of them. I went all the way back to their high school yearbook. Riley was a cheerleader, on the debate team, you name it. She and her brothers are all over every yearbook during their time there. Vivi is in none of them. She is listed as 'camera shy' every time.

Again, you can see her in the background but never in a full picture. It's really fucking weird."

"Who is this fucking girl?" Nox snarls, standing to pace. None of them look pleased.

"She is exactly who she says she is. I don't know if it's her uptight parents or a quirk of hers, but she's off the grid." We all let that settle for a few minutes before he continues. "So anyway she graduated with honors from RISD and then went to work for an art dealer, Phineas Paul. There's not much about her job that I could find, which could be deliberate since they deal with some expensive shit. Rich people like discretion. I looked into his stuff too, and he's clean. Not even a parking ticket. So unless Trace was looking to fence some art, I don't think that's the connection." I snort. Trace couldn't tell Picasso from a finger-painting.

"Let's move on to Vegas. So I was able to hack into the hotel security system, and based on what she said about it being the grand opening, I dialed down the date. I found her and Riley pretty quickly. Now look and tell me what you see." He walks over to my desktop, presses a few buttons, and then spins the monitor around. We all gather around and look at the split screen. Fallen adjusts something, and the camera zooms in on Riley, looking hot as fuck in a tiny red dress. She is tearing up the dance floor, two guys grinding on her from both sides. "I know those guys," Cage says sourly. "Trace's crew."

"Yup, and here is Vivi. Look around carefully." He taps the mouse, and the screen fills with the round bar area. Vivi is sitting right across from the bartender, doodling on a napkin. Her previously blonde hair is a wild mess around her shoulders, arms and back exposed by her black dress. She looks gorgeous.

"Damn, Scoot looks good," Daze grins, and I shoot him an evil look. "Wait a minute, isn't that Stephen right there? And

Cash?" We all move closer to the screen and where Daze is pointing. "Fuck he had the whole crew right under her nose."

"Yup, and there's Trace." Only about ten feet from Vivi is sitting, watching her like a hawk. He's fending off women left and right, but his sole focus is on the girl sitting at the bar. A large number of dickheads had approached her, and she seemed annoyed by all of the attention. At one point, Riley showed up to guzzle a drink and then left for the dance floor. We all watch as Cash slithered up to Vivi, who looks supremely disinterested until a devious look crosses her beautiful face. Nox snickers at her expression, and soon enough, Cash is balling up a napkin and throwing it at her. He disappears into the crowd, but from our view, we can see him link up with Stephen in the corner. Trace moves in smoothly, and I grit my teeth at how attracted she is immediately.

"Can we zoom in a little more without it getting grainy?" Fallen hits a few keys and then moves the mouse. "There's no audio?"

"Nope. The audio function went down the morning of. Convenient, huh?"

"I wonder what he is saying? Look at her face. She looks shocked, even a little alarmed," Kaz says, frowning.

"She still wanted to fuck him, though," Nox drawls. I glance at him, and the smile slips off of his face. "Sorry."

The action concluded quickly after that. Riley shows up and runs out of the club with a giant grin. Stephen and Cash follow behind her. Trace holds out his hand, and Vivi takes it, trailing him out of the club.

"Hold on. Rewind that last part. Maybe thirty seconds." The picture blurs and Vivi walks behind Trace with her head down. "Right there."

"Why does that guy look so familiar?" A tall, bulky figure with a headful of bleach-blonde hair slams into Vivi. Trace immediately got in the guy's face and shared some short words. Trace pulled her out quickly but didn't turn to see the asshole glaring suspiciously behind them. He pulled out a phone and typed quickly before slipping into the dark.

Pallas' gravelly voice splits the silence. "We have crossed paths with him before. He works for Koslov. And he recognized Trace."

CHAPTER 38

FREE

Fuck.

Fuck.

Fuck.

"Pallas, are you sure?" A stupid question—Pallas never opens his mouth unless he has something truthful to say.

"Yes. I am sure. I saw him at a drop, maybe seven or eight years ago. He said nothing—just oversaw the transaction, but it is him. I never got his name, but he is unmistakable. He was high in the organization."

"Fuck," Kaz spits out, and we all nod gravely. Koslov is the worst of all of the Russian mafia bosses to have Vivi on his radar. The evilest of the evil. He had his fingers in everything-drugs, trafficking, murder for hire, slavery—if it was the lowest a human could go, he was into it. He made billions of dollars preying on the most vulnerable people imaginable, catering to every kink and vice. He had no scruples, just a twisted form of morality that shifted like the tide. We never did business with him, making it known that we weren't interested in any affiliation with the *Chernyy Drakon*— The Black Dragons.

"I heard they chose Dragons because he burns people alive for sport," Nox said. Cage nods, and Kaz looks ill. "How could Trace let this happen?"

I could say a thousand things. That Trace never cared for another person in his life. That he didn't care what happened to all the women he used—though this is the first time I've heard about any death being involved. I know for a fact there was emotional collateral, hell, even financial. Trace and his crew give zero fucks about anything except their endgame— whatever that may be.

I'm not a good man. I never have been. I'm sure my mama told me I was born bad more than once. I've done things that guarantee I will never see the right side of heaven. But even with all the darkness in my past, Trace is far, far worse.

"That's the fucking question. Unless there is another mafia family on the radar, I'm going to assume that The Dragons were after her. The m.o fits—I read the police reports, and her family and friends were being terrorized. Her injuries were horrific- way worse than what we saw when she got here. Her hospital records said she was lucky to be alive— she coded twice in the ambulance. And that little girl she's got is a warrior--she could've easily lost the baby with how badly they beat her. Plus the police reports for her attack say nothing except that it was a simple robbery—not an attempted murder."

"What about the friend?" Devin asks. He's been silent this whole time, but that's his way—he likes to get all possible information before making decisions or comments.

"There's not much in that police report either, which I find hella strange. There was an explosion that took out the whole house—there must have been some sort of accelerant. And though no bodies were recoverable because of the high heat—both girls were declared dead."

"Both? They think Vivi is dead?" Fallen nods with a grimace.

"Yeah, but like I said, the police report is weirdly scant on information. It's been sanitized, but I can't figure out by whom. I don't like it. There should've been a huge media presence and an official fire inspection report. There is nothing. The girls were given a joint funeral, and that was it. It's really uncool how low-key the whole thing is. So it's by design."

"So even though there's a report that she's dead, she could still be in danger?"

"I would say so. We don't know who bleached out those reports. And we still don't know what Trace wanted from her-hell, she might not even know. We've got to put some safeguards in place. And Free? We are going to have to tell her about Koslov. She can't walk around in danger and be ignorant of it. She made it this far, beaten half to death and alone—she can take it."

"I think," Devin says in his quiet way. "I think it's time you made a phone call, Free. We can game plan a reason and go from there." All eyes are on me, as I agree.

"Let's set it up."

CHAPTER 39

HARLAND

The burner phone in my drawer rings, catching my hacking cough by surprise. It hasn't rung in years, but I keep it active anyway. Only two people on the planet have this number— and I pray it is not the person I think it is.

"Go secure."

"Fuck you," Free's voice drawls over the line. I chuckle, which, of course, turns into a cough.

"I'd tell you to get that checked out, but I don't give a fuck," he says as I get myself under control. I've been dreading this call for weeks. I sit back in my chair and light another *kretek*. "Why am I being granted an audience with the great devil himself?"

When I first met Free and Trace, they were young—full of fire and anger. Their daddy raised them in the worst of ways, and when he died, I swooped in and tried to get them both. Trace fell into it like a duck to water, while Free told me to stick it where the sun don't shine and took off. One of my biggest regrets was never getting him on my team. The man is brutality incarnate.

"I haven't been able to get any information about my mama. I need to know if Trace has checked on her. Where is he?" Fuck. This is not how I wanted this conversation to start. But Free is nothing if not practical. He would have anticipated this years ago.

"Free...there was an accident..." I start, then stop. There is no reason to spare this man's feelings—he has none, especially not for his brother.

"Spit it out, Harland. I don't have time for bullshit." His voice didn't even change inflection. Yup. Cold as ice.

"He was in a job. Supposed to cozy up this artist chick and get her to do something for us. I thought it was a long shot, but Trace was convinced he could do it. Somehow, he got made by our main target, and they ambushed the team while they were on their way out of town. Got Trace first, then took out Cash. Stephen got out, but he's not doing too good. Doc don't expect him to make it." I don't offer any apologies, though I am sorry. I practically raised Trace.

There is a long silence before he asks, "Why would you let him take a job you thought he couldn't do?"

I snort. "Your brother had a perfect record—he always accomplished his assignments. We had no reason to think this would be any different, though after the first time they fucked, I started to have my doubts. There was something about this girl—I can't explain it. She wasn't as gullible as I expected her to be. And no matter what your brother pulled out in the bedroom, she wouldn't crack. I told him I would go the old-fashioned way if he couldn't follow through."

"Old fashioned way?"

"Rendition. Or threaten her family. Anyway, he wasn't keen on that, which I didn't like. I think this girl might've started getting under his skin. Stephen thought the same thing, and then we started hearing rumblings that he was made. I pulled him out after one last chance with the girl. But it was too late." When Stephen told me he thought Trace was starting to catch feelings for that Vivi girl, I sent Cash to collect him. One of Trace's best qualities was his ability to work with no emotion. It's a trait both boys share.

"What about the girl? She make it?"

"Nah. They took her and her friend out. Blew up her house. Damn shame too. She was a looker." Very few women make my old dick stand up and take notice, but that girl made me wish I was young again. There was something lush about her—mysterious, even. Though I knew all of her secrets. Criminals often make the best bedmates.

"So that's it? You're just going to let my brother be killed and do nothing about it? Have you told my mom yet?" His voice is slightly annoyed but again frigid.

"I'm waiting to see if Stephen makes it or not. If I tell your mama, she'll tell Stephens's mom, who will then start asking questions. I need to see if I have to report it as a one-off or a double accident." He snorts but says nothing for a moment.

"Who was the target?"

"Free, you know I can't tell you that..."

"Harland, fuck you with that shit. I'm not one of your little crew of lost boys. Just because I keep it civil don't mean you should forget who I am." Icicles reach through the phone, and I shudder. Once again, I regret not being able to recruit him. I could've moved mountains with his darkness.

"I thought you gave all of that up? Trying to be a respectable rancher and all that." I still laugh at the thought that Free and his men are trying to walk the straight path. They should be locked up—the whole lot of them.

"I am a rancher. That doesn't make me any less dangerous. Is my mama in danger?"

"She should be fine. Koslov only knows Trace through his..."

"Koslov? What the fuck, Harland? You got people killed trying to take him down? Don't you know not to fuck with him?" Free spits out the admonishment, and I nod, though he can't see me. There is a long list of idiots who took on Koslov and lost. We had some iron-clad intel but needed to source an off-the-books accomplice. Someone so profoundly off the radar, so unlikely, we could sneak past Koslov's defenses. Vivi Duplantier came up in an obscure file, and we ran with it.

"We had a solid plan. I don't know how your brother got made, but it doesn't matter. You and I both know that mother-fucker needs to be taken out. The way he runs his organization, there isn't a suitable replacement. The whole thing will crumble without him at the top. Just because there were a few causalities doesn't mean we stop."

"A few casualties? You never change, Harland. I want men on my mama immediately. If I have to do it myself, I'm sure you and I will wind up having a different conversation." The threat is always there. Free is one of the most dangerous men in North America. If he has to step in and protect his mother, which has been Trace's job, it would mean a resurgence of his power.

No thanks. I have enough demons to fight.

"It'll be done. Free..."

But the line is dead.

CHAPTER 40

VIVI

"*Ma bébé, en veux-tu plus?*"

Carnage snorts and rubs his creamy, I mean dun-colored head along my face, nudging my belly lightly. Devin has been teaching me about all the different horses in the stables—the racers, the broodmares, the working horses, even ponies. All of them have different jobs on the ranch, though they are all spoiled. Free is building a state-of-the-art facility, moving from barn stabling to traditional. All the horses are together, but Devin said it can be stressful for them and that each of them having their own stall was much better. He and his team are gridding out who needs to be near whom since they are social animals and have clear family units. I've taken to coming out every morning and feeding them treats (though I think I am messing up their strict diets; Devin hasn't said anything yet) and giving them rubs. My favorites are Lily, the newest addition to the ranch, and Mongoose, an old horse with a sense of humor. I tried to warm up to Harley, the great big hope, but Jesus. That horse was as snooty as they come. He turned up his nose at an apple I offered him and won't even come over for a nose rub. He gets excited for Free, though. I watched from around the corner when he strolled into the training area, and Harley pranced around like the king himself was coming to visit—jerkface horse.

"Ah mon bébé, il n'yen a plus..."

"What the hell are you doing in here?" The gruff voice sounds behind me, and Carnage's ears lay flat against his neck. His right hoof starts tapping, a sign he is unhappy.

"Change your tone, please," I sing out lightly. "He doesn't like when people talk to me like that."

"Didn't Devin tell you that he is dangerous? He's injured three of the stable hands already," he spits with a gentler tone. Carnage is still eyeing him, and I continue to rub his nose.

"Yes, he did. But I was in here one day trying to cozy up to your asshole prized possession, Harley, and Carnage here was whinnying and trying to get my attention. We've been besties ever since. He has never been anything but sweet to me, right, *mon coeur*?" I kiss him and then gather up a handful of oats for him to munch on. He chews with one eye on Free, and I grin at his protectiveness. Free is watching me with an amused look on that face. "Harley is an asshole?"

I snort. "Yup. He looks at me like I'm something the cat drug in. Won't come near me, even if I have peppermints. He's a jerk," I say meaningfully, giving Free the stink eye, too. The last two weeks have been tiring. I've been called back to the interrogation room, I mean the living room, two more times, the whole gang of them asking me a million questions. I tell them the same stuff over and over, and I can tell they are getting frustrated. There has been so much activity in the house, between the boys coming in and out, Dulcie appearing with paint samples and decorating books, and Kaz (and Fallen) coming in daily to ensure I am "ok." Through it all, Free and I still managed only to say a few words to each other. I guess that's over with.

"Were you speaking French to him?" He asks, sweeping the floor quickly and patting the only other horse on this side, Mabel.

"Yes, he likes it. Mabel does, too. Why do you have him isolated like this? I don't think he likes it. He's been an angel since I've been visiting him every day. The only time he acted up was when one of the guys yelled at me. He showed his ass that day," I laugh.

"Who yelled at you?" He stops his sweeping to glare at me. Most of the guys, hell, almost all of them, wear jeans and cowboy boots. I haven't seen so many pairs of Wranglers in my life, and all of them wear cowboy hats. I swear I feel awful for whoever has to do laundry because it must be a bitch getting all the smell out. I swatted at Evonne when she tried to do my washing—I don't want anyone subjected to that. But Free is never in anything but black. Black shirt, black jeans, black boots. Never cowboy, either; usually some sort of work or hiking-type boot. His hair is always a mess—curls all over the place and sticking up. He's forever running his hand through it — though it doesn't make him less hot. And his days-old scruff just makes it hotter. Yikes. "And he's over here because he doesn't get along with the other horses. He bullies them. Mabel is old, so he leaves her alone. Now, who yelled at you?"

"I don't remember his name, but Pallas said something to him. You know, my shadow?" I smirked at him, and I swear I saw the glimmer of a smile crack his stern lips. Pallas has been following me from the beginning. I first peeped him when Dulcie and I had our first tour around the ranch. I didn't say anything at first, but at this point, I just talk to him like we are friends, though he is always ten feet behind me and silent as a tomb.

"He is especially protective of women and children. Even if I called him off, he wouldn't listen. He likes you." He puts the broom up and crosses his arms across his broad chest, leaning against a post. Christ, this guy is lethal. I turn around and fuss with Mabel's door so he won't see my red face. These pregnancy hormones are killing me.

"...anyway I was looking for you because we need to talk." I peek at him over my shoulder and swear he is checking out my ass, but he hates me, so that is definitely not the case. "We do?" His eyes drift slowly up and meet my face, pausing at my mouth.

"Yeah. I think it's long past time," he says, yanking on his curls and clicking his tongue ring. Riley dated this drummer once who had a tongue ring, and I swear she was cross-eyed for weeks after experiencing it. Every time I hear that noise, I have to hold back a groan.

"Um, ok. Do you want to talk here or go back to the house?" I shove my hands into my overall pockets, shoulders creeping toward my ears. What could he have to say?

"At the house. Daze and Devin are going to meet us there." Oh. Why would they need to be there? I cup my stomach, a habit I started after Kaz told me I was having a girl. I can't feel her moving or anything, but he said it could be any time now. I'll tell you what though, my belly sure is making itself known. It popped out overnight, and every day, it sticks out more and more. And it's a damn magnet. Devin is constantly patting it, and Nox even absently rubbed it when he stopped by this morning.

"She alright?" He asks, pointing at my stomach. I laugh lightly. "Yes, she is. Maybe a little hungry. Did you want to ask her yourself?" I quirk a brow at him, and he grins. "Maybe later. Let's walk." He gestures at me to go ahead of him, and I start, before turning around and blowing a kiss at Carnage. He jerks his head and snorts at me.

"Bonne nuit mon petit chou."

"What did you call him?" Free asks, amused again. I side-eye him and grin. "My little cabbage."

"Vivi, that horse is eighteen hands high. He's not a little anything. There's a reason we named him Carnage."

"Whatever. He's my little baby. Leave me alone."

"Jesus, I don't know who's worse, you or Dulcie."

DAZE AND DEVIN are already at the house when we get back. Evonne has a tray of snacks out for them, and Devin stops chewing long enough to ask if I want anything. I peep over at the tray and point at a hunk of cheese and some of the herb crackers I love. He slices some for me and hands it to me on a napkin. Daze drops a glass of apple juice beside me and props my feet on a leather ottoman. Free rolls his eyes, and I smirk at him. Dulcie keeps telling me the baby will be spoiled rotten, and I am starting to believe her. Daze sits beside me, with Free and Devin sitting across from us. I chew and raise an eyebrow, waiting for them to start. Free looks like he'd rather be having a root canal, and Dev nudges him. He swallows and then leans forward, dark eyes lasered to mine.

"I need to tell you about Trace." I blink and put down my cheese. I suddenly don't feel like eating.

"Trace and I didn't grow up the best way. Our dad was into some bad shit. He tried to shield us all from it, especially my Mama, but it spilled over anyway. We wound up getting dragged into stuff we had no business being in. Our dad died, and Mama moved away for her safety."

"How old were you when your dad died?" I ask.

"I was fifteen, and Trace was seventeen." Wait, Trace is older?

"Yes, he is," he says, amused. I didn't realize I said that out loud. "How old are you now?" I chew an old callus on my thumb.

"I'm thirty-six." My eyes bug out of my head. Trace didn't look a day over thirty, but he was knocking on forty. I blink a few times, and Devin coughs for him to continue.

"Anyway, when my dad died, a man came to see us. We were still living in our old house, and Riggs was checking on us every day, but we always worried about DCFS coming to grab us. So when the man showed up, we were prepared to fight—it turned out that the man, Harland, wasn't from DCFS. He told us that he was an old friend of our dad, and he wanted us to come with him. He asked us to keep it a secret because he didn't want to alert any authorities. We both told him to kick rocks, but he kept coming back. One day, I called Riggs and told him anyway. He showed up at the same time as Harland, and they had a big fight. Because Harland wasn't an old friend of my dad, he worked for the government."

"The government?" A cold hand reaches down my spine, and I shiver. Daze grabs a blanket and wraps it around me, but the ice won't leave.

"Yeah. My dad had run afoul of him a few times, and when he heard he died, he used it as an opportunity. He told me and Trace that we had a choice- we could go with him and live a long life or stay where we were and probably die young. He tried to sell us on this glamorous life, but my daddy didn't raise a fool. I told Harland to fuck off, but Trace didn't. He packed his bags and went with him. I stayed with Riggs."

"Wait, so what? Trace works for the government?" I'm fully shaking now. Daze pulls me into his lap and holds me tight. I feel faint. Free watches the movement, and though I see anger swirl in his eyes, he says nothing.

"Yeah. He started in the FBI. Harland put him through school, and he joined right after graduation. He was only there for a few years when he got recruited by an offshoot of the NSA. I guess you could call them spies. Harland is in charge, but Trace is his top agent." My mind whirls, and I try to fit all the pieces together.

"So when I met him in Vegas..." Free nods and Devin picks it up from there. "It was a set-up. That's what Trace does. He and his crew target women, Trace seduces them—usually for information—and then they use it in their investigations. Then, they move on to the next target. They were working on a big case this time— a man named Koslov. For some reason, they felt like you could help them. Do you know why they would think that?" I blink a thousand times in a row. I know exactly why, but I say nothing.

"Anyway, that night, you and Trace bumped into someone at the club. Do you remember?" I think back, frowning. I vaguely remember a tall guy with blonde hair, but that was it. I tell them that, and Devin nods. "That guy works for Koslov. Somehow, he recognized Trace, we don't know how, and that put you on their radar. They followed Trace to Seattle and started targeting your family to send you a message. They had no idea that you didn't know who Trace was. Stephen got wind of Koslov's men in town, and they pulled Trace out." He stops and looks at Free, who nods at him.

"We think Trace was worried that they would still go after you even with him leaving. That's why he told you to run. He knew that if things escalated, you would be safe here. But these men they are...not human. They don't care about innocent or guilty, accomplice or victim. To them, you are an asset they need to eliminate. They are the ones who attacked you in the parking lot. And they are the ones who killed Riley." A sob chokes up my throat, and I start crying. Daze pulls me closer, but I'm suddenly lifted, and the spearmint and sandalwood scent drags me in. I bury my face in his neck, and Devin continues behind me.

"It didn't matter if you were in Vegas or somewhere else. He would have approached you another way, Vivi. They would have been shadowing you for weeks. They would have known all of your habits and routines. Did you say some girls gave you those club passes? They probably worked for Trace. That is how insidious their plans are. "

"So everything he told me was a lie?" I know it intellectually, but I need to hear it. Free speaks from above me. "Yes. He would've tailored his whole approach around what he knew about you. The only thing he wouldn't have anticipated was you getting pregnant. It wouldn't have mattered anyway— Trace would still have disappeared on you. We are just grateful he gave you an escape clause." I am, too, but the guilt is eating me up from the soul out. If I had never made those mistakes when I was a stupid kid, I would have never been on Trace's radar to begin with. Riley...

"Who is this Koslov guy? Like a mob guy or something?" I feel Free nod. The heat from his body is slowly warming my frozen limbs. I hear a few clicks, and then the heat from the fireplace touches my back. I peek over at Daze and smile a little. He winks at me, puts my feet in his lap, and tries to rub them to life.

"Yes, that's exactly who he is. He's Russian mafia. And the worst of the worst. He's got his fingers in every terrible pie you can think of. Harland and Trace have been after him for years. Lots of other alphabet agencies have tried to take this guy down, and they've all failed. He's on Interpol's most-wanted list, but everyone knows where he is. He's that powerful. But the fatal flaw in his organization is that he has no children. No one to take over if he dies. His powers are so absolute that the whole engine will fall apart if he's gone."

"How old is this guy? He can't live forever."

Daze snorts. "He's no more than thirty-five." Damn, that sucks. He could live till he's a hundred and wreck lives the whole time. "So, do you think Trace will show up here? I mean, since he sent me here?" I can feel Free stiffen below me, his arms tightening around me.

"Vivi...the day that Trace left you, his car was ambushed. He and one of his crew were killed." I choke and feel my lungs spasm suddenly. I can't breathe. This is all my fault.

"Fuck. Vivi, your head between your legs and breathe shallow. Dev, send for Kazimir." Free barks out orders as I try to get my bearings. My vision swims, and then the blackness tries to take me.

"Don't you dare pass out. He is not worth it, you hear me? He has done this shit for years. He uses women—fucks them and manipulates them. I don't know what he wanted from you, but I can imagine he was pissed he didn't get it. He is not worth one of your tears, Vivi." I struggle to get my breathing under control and nod. I'm sure the anger will come later, but right now, all I can think is that my baby will have no father.

"She will have me. Fuck she will have all of us." I really need to stop thinking out loud. "He would have left you anyway, Vivi. Baby or not." Free shakes me slightly, and I suddenly get annoyed. "Maybe, but I am still allowed to feel some kind of way about it," I snap. He smiles suddenly, and my annoyance grows. Damn, his teeth are nice.

"So, how do I fix this? I mean, what do I do?"

"Well, the good news is that we think Koslov thinks you are dead. The police report states that you and Riley passed in the fire. So that should give you some cover. The bad news is that you will have to stay dead. You will not be able to go back to your old life." I sit up and stare at him. "But my parents.."

Daze looks at me gently. "They think you are gone, Vivi. They've already buried you and have had closure. Maybe in a long time, that can change, but for now, you have to build a new life here with us. You will want for nothing, and neither will little Dazita." My lips twitch, and Devin looks appalled. "Dazita? Dude."

"What? She can be named after her Uncle Daze. I'm going to be her favorite anyway; kids love me."

"Daze isn't even your real name, you ass." Daze shrugs, and his dimples flash at me. "I like it," he says, squeezing my cold fingers. "I know this is a lot for you, Vivi, but I promise you, you will get past it. It'll just take time.

"Meanwhile, Fallen will work on making you a whole online past, complete with a new last name, etc. I'm sure keeping your name as Vivi will be easy—we will just drop the Vivienne. That will help add more layers between you and your old life." I nod sadly. He taps me under my chin, and I give him a weak smile. A thought pops into my head, and I turn to Free.

"Wait, you said that you stayed behind when Trace left? What happened to you after that?" How could a fifteen-year-old kid with no family come to own a whole mountain? I was missing something here.

A lazy smile stretches across his face, and I swear I thank god I am already pregnant because I would've been expecting quadruplets after witnessing it. "After that? Baby, I became Death."

CHAPTER 41
FREE

"You gonna stay silent the whole ride? Or you gonna tell me what's on your mind?" Nox's thick tattooed wrist is draped over the steering wheel while I ride bitch in the passenger seat of his giant red six-fifty. I wanted to take my truck, but Daze pointed out it was too well-known despite my new profession. This monstrosity of a vehicle would be less noticeable where we are going—the middle of fucking nowhere in Kansas. I send him a side glare and shake my head.

"No? Nothing you want to talk about?" I look at him again and see the smug grin quivering at the edge of his lips. I've known Nox for many years, been to war with him, seen him fuck women, and kill men. But I never wanted to knock his teeth down his throat. Until now.

"I mean, if I were you, I would have lots to talk about. Like the fact that I've got a fucking knockout living in my house. Or that the knockout was messed up with my brother, but I would love to sink my di—"

"Nox, if you don't shut your mouth and drive, I'm going to grab the wheel and push your head into the window." I shut him down as he chuckles. We drive silently for a few miles, Nox whistling to a Luke Combs song and me in my thoughts. I restlessly tap my fingers against my pant leg, mind whirling with the shit going on.

"She's going to be alright, you know. Vivi. I know we threw a lot on her, but she's going to come out okay in the end," he says quietly. I sigh and roll my eyes. I swore I got my message across, but he seemed determined to have a moment.

"I know she will be. She's strong—and she's got us. I'm actually the least worried about that." I shrug. Vivi took everything we told her about Trace like a champ--after all the tears and freakout, she seemed determined to put it all behind her. She's been working with Fallen on her new identity all week, though he thinks she is still upset. If she is, the girl is a world-class actress.

"What is it then? Koslov? Something on the ranch?"

I'm silent. Fuck it. "I'm worried about the baby." There, I said it. I don't know shit about kids—we never had any around much, and even those I stayed away from. How the hell am I gonna deal with one?

"The baby? What about it?" I can hear the laughter he is trying to hold back, and I bare my teeth at him. This is why I hate the talking bullshit. "You're scared, aren't you?"

"Fuck yeah, I'm scared. I know fuck-all about kids, and now I gotta take care of one. Is the ranch even safe for her? What if something happens? What if the kid gets injured or something? Fuck, what if they come for Vivi and get the baby?" I'm panting now, and he shoots me a quick look.

"Free, it's not like the kid won't have a mother—Vivi is right there. And no one will get near that kid—she's got a whole army watching over her. The ranch is perfectly safe—you act like landmines and wild animals are everywhere. I can't believe you are this worried. Is there something I don't know?" He peers at me suspiciously before pulling his eyes back on the road.

"There's nothing." I go silent again. Lies. All lies.

"Okay then. Chill out." I hear him mutter something under his breath, but I don't catch all of it. "We need to tell Vivi about us, though, don't we? That's not something she needs to find out later or for someone else." I nod my head. I started to tell her the rest, but after Vivi's reaction about Trace, I figured she had enough. She may have acted like she was handling everything well, but telling her our history might send her over the edge. Kaz even said having too many shocks at once wasn't good for her health.

"There's a lot of stuff she still ain't tellin' us, ya know." I shrug and nod. "I'm aware. We'll get it out of her eventually." I lean back and close my eyes, hoping this will stop his incessant talking.

"Soooo. This meeting. You don't think it's playing with fire, do you? I mean, we haven't had any contact with Silver in years now. He may not feel the same about us, ya know." I nod my head with my eyes still closed, peeking at him when I answer.

"That may be true. But I am still me—and I don't have a problem reminding him of that. Plus, he hated Trace, too." Nox snorts, and the truck speeds up to pass a minivan. "We all did. If y'all didn't look so much alike, I would've never thought y'all were related." That's not the first time I've heard that. Trace and I were nothing alike, aside from our cruelty.

"Anyway, we got a long drive ahead of us. Where do you want to eat?"

～

The Shelter has been around since the eighties. Situated in the middle of a cornfield in Canton, Kansas, you would never know the debauchery that has gone on inside its cinder block walls. It used to be a hardcore punk club where all the most famous bands would appear to perform—no notice given. People came from all over to see what acts they could catch any night and never left disappointed. The original owners weren't known, and lots of rumors floated around— from the Mafia to the Kennedys. Only a chosen few knew that the Shelter was started by some of the most infamous men in the US— The Crown Prince's MC. The old, old President, Damn Doug, opened the doors as a front for some illegal shit he was doing at the time. Somehow, the word got out, and The Shelter became notorious— for the right and wrong reasons. When Damn Doug died, the Club kept control and expanded the music acts to all music genres, though punk continued to be the main attraction. When all the internet fucked up the anonymity aspect, the Princes flipped it over to its current venue—a BYOB strip club.

Nox swung the big body truck to the edge of the dirt parking lot, front facing out. I hop out, stretching my back out and stomping some feeling into my legs. I tuck my favorite Walther Arms PDP nine-millimeter into the back of my jeans and see Nox do the same with his Sig. We walk to the steel doors in front of the long line, and I spot Jessie handling the door. He's an old head—been a Prince for years. His long beard is liberally sprinkled with grey, the same shiny bald head, with a crown tatted above his left ear. He's arguing with a few kids at the door when he spots Nox and me does a double-take. A wide smile stretches his face, and he reaches around the stupid kids to shake my hand.

"Free? Well fuck a cow, what are you doing here?" He pulls

me in for a back/slap hug, and I grin. "And look at this idiot. Still braiding your hair like a fucking girl." He gives Nox the same kind of hug and tugs on his long blonde braid. "Y'all here to catch Silver?"

"Yeah, he around?" One of the kids at my back is griping about us cutting the line, and Nox turns around with a sneer. "Shut the fuck up, assmunch."

Nox has about seven inches on him, but the fool puffs up his chest in defiance. He takes a quick glance to his right, and I see a girl standing there watching him. I roll my eyes. Pussy will get you killed every time. "We were here first," he squeaks. Jesus, have his balls even dropped yet?

"I don't give a shit if you've been standing here for two years. We are here now. And unless you want this little girl you are trying to impress watch you bleed out at her feet, I suggest you close your mouth." Nox stands about one inch from him, leaning down into his face. The zygote squeaks again, nodding and moving backward. Jessie shakes his head.

"They get worse every year. Go on in and head back. Silver should be in his office. Do you remember the way? I'll tell him you're on your way back." He murmurs into a walkie as we walk down the long, dark hallway. The thump of a Dua Lipa song remix greets us, and we push through the beaded curtain to the flashing lights of the stage.

"Nice," Nox says, nodding toward the blonde with big pierced nipples who is gyrating on the stage. She is nude except for a sparkly mask, and her hips move to the beat sensually. The crowd is screaming for her, dollars strewn across the stage. We push through the throng and turn down a hidden nook leading to the offices and kitchen. The door at the end suddenly swings open, and a thin, bald man with a goatee steps out. He's got a cigarette hanging from his lip, the smoke obscuring his eyes.

"Free. Nox." He steps to the side, his leather vest moving slightly, showing off his gun in his waistband. I know he's also got a knife on his right side and one tucked into his boot. I'm not sure if this was intentional or not, and I glance at Nox, who raises his eyebrows with the same thought. A power play already. Interesting.

The room is well-lit, with a couch to the right and some chairs to the left. There's a tan rug under our feet, free of stains, and Silver's desk is backed against a wall—right in the sight line of the door and nothing behind him. His blue eyes watch us dispassionately, and I silently stop short of his desk. "Free."

"Silver. Long time and all that." Nox is at my back, facing somewhat sideways. Bent, the guy at the door, stands in front of it, blocking our exit as if he could. I'll allow the thought for now. I stare at Silver, waiting for him to make a move. We stay that way for a minute before a giant smile splits his handsome face.

"You cold son-of-a-bitch, you haven't changed a bit. What's it been, five, six years? You still make grown men quake. Get over here, you bastard." He jumps out of his chair and strides around the desk, grabbing me into a back-breaking hug. He thumps my shoulder a few times, his grin never fading. "Damn, it's good to see you. Nox, you big-ass Leif Erickkson-looking motherfucker get over here." Nox cracks up and gets some of the same treatment. They break apart, and Silver crosses his arms over his chest. "Fuck, it's good to see y'all. Sit down, sit. Bent, Get us some beers." Bent salutes him and closes the door behind him.

"How is everyone? Fallen, Pallas, Devin? Is Evonne still taking care of y'all?" He fires off the questions, and I laugh. When Silver was part of our crew, he rivaled Daze for the most outgoing of all my men. Being in the room with both of them was a lesson in patience. They could talk the paint off the walls. "Is it just you two?"

"Yeah. We're only here for a day or two and then heading back. Everyone is good." Bent returns with an armful of long necks, handing us two each. He walks back out, closing the door behind him. I take a sip and grin at Silver. "Look at you, Pres." I gesture to his cut, the big PRESIDENT patch situated above the gold and red crown. His wavy brown hair has been shaved down, and his head from ear to ear is tatted with a thorny crown dripping blood. His old man had the same one, except for the blood, which I know signifies each life he's taken.

"Yeah, I look good, don't I?"

Nox cracks up, and I smile. "You do. How are things?" He starts rattling off gossip like he always did, and I listen with half an ear, watching his animated face. Silver patched in with us years ago when his old man kicked him out of the house 'cause of some dumb shit. He was one of our best prospects and rose quickly in the ranks. When everything went down, he chose to go back to the Princes and made VP in a year. When Havoc, his dad, died, he was made President. From everything I hear, he's doing a hell of a job. The Princes are one of the largest MCs in the Midwest and are not an easy group to manage.

"...anyway, I'm sure you're not here to play Wendy Williams. What's up, Free?" Wendy who? I shake my head, making a note to ask Dulcie.

"We need your help, Silver. And I need to make sure the Princes will have our back if shit goes down."

He frowns. "Always Free. Tell me what you need." I look at Nox, and he nods.

"Well, it's about Trace..."

"THAT ROTTEN MOTHERFUCKER." Silver spits out.

"Pretty much. He's a dead motherfucker, though," Nox drawls. We caught Silver up on everything, and he sat with his mouth open through most of it. When we got to the part where Vivi showed up, half-dead and pregnant, he threw a bottle at the wall.

"So, according to Harland, the Russians think she is dead, but you ain't feeling too confident about it? Why not?" He paced the room several times and sat on the couch next to Nox.

"Because Harland didn't own up to sanitizing her files. Fallen says that with all the shit that happened to her, there should have been piles of paperwork, and instead, there was almost nothing. I don't like it," I slam my beer down. I can't think of a time when Koslov would care about erasing evidence because he is so far above the law. But with Trace gone and Stephen basically a vegetable, no one was left to do it. And Harland doesn't give a shit who he hurts when he's on the hunt.

Silver nods. "How is the girl now?"

I frown. "She's fine." There is a small silence, and I glance up to see Silver grinning at me. "Just fine? You got a picture?"

"I do," Nox pipes up, and I sit up with a growl. What the fuck? Why does he have a picture of Vivi on his phone?

"I was braiding her hair, and she wanted to send a pic to Dulcie," he flips through his photos, stopping on one. When the hell was he braiding her hair? I know he does it for the chatterbox, but had no idea that he included Vivi in his hair crap.

"Here she is." Silver leans over, whistling. "Jumping Jesus. Even with those bruises, she's a fucking goddess. Her back would hit every wall in my house. Tits?"

What?!

"Big. She ain't but a little thing, but she's got some nice ones. Natural, too." Nox holds his hands out in front of his chest and jiggles. Silver makes a weird sucking noise, and Nox laughs. "She's got an ass on her too. Whole package is a test of respect. Girl's been through it, but damn, does she look good."

"Y'all have about ten seconds before I forget we are friends," I spit out. They both have stupid smirks on their faces, and I feel a wave of violence swirl up my throat. They grin bigger at my threat, though Nox watches my fingers flex and inch toward the knife he knows I have at my waist.

"Alright, so I will have my men put an ear to the ground to listen for any information that Koslov might be after your girl. When I call church this week, I'll let everyone know that we are on alert. I've got a small chapter that just started up in Oklahoma—they'll be the first one to you. VP is Atlas—he's a good man in a fight. Remember Havoc's bitch from New Orleans? He's her first kid. Not my brother, but close enough. Y'all still equipped up? Need anything?" Nox snorts, and I shake my head. I may have given up the lifestyle, the violence, the darkness, but I never gave up my arsenal. It's in a shed behind Cash's garage, guarded by about three hundred layers of security. "We're good."

Silver nods and leans back. "She knows about y'all?"

I shake my head. "No. I was waiting until we met with you. Not sure how much more she can take, but at least she will know we can keep her safe. She thinks we are just ranchers." With us now linking up with the Princes, it will be time. There will be no way to explain a bunch of bald men in cuts with tattoos all over their heads running around the stables. "I'll tell her when we get home."

"You know, Free, there is a simpler way to keep your girl

safe. I'm surprised you haven't thought of it yet." Silver sits up, his platinum-capped canines flashing in the light.

"What?" I'm already dreading his answer.

His smile gets bigger.

Fuck.

CHAPTER 42

VIVI

"I'm sorry. What the hell did you just say?" I'm sure I look like a complete idiot with my mouth hanging open and an armful of corncobs and carrots. I have a coconut tucked into the bib top of my overalls, and my pockets are full of peppermints. Devin told me that Free gave them the go-ahead to try and train Carnage again and asked if I would be present since he only seemed to respond to me. The little gremlin initially gave them all kinds of hell but started listening when I bribed him with treats. He was doing some fast work, and I was cheering him on when Free came out of nowhere. He's been gone a few days, so the house has been quiet. I was about to brag about how well my Little Cabbage was doing before he dropped a bomb on me.

"I said we are gonna get married today." Yeah, that's what I thought he said.

"Uhhhh, no we aren't." My mouth is still open, and I don't even know if my words come out in gibberish. Why in the peanut butter fuck would he think I would marry him? Is this some sort of joke? I would rather marry Carnage.

"I've heard of people marrying their horses, but that is not an option for you," he drawls with a lazy smile. Goddammit, I really need to stop thinking out loud.

"I am not marrying you, Free, are you crazy?" Am I crazy? There is no way.

"Why not?" That smile is still in place, and dammit, it's getting bigger. What the hell is going on?

"Why not? Are you okay? Like did you hit your head or something? Maybe you ingested some Amazonian mushrooms and are hallucinating. Free, I am pregnant with your brother's baby. And we hate each other. We cannot get married. I think you need to sit down—maybe you need some water or a vitamin." I drop my horse goodies to the ground and start toward the stable kitchen. Free reaches out, wraps his fingers around my bicep, and gently tugs me toward him. He maneuvers me to the side of the training circle, backing me up against the fence. He cages me with both arms and leans down into my face. Heaven help me, he smells like mint, man, and hay. MintyHay-Man. I gulp and stare at him. This is the kind of man that has you seeing sounds and hearing colors.

"First of all, I do not hate you. I never did. I also did not hit my head or eat any weird food. I have put all kinds of shit in place to keep you safe, and a friend reminded me that the easiest way to protect you is to claim you. So I am. Close your mouth." He puts a finger under my chin and pushes gently. It falls open again anyway.

"Claim me? What the hell? And you may not hate me, but I hate you." I growl and try to twist away, but damn, those giant muscles won't budge.

"No, you don't. And I'm not giving you a choice. No one with a fucking lick of sense the devil gave them would touch my wife. Not even Koslov. He might think about it, but the thought would be gone before it formed. As for the baby, she will be mine. That same protection extends to her. No one will want to get near her. You will be the safest girls in America." The same finger sweeps around my ear and tugs a strand of hair to tuck. It continues to my eyebrows and smoothes the crinkles between.

"That makes no sense. Why would anyone be scared of a horse breeder? I mean, you're big, really big," he smiles again as I scowl, "but you're not scary." He moves closer and whispers in my ear, tingles dancing across my neck. "I used to be someone else. Remember I said I became Death? I meant it." He pulls back and stares into my eyes, nodding.

"What does that mean, Death?" I gulp because I think about some of the stuff he said about his dad and some weird things that I've been ignoring on the ranch. Things like a gun I saw strapped to Pallas' waist and the fact that although these men treat me like gold, there is a weird undercurrent there. Not to mention the amount of security on the property. It's like Fort Knox around here.

"Come with me, and I'll tell you."

"When Trace left with Harland, I stayed behind, remember?" We are in Free's bedroom, a monstrosity of a room with a bigger-than-king black-clad bed and lots of raw mango furniture that matches mine. The bad part of me wants to poke around his stuff, maybe sniff a shirt or two, but the current me, the one who is still gobsmacked that this fool thinks I am going to marry him, is too busy trying to listen.

"Yeah. You stayed behind with Riggs, right?" I frown when he nods. He's got a stone-hewn fireplace against one wall, and I'm parked in front of it. He leaning on the mantel, all long, bulky limbs and dangerous vibes. The tattoos on his arms flex and undulate with his movements, and that damn tongue ring is clicking a siren's song. I try not to stare at his thighs, which are molded in his black jeans in a way every woman but me should want.

"Riggs was my dad's Enforcer—when he died, the old VP took over, and I became a prospect. I was young, almost too young. But even at fifteen, I'd seen and done shit that made me grow up fast. When I was eighteen, I patched in. Daze, whose dad was also in, patched in with me."

He watches my face, and I shrug in confusion. "Is all of that supposed to mean something to me? What does patched-in mean? What is an Enforcer?" He grimaces, shoveling his hand into those crazy black curls.

"They are MC terms. My dad had been the President of the Ghost Nomads MC. Motorcycle Club."

There goes my mouth again. Any minute, something is going to fly in there. "You mean you and Daze were in like a *Sons Of Anarchy* type thing?" I never watched the show, but I cannot tell you how many times Riley pulled up pictures of some of the actors in their gear. Even Mama Mansour was in on it.

Free grimaces but nods. "Yeah, that shows a little sanitized, but it's the gist. It wasn't just Daze and me; it was all of us. Pallas, Nox, Devin, and eventually all of us. Even Kazimir. Most of us were kids or relatives of older members. Evonne was the old lady of one of the members—she's been with us forever. We were out on a drop one night, and a rival club rolled into the clubhouse. Most of the brothers were taken out. When we got back, almost nothing was left except what we had on us. Riggs was almost dead, but he pulled through. He recognized the cuts on the killers and me and the remaining boys got retribution. We left none alive." His face is impassive, not a snippet of remorse in his dark eyes. A cold shiver touches my spine.

"We got offers to join other clubs but decided to form our own. I was elected President when I was nineteen. We called ourselves Gods of The Apocalypse." He holds up a ring on his right middle finger and squinting; I can see the letters GOTA swirled in gold.

"It didn't take us long to establish ourselves. We'd taken out a huge crew, and word got around. I wasn't happy with our turf and we kept, ummmm, expanding. Aggressively. We were into all kinds of shit, and it was known that if I didn't get what I wanted, then people would pay for it. Our reputation was Death—give in or meet it. At the same time, Trace was rising in the ranks on the government side, though no one knew his brother was the leader of the GOTA. Harlan was able to clean up his background somehow. Anyway, one day, we were about to act on some intel we got on another club, and instead, we ran into a set-up by Trace and his crew. He pretended he didn't know who I was, but I blew up his spot. I told him if he even thought about coming after us, I would let all his little federal buddies know exactly where he came from. Stephen, too, since he grew up near us. He got pissed, but we came to an agreement. Every so often, he would reach out and ask for information, and once in a while, I'd give him a taste if it suited my needs. The last time was a few years ago. We'd just come out of some bad shit and decided to go legit, and Trace wanted one more favor. I knew what he was all about and made him promise to keep looking after our mama in exchange. He agreed, which was the last time I spoke to him."

Wait a minute. "Your mama is still alive?"

Free nods. "I haven't seen her in years. She probably thinks I'm dead or in jail—I don't know what Trace was telling her. Anyway, he put her up in a house, and she told all her friends about her son and his job, though she has no idea he was a government honeypot." I wince. "I would get a text from an unknown number every so often with pictures of her, so I know she's doing okay."

"Does she know that Trace is, um," I wave my hand at him.

"No. Trace's boss, Harland, wants to wait for some other things before he tells her. She will be devastated. He was her one good thing. She fell in love with my dad and knew what he was, but she always thought she could keep us out of it. If anyone asked her which of us would've turned out bad, she would have definitely said me. I was wild from birth." I snort. My mama would've said the same thing about me.

"Anyway, one of my old brothers, Silver, reminded me that I may not have my club anymore, but I am still me. No one would ever think about going up against me. There's a bunch of people who are still worried that we will re-form, though we've been out of the game for years."

"So we don't have to really get married then? We can tell people we are. Wait, why are you looking at me like that?" He's got a cross between a scowl and a grin on his face. It looks painful. "No, we need to do it all legally or as close as we can to your new identity. Fallen will take care of it. If anyone goes looking, we have to make sure they know it's for real."

I stand up and start pacing around the room, yanking on my hair with one hand and cradling my belly with the other. "So let me get this all together in my head. You, Daze, Pallas, Cage, Nox, Devin, and Fallen were all like some criminal badasses in a motorcycle club, and you want me to marry you because you were SUCH a badass that people would be too scared to mess with me? And your mama doesn't know that her one son is gone and the other is like this horse person? Did I get the gist of it?" I stop and glare at him because he is grinning at me, and I don't like it.

"Kazimir was in it too. We had a lot of members, but those are the ones that decided to go straight with me. Everyone else joined other clubs or is dead," he says calmly, and I throw my hands in the air. "Dead? Just like that?"

"Vivi, that's part of the life. No one expects to live to an old age, and most of us would rather go out fighting anyway." Great. "Do I have time to think about this?"

"No. The sooner, the better. I want our marriage established before the baby comes. Once it's all on the books, then Silver will let it leak through the grapevine. He's a gossip, so it will seem natural." His arms uncross, and he takes a few steps toward me. "I know this isn't how you pictured getting married, but it will keep you safe." I snort again. I never really thought about being married. Ever. I was content to work on my art and maybe be an auntie to Riley's kids. Now look at me. A baby on the way, and one hot, killer of a husband coming right up.

"Well, this explains the names," I mutter. "Is Free even your real name? Or is it like Horace or Nathaniel?"

"It's Free. Now and forever. Come on, you. Let's go get married."

CHAPTER 43
VIVI

Holy Shit. I'm married.

CHAPTER 44
FREE

Thank fuck. I'm married.

CHAPTER 45
FREE

"Daze, where is my wife?"

We've been married two days, and I can honestly say my wife is the biggest pain in the ass in the world.

First, she wouldn't budge until she and Dulcie could devise a suitable outfit for her. I was ready to marry her in her dirty overalls, but when I told her that, she gave me a look that should have withered my balls into a knot. Once they finagled a cream-colored dress that did wonders for her tits (she's my wife, I can look), then she wanted 'Noxxie' to come and braid her hair. He came in from the construction site and waggled his eyebrows at her cleavage but agreed to give her what she wanted. Then, of course, Dulcie wanted a matching hairstyle, so he had to indulge her too.

Then, she wanted all the guys to be a witness, not just Daze. Judge Takis owed me several favors, so he waited patiently while she rounded up all of my brothers, all in different stages of filth. Pallas was elected to walk her 'down the aisle,' which was just the hallway outside my office. She pulled Daze from the couch and made him stand beside me, and then Dulcie lined up beside her. I even saw Evonne in the corner. She was sure throwing out orders like a real bridezilla for someone who never wanted to get married. Judge Takis thankfully thought she was adorable and let her do whatever she wanted. We had already signed the marriage license, and even though he gave us the most basic ceremony, Dulcie and Evonne still sniffled through it. Vivi was clear-eyed, listening intently to his words, while I spent the few minutes staring at my soon-to-be wife's face. I said, 'I do' at some point, slipping a thin platinum band on her finger, which caused her to freeze in shock. "I don't have a ring for you," she whispered.

"It's okay. We can get one later," I whispered back. She still looked upset, but I squeezed her fingers in assurance. A long time ago, I had decided on the last name 'Kelly' as an homage to the Kelly Gang and because Dulcie liked how it sounded. Plus, it was far away from my real name.

When Judge Takis said I could now kiss my bride, I saw the panic in her face and gave her no choice. I gripped her around her waist and caught her supple mouth with mine. Her lips opened in protest, and I slipped my tongue inside, stroking hers with a gentle rhythm. The garden flowers she had in her hand fell to the floor, and she kissed me back, leaning in heavily. Someone cleared their throat, and everyone laughed. She sprung back, face fever-red with embarrassment.

I give no fucks. If I want to kiss my wife, I goddamn will.

Since then, I have seen her for a total of twenty minutes, tops. Evonne had made us a wedding dinner, but something in it set her off because she got sick immediately. Kaz jumped in and sent her straight to bed, and just like that, the reception was over. The next day, I went to check on her, but apparently, she was up and at 'em with Dulcie, and I was too busy to look for her. I asked Evonne to make sure that Vivi's things were moved into my room and the nursery planning was transferred to the room across the hall. When I went to check, nothing had been moved, and Evonne informed me that my wife's exact words were "hell no." So this morning, I have been looking for her, but it seems no one knows where she is.

"Wow, you lost her already?" Daze smirks at me and I think about how many ways I could get rid of his body on all this acreage. "Not a very good husband, are ya?"

Yeah. I could make sure the vultures couldn't even find him. "I didn't lose her, you maggot. Have you seen her?" His smirk deepens, and I take a step toward him. He holds his hand up, laughing. "Okay, okay. She's with Whistler."

Whistler? What?

"Daze, why is Vivi hanging out with our farrier?" Whistler is harmless, an older dude that's worked on some of the best ranches, but I don't want my pregnant wife around animals that are being treated.

"I can't tell you that. It's a surprise." I don't like surprises. I start backward toward the pen where Whistler normally works. He's got a shed where he stores his equipment, though I don't think I've even been in it. Devin is his normal contact. It is a bit back from the stables, and I walk quickly, sensing Daze on my heels. "Can't you just let her have this?" I stop in my tracks. "Have what?" He hesitates, and I keep walking. In the short distance, I can hear the whine of some equipment and frown when I see sparks coming from the shed. "What is that?" I look back at Daze, who is shaking his head at me. I walk faster and see Whistler leaning against a post, a small smile on his craggy face. If he's not in the shed...

"What the fuck?" The sparks stop, and Vivi raises the

welder's helmet around her head. She's got a torch in her hand and a gigantic grin on her face. "What are you doing?"

"I'm making you something. See?" She leans forward and plucks something from between two clasps. She holds it out to me, and I see it's a ring. "I thought I'd make you a wedding ring instead of buying one—I mean, let's face it, I don't have any money, but this is better anyway. Whistler let me use his stuff." She puts the ring back into the clasps. "I just need to sand down some of the edges, and it'll be ready."

"Vivienne Kelly, put that torch down right now." I point at the floor and glare at her. "You are going to hurt yourself." She grins wider and shakes her head. "Free, I totally know what I am doing. It's okay. Now go away and let me finish." She pushes the helmet back down and expertly flicks the gas to start the torch again. It sparks around her little body, and she leans forward to touch it to the small ring.

Whistler touches my back and motions me to step back. My breath is coming out in worried pants, but he smiles at me reassuringly. "Your little lady knows what she is doing, Free. She's been poking around my shed for weeks now. She probably knows more about all of this than I ever could. I dunno what she did before, but she knows her way around metals." He walked off, and I turned to see Daze watching me.

"Well, we knew she was keeping stuff from us," he shrugs. He eyes my terrified face and pats my arm. "I know, Free. But she's happy. I don't think I've seen her this happy since she's been here. Bout scared the shit outta me too when I first saw her pick that torch up. But she's a master at it. Hell, Whistler himself picked out that helmet for her." I scowl. I don't want anyone buying her anything but me. Wait what?

"Let her have this. She's not in any danger."

"Finished! Let me see your hand." Vivi bounds out of the shed, wiggling around. I stare at her flushed, exuberant face and sigh, holding out my left hand. She slips off the ring on my middle finger, pocketing it, and places the heavy metal piece on my ring finger. It's a perfect fit. "I made it out of one of Sea Voyage's horseshoes. Daze said that he was the first racehorse you bought." I thumb the smooth surface and stare at her in silence.

"Do you like it?" She bounces on her toes, a whole fire-cracker—sparkling and sizzling.

"Yeah, I do. Thank you." I eye her. "How did you know my ring size?" She grins again. "I stole your ring when you were in the shower." I try not to think about how my dick wishes she would've stolen him instead. "Little thief. How do you know so much about welding?" I watch in fascination as a veil comes down over her eyes, and I mourn the happiness that just dimmed.

"It's a hobby, I guess. So, is it okay if I come out here and play around? Whistler said he doesn't mind." I bet he doesn't. He may be old, but he ain't blind. I glance at Daze, who lifts his eyebrows at me and gestures with his hands.

"Will you promise always to wear your helmet? And will you wear better shoes? Those things that on your feet aren't even close-toed. And will you come to me to buy you what you need? I want to know what you are doing." She starts bouncing on her toes again, nodding her head happily. "And you need an apron, too. We will make you a list when we get home." She squeals and throws herself at me, and I catch her with a low grunt. Her breasts are pressed into my chest, and her small belly nestles against me. Her soft lips peck kisses all over my face. "Thank you, thank you! Whistler! Imma need more room!" She slips away and scampers after him, skipping every few steps. I watch her careen around the corner and smile.

"You may want to fix your face, my friend. I don't think you want anyone to know your secret." Daze drawls, sauntering after my wife.

"What secret? I don't have any secrets." He laughs loudly and keeps walking.

Whatever. I don't know what the hell he's talking about. Now I just have to move all of my wife's shit into our room. Immediately.

CHAPTER 46
VIVI

I twist my hands nervously, then start biting on my thumbnail. I glance at the clock and see it's a little after eleven pm. I should be asleep; this baby is making me fall out around eight every night, without fail. But tonight, I am not sleeping alone. I chew the hangnail I created and jiggle my leg under the thick, dark covers.

When I returned from making Free's ring and visiting Carnage, I just wanted to soak in a tub and eat. I'm slightly out of practice with the labor and discipline of creating something, so my muscles are sore, and I am hungrier than usual (go figure.) I walked into my bedroom and was half undressed when I noticed the bare room. The bed sheets were stripped, and the top mattress was gone. My meager belongings were missing, and a quick check of the closet and bathroom showed that my clothes and toiletries were also missing. Dammit. I called out for Evonne, who was already upstairs.

"Let me guess; your boss asked you to move all my stuff anyway?" I huffed and crisscrossed my arms, which did nothing because nothing rattles Ev, no matter what you do.

"No, your *husband* asked me to move your things. He was not happy that your clothes and things were not in his room as he requested. He had Devin and Dulcie do it while you were out playing in the stables," she huffed back with a raised brow. "Stop your sulking now. There are much worse fates than sharing a bed with a man like Free." She patted my arm and went downstairs. "I'll bring you a tray when you are ready," she called over her shoulder. I stared after her, stomped off to the room down the hall, and pushed the door open with force.

Luckily, Free wasn't in there, and I was able to give in and poke around his bedroom. I opened every drawer in his dresser, discovering that most were empty except two, which were filled with stacks and stacks of black t-shirts and one stack of white. I pulled one white one out and tossed it on the bed. There were two nightstands, again one empty, the other filled with a few magazines, a pack of cigarettes with three missing, and two boxes of condoms. I snicker when I notice they are extra-magnum sized, because WHY WOULDN'T THEY BE? The man is already a giant column of hotness; it would stand to reason he'd have a tree trunk for a dick. Riley used to say there was no such thing as too big, but I dunno. At least he's being safe, I guess. The bottom drawer makes me pause and slam it shut because there are guns in there. Not just one, either. The closet is next, and I see that on one side are rows of leather jackets, black jeans, and racks of boots. Some drawers are built in, filled with underwear and socks, all neatly orga-nized. Oh, and two more boxes of condoms. Jesus. I grab a chair and check all the upper shelves, discovering four more gun safes and matching ammo boxes. I am disappointed there is nothing more juicy, but I see that the other side is my pitiful wardrobe, complete with all my overalls and a few dresses I don't recognize. Dulcie, I'm sure.

The giant bathroom is all black and granite, and I go

through everything there, too, discovering that the scent that clings to Free is his body wash and matching deodorant. He uses a charcoal toothbrush, which I find hilarious, and likes spearmint toothpaste. All my stuff is neatly lined up around one of the double sinks, and my shampoo and conditioner have their spot in the shower stall. I turn on the water and see he has a rain shower head (score!), and other jets are sticking out of the wall. I fiddle with the levers until I figure out the pattern and then turn the water off. This bathroom doesn't have a clawfoot tub, but it does have a huge soaker tub with one window that looks over the land in the back of the house.

Don't mind if I do.

After the best soak of my life, Evonne brought me a tray with fried chicken and an avocado salad, which I hoovered up. My eyes started getting heavy, so I lay on the bed but couldn't fall asleep. I tossed for a bit and then grabbed some paper and a pen that I snagged from Dulcie's office. I started sketching out some designs, and before I knew it, it was late, and Free still wasn't upstairs. I put my drawings aside, and that's where I am now—nervously gnawing on my body parts and waiting for him to come to bed. My eyes started drooping again but shot open when I heard heavy footsteps coming up the stairs. I sit up and scratch at my hair, tucking the blankets around my lap and fidgeting with the pillows. The walking stops, and I wait, holding my breath when they slowly head in my direction. The door which is partially closed, pushes open quietly, and Free's head pokes around it. We stare at each other momentarily before he comes all the way in, closing the door behind him. "You're still up?" He walks over to my side of the bed, his body slinking smoothly. I never noticed how he moved —like a giant cat about to leap on you silently.

"Umm, yeah. I couldn't sleep," I watch as he comes closer and sits beside me on the bed. I gulp at his smell and the just sheer overwhelmence of his presence. "How tall are you?" I blurt out, and he gives me that slight smirk. Damn him.

"About six-four or five. You?" He plucks at the sleeve of the white t-shirt I stole, and the smirk kicks up again.

"Uhhh, five-two or three." Liar. I am a whole-ass five-foot-one. Maybe.

"Really, Little Thief? I swore you were smaller than that. Is that my t-shirt?" He traces the neckline where it slipped off of my shoulder. Goosebumps follow his trail, and my throat goes dry. I can feel the squelch of my awkwardness about to make itself known. Uh oh.

"Uh, yes? I don't have pajamas, and you're really big, I mean, your clothes are. I can take it off if you want?" His eyebrows shoot up, and a dark light edges his pupils. "Wait, I didn't mean it like that! I meant that I can wear something else." Kill me now.

"We're married, Vivi. What's mine is yours." His fingers are now on my collarbone, and I swear the roughness of his fingertips, combined with the heat from his body, is about to make a hormone jump out of me and attack him. God help me.

"What are these sketches?"

Sketches? Huh? Oh! "I'm going to make the baby's crib instead of buying one. I want it to be more personal, you know?" He flips through the pages, peering at me every other one. "Vivi, these are incredible. What can I do to help?" I feel a sting of a tear at the corner of my eye and sniffle. Damn hormones. "What's wrong?" Free puts the papers down and moves closer, wrapping his hands around my hips and pulling me to his lap.

"Nothing. Just you are being really nice to me, and I didn't expect it, I guess. Especially since you told me all about how you used to be this psycho motorcycle person." He chuckles at that, and his fingers tighten into my flesh.

"Again, you are my wife. I will do whatever you need me to do," He brushes a tear away from my cheek with a frown. "Make sure you leave me a list of everything you need." I nod, and he pulls away, standing up. "Lay down. I'm going to take a shower and come to bed. You don't have to wait up for me—I will always find you." I scoot down as he pushes his boots from his feet and takes them to the closet. "Free?" He glances over his shoulder at me. "Yeah, Little Thief?"

I smile at the nickname. "I left your other ring on your nightstand. Um, I may have also gone through all of your stuff." He smirks and leans on the doorway. "Find anything interesting?" I barely have the wherewithal to stop ogling his perfect face.

"Lots of guns and condoms. I guess that tracks, though." I say a bit more sourly than I intended. That pierced brow quirks up at my tone, and I curse myself. I sound like a *femme jalouse*. Ugh.

"I'll make sure all of the guns are put up before the baby comes, don't worry. As for the condoms...I was a single man, Vivi. I won't apologize for my past. But luckily, I'm married now; I can throw those all out."

WHAT?!

He grins at me and saunters into the bathroom, unbuckling his pants as he goes. "Free?" He pokes his head out as he closes the door. "Yesss?"

"What does the FTW stand for on your ring? For the win?" He shakes his head solemnly.

"No, baby. It's First To War." He closes the door behind him with a soft thud.

CHAPTER 47
FREE

'm in hell.

I've thought that in the past. I've been in situations where I felt I wouldn't make it or that one of my brothers wouldn't. I've brought death to innocent people and sent others straight to the netherworld.

Nothing. And I mean, nothing is as torturous as being married to Vivi Kelly.

The first morning I woke up from her being in my bed? She'd scooted across the bed and wrapped around me like a creeping vine. Her leg was thrown over mine, full tits pushed against my bicep. Her crazy hair was in my face, and her belly was wedged between us, her arm thrown across my torso, too close to my dick, which was awake and looking to play. I crept out of the bed and took another shower, this time a cold one. When I stepped out, she was sitting up, a rumpled gorgeous mess whose mouth dropped open at the sight of me in just a towel. I smirked at her when she dove back under the covers, but it was too late. Her reaction caused me to need another cold shower, and I practically ran out of my own bedroom. I figured it was a one-time thing, but no. No matter where we start in the bed, she always winds up on top of me, her body finding me in the dark and fusing itself with mine in the most excruciating ways. The past three weeks have been awful, and now my subconscious is claiming her, sliding under her panties to grip her juicy ass, or worse, a hand gripped between her legs. She hasn't said a word either, and I know she's woken up a few times to me groping her in my sleep. My poor dick has been yelling at me, and no amount of jerking off in the shower is going to substitute for ramming into her slick heat.

"Boss, you got a sec?" Fallen knocks on the doorway's frame, one of his many laptops clutched in his arms.

God yes. Please talk to me and get my mind off of my gorgeous wife. "Yeah, come in. What's up?" I ask him, frowning at the look of anxiety on his face. "Is something wrong?"

"Um, no, not really. Where's your wife?" My frown deepens. "She out at her workshop. Why?" Vivi had given me a long list of things she wanted for her 'hobby,' I took one look at it and knew that we couldn't invade Whistler's domain with all this stuff. I didn't even recognize most of it, so I gave the list to Cage, who ordered all of it from his connections. He offered a small shed used to house equipment near his garage, and Vivi pounced on it. She commandeered him and Pallas, and before long, she had a whole little spot staked out for herself. The day I took her to a salvage yard to pick out metal for the baby's crib might've been one of the best days of my life.

"I just want to ensure we are alone when I give you this information." He sits down gingerly, balancing the laptop on his leg.

"Should I be pulling in Daze and the other guys?" I reach for my cell phone, but he shakes his head quickly.

"No, this is more personal. It can be just us." I sit back and wait, Fallen squirming in his chair. His slim fingers tap his jean-clad leg, then reach up and tug at the neckline of his Metallica t-shirt. "That's a nice sculpture." He points at the metal piece Vivi made for me last week--Konabos and Ares from a painting Vivi said she saw long ago.

"Yeah, you said that last week when you saw it. What gives?" I'm getting impatient, and anything involving my wife can put me on edge.

"Well, I kept thinking about it after I saw it. I mean, Vivi keeps saying that her welding stuff is a 'hobby,' but she's way too skilled for it to be something that she does in her spare time. Aside from your wedding band, she's produced that sculpture, the crib, and now I hear she is working on a top-secret thing for you, too."

I heard the same thing, and she won't budge or give me a clue. Last night, I threatened to tickle her, and she informed me that she would definitely pee if I did, and with such a solemn little face that I had no choice but to laugh.

"My point is, that's a lot over a few weeks. I couldn't stop thinking about it. Then I remembered that I had never done a reverse image search when digging into her background. So I took a pic of her and plugged it into a program." He turned his laptop around, and I stood up in a fury.

"You took a picture of my wife?" I stepped around the desk, and to his credit, Fallen didn't budge. "Yes, I did. It wasn't anything salacious. And I was very, very cautious. I know how much she means to you. Do you want to see what I found?" He sits calmly while I pant like a bull, standing beside him.

"What?" I bite out.

"Well, first, it was just the usual. I found her school IDs and her driver's license. See?"

He shows me a few pictures of a younger Vivi with her old blonde hair, and I smirk when I see her license has her listed as five feet tall. Little liar.

"Then I sorted through a few that weren't her, and right at the end, I found this," he clicks on an image of what looks like a flyer or newsletter. There is a bunch of words, but in a small square, there is a picture of Vivi. She's smiling—not her normal one, but more...professional. I see the name under the image and frown. "V. Woods? Who is that?"

"It's your wife. V. Woods is like this uber-famous metal sculptor. Look." He clicks on more things, and I sit reading through them. "She did all of this?" I point at a tall interpretation of a man holding an umbrella. I squint when I see what the piece sold for. "Holy fuck. Her shit was selling for that much?" Fallen nods. "Yeah, she is, was pretty in demand. That guy Phineas was her main gallery, but she showed all over, including London, Tokyo, etc. There isn't much of a bio, just a few sentences about being a prodigy, etc. There's speculation that the photo is fake, though we know they're not. She did almost no press for her work. She was pretty much a mystery."

"He was supposed to cozy up this artist chick and get her to do something for us." That's what Harland said."

"But Trace and his crew knew the truth. That's how he got in with her."

Fallen nodded. "I couldn't find any evidence of a studio anywhere, meaning it was in her house. And if Trace was spending nights there, sorry, then he must've known." I scowled at these words—I don't like to think of Vivi with Trace. At all.

"Why wouldn't she tell us that? Or me?" We've grown close over the last few weeks.

"I don't know. But I think your girl has been living with secrets for a long time. According to this little write-up, she's been sculpting since she was a little kid." He stands up, shutting the laptop with a snap. "Talk to her, Free. Maybe she has a reason."

I see the sparks from her torch and smell the chemical scent of something she uses to strip stuff down. I almost had a heart attack when I saw some of the stuff she asked for, but she promised to wear a thick mask and gloves when handling anything substantial. I asked Kaz to make sure, and he carefully checked and said a mask would be fine if she didn't have prolonged exposure. Cage installed some industrial fans for her, and the whole southern side of the shed rolled up for full ventilation. Some weird old song is playing, probably from the nineties, which she proclaimed was 'the best music decade ever,' so she doesn't hear me walk up.

"Vivi!" I shout over the music, and her head snaps up from whatever she is meshing together.

"Hey, you aren't supposed to be in here! I told you that it was a surprise," she says, pushing her mask over her head. She straddles something and swings her legs over it to stand up straight. Her belly, which is getting bigger by the day, is prominent in her conductor-striped overalls. I smile at her flushed face and reach out to pat her tummy.

"I'm not looking, I swear. But you've been out here for a while, Little Thief, and it's time for you to eat something and take a rest." I've discovered that once she starts on something, she has a hard time pulling away, and I have to force her to stop, or she will go all night.

"Damn, has it really been four hours? Jeez." She strips off her gloves and smiles up at me. "I think the baby finally moved today."

"Really? You didn't call me?" Kaz told her that the kid should be kicking by now, and Vivi admitted that she had been feeling things but didn't know if it was gas or not. I howled at the look on her face, and she swatted me in embarrassment.

"Well, I wanted to make sure it wasn't a fart, okay? The last two times were false alarms." I chuckle and watch as she carefully puts up all her tools, covering her latest project with a tarp. 'What are we eating?"

"I think Ev made lasagna. Let's walk a bit first." I take her hand and lace my fingers through hers. She stares down at our hands and looks up at me in confusion. "Um, okay." We pass the building where Cage and his team maintained all the ranch equipment and nod at Riggs, who is stacking some tires. It's a bit of a walk back to the house, but I think the time will be good for us. I think about how to start and then decide to go for it. Fuck it.

"Vivi, you know you can tell me anything, right?" I look down at her as she stares at her feet as we walk. "You do know that, right?" She shrugs one small shoulder and nods. "I ain't in no position to judge anyone. You know all of my shit—maybe not specifics, 'cause I will never tell you those, but you know the big shit. So anything you got going on will not matter to me, alright?" Another shrug and nod. "Tell me about V. Woods." Her head snaps up, halting in place, her mouth dropping open. "Close that mouth," I push it shut and tug her closer. "It's okay."

"How did you find out?" She's wringing her hands together, and I grab them tightly. "It's okay, I said. Fallen got suspicious and did some digging."

"Damn him," she mutters and starts stomping toward the house, her crazy hair blowing in the warm breeze. "Why is he so nosy?" She shouts at me from over her shoulder, and I can't help but laugh. I jog to catch up to her and grab her arm, swinging it around.

"Vivi, it's his job to find out information. It's what he did for the club; now, he keeps all our security equipment and computers running. It's his specialty." I see a flash in her eyes, the green tinting more than usual. "Anyway, what's the fucking big deal? You were a famous artist. That's nothing to hide." I rub my hands up and down her arms as she sags. "Come here." I pull her into my arms and squeeze her gently. "I'm proud of you." A sob comes from her, and I try not to laugh. My wife is emotional at the drop of a hat. Hormones. "None of that, now."

"You are one of the only people to ever say that to me about my art," she mutters, wiping her snot on my shirt.

"Really, not your parents?" Fallen said they seemed stuck up, and Vivi talks about them very little. She is silent for a moment, still standing in my arms.

"My, um, Maman and I didn't really get along. She wanted a little prissy miss, and I was...not. I was a whole troublemaker as a kid. I didn't straighten up until around the time I met Riley, but I still was...problematic. Anyway, when I started getting into metal sculpting, she was horrified. She was okay with me taking art classes because that seemed innocuous, but when my talent led me in that direction, she refused even to acknowledge it. I sold my first piece when I was seventeen. Phineas, who was my agent, got me a really pretty penny, and it's what paid for RISD. My parents wanted me to stay home, where they could watch me and take something basic at college, but they couldn't do a thing when I could pay for it on my own. She never went to my shows or told her friends anything. My dad came to a few, but she made him pay for it when he got home. Riley was proud of me but would've felt the same if I were a cashier. She loved me no matter what. I've always avoided attention, so having a pseudonym made sense for many reasons. And my mama wouldn't be embarrassed."

"But I saw all kinds of cool shit about you. Why would she be ashamed? You're a badass." She's quiet again. "My parents didn't want a badass. They wanted a conformer, a robot.

Someone who would marry someone boring and safe and would fall into line." I snort.

"So I'm guessing they would not approve of me?" I'm amused at the thought. I can only imagine what a pair of uptight French parents would think.

She laughs, the deep, raspy one that always shocks me can come out of such a small body. "My mother would probably scream and call the cops on you. My dad would cry. Riley would cheer. She hated how I lived in seclusion."

Her voice is sad, and I hold her tighter. "I don't believe in the afterlife, but if there is one, Riley is up there doing backflips. You alright, now?" I tilt her beautiful face toward mine, ghosting a kiss over her nose. She sighs and nods before a loud growl comes from her stomach. A giggle breaks loose, and I chuckle. "Our kid is hungry. Let's go see what Evonne has cooked up, Mrs. Kelly." I take her hand, and we walk back home in the gloom.

CHAPTER 48
VIVI

"Can we stop at the next rest stop?" I ask, chewing on a finger.

"Again?" Nox asks sarcastically from the front seat. I flip him my middle finger, and he laughs. Pallas smiles from next to me, silent as always. "I'm six months pregnant, Noxxie. That means my bladder is squished like a grape right now. And this little girl has been kicking me to death for the last hour. So unless one of you wants to clean up pee, I suggest you hush it and stop when I ask you to." Free smiles at me in the rearview, making my grouchiness lessen. Damn, that man is pretty.

"There's a Buc-ees in about five miles, Little Thief. You think you can last that long?" He taps the nav system, and indeed, we are about to roll up on one soon.

"Yeah. I need a snack anyway."

"You just ate a pi—"

"Shut it, Nox! Part of the pregnant thing is I like to eat, okay?" He grins wolfishly and chuckles. "Just pulling your chain, Lil Mama." I pluck the back of his head and tug on one of his braids. "I need you to do my hair like this next time." He's got three braids going straight down the back of his head, each hanging shorter than the next. It's amazing.

"You got it." Free looks at him with a frown, so I pluck him, too. He grunts as he switches lanes. He gets extra grumpy whenever Nox braids my hair. I don't know what he's worried about. No one is looking to get laid by a pregnant chick with a bad attitude.

"So this horse we will get, she's for Carnage?" Free asked me a few days ago to accompany him to a ranch near Dallas, where he wanted to buy a two-year-old filly named Judy. Once the owners learned he was married, they insisted he bring me along. The giant hitch attached to the truck bed could hold an elephant.

"Yeah. Since your boy is acting right, we should start thinking about him siring some offspring." Carnage has been doing fantastic in his training, and just last week, Devin said he is ready to enter some prequalifying races. I hope he smokes Harley, who is still a stuck-up twat.

"Does that mean you will sell his babies?" My eyes water up, and Pallas groans.

"Vivi, we have been over this. If Carnage ever breeds successfully, his offspring will be very valuable. But I promise you we will keep some of them, okay?" Free tells me with a smile as I sniffle and nod. I don't want any baby Cabbages going anywhere. Maybe I can change his mind later. The big truck slows down, and my bladder announces it has waited long enough.

"Pally, help me down. I gotta go." He jogs around the truck and lifts me down, hustling behind me as I rush to the bathroom. "Wait." He says the word quietly, and I jump and jiggle while he checks out the empty stalls, disregarding the angry exclamations from the women using the facility. "Okay, go.

Here." He points at a stall closest to the entrance, and I scamper in, knowing he will be waiting for me just outside the doors. I feel instant relief and pat a bump where Little Miss sticks out an elbow or foot. She is an active baby and responds instantly to food, music, or the sound of Free's voice. Seeing such a big, dangerous man leaning over my stomach is funny, telling her about all the horses she will ride when she is old enough. I wash my hands, and sure enough, Pallas is leaning against the wall. I slip my hand through his bent elbow, headed straight for the beef jerky wall. "I want some Cherry Maple jerky. And a hotdog. And some strawberries." He chuckles and taps his phone to let Free know we are heading toward the snacks. He quickly gathers all my requests and heads to the cash wrap. I get sidetracked a few times, and Pallas gently pulls me along.

"Where are Nox and Fr-" I start before stopping dead in my tracks. Pallas stops next to me with a grunt. What. The Fuck.

Look, I know my husband is hot. Okay, he's gorgeous. He's got a ton of sexy mixed with bad boy and a whole lot of dangerous. And yeah, we didn't marry because we were in love and haven't done anything in the bedroom. I know all of this. Intellectually. But right now, I'm seriously about to pop off.

Free is leaning against a barrel of peanuts, his long legs stretched in front of him, inked-up arms crossed over his chest. His head is tilted to the side as he listens to the woman standing before him, straddling his left leg. I take her in, all cheap bleached hair, her flat ass barely covered by the toddler's denim skirt she is wearing. Her boobs are about a donkey's hair away from popping out of her tank top, and she teetered in four-inch stacked heels. Her legs are long and thin, and her stomach is flat. She's got a cigarette in her hand, and I watch as she takes a long drag, pursing her lips so that the smoke forms a ring. Something Free says makes her laugh, and she runs a long fake nail down his arm.

Hell. No.

"Do not consider her at all. She has nothing on you." Pallas tells me quietly. She may not have anything on me, but I'm about to put something on her. Like my foot on her ass.

"You are pregnant. There will be no feet in asses for you. Come." Goddammit, did I say that out loud again? About two feet away, I see Nox chatting to a replica of the floozy in front of Free, and when he sees me coming, he straightens up and clears his throat. Free looks up and smiles at me but frowns when he gets a look at my face. "Vivi?"

Don't you Vivi me, you ass. I give him a long look and turn to glare at this hoe. She doesn't look fazed as I mentally turn her into stone. The baby kicks in solidarity, and I don't care what Pallas says. I'm about to open up a can of whoop-ass. "When you are done taking out the trash, I will meet you at the truck. Pallas. Nox." I snap my fingers, and they follow me to pay before escorting me back to the six-fifty. I climb in the truck and viciously take a bite of jerky, thinking about what tools I would need to weld that bitches legs shut. I slam the door and take another bite.

"Vivi." I keep chewing, looking straight ahead. He can go kick rocks.

"Vivi, you gonna look at me?" I say nothing, taking a long sip of water. He's standing outside my window, arms leaning on the sill. "Little Thief, are you jealous?" I stop eating and slowly turn my head, laser beams about to come out of my eyes and roast him on the spot. "I was waiting for you, and she just approached me. I told her I was waiting for my wife, but she kept talking. I didn't invite her." I roll my eyes and look at the back of Nox's seat, who just sat back down and turned around to stick up for his friend.

"It's true. We were just standing there." I shoot him a glare, too, and he shuts up quickly. "So her humping your leg and stroking your arm with her paws was an accident? I don't think so." I say, looking at Nox but addressing Free. He chuckles, and my hackles go all the way up.

"I think I like this side of you." He reaches in and tugs my ear. I pull away and shoot him another death stare. "Let's get on the road." He strolls around the truck, and I growl. "It was nothing, Vivi, I promise you," Nox says before Free returns.

"Nox, have you ever had your hair set on fire? No? I suggest you be quiet." He makes a zipper motion across his lips and turns back around.

I say nothing for the rest of the trip.

"AND OVER HERE, we have our guest houses. Isn't the architecture insane? We had an outfit out of New York design them. Cost us a little bit, but anything Traddy wants, Traddy gets." I fight back the urge to pull my eyes out of my head and nod with fake enthusiasm instead.

"And right here is Traddy's mama's prized tomato garden. She won all kinds of awards for 'em. She made up her own special gin trash—these are the best you will ever taste." I eye the juicy red fruit, and no lie, I kinda want to try them, but... "Tomatoes and my baby don't get along. I haven't been able to eat a plain tomato since I've been pregnant."

Mrs.'Call me Vanna' Eames clucks her tongue in faux sympathy. "Oh, I'll just have to send some along once that little one comes. Now this building...." I turn around, looking at Pallas to save me, giving him my best look of suffering, which he ignores. I just want to go home.

When we were about ten miles from the Eames Ranch, Free

pulled over so that I could change my clothes and clean up. Dulcie warned me that the Eames family was one of Texas's oldest horse breeding facilities and one of the most revered in the country. They are super selective about who they do business with, and the fact that they are even giving Konabos the time of day is a big deal. She sent me a deep turquoise dress with cap sleeves and a slim fit—it's not a maternity dress, but it does wonders with my belly. I let my hair go loose, though I wanted to die with this humidity, and decked myself in all the jewelry she sent along. I even hit the lashes with mascara and added a light pink gloss. When I exited the rest stop bathroom, Pallas gave me a big smile and Nox a low wolf whistle. Free stared at me while a slow grin crossed his stupid, handsome face. I ignored him. I'll wait until I have to behave to acknowledge him.

I first noticed the massive iron gate when we pulled up. It had "Eames" in an elaborate script with what looked like bunches of bluebonnets and roses. I smile, thinking about my little project back home. The second thing I notice is how long the driveway is, lined with pecan trees and more fencing. We drive a ways until a large Georgian-style building comes into view. It is at least three stories tall, with green shuttered windows and rose vines climbing up the facade.

"Jeez," Nox mutters under his breath, and I nod. "They definitely want you to know they have money." A tall man in a white Stetson, clean creased jeans, and a pearl button shirt steps through the doors approaching our truck. Free comes around to help me down, and the man stops a foot away.

"You must be Free Kelly. I'm the Eames ranch manager, Thompson. Welcome." He shakes Free's hand and then Nox and Pallas. He tips his hat backward when he approaches me and lifts my right hand for a kiss. "Ma'am. You must be Mrs. Kelly—a pleasure," he grins, making my husband stiffen, and me want to run away. Thompson is attractive in a very Texas way—lean build, weathered skin that creases at the eyes, and gleaming white teeth. Yikes.

"Please call me Vivi," I smile, and his teeth multiply. "Vivi, then. Mr. and Mrs. Eames are at the stables. I've been tasked with walking you through the welcome center and ensuring you have refreshments." He waves a hand to the building behind him. Welcome center? This isn't their house?

Yikes again.

We follow him into the building, which looks like a museum. It's filled with photography and TV screens depicting the history of the ranch and family. There are cases of trophies and awards and even a genealogy wall—showing the growth of their programs from the first horse. "Please follow me. Can I offer you some lemonade? Something stronger?" He escorts us out of the back of the building, which opens to the whole property. There is a vast stable to our left; in the long distance, you can see training rings and open pastures. There are more buildings to our right, and in the far distance is a mansion, twice as big as the welcome center but with the same architecture.

"I'm sure my wife would love some lemonade." Free shakes me out of mouth-open perusal, and I jump to smile winningly. "That would be lovely."

Thompson gestures to a woman in a pristine white apron, who sets a large silver tray on the table. She pours me a frosty glass and places two macarons on a delicate china plate. After she puts a lace napkin in my lap, she bows and disappears. I take a sip, and it's perfectly tart and cold. I nibble the macaron and find it has a fresh pecan flavor—probably from the trees in the driveway. My maman would be in hog heaven right now.

"Once Miss Vivi is refreshed, we will meet Mr. and Mrs. Eames. Please take your time. I know the Dallas humidity can be rough." He gives me those teeth again, and I smile politely, peeking at Free, who looks like he may be contemplating murder. Thompson engages the guys in conversation, and I see Free visibly relax. There is a sneaky smirk on Thompson's face like he knows he's riling my husband up and is enjoying it. What an asshole.

I place my empty glass down, and Thompson gestures for us to follow him down the marble steps. The Eames have the traditional stabling that Free is building at Konabos. All the buildings are painted a stark white, and there is a black ceiling fan every few feet, smoothly moving air. Each stall has a horse with a brass plate outside, giving its bloodlines, awards, and breed. Thompson tells us that each stable houses different breeds: Arabians, Shires, Thoroughbreds, etc. Most people know what kind of horse they want, and he tells us it's easier to separate them. The family horses are on a different part of the property, housed in even more luxury.

"Ah, here they are, with Judy." I pull my eyes off the expensive tack hanging outside one of the stalls and turn toward a couple standing to the side. I blink. And then blink again.

"Traddy Eames and his wife, Vanessa Eames. This is Free Kelly and his wife, Vivi. These two gentlemen are part of Free's program. They own the Konabos Ranch, south of here," Thompson tells the two...people. Free steps forward to shake hands, and the old, old, old man looks him up and down, staring at his tattoos and piercings, before sticking his hand out stingily, like Free might be contagious. He gives him a one-pump shake before yanking his hand back and wiping it on his tan slacks. His tan Luccesse hat was pulled low over his ears (which have hairs sticking out of them—just saying), and the skin on his face was stretched as tight as a drum. He's got maybe six cream-colored teeth left that are natural, and the rest are giant veneers that are in no way the right size or color. His neck is covered with liver spots, and his thin frame is stooped at the left shoulder. He's got a thick leather bolo tie around his neck with a how-many-carats diamond in the center— an "E" engraved in gold filigree. His mouth opens, and he gestures to the woman beside him. "My wife," he croaks out, and bless Free; he doesn't flinch when the decades-younger floozy eyes him up and down and stops on his crotch.

Mrs. Eames is dressed identically to her husband, from the tan hat down to the matching tan Lucchese boots. So. Much. Beige. Her bright red hair is curled around her shoulders, falling on top of her rock-hard boobs that look like torpedos under her skintight shirt. Her hips flare from a tiny waist, and she also has veneers, but hers at least cover every tooth. She has to be at least forty years younger than her corpse, I mean husband.

"Such a pleasure to meet you," she purrs, barely glancing at me, probably because she is drooling over all the boys. She looks like she's about to lasso them into her lair and never let them go. She runs her fingers across her bright red lips, showing off the meteor of a wedding ring she is sporting. "Call me Vanna. No one calls me Vanessa anymore," she bats her spider-web lashes at Free and turns to me with a giant fake smile. "Oh, you're pregnant! How cute." Cute?!

"Gotta breed them when you're young. Then get you a younger one in your old age. That's the way to do it," Traddy says with a cackle and wheeze. I pinch my lips together and stare at Free, who has a slight tic at his eyebrow.

"Oh, Traddy honey, you're so full of good advice," she coos. "Now, I'll take Miss Vera with me on a little tour of the property, and you can have your man-talk."

Vera? Who the fuck is Vera?

I look at Nox, who is coughing into his hand and won't meet my eyes. Free gives me a wink. "That sounds wonderful, Vanna. You won't mind if Pallas joins you? I don't trust any man not to be tempted by all the beauty between you and my wife." He gives her a lopsided grin, and I swear I hear her vagina growl.

"Oh, honey, I sure don't. Pallas, is it? He's more than welcome to escort me around." She winks, and poor Pallas looks like he wants to dig a hole and dive in it. "Those eyes are amazing." She eyes his crotch, too, and he discreetly moves his arm to cover it. She sways her ass out of the stable, and Pallas and I follow behind. We are two hours into this tour, and I am about done. Not only has this woman visually assaulted my husband and friends, but she has also called me the wrong name three times, implied that I am fat and that Konabos is poor. I don't give a rat fuck about these tomatoes except what she will look like covered in them.

"You know, you are not the only people interested in Judy. We've had several other ranches out here. Luckily for you, the decision rests with me." She gives me an evil smile, and I stop in my tracks. "What do you mean."

"Well, Traddy lets Thompson and I make most of the choices on where our precious babies go. None of those other ranches had anything to offer us except money, and well," she waves her hand around in a circle. I notice that her polish is a bright crimson red. "We have plenty of that. There are other... things to consider, however." That smile brightens, and I half expect a hiss to come from between those lips. 'What other things?" I cross my arms around my belly and face her head-on. My bullshit tolerance meter just plummeted to negative ten.

"Well, honey, you are young. Early twenties? What does a girl like you know about satisfying a man like your husband? He's probably got needs that you could never imagine. Now you let me have a turn with him, show him a thing or two, and maybe I'll consider your little ranch for Judy. You might up your chances if you throw in the Viking or this creamy piece of chocolate," she gestures at Pallas, standing about ten feet away, but I am positive can hear her.

"You want me to...let you sleep with my husband?" I say carefully, taking a step toward her like we are girlfriends confiding in each other. She nods excitedly, and I give her a slight grin. Yeah, that can of whoop ass is about to make a comeback.

"Vanna, honey? I know you married that gross old man, hoping that he would leave you all his money, and maybe there are people desperate enough to take you up on your disgusting offer. But if you ever fix that groundhog hole of a mouth to ask me to fuck my husband again, I will ruin you. Literally, destroy you. Don't fuck with me. You have no idea who I am or what I am capable of. Now Pallas and I are going to turn around and find our family and get the fuck out of here. I won't tell your husband what you said, but if you say one word I don't like, I will make sure all of Texas knows about you. *Capice?*" I snap my fingers in her furious face and stalk backward.

"Good luck getting any other breeder to work with you, then! I can make it so your hovel of a ranch gets blacklisted," she calls out, and I turn to see her tapping her foot in spiteful glee.

"You just made a mistake, Vanessa." I give her a long look and grab Pallas' hand. "I want to be out of here in ten minutes," I tell him. "And I don't want to hear shit about shit. And I want donuts." Pallas says nothing, squeezes my hand, and hustles next to me. About halfway to the welcome center, I see Free and Nox, both with grim expressions on their faces. Free looks at me and then looks at Pallas, eyes narrowing. "Y'all ok?"

I don't stop walking, just pass him, and gesture. "Yup, we are leaving. Now." God love him, he says nothing and follows me. We are in the truck and pulling off the property in less than eight minutes.

"Vivi? Tell me what happened." Free is in the passenger seat, and he turns around, frowning at me. I glance at Pallas and smooth out my face.

"Nothing. That lady was rude. I just want to go home." He gives Pallas a long look. "That's it? She was rude?" I nod and look out the window.

"Well, that old fossil insulted us ten ways until Tuesday. He basically called us trash and then said they would be in touch. I guess Judy is off the table," Nox tells me in the rearview mirror. "Good riddance."

"Yup," I say, mind whirling.

She can't say I didn't warn her.

CHAPTER 49
FREE

"Uh, Free? You got a minute?" I turn around and see Devin and Pallas standing in the nursery doorway. Vivi finally decided on a color for the baby's room, and I want to hurry and finish it before she changes her mind. The deep, rich cream color warms up the room, though I know Dulcie is furious that we didn't go with pink.

"Yeah, grab something and help me out. I only have this one wall to do." Devin grabs a clean roller, and Pallas takes a brush to polish off the wainscoting. We make quick work of it, and I open the rest of the windows to help with the drying. "Dulcie still pissed?" I chuckle, and Devin joins me.

"Yup. She had already warned me that we would only go for blue or pink when we have our own kid. I don't think I will have any say anyway." He grins and pulls the drop cloth off the floor. We cleaned all the paint supplies and loaded them by the back door. "I'll have Riggs come grab this stuff later. My office good?" Devin nods, and Pallas, as usual, has a blank face.

"Fallen, what are you doing in here?" I stopped in the doorway when I spot him sitting at my desk. He's tapping his pant leg, looking like he's about to come out of his skin. "What's wrong?"

'Nothing, um, nothing. We are just waiting on Daze." His eyes flit to Devin and then back to me. "I checked. The girls are still in town with Cage. I sent him a text to stall as long as he can." I stare at him a moment and his fidgeting increases.

"I'm here," Daze enters, flinging his hat on the desk. He sits beside Fallen and pulls a granola bar out of his pocket. It crumbles in bits, and he plucks them off his shirt, chewing. "Okay, let's tell him." He grins at me and points at Devin.

"Okay, I got a call from Eames Ranch today. They want to sell us Judy," Devin leans forward, clasping his hands. I frown.

"Two weeks ago, they told us to go to hell. Why the change of heart?" I'm thrilled about it, but given how shitty our visit went, I never expected this.

"I guess you haven't been following the grapevine. They ran into some weird financial problems. Bad stock trades, investment failures, IRS knocking on their door. You name it, it went down. Their website went haywire; instead of horses, it was filled with pictures of cats. Each page is just a montage of them. Even their socials went nuts. They are desperate for cash and have reached out. I've heard they are calling anyone and everyone, offering up horses left and right," he waves a hand, sitting back in the chair. "I told them we, of course, still wanted her. Thompson? That's who you all met? He said we could pick her up when the wire transfer clears. I'm going first thing in the morning."

"Fucking A. What's this all about, then?" I'm confused.

"At the end of the conversation, some woman got on the phone and was screeching in my ear. She said, and I quote, "Tell her I'm sorry and to stop it." Then they hung up. I couldn't figure out what she could be talking about, so I asked Pallas what happened." He stopped here and gestured to

Pallas, leaning away from us, as is his habit. I'm somewhat surprised he didn't accompany my wife, but now I realize why.

"I am going to play something for you." He pulls his phone out and taps the screen. He holds it up, and Fallen does his thing so that it airplays to the speakers in the room. I listen as that old man's bitch of a wife propositions Vivi for my dick. I knew she was about bullshit when she licked her lips and pinned her eyes to my zipper. If there were a billboard for easy pussy, her face would be on it.

"Vanna, honey? I know you married that gross old man, hoping that he would leave you all his money, and maybe there are people desperate enough to take you up on your disgusting offer. But if you ever fix that groundhog hole of a mouth to ask me to fuck my husband again, I will ruin you. Literally, destroy you. Don't fuck with me. You have no idea who I am or what I am capable of. Now Pallas and I are going to turn around and find our family and get the fuck out of here. I won't tell your husband what you said, but if you say one word I don't like, I will make sure all of Texas knows about you. Capice?"

"Good luck getting any other breeder to work with you, then. I can make it so your hovel of a ranch gets blacklisted."

"You just made a mistake, Vanessa."

My wife's voice is cold, calculating even. I don't think I've ever heard him speak like that before. Devin lets out a low whistle. "Damn, Vivi is scary." Pallas nods.

"She was furious. I think she had enough between the woman at the gas station and this creature insulting her."

"What woman at the gas station?" Daze asks, eating yet another granola bar. I wave him off and tell Pallas to play it again. Damn. Her anger is making my dick hard.

Fallen picks up the conversation. "I looked back at when all of the Eames issues started, and it was the morning after y'all got back from Dallas, like within hours. I thought that was too much of a coincidence. Way too much. Plus, with how that harpy was screeching...well, I started doing some more digging. I asked Daze over, and we reviewed their websites, etc. There was one common thread—the cats. And the sound."

"What sound?" I ask. He types on his laptop, and I hear nothing but a soft "meow." He types more, and it's the same thing over and over again.

"That's the only thing that comes across the audio. Every webpage and social media site, it even popped up on their phone calls. They've got their best security team working on it, but they can't seem to get it to stop. Someone has complete control of all their tech, and they won't let it go. Hell, even I can't crack it," he grins in admiration. "All of this kinda rang a bell. So, I contacted some hackers on the dark web, and the result immediately returned. Salem."

"What's Salem?" Devin asks. I nod, too.

"Salem isn't a what, it's a who. A long time ago, like almost twenty years, when hacking was newer, Salem came on the scene and took out everyone—overriding hacks, spoofing other people, inserting malware. They were a beast. And after every attack, there would be only one sound. A meow. I played it for someone I know, and he confirmed. Only Salem used that signature. Then, one day, they just disappeared. There were lots of rumors that Salem got into some government agency and got caught. Never to be heard from again. Until now." The room goes silent.

"I checked all of our network sign-ons for that day. Your office had one at two am. It only lasted three minutes, but I know that was planted. I had Daze pull up the cameras." He stops and watches as I connect the dots. "She spent two hours. Non-stop. Only someone at an elite level could pull off what she did. I can't even fucking do it." He handed me his laptop and a video was playing. My wife sits at my desk, a gallon of milk next to her and a huge bag of Charleston chews in her lap. Her face is intent, fingers flying over the keyboard at a rate I can't imagine. "You said Salem was active how many years ago? Twentyish? She would have been a kid. Just a baby."

"Yeah. But it lines up. She would've been around ten-ish. She's repeatedly told us how isolated she was—hell, she barely watches TV. When I gave her that new cell phone, she looked at it like it was a snake. I haven't seen her touch anything tech since she got here. It would also explain what Harland was talking about. They must have pulled her file and wanted her to hack something for them. No one would think to check on an artist from Seattle."

"So you're telling me that my wife, all five feet of her, is some crazy hacker?"

"I prefer the term information freedom fighter." We all turn around and see Vivi and Dulcie standing in the doorway, arms full of shopping bags. Cage is behind them, a full apologetic look on his face.

"I guess I should explain."

CHAPTER 50

VIVI

"I think I told you how much of a pain in the ass I was when I was little," I start. Daze asked all the other guys to come into the office so I would only need to tell my story once. Hell, even Riggs is here. Evonne brought in a large tray of snacks, and I have some strawberries in a bowl on my lap. Free is parked next to me, muscled arm stretched behind me. Every so often, he strokes my shoulder, nudging me with his knee. If anybody were going to understand, it would be this group.

"I mean, you're a pain in the butt now, Scoot," Daze drawls, and I throw a strawberry at him. He catches it deftly and shoves it in his mouth. "Shut up, fool."

"Anyway. I was a handful. My parents are strict French. Very proper, very mannered. I was such a throwback—always into stuff, dirty, never listened. My *maman* tried everything. She put me in all kinds of behavioral lessons, kept me in the house, hired a nanny, you name it. The nanny didn't last, but she told my parents that she thought maybe I was bored. That they weren't wearing out my energy in the right way. She said the only time I was ever still was when she took me to the library—I would read for hours. My mom jumped on that and bought me every book imaginable, and when I went through those too fast, my dad suggested a computer. His family is big into education, so he thought this was the perfect solution. I took to it like a pig to slop." I pop a few more berries in my mouth, dipping them first in the whipped cream. Free leans forward, opening his mouth for one, too. I give him extra cream and smile.

"But that didn't make my mom happy either. Because instead of falling into line and being her perfect little *Mademoiselle*, I stayed in my room. She couldn't figure out what I was doing; it was driving her crazy. She kept coming in and checking on me, and all she saw were lines and lines of code. She didn't know that I was breaking into all kinds of stuff and leaving a trail of mess behind me."

"How did you learn to code like that? You were how old? Ten?" Fallen asks. He looks like a kid meeting Santa Claus for the first time.

"I watched a video and thought, I could do that. I read a couple of books and then went for it. It was easy. At least for me, it was. The first place I hacked into was Microsoft." There are gasps in the room, and I smile. "Sabrina the Teen-Age Witch was still popular then. And I always wanted a black cat, but my mom said cats were disgusting. So that's where Salem came from."

"My parents had a party one night. My mom bought me this fluffy pink dress and tried to tame down my hair. She warned me that I was expected to act like a lady and she wouldn't tolerate any misbehavior. It took me twenty minutes to spill juice on my dress and mispronounce some words in *patois* to make it sound like I was cursing everyone out. I was sent to my room, where I wanted to go anyway. Later that night, I heard my parents talking, and mom was planning to send me to France, Aix specifically. Her mother lived there, and she was mean as hell. I was so mad that I stopped talking. My mom yanked me around, trying to get me to communicate: no supper, no privileges, no playing. I was locked in my room. That lasted two weeks. I spent that time breaking into the one place everyone on the dark web said couldn't be hacked—the White House."

"YOU HACKED THE FUCKING WHITE HOUSE?!" Free shouts from next to me, and I wince, nodding. "Plenty of people tried to get into the POTUS mainframe, and I managed to take it down for four seconds. Just long enough to plant a 'meow' and then get out." Daze is cracking up, and Fallen is about a minute away from crying. I peek at Free, and he is staring at me with a look that's the child of admiration and horror.

"I was so excited, so proud. Of course, I couldn't tell anyone, but I did come out of my room and start making nice with my parents. It was great--until we got a visit from the FBI."

"You got busted?" Dulcie hisses. I nod ruefully.

"Yup. I must have missed something on my way in and out. About ten FBI and Secret Service agents showed up at my parent's house. I thought my mother was going to die on the spot when they told her that they had traced an incursion to our home computer. Luckily, they couldn't find my signature, just the IP address. They were prepared to arrest me and throw away the key, but the SAC, Janes, gave me an ultimatum. He would spare me that one time, but I could never touch a computer again. He would take me and my parents in if I even thought about one. I was ten years old. They scared me within an inch of my life. I swore off everything: TV, radio, phones, everything. My parents, especially my mother, never forgave me. I spent the next twenty years trying to convince her that I wasn't going to hulk out and start robbing banks. She never believed it, though. To her, I was just one bad decision waiting to happen."

"So you just stopped cold turkey?" Fallen is shocked. I can only imagine. Most hackers need the adrenaline hit to survive.

"I had to. Luckily, right around that time, Riley moved to Seattle. I told her and her parents immediately; weirdly, they didn't care. They actually helped out by getting us into all kinds of activities. Eventually, we took an art class, and that's when I found my calling." I sip some water and look around the room, relieved not to see a single ounce of judgment.

"I broke the seal when I ran from Seattle. I waited outside of a survivalist store, and when the manager came to open, I begged him for help. He gave me the GPS and let me use his computer to learn how to get rid of VINS and hack a SatNav system. I did the rest myself." I smile, thinking about the young kid who looked horrified at my injuries. I think he would have taken on the Mafia by himself on my behalf.

"The rest, you know. I changed plates six times on the way here. The last time was in Utah. I deliberately took the wrong turns and let the GPS reroute me in case anyone followed me. I had Riley's wallet and mine— I never used credit cards, so mine had plenty of cash. I would have probably gone on the same, but that Vanna woman sent me over the edge. She wanted...well, she wanted something, and when I told her no, she threatened me. She said she would fuck with the ranch. I felt old me come up and warned her that she was messing with the wrong person. She didn't listen, so," I shrug. I suddenly feel exhausted. I sag back against Free's chest.

"Vivi, I always knew you were hiding stuff but shit girl, I never figured this was it. I am in awe of you girl. I love that you are a criminal, too." Daze reaches over and pats my leg. Free scowls and kicks out at him. I roll my eyes but then get worried.

"You are not mad at me, are you? I figured out pretty quickly that Trace probably wanted me to hack into this Koslov guy's network. It made sense once you said he used to be in the FBI; they would have had my file. I'm sorry I didn't tell you, guys, though. I've lived under this for so long, I didn't know how." I wring my hands, and Free grabs me to stop.

"Hell no, we aren't mad. I never thought Free would get married, but it makes sense that he would pick the most badass chick ever. The White House... phew." Cage says, and all the others nod. I relax, and a genuine smile comes out. "Thanks guys." I feel like a giant boulder just rolled off of my shoulders. And also feel like I would like Salisbury steak.

"I think Vivi has shared enough with us. Everyone get out." Free stands up, and each one of the guys comes over and gives me a big hug. By the time Pallas comes and holds me gently, I am a blubbering mess. Dulcie laughs and wipes my face with her shirt. "I'll come over tomorrow, and we'll start ordering the nursery furniture, ok?" I nod, and she gives me a big kiss on the cheek. Before I know it, Free and I are alone. He's standing with hands in his pockets, regarding me carefully.

"Anything else I need to know, Vivienne?"

Ouch, the whole name? Is he pissed?

Crap.

CHAPTER 51

FREE

I'm torn. I don't know what I want to do first.

Grab her and kiss her for being so fucking gorgeous, even with her sweaty hair and strawberry-stained dress? Bend over her and spank her for keeping this from me? I've been dreaming of turning her ass cherry red for months.

Or.

Fuck the living hell out of her. Because I am so fucking turned on right now, I could explode.

"Anything else? Like what? You might be the only person in the world who knows everything about me." Her little hands prop on her hips, juicy lips pursed in defiance.

That's all it takes.

I take three giant steps forward, grinning at the alarm in her eyes, and snatch her into my arms. I carry her up the stairs and into our bedroom, locking the door behind us. She stands right where I leave her, those blue-green eyes watching me warily. "What is that weird look on your face?"

"Greed." I walk forward and slide my hands down her sides, running my nose from her neck to her ear. I have been obsessed with her scent from day one. She's got a natural vanilla flavor mixed with roses and something else. It drives me crazy.

"Greed?" Her sweet breath comes in short gasps as she unknowingly arches into my touch. Her hands tug on the end of my shirt, and I smile into her skin. "You want me to take this off?" She gulps, and I hold down my laughter. "Yes?"

I step back and yank it off from the back of my neck, the satisfaction of her infatuation coursing through me. I watch as she takes a long look at my body, lingering on the giant stallion tattoo that splays across my chest. My dick lengthens, and her eyes get wide when she sees it move. I kick off my boots and socks and unbuckle my pants. She hasn't moved an inch. I press closer to her, staring into her beautiful eyes.

"You like what you do to me?" Her mouth opens, and I take it. I let out all of my pent up need, all of the want. Her tongue tentatively duels with mine, letting me set the pace and eventually meeting with equal force. I pull on her hair, tugging her head back, bending her gently over my arm. "Jesus, I love your mouth." I drag my lips down her neck, my hands restlessly wandering over her body. My tongue reaches out and tastes every inch, and I nip at the vein pulsing in her neck. She jumps at the pain, which I soothe with my tongue.

"Easy, baby," my fingers run down the buttons at the front of her dress, and I flick them, one by one, exposing the black lace bra that barely covers her breasts. The buttons snag on her stomach, so I kneel, placing a few kisses on her belly button. The dress slips off on its own, leaving her in just a pair of boy shorts and that overflowing bra. "You are the most beautiful woman I have ever seen." I lean forward and bury my face between her legs, the tangy scent of pussy, twisting my guts with desire. Her knees buckle, and I catch her, sweeping her onto the bed. I pull off my jeans, and her eyes widen when she sees I'm already hard and bare.

"Why wait?" She snorts, and I climb on the bed, kneeling between her legs. Her stomach is in front of me, and I lick it from her navel down to her clit. She lets out a wail, and I smile. I flick out my tongue, letting the ball in my piecing tap her again. Her legs are trembling, and I can sense them tightening.

"That's all it takes, baby? You still have your panties on." I yank them to the side, exposing her pulsing pink flesh. "Damn, you're pretty here too." Her glistening arousal beckons me, and I scoop it all into my mouth. Her scream echoes in the room, and I feel the swell and break of her orgasm. Her hand has a tight grip on my hair as she yanks me closer. "Free, please."

"Please? I think I like the sound of you begging me, Vivi. It's sweet." I rub her clit with one finger, letting the soft motion keep her trembles going. She's got both hands in my hair now, her legs spreading wider on their own. "You like that, hmm. What about this?" I slide two fingers slowly inside of her, the walls of her pussy tight with their recent work. She's warm and slick, and my dick starts jumping with need. "Jesus, Vivi, you feel like a fucking dream." I pump my fingers in and out, smiling when her hips match my rhythm. "That's it, girl. Use me. Make yourself come." She moves faster, but I keep my slow pace, feeling the wave about to hit her. She grabs the pillow and yells into it as she crests again. "Fuck look at you. You're going to ruin me." I pull out of her and yank her panties slowly down her supple legs. I turn her on her side and then slide behind her. She's out of breath, and I bite her shoulder as I lift her leg over my thigh. I line up my dick with her wetness and slide in, one single thrust. She cries out and tries to pull away, but I hold onto her hip, keeping her still.

"Free, it's too much. I can't." She wiggles under my hold, pushing closer and making me groan.

"Yes, you can," I whisper into her ear. "All of this, it's all yours. I need to mark you with every inch, so I know you are mine, too." I pull out and then thrust in again. She groans, sinking backward and giving me another inch. I reach around and pinch one of her perfect mocha nipples, pulling at it harshly. I can feel her wetness slipping and sliding between us, and I quicken my pace, alternating each pull with a pump.

"You feel so fucking good, wife. I don't think I'll ever get enough of you." I pull out, laughing at her grunt of anger, and flip her over to her knees. I carefully place a pillow under her stomach, positioning her until she is comfortable and her pussy is wide open. I rub my hands roughly over her delicious ass, smacking it lightly and then harder. She moans, and I can't help but lean in for a bite. I slide back into her carefully, knowing this will be deeper than before. My eyes close, and my head falls back as I pick up a pace that feels like heaven. My fingers dig into her hips, and I grip her harder, wanting to see my marks at the end.

"Thief, you are in trouble now. I'm never gonna leave this pussy alone. FUCK!" She sucks me in deeper with every thrust, and I can feel her body tense for its release.

"Don't fight it, baby. Let it happen." I lift her slightly, her knees no longer touching the bed, brutally pounding into her.

"Free! Ahhhhhhh!" A long scream comes from her throat; I keep going, feeling the push of my come boiling out of me. I rut into her, yelling uncontrollable things, as my heart thunders in my chest.

She is perfection.

She is every wish I never expected to be granted.

She is mine.

"Are you okay?" She is silent, her head resting on her arms, ass still in my face. I smack it again and carefully pull out, watching in fascination as my come seeps out of her. Fuck. My dick is already stirring again. "Vivi?"

"I'm schmokay." Her eyes are still closed, and I laugh lightly. "You need a break?" One eye pops open as she eases onto her back. "A break?"

"Yeah, before we do that again." I head to the bathroom to grab a washcloth and then change my mind. I want to keep all of me in her.

"Do it again?" She lifts onto her elbow and glares at me. "Are you serious? Oh." She stares at my dick which is pointing straight at her. "You are, um, still ready to go." Her nipples peak despite her apparent shyness.

"Baby, I have been ready to go since you got on this ranch, Rocky Balboa face and all," I chuckle as she scowls. Her eyes eat me up, leaving no crumbs. She lies back, a temptress with messy hair and a stubborn chin.

"You got any other tricks you can do with that tongue ring?" I grin.

"Oh, girl. You have no idea."

CHAPTER 52
THEM

"What about Clementine?" We are sitting up in bed, both naked, after I decided that making my wife orgasm was better than dessert. She's got a baby name book on her lap while I stare at the ceiling, listening. "What would her nickname be? Clem? I don't like that." She giggles and turns the page. "Dauphine? Emeraude? Florentine?" I grimace and shake my head—none of those. I slink down and rest my head next to her belly. "What do you think, Pendophilius? Do you like that name?" I caress the smooth skin and laugh when a foot sticks out. "She says those names are awful."

Vivi is giggling uncontrollably. "What about Genevieve?" She pronounces it in the decidedly French way, and I contemplate it. "I actually don't mind it. It's close to your name." She nods but grimaces. "Yeah, but I want her to have her own identity." She keeps flipping, and I poke at the little foot that keeps popping out.

"I've got it. Theodora. We can call her Teddy."

This time, the baby kicks twice. "I like it. And so does she." I kiss that spot and rub my face against her skin.

"Theodora it is. We can't wait to meet you."

"Absolutely not." Dammit.

"But I'm a good driver. And think about how much faster I would get back and forth if I were in something like this." I pout, and Free rolls his eyes.

"Baby, you are a terrible driver. That's why Cage only lets you drive the pickup. You've put dents in every car that we have."

"I have not!" I totally have.

"No?" He looks down at me, his hands on his hips in accusation. "There is no way in hell you will drive my Demon anywhere. Not even on the property."

Cage finally let me into part of his garage where the boys keep their toys. My jaw hit the floor when I saw the rows of cars, and I zeroed in on the beauty parked by herself in the back left corner. The entire vehicle is mob-tint black, without a speck of color anywhere. Even the lights were black. It looked like the Batmobile. "That's Free's pride and joy. Completely illegal on the road, it's got a souped-up V-8 engine and a jailbreak package. That baby can go zero to sixty in two seconds." I drooled away, but when Cage told Free, he shot me down. Hard.

"How about if you take me for a ride then?" I put my hands together in a praying position and bounce up and down. He eyes me in amusement and then zeros in on my big belly. "When Teddy comes out, maybe. Until then, you will continue to drive the Chevy." I stamp my foot and throw my head back in annoyance. The pickup is old and reliable. Ugh, I might as well be driving a minivan.

"Fiiiiiine." Hmmmm, I wonder if I could hot-wire it? Dulcie can be my lookout. I can google it and....

"Um, Vivi. You are not hot-wiring my car, Little Thief."

Drat! "Did I say that out loud?"

"Yeah, you did."

MY FINGERS DANCE down his brick-like abs, and I linger on the tattoo of a stallion that splays above his groin. I trace it in small circles before Free groans with a laugh. "Are you trying to kill me, baby?" His cock is pointing up and at me- its glistening head twitching and throbbing. "Of course not. You're too mean to die, anyway." My head is resting on his bent leg, and it takes me little effort to lean forward and slip my tongue along the slit. He back bows off the bed and grips the sheets tightly. "Vivi, God..."

"You like that, hmmm?" I lick it again, this time sucking him in, pumping my hand in time to the rhythm. The stretch around my lips is a little uncomfortable, the thickness of him almost too much, but I forget that quickly as his groans get louder.

"Don't stop, baby, never stop, GAH!" I swallow two more inches, and I'm at my limit. He's too hard, too thick, too long for any more.

"Yeah, take it, take it all." All? Hell no. A sword-swallower couldn't get all this dick in their mouth. I flick my tongue like a swarm of butterflies and then go in for a hard pull.

"FUCK! I'm going to cum, baby," he groans out. "Baby, do you want it in your mouth?" He rubs a thumb down the side of my face, and I watch in fascination as his face contorts in ecstasy, timed with the hot spurts that slide down my throat. I keep up my hand motions until the last drop lands, and his thighs twitch in sensitivity. I pull away and roll onto my side and then up. His big body is sprawled out like a snow angel, and I snort at the smile on his face. He's the perfect picture of bad boy satisfaction.

"I'd return the favor, but I'll need some recovery time."

"Well, I can think of another way you can thank me..."

"No."

"You don't even know what I was going to say!" I cross my arms across my chest and glare at him.

"Baby, I know you. And the answer is no."

Dammit!

"Vivi, what the hell?" I crack up as my wife looks up at me from the floor. She's parked in front of the fireplace in our bedroom, stark naked with an empty bowl perched on their stomach. She's at the point in her pregnancy where everything makes her uncomfortable, which makes me uneasy. She's barely sleeping, though she's exhausted.

"I couldn't get up, so I figured I'd wait for you to help me, but you took too long, and I got hot. So I stripped and then just stayed here."

"Oh, baby. I'm sorry. It's almost over." Kaz said she could go any day now, and the whole ranch is on pins and needles. I bend down and lift her to her feet, and she immediately ambles to the bathroom. I hear a deep sigh of relief as she pees with the door open.

"Are you sure you'll be able to handle the labor part?" She peeks around the corner, slipping one of my t-shirts over her head. The middle is stretched to death.

"Of course I can." I've killed and tortured people for sport. I can handle anything.

"Are you sure? Because Fallen told me that he sent you a video, and you threw up?" That motherfucker. "I didn't throw up. I was just caught off guard."

She eyes me skeptically. "Okay, big guy." Was that sarcasm?

"You don't believe me? Just watch"

I'M OFFICIALLY A PUSSY.

"Okay, Vivi. Push!" My wife is a fucking soldier because she is pushing with all her might, face red and quivering. And I'm behind her, sobbing like a little bitch. She slumps back and takes an exhausted breath.

"You are doing amazing, honey. A few more, and this little girl will be out, right Daddy?" The nurse glares at me, and I nod weakly. I've been nothing but a mess since Vivi woke me up last night to tell me that her water broke. My poor wife watched me run in circles like a headless chicken while she stood at the door, her go-bag in hand. Dulcie had to drive because I was shaking like a leaf, and I wanted to hold Vivi's hand. The first time she squeezed it because of the pain she was in, I about passed out. Devin was in the front seat crying laughing, and the only thing that saved his life was that I didn't want us to crash.

"Push again now!" She bears down as Kaz comes into the room, all smiles and confidence. "Hey there, lady. You ready to have this baby?" I scowl as he takes a stool between Vivi's legs, but let it go when the monitor beeps another contraction.

"Ah, this is a good one. On three, push for me, okay? One, two, three, and push.." His voice is calm, and I see him doing something--down there. "Ah, there's the head. Free? Take a look." He holds up a mirror...and that's the last thing I remember.

"I can't believe you," Vivi says tiredly but with a chuckle. I'm sitting in the chair beside her bed, my feet propped up and my daughter in my arms. Her face is perfectly still as she sleeps, and she's the most beautiful thing I've ever seen.

"Don't start," I warn. "I wasn't expecting that. He coulda warned me or something." I lean down and take a whiff. She smells like heaven and everything I didn't know I wanted. "We are gonna have some serious problems. This kid looks just like you. Down to her little dimpled chin." Teddy takes that moment to squirm around, and her chubby face scrunches as if she were about to cry. "Shhhh," I rock her a bit and lean closer. "She's got a dimple in her cheek, too. It's official; she's not dating until she is thirty-five." Vivi snorts, and I get lost in the look in her eyes.

"You are going to make a perfect dad. Even if you passed out before she was born." I scowl and snuggle Teddy closer.

"Knock, knock." I see Daze and the other guys crowded in the doorway. "Can we come in?" He doesn't wait for an answer; instead, he marches straight to the bed and kisses Vivi on the forehead. "You okay, Scoot?" Pallas and Nox are crowded around me, each pushing to get a look at the baby.

"Damn, that's a pretty baby. Looks just like her mama," Nox whispers. He runs a finger down her cheek, and she twitches. They take turns staring at her until Daze comes over and snatches her clean out of my arms. "Hey!'

"Hey, nothing. This baby is for all of us. You're hogging

her." He sits on the couch, and Fallen sits next to him, gently touching her foot. "Theodora, right?"

"Yes. Theodora Starla Kelly." Vivi sniffles, and Pallas, lying beside her, pats her hand. I know that she is missing Riley, something fierce.

"Dulcie said she had to cut the cord," Daze says innocently. I narrow my eyes on him.

"Oh really? Why is that?" Fallen asks in a droll voice.

"I dunno. Free? Wanna tell us why?"

"Hey, Free? Why do you have that bandage on your head?" Nox is snickering, and even Pallas's face is twitching.

"Fu-"

'Hey! Language," Daze points at the baby and grins.

Motherfuc****

CHAPTER 53
FREE

"Look at you, Daddy!" Silvers got a smile a mile wide, his canines glinting in the sun. He made a quick trip down with Bent and his Enforcer, Mako. So far, there's been no chatter about anyone looking for my wife, and I've been breathing a little easier. This trip is all about him being a nosy motherfucker. "Daze, you bitch get over here." The two of them hug and pound each other's backs. He takes turns greeting all the guys, and the ruckus in the courtyard is deafening.

"Fuck, it's good to see all of y'all. Look at this place. Y'all have really done it, haven't you, King? I read about a couple of your horses tearing up the prelims."

"Yeah, that would be Harley and Vivi's horse, Carnage. Shocked the fuck out of all of us." Her "Little Cabbage" has turned the corner. He tore the cover off the track, setting a record on the flat. I've had calls for weeks about him, and Devin has been busy with the trainers prepping him for the next go-round. Harley placed first in all his races, too, but I try not to celebrate too much in front of my wife—she and Harley still don't like each other.

"How's the Princess? She's a few months old now, yeah?" We head toward the stables, and I smile big. "She's perfect. A whole hellion just like her mama. Spoiled as can be, but a real sweetheart. Vivi will bring her down when she gets up from her nap." I take them to the new stables, where we've been putting the finishing touches on the whole building. "This here is Harley." We stop at my boy's stall, and he comes out for a pat. He snorts and throws his head up at the crowd around him, showing off.

"He's a beauty. This set-up is the shit."

I smile. "My wife and Dulcie did it." The girls brainstormed for weeks after Carnage won his prelim about how to put Konabos on the map. We were getting requests for interviews and turned them all down because, according to Vivi and Dulcie, "that's like trying to impress a girl with a dirty car." So they got to work researching and designing, and now most stalls were complete. Vivi made a nameplate on each wall underneath a tablet that looped video of the horse in action. They were motion-censored and hooked up to solar panels, so they never ran out of juice; all of the racehorses had personal sculptures perched above the doorways. It was way more than I could have ever imagined, and now they are working on our social media. The first picture they posted of Devin working with Harley got over ten thousand likes—though most were requests for Devins's phone number. They cackled like hens over the comments, some of them so dirty that even I blushed. But it got attention, and now they plan each post like generals mapping out a war.

"I saw that fancy-ass front gate too. That must've cost you a pretty penny." I shrug, and Daze chuckles. A few weeks ago, Cage called me out of his garage, and I found Vivi with a big ass smile on her glowing face, Teddy in a sling across her chest. "For you," she said, and my mouth dropped when I saw the fifteen-foot-tall scrollwork with "Konabos Ranch" spelled out with horses pulling a chariot behind them. I yanked her into my arms and gave her a kiss that should've scorched the earth. "Thank you, baby." She blinked some happy tears away, laughing. "A world-class farm needs better than a plain white fence." I kissed Teddy, too, and Cage left us alone momentarily. Daze and Fallen spent a week hooking it up to the security system, and now we have plans to secure even more of the perimeter with matching fencing.

We walk around the rest of the stables but only look at Carnage from a distance. He's still not good with people invading his turf, and now that Judy is next to him, he is even more protective. God forbid Vivi and Teddy are around—he goes manic. "My wife's horse, according to her. He's her baby, but he doesn't like strangers. Maybe later she can bring you down alone. I'm not good enough to introduce him to anyone. And that's his girlfriend. Hoping to breed them next year." We walk around the training circle before Silver announces he's hungry.

"Ev has some grub cooking at the house, and Teddy should be up by now. We walk down the path to the house, and when we round the corner, I see Vivi coming down the stairs; she and Teddy have matching smiles.

"Damn, King. That's a sight right there," Bent says in a low voice. Silver strides ahead and struts right up to my wife, giving her a big kiss. He says a few words and then takes Teddy from her arms. It's funny seeing a guy as hardcore-looking as Silver cradling a pile of squishy goodness decked out in a tiny set of overalls. My daughter stares at him for a full minute, and when I think she's going to scrunch up and cry, she lets out a belly laugh and pops Silver in the face with a wet fist.

"Ah, my little Princess. If your daddy weren't burning holes into my head right now, I'd snatch you and your beautiful mama right on up." Vivi laughs, and he gives her a big smile. "My Queen," he bows his head, and they walk inside together. We follow behind, and the smell from the kitchen permeates the house.

"I know that damn smell. Where is my girl?" He bellows, and Evonne scurries around the corner, squealing when she sees him. I quickly snatch my kid as he reaches over and lifts Evonne off the floor, twirling her in a circle. "Girl, you are a sight for sore eyes. Ain't aged a day and as sexy ever." His eyes twinkle, and she laughs, slapping his cut. "And you are as smooth a talker as ever. I've got your favorite making in the kitchen."

"Cowboy casserole? Mash potatoes? Biscuits?" His voice takes on a pitiful note, and we all chuckle.

"Of course. You all get set up in the dining hall. I'm gonna start bringing it all out. Vivi? A hand? Dulcie is already getting the table set." They scurry off, and I lead everyone through the archway, placing Teddy in her swing and turning it on. She gurgles, squealing and babbling to herself. The food starts coming out, and we all grab plates and start in—family style. Ev has more than Silver's casserole—there's also a roast, tons of vegetables, and some fried chicken. She must've been up since dawn.

"Ev, this is great. Thank you." She flusteredly nods and continues bringing out dishes. The girls finally stop and start serving themselves. Vivi sits next to me, her plate rivaling mine in height. My eyebrows raise, and her eyes narrow. "I'm breastfeeding. You shut it." I laugh, kiss her, and catch Silver's eye.

"King, I never envied you a thing until now. I don't know what you did to deserve these two beauties— but you hold on to it. I mean that shit." He points at me with his fork and then shovels another bite into his mouth.

"Why do you call him King?" Vivi asks, chewing slowly.

"Because that's who he is—King of The MC's. We took over so much territory and eliminated so many clubs; we were the biggest and worst. No one wanted to fuck with him, not the law, not the underworld. Don't matter that he went straight—he's always going to be the King. And that makes you the Queen, baby." She says nothing, raising her eyebrows and staring at me. She's asked me a few times what made us leave the life, and each time, I distract her— usually with my tongue. There will never be a time that telling my wife the horror we went through will be right. I'll go to my grave with it.

"So nothing?"

Silver leans back, flipping a toothpick in his mouth. "Nah. There ain't a peep out there about Queen Vivi. I let it slip that the King has settled down with a wife and kid. Lots of surprise, some bullshit, but nothing else. I think she's safe."

My chest loosens an inch, but not all the way. I've been on both sides of this kind of fuckery— the one doing the hunt and the one being hunted. And one thing I've learned is that until one side is dead, there is no relief. This was as close as we would get, short of killing Koslov myself. I know that Vivi chafes a bit at the restrictions, the constant guards, and the lack of privacy in some ways. The club rule has always been to keep shit away from old ladies and family. The only problem is my wife is an off-the-charts genius— if I don't tell her what she wants to know, she will find it out for herself. "You still worried?"

I click my teeth. I don't think I'll ever *not* be worried. I've never had two people who meant more to me. And the thought that something might happen to them don't sit right with me. "Fuck yeah. I don't think I'll ever sleep right again." Silver laughs with a nod. "That's love, man." My office phone rings, and I click the intercom button. "What?"

"Uhhhh, boss, you may want to come out here?" Daze's voice comes over, and I feel a shiver like a ghost passing over my grave. "What's up? Everything alright?"

He hesitates. "Yeah, we just got company. Front driveway." The line goes silent, and I glance at Silver, who is frowning. "I'll go with you. We were gonna head out in a few anyway." I stop for a beat, then slip my Walther out of my desk drawer and tuck it in the back of my jeans. Silver twitches in his cut, and I see he is packing his favorite Sig Sauer P226. Bent and Mako meet us at the front door, and for a second, it feels like old times—my brothers at my back as we meet danger head-on. I know Pallas is with Vivi and Teddy; by now, he's got them and Dulcie tucked away somewhere.

I see Daze shading his eyes with his hand, looking out in the distance. Nox is next to him, watching a black Mustang pull up the drive, fishtailing in its speed and kicking dust in its wake. "Who the fuck is that?" The car zips to within one foot of our standing, and the driver's door flings open. A flurry of bright red hair and long limbs flies out, and suddenly, my arms are filled with woman, the scent of lilies and grass wrapping around me, along with a pair of lean, bare legs.

"Free! I'm home!" The voice squeals, raining kisses over my face.

Fuck.

CHAPTER 54
VÍVI

Her name is Mallory. In French, it means 'unfortunate' or 'unlucky'.

Go fucking figure.

"...so then she left. She hasn't been around in years." I listen with half an ear as Dulcie quietly tells me all about this chick who had her legs wrapped around my husband like a Twizzler. I walked around the bend from visiting Carnage and Judy, Dulcie pushing Teddy in her stroller beside me. Pallas was hurrying from the opposite direction, but it was too late. I saw this dirty car do a donut and stop next to Free, and the next thing I knew, an Amazon jumped out and attacked him. She was slobbering all over his face, and that jerk didn't even stop her. He held her up by her ass for a full minute before she slid down his front, all of her scrawny bits pressed to his. She then jumped on all the other guys, including Devin, which made Dulcie hiss like a rattlesnake.

"I never liked her. I couldn't understand what Free saw in her." I could. The girl was a looker—what Riley would call an "Insta-thot." She was slim and long-legged but had a rack on her. Judging by her eyebrows, she is a natural redhead, her skin is clear and bright. She's got to be close to six feet tall because she came just up to Free's chin. Perfect.

"...I saw her in a few magazines, nothing big though. We all thought she had made it. I guess if she's back, then her career didn't pan out." Or, more likely, Silver did too good of a job, and this girl came scurrying back when she heard Free was married. The timing is too coincidental for me. I'd stopped about five feet from Free, who had a stupid-ass smile on his face, and waited for him to notice me. It took way too long. Teddy finally screeched for his attention, and he whipped around—I'll give him credit for looking a little ill at the expression on my face. He stepped toward us, but Dulcie whipped the stroller around and stalked toward the house. I gave all of the guys a long glare and followed behind her. The silence behind us was broken when I heard Silver say, "Oh shit." He and his guys left about twenty minutes ago, but not before he came to tell us goodbye. He gave Dulcie a tight hug, admonishing her not to be mad at Devin. He slobbered on Teddy and then turned to me. He reminds me of Daze in a way. He's a jokester, always laughing and chatting, but there is a black wall in his eyes. If I were ever in a bind, I'd call him.

"My beautiful Queenie. I want to tell you not to sweat Mallory, but I'd be a liar, not because of Free, but because I know that girl. Never trust her. And if you decide you want help burying the body, I'm your boy," he whispered into my hair as he hugged me. "My money will always be on you." He chucked my chin, pinching the dimple, before climbing onto his ridiculously tricked-out Harley 1250. It's all shades of silver with a streak of gold around its tailpipes. It growls and spits as he turns it on, its loud song, matching its owner. He gives me one more salute before they thunder out the front gates.

Now we are hiding at Dulcie and Devin's house, Teddy on a blanket on the floor, kicking her feet at the shadows.

"I'll tell you one thing— she ain't staying with me and Devin." Mallory grew up with a few of the guys, her dad being high up in the Ghost Nomads. She and her mom had been out shopping with Evonne when the clubhouse was been attacked. Her dad didn't make it, and her mom stayed close to the GOTA when they formed. Mallory spent a lot of time at their place, and Evonne had even babysat her. Sometime after she turned eighteen, she dated Devin a little, but her sights were really on Free. She wanted to be the main woman in the club—not the girl of a soldier. She left Devin one night and threw her ass in Free's bed. That's all it took. They became A THING. That was until a model scout spotted her at a mall and offered her a contract. She threatened to leave Free and move to New York if he didn't make it official between them. But Free was caught up in all of his shit, so he told her to go. And now she is back.

"You're really quiet, Vivi. It's making me nervous."

"I don't know what you want me to say. Free and I are married, but only to protect me. He can do whatever he wants." Like hell, he can. I will skin his ass alive.

She purses her pretty lips and props a hand on a hip. "Don't you give me that shit. You took down a billion-dollar farm because that lady asked if she could lick up on your husband. You want me to believe you won't make that girl disappear if she steps out of line?" She snorts and tosses her braid over her right shoulder. "All I'm asking is that you let me get a few kicks in. I was young when she was pulling her bullshit with Devin, but I will snatch her bald if she touches him again." I believe her. And Devin knows it, too. He has texted her no less than twenty times, sweet and worried, though she refuses to answer him. I check my phone and see my message box sitting on a fat zero.

"I'm assuming she will stay with Evonne at her place." If I thought Ev was excited to see Silver, it was nothing compared to when she saw Mallory. She fell on her like a collapsed wall and blubbered like a baby. The last thing I heard was that she was going to make her a special meal, including homemade ice cream, something she had never made me.

Does that make me a petty bitch? Yup. Do I care? Nope.

The front door opens, and Devin steps inside. He snatches his hat off his head, eyes glued to Dulcie's face.

"Baby?" He looks like he's approaching a cobra. He's not far off. "Can we talk?" Dulcie stares at him, a sour look on her face. "I don't know. Can we? Or will Mallory be joining us?" She snipes with a glare. He gulps and says nothing.

Yup, it's time for me to go.

I bend down and pick up my kid, who squeals, sucking on her fist. I checked the time, and see she was due for a feeding. I strap her into her stroller and grab her diaper bag. "Dulcie, I'll see you tomorrow." She is still staring at Devin.

"Okay, Vivi."

That's all I get. I almost feel sorry for him, but considering I'm close to committing murder myself, it doesn't last too long. I close the door behind me and almost instantly hear a screech of anger.

Get him, girl.

I pause on the porch, not knowing where to go. Right at this moment, I don't feel like my home is my own. I'm assuming Free and Mallory are there together. Doing stuff. My chest tightens, and I walk briskly down the lawn. I'm not too far from my workshop. I can feed Teddy there, wait until later, and then sneak into the house. Hopefully, he hasn't already moved her into his bedroom. I can sleep with Teddy until I can make other living arrangements. Yes. That is what I will do. I whisper to myself, not even noticing the tears tracking down my face or that Pallas is following behind me.

CHAPTER 55
FREE

" S he is at her workshop, but she is not working, you stupid motherfucker." Daze gives me the death look mirrored on everyone else's face. "She is feeding the baby. Are you going to go down there and get her? Pallas says she is crying."

Fuck. I sigh and run a hand down my face.

When Mallory jumped out of that car and threw herself at me, the first thing I thought was that I prayed my wife wasn't watching. Of course, I am not that lucky, and after Mal's Oscar-winning performance, I heard my daughter yell out and turned around to three outraged female faces. It took them thirty seconds to scorch all of us with a look and less than that for me to know that I'm fucked. Once Mallory untangled herself, I sent her off with Evonne, letting her know she could stay with her for a few days. Her amber eyes flashed in disappointed anger, and I knew then that I would have to put her in her place. "I'll go get her."

"You'd better. And you better make sure that girl is gone as soon as possible. She's always been nothing but a troublemaker—it don't look like much has changed," Cage huffs. I got caught up in Mallory and her drama a long time ago. She was seeing Devin, but that didn't stop her from eye-fucking me every chance she got. I won't lie; I got off on it. She was a beautiful girl, lean with curves, and she put it on a platter for me. The first time I fucked her, she squirted, and I made it my mission to get her to do it again. I didn't let her off her back for months, and while I was in it for the challenge, she was in it for status. Every time I sunk my dick into her pussy, she thought it was a stepping stone to being First Lady. When that model scout recruited her, it was like a sign from heaven. She was causing all kinds of problems with the hangers-on, and Pallas' old lady scrapped with her more than once. She threatened to leave for New York, fuck other men if I didn't elevate her. I told her she could go with my blessing, taking one of the other girls to my bed that night. The following day, she was gone. After we got into our shit and went straight, It never occurred to me to send for her— I practically forgot she existed.

"You know she only showed up because she heard about Vivi and Teddy," Kazimir says in an even tone. The timing is too right." Silver had said the same thing. He gave me a long look before he left but didn't say a word.

"Pallas just texted that she seems to be preparing to spend the night there." I stand up and stride toward the door. "Y'all be gone when we get back," I order and hear some grunts in response. The dark has started to fall, and the horses are making their normal huffs and stomps. I glance to the back where Evonne's apartment sits, all the lights on and music playing. When the Nomads were wiped out, Evonne had been pregnant. Upon hearing the news of her man, Hogan, being gone, she fell out and lost the baby. Mallory was the closest she had to raising a kid, so I know my asking Mal to leave, will not go over well.

I see the meager light from the workshop in the distance, the rollup door tightly shut. The temperature is dropping, and I don't like the idea of my girls being out here. I knock once before pushing the door open, my heart seizing. Vivi is stretched out on the old futon Cage had left in there; Teddy curled into the small space between her mama and the cushions. They are covered with a blanket, but it's still cold. I hear a noise behind me and see Pallas in the doorway.

"I will take the little one. You get your wife," he says quietly. I lift her in my arms, and she immediately awakens, confused. "Free?"

"Yeah, baby?" I hear Teddy snuffle in her sleep, and Pallas wraps her up and burrows her close to his chest.

"Where are you taking me?" I grip her tighter. "I'm taking you home, baby. Where you belong." I nuzzle her hair and sigh.

"What about Mallory?"

"She is with Evonne. She will only be here a few days."

"Oh." Her voice is small, and I know that I really messed up. I should've done what Devin did and gone after her immediately. I'm failing at this husband thing.

"So you don't want me to leave?" Yup, a complete failure.

"Never, little thief. Never."

PALLAS TUCKED Teddy into her bed, changing her into pajamas with a fresh diaper. One thing about my kid is that she sleeps for Texas. She barely moved when he wiped her down, drool coming out one side of her mouth. She's been this way since birth, which was a blessing because neither I nor her mother would have known what to do with a baby that woke up several times in the night.

I put a sleepy Vivi into the shower and check on the baby.

Pallas was in the middle of closing her door, with a finger up to his lips for silence. "She is out now." I nodded and peeked over his shoulder to see that he had turned her night light on. He moved toward the top of the stairs, pausing before heading down.

"Free, I would give anything to have my lady back. For us to have had a family. Do not mess this up with Vivienne. I know it's new for both of you, but you can have something beautiful if you reach for it. And once you do, cherish it. And never, ever let it go." He gives me a sad smile and pads down the stairs. I stare after him before walking into our bedroom. The shower has stopped, and there's little noise behind the door. "Vivi?" I knock lightly and hear a shuffle. The door opens, and she comes out, head to toe, in a sweatsuit. "What the hell are you wearing?"

She shrugs with a look of defiance on her face. "You know I don't have pajamas." She stalks toward her side of the bed, throwing back the covers and wrapping herself in the quilt. She looks like a human burrito. My anger snaps, and I follow her, ripping the blankets off and grabbing her by the ankle. She screeches, and I pick her up from under her arms and set her on her feet. I quickly pull her sweatshirt off and toss it across the room. I bend down and pull behind her knees, causing her to fall backward on the bed, and make quick work of the matching pants.

I lean down close to her angry face and snarl. "When you are in my bed, you wear my shirt or nothing." She scowls and tries to scamper away, but I drag her back, pinning her arms next to her head. "Look at me, Vivi." She closes her eyes and turns her head. I lean down and bite her neck, her yelp making my dick hard. "Unless you want me to put another one on the other side, you will look at me." Her eyes snap open, the blue flames reaching out to burn us both. "I'm sorry." She stills her struggles, staring at me with anger and desire. I know she can feel my hardness, and I move my legs around until my dick is settled between her legs. I push a bit, watching her pupils blow with the movement. "I'm sorry. I should've handled Mallory better. I was caught off guard—I hadn't seen her in years. I know it probably looked like I enjoyed it, but trust me, it was a shock." I nibble on her chin and glance up at her through my lashes.

"You were smiling," she bites out, and I hide a grin.

"I was. I've known her since she was little. We dated for a bit." In no way am I saying more than that.

"You had your hand on her ass." I lick the area between her jawline and ear. "I was holding her up; she didn't seem steady. I wasn't feeling her up or anything."

"She's very pretty And tall. And skinny."

I pull back and stare at her. "She is. But she is nowhere near your level." I let her hands, and sitting back on my feet, I rip my shirt off, watching her greedy eyes take in my chest. "If I could have built a woman perfect for me, she would come out exactly like you." I grab a handful of her dark, messy hair. "I would give her this hair. I love how it curls and waves." I tug it before cupping her face in my hand. "I would give her this face. You are the most beautiful woman I have ever seen. I could get lost in these eyes. Every day, I wait to see what I have say to make them green. I love how you look at me and our daughter."

I kiss her eyelids, which flutter under my lips. "I love this mouth. The puffiness, the sweetness of your lips." I press my mouth to hers, groaning when I feel the pliancy of her lips, slipping my tongue against hers, stroking her lightly. "And this chin." I bite the dimple again. "I love that our baby has it too." I run my lips down her neck, licking from one side of her collarbone to the other. I raise on one arm, grabbing one of her breasts in my hand and squeezing it roughly. "And you know I love these. I couldn't make up better tits in my imagination." I tweak one nipple and then the other, watching in fascination as a bead of milk pops up on one. I lean down with a groan and lick it up. I stand up and pull her to the edge of the bed, shedding my pants at the same time. My dick is like a stone waiting to be thrown into a pond.

"And this pussy." I give it a long, hard lick, making sure my tongue ring flicks over her clit. "I couldn't make a hotter, wetter, tighter pussy than yours. The way you take me..." I flick her clit again, dipping into her channel and lapping up the wetness seeping from her. I slide my hands under her ass and bury my face full between her legs, biting and sucking every inch. She screams as the first orgasm hits her, and I smile to myself.

"I love the way you look when you come. Like you are desperate for every inch of my touch." I press the ball in my mouth against her clit again, pushing it until I feel her tremble again. I pull back and run my finger over the throbbing nub, watching as it swells with her need. Just before she breaks, I roughly sink two fingers into her, lightly kissing her— the hard and soft sending her over again. Her body goes limp, and I turn her over. "Oh no, baby. I'm nowhere near done with you." I pull her up onto her knees, lining my dick up with her dripping hole. "Goddamn baby. You are so wet for me," I growl, slamming into her in one thrust. She screams into the pillow as I plunge forward and pull back before giving her more. She comes again, and I want to beat my chest. "You hear me, Vivi Kelly?" I raise on one knee, my hands gripping her hips in a vise. "I said, do you hear me, Vivi Kelly?" I slam into her over and over. I could conquer the world.

"Yes, yes, I hear you," she sobs, her hands clawing at the sheets for purchase. I'm completely in control of her body, her pussy at my mercy.

"I am yours. Do you hear that? And I want to be. There is no one who can take me from you. Not even Death himself." A burn starts in my balls, the fire of ten thousand suns, a streak of hell. My breath catches in my throat as the heat overwhelms me, and I come and come. I distantly hear her yell, her last explosion overwhelming both of us. I collapse on top of her, panting as a few last spurts of come leak from my dick.

"I think I may die."

She chuckles tiredly, making a choking noise to get me off of her. I move over but keep a firm grip on her leg. We are both silent, and I raise my head to stare at that face.

"I'm not stupid, Vivi. I know Mallory is probably out to cause trouble. I promise you that no matter what she pulls, it's you and me." I squeeze her to get her to look at me.

She stares at me, a look of trust and something else on her face. "And Teddy." I smile and kiss her on the nose. "Yes, and Teddy. It's going to be okay, baby. I promise."

CHAPTER 56
VIVI

I knew it would be too much for this bitch to be gone by this morning.

Free kept me up (and on my knees) all night, alternating between trying to imprint his body on mine and telling me about him and Mallory. Sometime before dawn, he finished up, and we finally fell asleep. He was up a few hours later; I could barely move. He slapped me lightly on the ass and told me he would take care of Teddy until I got up. I gave him the thumbs up and fell all the way back asleep. When I finally opened my eyes, it was after nine, which meant Teddy had been up for a few hours. I took another shower and dressed in jeans and a denim button shirt Dulcie bought me last week. I slapped my hair into a top knot and tugged on some Uggs. I could smell breakfast, and my stomach growled while my boobs tingled. I need to either feed my daughter or pump.

I turn the corner to the kitchen and pause with a glare. Mallory is feeding Teddy, a slick smile on her face, while Dulcie shoots daggers at her with her eyes. "I'm sure Vivi won't mind. From what I understand, everyone has a hand in raising Free's daughter. What's one more person?" You know how when a cat is about to attack someone, their hair stands up, their tail poofs out, and their ears lay flat? That is precisely what Dulcie looks like.

"First of all, Vivi and Free raise their daughter. We all love Teddy, so we fight over her, yeah. But whatever you are trying to imply, you best not. And I don't think Vivi would like you touching that baby." Mallory scoffs with the same smile.

"Free doesn't mind, and that's all that matters. You know, Dulcie, I don't remember you being this hostile the last time I saw you—all scrawny legs and frizzy hair. I really despaired for you; your whole family is so good-looking, and you were just this odd duck. I'm so happy that someone helped you clean up."

No. She. Didn't.

Dulcie is just blinking, a red flush spreading up her neck. "You bi-"

"Is this about Devin? Are you jealous? I mean, yeah, I fucked him good, but that was before you. You can't be holding on to that, can you? I mean, I'm sure he does all the same dirty things to you."

Teddy hiccups, and Mallory turns her onto her shoulder, patting her back. My daughter sees me behind her and grins. One of the pats was too hard, and she scowled, looking at me with the 'get me away from this heifer' look on her face. I step forward and snatch her away before Dulcie can leap over the table and choke her.

"I think it's time you got out of my house." Teddy finally burps, and I hand her to Dulcie. "Take her to your office, won't you? I'll meet you there. Have you had anything to eat?" I don't see a plate, but Mallory has what looks like the Last Supper in front of her. Dulcie shakes her head. "No, I didn't feel like eating this morning. My appetite is gone." She points at Mallory's face and flounces out. I hear a low laugh, turning toward the sound. "She's still a spoiled little girl." I raise my brows and sit across from her, just staring.

"I suppose you want a piece of me, too. Look, I've been away for a long time, but now I'm back. This place should all be mine. That ring should be mine. I was here first." She sips at some coffee, peering at me over the edge of the cup. I still say nothing.

"Alright, let's get it all out on the table. Free was mine first. See, I had to play the long game. First, I was too young—I had to wait years, watching him take one woman after another to his bed, sometimes fucking them right in my face. Then, once I was old enough, he was taking over territory. He didn't have time for me. But Devin did. He was my in—I got to stay with the club and in Free's attention. I made sure he knew I wanted him, and I knew he wanted me. The first time he fucked me..." Her eyes go distant, and I see her nipples peak under her thin sweater. My stomach knots, but I let her talk. "It was almost too much. I mean, he's fucked you, right? You know how he is. The way he takes command and how rough he is." Okay, maybe I don't have to let her talk.

"Yes, I'm aware of how good my husband is in bed." I smile thinly, tapping my wedding band on the table. I mentally measure the distance. Yeah, I think I could swipe her in one jump.

"Then you know why I won't give up on him. I mean no offense to you; you seem like a decent person. But I put in a lot of work and won't step aside for someone who's only known him for five minutes. If you had any pride, you'd leave before he kicks you out. You don't have to go far, just off the ranch. You can see the baby sometimes. I'm sure Evonne wouldn't mind bringing her around." She waves her hand around like she has everything figured out.

"I repeat, it's time you get out of my house." She doesn't budge, just smirks, chewing slowly on a sausage link. I keep my eyes on her, watching as she eats another sausage. "If I have to get Free, you won't like what happens. See, he told me all about your little affair. And the thing that stuck out was how you tried to threaten him with other men, and he told you to go ahead. You showing up here after he is married and a father smacks of sour grapes. Like someone desperate. Like someone who can't let the past go. If a man told me to go ahead and sleep with other people, I would never want to see him again, so I don't think I'm the one who lacks pride. You aren't a bad-looking girl; I'm sure plenty of men wouldn't mind having you around. But that man is not my husband. Nor is it Devin or any of the other boys. They are all mine."

I stand up, smiling again; I'm sure I look like a crazed clown. "Now I know that Evonne has missed you, and I don't want her upset because she means a lot to me. So I will let you stay on the ranch a few more days, let's say until Friday morning. After that, I will personally escort your skinny ass off the property." I walk around the table and take the plate from in front of her. I take a big forkful of fluffy eggs and grin at her expression. "Mallory honey, I'm going to tell you something I recently told someone else—don't fuck with me. You don't know shit about me. I will destroy you before you even see me coming." I take her coffee cup and swig the rest. I lean in until my face is one inch from hers.

"Get. Out. Of. My. House." I push her chair with my foot, the scraping sound bringing Pallas from wherever he was.

"Vivi? Is everything alright?" He stands behind me, and I see Mallory gulp.

"Everything is fine, isn't it, Mal? She was just telling me how she is going to stick to Evonne's place until she leaves on Friday. Right, Mal?"

"Uhhhh, right. I'll just be on my way." She stands up suddenly, and I see she is wearing a skirt so tight that her liver should be popping out any minute. I roll my eyes, taking another chew of eggs. She takes one more long look at me before sauntering out the door.

"You threatened her, didn't you?" Pallas's handsome face is amused. I shrug.

"Words were said. Let's just say I gave her a heads-up. Let's go check on Dulcie, shall we?"

VIVI

"I still can't believe the nerve of that bitch."

It's been a few days since I had the blow-up with Mallory, and tomorrow is Friday, the day she is supposed to high-tail it out of town. But Evonne came to me and Free, tearfully asking if Mallory could stay until Evonnes birthday the following week. I said nothing, but Free agreed, gripping my hand tightly. I started feeling twitchy until I saw Evonne's face light up with happiness. Free laughed at my grumbling curses, kissing me until I was dizzy. "It's alright, baby. One more week, and then we will never see her again."

Fat chance. Maybe Mallory has stayed away from the house, but that doesn't mean I haven't seen her crazy ass around the ranch, harassing the guys and flirting with every stablehand imaginable. I even saw her talking to Whistler one day. Luckily, she spends more time in town, shopping for god knows what. I swear her car is packed to the gills every time I see it. I don't believe for one minute that she has changed her stripes. Dulcie is still smarting over Mallory's words even though all of us have told her to let it go.

"Don't let her get to you. She's just a jealous cow," I tell her while adjusting Teddy, who is munching away at her breakfast, namely me. On my way to my workshop, I stopped at the stable office and found my friend in a snit.

"I'm trying not to; I am. But I can't get over what she said about Devin." She sniffles, and I groan.

"Girl, come on. Devin can't keep his hands off of you. I swear you guys have more sex than cats in heat." One afternoon, I stopped by their house and could hear them groaning through the door. I ran out of there as fast as I could. When I went back a few hours later, it was dark, and they were still at it. Free even told me that Fallen had caught them on the security cameras. "What if there are things he wants that I don't do, but she did? Do you think he compares us? What if they did ...butt stuff?" Her cries get louder as she whispers, and I stare at her.

"Dulcie?" I get up and pour her a cup of tea from the tray Evonne brought from the house. I notice that her plate hasn't been touched. "Why haven't you eaten your breakfast? Are you not hungry?" She shakes her head miserably. "No, I just don't want it. It smells weird."

It smells weird. I peer closer at my friend and see that she looks like she's gained a little weight—not much, but her face looks fuller. She sips the tea and then makes a face. "Didn't you put any sugar in here?" She jumps up, dumps about two tons of sugar and milk in, and then takes another sip, sighing in happiness.

"No, I didn't. Because you don't like sugar in your tea *or* milk," I tell her slowly. She pauses before shrugging. "Well, I do now," she snaps. I pull a Charleston Chew out of my pocket and lay it on her desk. She snatches it up, gobbling it down in one bite.

"Dulcie? You hate Charleston Chews." She pauses and

peers at me. My eyebrows are on the ceiling. "When was the last time you had a period?" Her eyes get big, and she started crying again. "Indeed. We need to get you a pregnancy test."

"Okay, I peed on all three of them. How long do we wait?" We are both standing over the bathroom sink, and I click the timer on my phone. "Sixty seconds."

"I can't believe this. I should have seen the signs earlier." She's quivering in excitement, and I smile at her. I know she and Devin are super happy with their current set-up, but deep down, my girl wants to be married with kids. She will make an excellent mother, though I pray they have a boy. I can only imagine the outfits she would put on a girl.

"I hope it's a girl. That way, she and Teddy can be best friends." I laugh as if she plucked my thoughts out of my head. "Whatever it is, it will be so lucky to have you as a mama." I reach out and hold her hand as the timer goes off. "Okay, let's look."

"I can't. You do it." She goes and stands in the shower stall, closing the door behind her. I crack up and pick up the first one —two pink lines. I smile hard. The second one is digital: pregnant. The third is a simple yes or no: Yes. "Dulcie?"

"Yeah?" Her voice shakes, and I move closer to the door. "Promise me you won't name this kid Dazita?"

"What do you mean you want to wait to tell Devin?" We are sitting in Teddy's nursery, and of course, Dulcie has sixteen thousand baby magazines in her lap. I don't even know where they came from.

"Only a few days. I want to make sure it's perfect. I wanted to have balloons and ordered the cutest little rodeo outfit. They race next weekend; as soon as he gets home, I'm going to have the whole thing ready." She calmly folds a page down. Every magazine has about twenty sheets like these. Poor Devin. "Plus, when I tell my Mama, she will have a hog-tied fit. This will be her first grandbaby. That means she will always be down at my house, even before the baby comes. I gotta make sure the whole thing is just right." She rips one page out and adds to another pile.

"Out of all her kids, there's no grandbabies?" Did I say poor Devin yet?

Dulcie shakes her head slowly, her attention divided. "Nope. My oldest brother, Deacon, is a career Air Force. He never had time to find a wife or anything. Then you have Daze, and we know that fool ain't never settling down. Third is the golden child, Ken, who lives in New York. A hedge fund genius. He bought Mama her house. The idiot in front of me is Porter. He's a will o' the wisp. Can't settle down anywhere. Daze keeps asking him to come out here and work, but last time we heard, he was in the Philippines, doin' god knows what. Then me. So Mama has all these boys, and not one of 'em is tied up. That's why I'm her favorite. Plus, she loves her some Devin."

Wow. "Uhhhh, your family is very eclectic." Dulcie beams. "My Memaw told my parents they needed to let their boys find their way in life. They followed her advice. Aside from Daze, they are all on the straight and narrow."

"What's Daze's real name?" She snickers.

"Dulcie.." We both yelp, jumping in our seats. Pallas smirks at both of us, his green eyes crinkling at the corners. "Your brother hasn't gone by that name in a long time. He will not be pleased that you are throwing it around."

"Oh, come on, Pally. I need to know. Is it awful?" His eyes twinkle, and I crack up.

"And you," he points at Dulcie. "You need to tell Devin about the little one." She screeches in a whisper, trying not to wake up Teddy. "How did you know?"

"You two are not very quiet. Also, you have been an emotional mess—more so than usual. He will be happy; why not tell him immediately?" He leans over the crib, stroking the baby's hair.

"Because I have a plan," she whispers furiously. And you better not say anything, Pally. Like not even a hint." She squints at him threateningly, crooking her fingers into a weird curse. He chuckles, then checks his phone and walks out. "My lips are sealed."

She claps her hands and then winces. "Sorry. This is gonna be epic!"

CHAPTER 58
FREE

"I don't know who will kill her first, Dulcie or Vivi," Devin says as we hitch Harley into his trailer.

"My money is on Vivi. She caught her out at the garage this morning and stepped out of her workshop holding her torch and a giant set of pliers. She just stared at her, swinging her arms, until Mal got the hint and took off." Cage tells us, giggling like a girl. I sigh and shake my head. I thought I was doing something nice for Evonne when she begged me to let Mallory stay a few extra days. I didn't know at the time that my wife had already given her a deadline, so I felt like shit when Vivi laid into me that night. She told me all the crap that Mal had told her, and I had to fuck her into a coma to get her to calm down. Knowing Mal, she put Evonne up to it.

"She fucked Kagan last night," Devin whispers. "All the hands are talking about it. I normally don't get into their business, but I tried to warn him off, and he gave me an attitude. He's been a problem for a while. He yelled at Vivi that one time, remember? I hate to lose him, but I think it's time." I remember her telling me someone yelled at her when she visited Carnage.

I'm not shocked that it's the same dude who thought hooking up with Mallory was a good idea. He's just lucky he don't have to see me about my wife.

"I'm fine with that. First thing Monday morning." I give Harley one last pat and a couple of sugar cubes. "We need him to place first or second to have enough points for the season. You think he's ready?" Devin snorts. "He'll smoke all of them. I heard some farms pulled their horses out when they found out he had entered. Then they tried to move them to Carnage's races and panicked again." I smile and groan when I see Mallory headed our way. She's spent the last few days trying to get me alone, and I'm not ashamed that I've been hiding in my office. My wife put enough fear in her that she wouldn't come within fifty feet of our house.

"Free and Devin? It's like someone dropped my favorite type of sandwich into my lap," she purrs from behind us. Devins's shoulders hike to his ears, and I see him surreptitiously checking to see if Dulcie is going to fly out of the shadows and kick him one.

"Mal. What do you want?" I don't look at her; instead, I spin away and check inside Carnages's trailer before we load him in. I hear her boots crunch in the dirt, stopping close to me. Her hands slide around my middle, immediately diving for my dick. I grab them, squeeze them hard, and shove her backward. I smirk at her cruelly. "You must have a death wish. My wife will kill you if you touch me again."

She scoffs and pushes herself against me. "I'm not scared of that little bitch. She can say whatever she wants. You and I know the truth. What I want to know is when are you gonna get rid of her?" She pouts, pushing her tits into my chest, her nipples like darts. I step back, and she follows. "And what is the truth?"

"You made a mistake when you let me go, and I made a

mistake by letting you. That we have never stopped loving each other. Free, I can overlook you having a baby with someone else, even marrying her because of it. As long as you do right by me, we can forget all about it." I stare at her for a minute and then laugh—hard.

"Mallory, I never loved you. Ever. You had a hot pussy that I enjoyed. You let me fuck you anyway I wanted. That was it. I never had plans to make you my old lady or have kids with you. You were never First Lady material. I just let you believe what you wanted until I got tired of you. Do you really think that model scout showed up by coincidence? I set that whole shit up. You were causing problems with my brothers and their women. Your leaving was the best thing that happened to me. Want to know why?" Her eyes are enormous on her pale face. "Because life is just a bunch of decisions you make—a choose your own adventure book—until you wind up where you are supposed to be. You led me right to my wife, who is the most ridiculous woman I have ever met. I may have thought I never wanted kids, but my daughter is why I get up every morning. So, in a way, I have to thank you, Mal. Thank you for giving me my family." She takes a step back, a sour expression on her face.

"So you think that's it Free? Do you think I will just let someone else have *MY* life? That should be my house, my farm, my kid." She screams, the veins in her neck protruding, face a violent red. Her hair is in a long braid, and she flips it over her shoulder, her pretty eyes narrowing into slits. "If you and Devin think I am going to let you play me like that, you have another thing coming." She points at me and then whips around, pointing at Devin, hiding behind a door. "How about if I tell your little whores all the ways you guys fucked me? Would they like to know about the times you shared me? I don't think that little idiot you are with will be able to handle it, do you, Devin? I see her walking around here with hearts in her eyes, calling you all those stupid nicknames. She thinks you are a choirboy, doesn't she? I'm sure she would love to hear how many times you fucked me in the ass." She slides a hand over her hip and slaps herself on an asscheek. Devin steps from behind the door, a cold look on his face.

"You'll shut your mouth about my sister, Mallory," Daze says from the left of us. He gives her his dimples, but his eyes are dead. "I think it's time to escort you off the farm, don't you? And I think this is me warning you that out of all of us, I have no problem making sure you are never seen again." He pulls his Stetson off, tapping it on his leg. "I didn't like you back then, and I especially don't like you now. What's going to happen next is you, and I are gonna take a stroll to Evonne's place, we are going to pack up all of your shit, and I'm going to find you a hotel in town. Ev can visit you there. And you will never fix your face to say a word about Vivi or my sister again. My mama still speaks to yours every once in a while, and I'm sure you don't want her to hear about how you whored yourself around New York to get your rent paid, do you?" His smile never changes, but his voice gets deeper and deeper until it's coming from the pits of hell.

She turns to me, sees my face filled with disgust, and even tries to plead silently with Devin, who is scowling at her. Cage stands next to him, his smirk as deadly as poison.

"If that's the way you want it. But don't think you can come crawling back to me when things don't work out with that midget tramp you married." She storms off, Daze in her wake. He winks at me and saunters behind her, whistling.

"She has always been trouble," Cage says.

"That she was. Now, let's get Carnage prepped. We have some races to win." I stare after her until she disappears into the wind.

CHAPTER 59
VIVI

"Free just texted me. They won all of their races. They should be home around six." We are in Dulcie and Devin's house setting up his surprise. We went into town right after the boys left and picked up about one thousand balloons and all the other paraphernalia that Dulcie had ordered. Five balloons spell out "DADDY" in alternating pink and blue colors. We even have a fog machine that I hooked up to her phone so she can turn it on from the doorway.

"Sweet. Evonne says that they wanted a big feast at your house to celebrate so I will drag him back here after that." She has stacks of diapers in the corner, and we borrowed Teddy's Moses basket and filled it with toy horses. "Did I tell you that my Mama called me yesterday? She said she had a dream about me with a baby carriage. I about died. I told her it was probably Theodora in that carriage, and she sounded so disappointed. She's gonna get me for lying to her."

"I think she will forgive you once you tell her a baby is involved. She might get after Daze for you going first. Oh! Did you hear that your brother threw Whatsherbitch off the ranch yesterday? Noxxie told me that he followed her off the property to town. And Daze told everyone that she wasn't allowed back. Evonne has been weepy all day." I hear a whimper and see Teddy stirring in her pack-n-play. Her little head pops up, thick curls plastered on one side of her head, a confused, sleepy look in her eyes.

"Hey, stinky." She swings her head to me, grinning. I bend down and pick her up, cuddling her close to my chest. She rubs her face on my shirt as I kiss her fat cheeks. She is growing so fast that I can't catch my breath.

"I can't believe how much she looks like Free. I mean, I know Trace is his brother, but she literally looks just like Free." I smile. Trace had straight dark brown hair, brown eyes, and an athletic build. Theodora is a supremely chubby baby with a head full of jet-black unruly curls, just like Free. She even scowls like he does. She does have my eyes, puffy lips, though, and chin.

"I hope our kid looks like Devin. I read somewhere that babies are supposed to look like their dads at birth because it helps the father bond with the baby. Like a biology thing." I snort lightly. I saw Dulcie's Amazon cart, and she ordered about fifteen schmoozy-boozy new-age birth books. I can't wait until she tells Devins she wants a water birth in the stables. Something about 'bonding to earthly animals.'

Help.

"I think this looks good, girl." She takes out her phone and takes a bunch of pictures. "We should head back and help Ev get ready for tonight." She clicks a last few and then starts sniffling. Oh, boy.

"Don't mind me. I'm just happy." She waves a hand in front of her face before reaching for Teddy. "Let's go, girlfriend. I think there are some bananas and oatmeal in your future."

"Give me another kiss, woman." I smile and stand on my toes, lips pursed. Free pulls on my chin until my mouth is open and swoops down to deepen it. My eyes drift close as one hand buries in my hair, and his other reaches around to grab my ass. He tilts my head to one side, stoking the sides of my mouth with his tongue ring. "Now, that's how a man likes to be greeted." I smack his chest and give him a tight hug. The guys got home a few minutes ago, and Dulcie and I came spilling out of the house, yelling with bottles of spewing champagne. Devin and Cage came out of the trucks, whooping up a storm, and Nox ripped off his shirt, chugging a bottle in one long sip. Free was all smiles, sweeping me off my feet and grabbing a bottle himself. The rest of the team emerged from the stables, shouting and celebrating. Harley qualified for a national race with this win and was the odds-on favorite. Carnage still needed more points, but he should be national in a month or two because he also won his entries.

Ev, Dulcie, and I set up tables in front of the house filled with the kind of spread I always picture in Texas: bowls of potato salad, fruit, and macaroni salad, dishes of cornbread and biscuits, and platters and platters of barbecue. We've been cooking all day, and when the boys told us they were an hour out, Daze fired up the grill and has been parked there since, wearing an apron that says "Fuck The Chef." There is plenty of beer, but not too much. "Don't want these boys to get stupid. They still gotta work tomorrow," Evonne told us with a smile. I checked to see if she seemed upset about Mallory being kicked out, but she seemed fine.

"I missed you." I freeze and peek over my shoulder at Free, who smirks at me. "What?" He pulls me back into his chest, wrapping his arms around my shoulders. "I said I missed you.

Didn't like sleeping alone," he says in my ear, nipping on my lobe and tugging lightly.

"You could have always snuggled with Devin. OW!" I rub my butt where he pinched it.

"Did you miss me?" He asks, spinning me around and peering into my face. My mouth drops open, and as usual, he pushes it shut. "Thief?"

"Uhh. Yes?" What am I supposed to say? That I was a miserable little bitch without him? That I sleep on his side of the bed because it smells like him? Hell no. I'm going to the grave with that.

"No graves for you, baby."

OH. MY. GOD.

"I said all of that out loud, didn't I?" He laughs like a jackal, nodding. "Brb. I'm just going to go hide in the pantry for a decade," I try to pull away, and he snatches me back, laughing and kissing me some more. "I like you being miserable because you missed me." I bury my head in his hard chest and sigh. "Okay." His smell envelops me, and I take a deep whiff. "Who has our kid?" I look up and around, finding Devin with Teddy on his shoulders. Dulcie is right beside him, stars in her eyes. I smile and snuggle closer.

"That should be the last of it." I dust my hands off and smile. We have been working hard all day to ensure the yard is clean quickly. Once all the food was gone, the hands went home, but the boys were spread around the living room, sprawled over every piece of furniture. Ev wanted to visit Mallory, so we feverishly helped her ensure everything was put away while the boys doused all the trash can bonfires. Dulcie is excitedly vibrating, jittering about, and speaking in long, breathless sentences. Devin has tried calming her down all day, but she is like a helium balloon drifting toward the ceiling.

"Okay, I'm going to round up Devin." She flits out of the kitchen, and I saw Ev slip out of the backdoor before I could say goodbye. I checked the time and saw that it's later than I thought. Teddy has long been asleep, worn out from being passed around like a tray of candy. I check her baby monitor and notice that she is face down with her pampered butt in the air.

I walk to the living room and see Free passing out rock glasses of whiskey. "We always said that when we made it, really made it, we would open this bottle of Pappy's. Here we are, boys. Let's toast." He holds his glass up, as does the rest of the crew.

"To fighting, stealing and killing. Fighting for what you believe in, stealing a woman's heart, and killing a bottle with your brothers!" He tosses the glass back with a yell.

Daze pops up and raises his glass, too. "Brothers! To a good selection, no rejection, a strong erection, a clean injection, and no infection!" I crack up and 'eeww' at the same time. Dulcie is wiping tears of laughter off her face.

"Last one! Here's to a girl in little red shoes. May she spend your money and drink your booze. She has no cherry, but that's no sin; she still has the box the cherry came in!" There is a shocked silence before I start howling. "KAZ!" The laughter busts out, and I'm doubled over. Cage falls off his chair, and Pallas has his face buried in his hands.

"Vivi," Dulcie whispers. She pulls me frantically to the side, a finger shushing me. "I forgot to put up the lights." I groan and push her further back. "The fairy lights?" She nods, her bottom lip trembling. "What do you want to do? Devin won't know they are missing."

"But I will know. I want it to be perfect." She tears up, and I sigh. "You want me to help you?" She nods, wiping her face. "They will be polishing off that bottle for a while anyway. It should only take a few minutes." She's bouncy again. "Okay, let me tell Free."

I walk into the middle of the melee, where Nox retells the last few minutes of Carnage's ass-whooping and lean over my husband. "Dulcie has a surprise set up for Devin, and we need to prepare it. I'll be back in a few," I tell him. He wraps his long fingers around my wrist and kisses me. "Okay, baby. Hurry back." I smile and hand him the baby monitor he sets on the table before him. I give him another peck and wink at Pallas, watching us with a smile.

"Let's do this and get back," I tell Dulcie, tucking my phone into the back pocket of my skintight jeans. We hurry out the back door and down the pathway, skirting the stables. We make it to her house in no time, and she pulls out the box of lights that she wants to frame the archway into her home. As she fussed with the placement and spacing, I grumbled but deftly hammered in nails for them to hang from. After about twenty minutes, she declared it perfect, and I took a deep breath. "Nothing else? This is it for real?" I ask her sarcastically, and she shoots me a teasing glare. "I think so."

"Girl, bye." I march out of her house, and she laughs, following me. We stroll toward the house, and I hear a loud whinny coming from Carnage's area.

"What was th-" Dulcie screams, and I whip around and see her being dragged into the night.

"Dulcie!" I start to run, and then I am lifted clean off of my feet—a hard, dry hand clamping over my mouth, muffling my screams and pinching my breathing. I struggle, but the arms around me tighten like a vise. A light sting pierces my neck, and I fall into a cold, exploding darkness.

CHAPTER 60
FREE

The first thing I notice is the silence. A farm is never this quiet, with animals stirring and equipment humming. Constant noise. Weird.

The second thing is the nasty taste in my mouth. If a cow's ass, liquor, and sauerkraut threw a party, it wouldn't be as bad as this. I smack my lips together, hoping to draw up some spit to help swallow it, but not a drop comes up.

The third thing is I hear my daughter crying. It's from a distance but also echoing in my head. Speaking of heads, mine is splitting from pain. Shit, am I hungover? I haven't been this drunk in years. Fuck, I'm too old for this shit.

"Vivi, I'd go get her, but I might throw up first." My arm is thrown over my eyes, so I can't see a lick of light. "Baby?" I roll over and grunt when I hit the floor, landing on something that feels like another body, too big to be my wife.

"Fuck dude, get the hell off me," Daze's voice is gruff, and he groans, pushing himself to his knees. I'm still lying where I landed. "Dude, I feel like shit. How much did we drink last night?" I frown. I only remember us finishing off that bottle of

Van Winkle. "Just the Pappy's, I thought." Teddy is still crying, and it's turned into the hiccups— the kind where she is almost inconsolable. "Dude, why is your baby crying like that?" He takes a crawling step forward and then collapses again. He lands with his head on Fallen's back, who is facedown on the carpet.

I hear another groan and squint in the light to see Pallas staggering toward the stairs. He's holding his head too, moving from side to side. "I'll go see." I vaguely recall that Vivi left the baby monitor with me, and brave an eye opening to look for it. Had she left it on the table? It's not there.

"Dude, wake up." Daze is shaking Devin, who is snoring like a buzzsaw. He shakes him hard, but he isn't budging. I pull myself to a squat position, finding Nox and Cage each under a table. Riggs is spread-eagle in front of the fireplace, one boot in the ashes. Kaz is half on an ottoman, the other half hanging to the floor. Something isn't right.

"Free?" Pallas stands at the top of the stairs holding Teddy, who is still hiccuping, her little face wet and red. She stutters, and when she sees me, she starts crying again. "She is soaked through. Her crib is wet, too."

"What time is it?" I stumble around, looking for a clock. It's past noon and a weird feeling wells in my throat.

My father once told me that fear is a phenomenon. Sometimes it hits you like a crash, crippling you, stealing your legs from under you, stinging you in the heart. Other times, it's like a small crack in the pavement. It seems inconsequential, foolish even. But soon, the crack widens, and it can eat everything in its path, including you.

Pallas gingerly comes downstairs, his balance still off. He brings Teddy to me, who smells like pee. I can feel how full her diaper is, and the poor thing is whimpering. "I'll get her bottle," Pallas says, and I peel off her wet clothes.

"It'll be ok, little one." I hold her little naked rump in one arm and kick at Kaz. "Get up." He wakes up with a shout, and I repeat the same with everyone else. Everyone slowly returns online, and Pallas reappears with Teddy's lunch. She lunges forward, almost falling out of my arms. She sucks hard, her poor little tummy growling. "Fuck, she's starving."

"Watch your language," Kaz says, standing up and stretching. He peeps around the room, frowning at everyone's state. "What is going on?" He starts toward Cage, who snarls at him, but Kaz grabs his wrist, checking his pulse. He pulls his ever-present penlight out of his pocket and flashes it into his eyes. He frowned deeper and did the same with everyone else. "Shit, we've been drugged. Pupils pinpoint and erratic pulses. We've probably been out a good twelve hours."

It's then that I almost collapse. "Where is my wife?"

"There is a bump in the feed. Only maybe a few minutes. They came through the South Gate, that much we know. They took the girls within site of the house—you can see where they leave Devin's house, and then there's a blackout. Five minutes later, they disappear." Fallen is gulping an energy drink, his legs jumping in fear and caffeine. "The feed to the front gate is undisturbed; they only messed with the ones on their route in and out." He pauses, and I turn around and see him staring at me. I stood in front of the window about thirty minutes after we realized the girls were missing. Everyone spread out, gathering information. Pallas went with Devin, who was in the chair next to me, his head in his hands. He walked into a house full of decorations announcing that he would be a father and almost lost it. Pallas had to virtually carry him back to the house.

"Are we all in agreement that it was the Russians?" Daze asks. We all nod, and I say nothing. "Silver said it's not another MC. Once the Princes let it be known they were allied with Free, the clubs came to him for alliances. No, this was too quick and clean. The Russians are the only ones with any business looking here." There is a murmur of agreement.

"Where did you find Vivi's phone?" Fallen clicks around. "About five hundred feet from the stables. A few of the hands said they heard Carnage going crazy last night. He's off the charts today. It's like he knows something happened. Free..." I shake my head. I need to stay above water. I don't want sympathy. I don't want solace. I'm treading in the darkness and need to stay here.

"So they knew she had a tracker on her phone. They let Dulcie keep hers for a few miles before it was tossed. Vivi's was almost immediate."

"What if they decide they don't need Dulcie because they really wanted Vivi? They could kill her." Devin's voice is a mourning cry. It's quiet, but I only have this to give him.

"Dulcie is a beautiful girl— a blonde. And she's pregnant. That makes her valuable. They would probably sell her before they would kill her." He sobs, and I put a tight hand on his shoulder. "We will find them before that even happens." He wipes his eyes, nodding, and I turn to Daze. "I want to ride out in an hour. We split up. Three groups: Daze, Riggs, and Kaz- you go west. Devin, me, and Nox are in another—we will go East. Cage, Pallas, you will ride up north and meet with the Princes. Fallen, you will stay behind and keep us all coordinated. Has anyone been able to find Evonne?" Her apartment was empty, though all her stuff was still in it. "No, she's nowhere." I shake my head. "No offense to her, but I can't afford to worry about her right now. Everyone saddle up."

I PAUSE OUTSIDE THE GARAGE, my fingers hovering over the keypad, shaking. This door is hidden in the corner of the room, concealed within the framework of a tool wall. If someone noticed it, they'd have to get past two more layers of security before they can even imagine what's behind the door. I don't come out here, letting Cage keep everything in order. "You gonna be alright?" Pallas comes up next to me, punching in the numbers. The door swooshes open, and the second garage lights up with motion sensors. The row of gleaming metal beckons to me, and I feel like a chameleon who is putting its skin back on.

"Vivi once told me that I made her feel safe—that she was finally free to be who she was always meant to be. That she was tired of hiding. I did that for her, Pallas." I take a deep breath as I walk over to the wall where our cuts hang neatly, welcoming us home. "I gave her all this security, and now she's gone. And I never got a chance to tell her that I love her." My heart cracks, and I fight it, sealing it up with hate and rage.

"You can tell her when we find her." He slips his cut over his shoulders, the black VP patch gleaming in the low light. He holds mine out, and I grit my teeth, peeling off my T-shirt. I shrug it on, a hug from an old enemy. "We don't need Free Kelly and Vivi's husband. We need the King. She needs the King. You can do penance later." I hear the murmur of the other guys coming in and the silence of them watching me become Death. I head for my personal gun locker and pull out the ammo for not just my Walther but for the Luger G18 9mm with the illegal thirty-three-round clip and the HK416 rifle that I strap to my bike. I have knives at each wrist, one ten-inch Bowie at my waist, and one in each boot. I pull out zip ties and a small spool of barbed wire that I designed myself. I walk over to my grave-black Dyna SuperGlide. Cage made sure all the matte black paint was pristine, and I popped open the saddlebag to dump my ammo, a GPS, and spare phone batteries. I slip a Bluetooth over my ear and tap it. "Fallen?"

"I'm here, Free. Teddy is right here next to me. Did you know she's got a tooth coming in? She's chewing on my fingers." I smile and swing my leg over the seat, turning the key and letting the loud rumble of the souped-up engine fill my soul. I see Daze put his twin swords in his back holster, his favorite knives at his waist. His "Enforcer" patch is pierced with a gold hoop, one of Dulcie's earrings.

"Fallen? Can you put the phone up to her?" I hear a shuffle and then the sweet sound of her breathing. "Teddy. I promise you that I will bring your Mama back or die trying. Be good for Uncle Fallen. Daddy loves you." I hear a sucking sound and then a loud gurgle. I smile for the last time, pushing a button that rolls up the back wall. I roll out, the deafening sound probably sending the horses into a frenzy. We creep down the driveway in a coordinated line, like wraiths fighting the sun. I click the earpiece one more time.

"Check in hourly. I want to know if you hear anything, no matter how small. Stay frosty." All seven matte blackheads nod, me being the only one not wearing a helmet. I want them to see me coming.

CHAPTER 61

VIVI

I watch Dulcie sleep and think about how I will get us out of this mess. I woke up in the back of a van, arms tied in front of me and ankles bound. I tried to get a look around and was promptly shot up with drugs again as soon as they saw me wiggling around. I woke up again a few hours later and pulled into a seated position. There were two men with us in the back and two more upfront. Dulcie is sitting up, too, but she has a gag in her mouth. Her eyes were red from crying, and I could faintly smell urine, which she let go in fright. All the men wore black ski masks, and the eyeholes were extra stitched.

"Ty sobirayesh'sya byt' khoroshey devochkoy?" The one closest to me poked me, and I looked at him blankly, though I recognized the accent. Russian.

"What?" I said innocently. He repeated the same phrase, and I just shook my head and shrugged my shoulders in confusion. They laughed, and he reached out, slapping me suddenly. My head snapped around, and Dulcie cried out from behind her gag. "Dulcie, quiet," I told her, feeling the immediate raw spot in my mouth. She sniffled in fright, trying to hold it in. The one near her slipped his hand up her dress, and she squealed.

"Ne trogayte tovar!" The driver said, glaring in the rearview. The pervert slipped his hands out, but not before giving her thigh a hard squeeze. *"Mozhet byt', pozze, my poveselimsya, net?"* I glare at him again and feel the pinch from the needle as I slide back into oblivion. Now I'm up, hands and feet free. We are in a room in what looks like a garage. There are hubcaps stacked in neat piles across from us, and the typical dirty window gives off meek light above us. There is a cot, which Dulcie is dozing on, and a few old desks piled on top of each other. I don't know what they've been giving us, but we are losing time, I calculate that we've been here around three days. Some guy comes in every few hours with a tray with two pieces of bread and a cup of water. I let Dulcie eat the bread but won't let either of us touch the water. I dump it in the small bathroom, filling it with the tap instead. The trauma of all of this is helping her stay asleep and oblivious, which is for the best. I can't keep her calm and plan at the same time.

There is a short knock on the door, and Dulcie shoots up, eyes wide. It's just our jailer bringing another tray. There are a few cookies with the bread and a sealed milk container this time. I eye him suspiciously, and he chuckles behind the black mask. "You eat this time, yah?" I give a small start at his use of English but say nothing. "The boss? He will haf a conversation with you, tonight?" I shiver but keep my chin up. He walks out of the room, locking it behind him.

"Vivi! What are we going to do?" I hold the cookies to Dulcie, who doesn't even chew them. I know she has to be starving. I gently hold the milk to the light and squeeze it, looking for needle holes. "This is fine. I need you to drink it. You need to keep up your strength." She pauses before sucking it down, leaving me a bit. I swallowed it and then dumped the water in the sink again. I come back, watch her eat the bread, and then lie down.

"Don't you think I didn't notice your fever? You were burning up last night," she says softly. I nod and go to splash cold water on my face. "It's my milk. I haven't pumped in days, and I think I've got milk fever," I sit on the floor and fight off exhaustion.

"Do you think the guys are looking for us?" I snort. "I think...that they are tearing the world apart right now." She nods. "You didn't know them before when they were GOTA. God, they were terrifying. People moved out of their way on the street—their aura was just that dark. Free will kill anyone and everyone who had anything to do with this. I almost feel bad. But not really." I snort again. "Go to sleep, Dulcie."

"Girl!" I jump awake and saw the main jailer guy standing in the doorway beckoning me. Dulcie is already awake and crying. A second guy is twisting her arm, and blood is coming from her nose. "Get your hands off of her right now." I advance on him, fists balling up. He laughs at me, shoving her down and kicking her in the leg. He grabs my bicep and drags me out of the room. They pull me down a long hallway lined with drums of something, and the space opens to an actual garage. I quickly look for the exit and see it in the distance. There are cars on jacks and loads of tools. There are also far more men here than I thought. I count at least twenty and can hear more in the back. A door opens ahead of me, and I am shoved inside. I fall to the ground, and the door slams behind me.

"Get up." I hear, and I push myself up. "Do you know who I am?"

I blink because sitting in front of me is the giant who bumped into me in Las Vegas. His hair is bright yellow-white, and I can see he is missing an ear. "No."

"Ahhh. I knew you would say that. We have met before, you and I. Do you not remember?" He smiles, and I would think it was charming if life were normal. His heavily accented English is thick, but I can understand him fine. I take small peeps around the room. There is hardly anything in here- just basic office furniture. The window behind him is blacked out and barred. There is a bank of camera screens to the left of the desk—I feel a small relief when I don't see our cell on the list.

"I think I would remember if we did."

He throws his head back and laughs. "Oh, I think you do. I remember thinking how charming you looked in that dress you were wearing. If my orders had been different, I would have taken the time to see what that pig was enjoying. But alas, I was just there to kill you. As my bad luck would have it, you survived, so I went after you at home. And I thought, "Ivan, what a shame you never got a piece of that beautiful little *kukla*." He smiles again, and I fight the shaking that is taking over my limbs. This was the man who killed Riley. "So imagine my surprise when I learned you were alive again and living on a farm." He spreads his hands, and when his suit jacket moves, I see the gun tucked into his waist. His cold blue eyes watch my expression. "Do you remember me now, *kukla?*"

"You killed Riley!" I shout out, clapping my hand over my mouth. I want to reach out and choke him. The level of violence in my soul is scaring me.

"Ah, the pretty blonde? Yes, it's a shame. I must say I don't care for your current color." He gestures toward me, and I move back an inch. "I have a boss. You know him?" I shake my head, biting my lip into blood.

"Maybe you do not. But I need to know that he has not

been compromised. Normally, I would turn you over to him, but I will keep you close for now. Maybe we can have some fun, no?" I take another step back. "Do you smoke?" He strikes a match from a bowl on his desk and pulls a cigarette from his jacket pocket. "No?" He takes a long puff and blows it toward my face. *"Seychas!"*

The door flies open behind me, and I yanked facedown onto the desk. A body braces against me, and another holds my arms over my head. I shudder when I feel the man behind get excited from the action.

"I'm going to ask you again, little *kukla*. Do you know my boss? You can make this easy on yourself by not lying to me." I scream when I feel the tight burn of the cigarette singeing the flesh on my arm. "Come now. Tell me." He burns the other arm, and I scream again but say nothing. He leans his face near me, and I can smell the rancidness of his breath. "I know a million ways to hurt a woman, Vivienne. This is only one." He holds the cigarette near my eye and dances it around until he presses it into my cheek. I screech but press my lips together to hold it in.

"Ah! A warrior! I like this game. Close the door, gentleman. We may be here a while."

CHAPTER 62
FREE

"Free?" I look up from where I sit on my bike, drinking water. We are in the middle of Tennessee, headed toward Chicago, where I know Koslov has his stronghold. Silver hooked up with Cage and Pallas, who are headed toward Seattle. We've got several offshoots of the Princes headed in different directions, and I've heard from a few ex-GOTA. But no one has seen my wife. "Yeah?"

"Phone. Fallen." Nox tosses it to me, and I catch it, putting it on speaker for Devin, who looks more ashen every day. "Go."

"I found Evonne."

I hear music in the background and realize it's the Wiggles. "She okay?"

"No. She was in the hospital. She had acute drug poisoning. Someone loaded her up on GHB and then left her in her car. She got found just in time; according to the records, she almost died," he whispers. "I had her brought back to the ranch and she had some interesting sh—um...stuff to say."

I frown. "Anything we can use?"

"I'll let her tell you. I'll do whatever you want me to. Ev!!"

Devin makes a face at that declaration. I hear him fumble with the phone and then a low whisper.

"Hello?"

I've known Ev for years. When we prospected with the Ghosts, she was one of the old ladies who cared for the clubhouse. Her parents had owned a diner, so after the first time she made us biscuits, she was relegated to being the club cook, though she didn't mind. She kept everything in order, all the hangers-on, all the other women and girlfriends. If circumstances had been different for her, she would have made some club an excellent First Lady. When GOTA was formed, she came with us, taking on the same role, and when we disbanded, she followed us to the ranch. She has always had a quiet way about her, putting her head down and working. We ensured she knew how much we loved her, though I always wondered why she never got another man after Hogan died. She was a pretty woman with a great rack and thick brown hair. One thing she never was was hesitant. So that's why her voice sends alarm bells off in my head.

"Ev, are you okay?" I hear sniffles and then a loud, wracking cry. Devin huffs in impatience. "Evonne, what is going on?"

"This is all my fault." The cries are almost deafening, her words a jumbled mess. Devin stiffens, his pale face slowly turning dead white. He hasn't slept or eaten in days, going off of pure horror—this might send him over the edge. "What do you mean?" More crying, and I hear Fallen trying to calm her down, but even he seems like he is getting stressed.

"I didn't think she would do anything, I swear. She was just so brokenhearted about the two of you being over." She cries but there is a defensive tone in her voice.

"Who, Ev?" God help me; I already know.

"Mallory."

"What did you tell her, Evonne?" Nox puts on his country boy charm, which is good because I would like to reach out through the phone and kill her.

"I told her she should hang in there because you only married Vivienne because she was on the run. That one day, you would leave her. And that Teddy wasn't your kid. She asked me what I meant, and I told her. About Trace, about Vivi and that Russian mafia guy. I told her how she showed up all beaten up and that you only married her because you had to." She pauses and waits for our reaction. We all say nothing, and she drives the final nail in.

"She was so happy, Free. I know that you have to keep up a performance so that everyone thinks your marriage is real, but Mallory truly loves you. She's been telling me forever that she just was waiting for the signal and she would be at your side in a minute. I went to see her that night, and she was packing up to go, saying that she couldn't bear to watch you play house with Vivi anymore. We sat in my car talking, and that's the last thing I remember."

"Who drugged the Pappy's, Evonne?"

She sniffled again. "Um, I dunno. I know that Mallory borrowed some stuff and I told her to put it back before you could notice."

I stare at Devin and Nox and brace myself against my bike, my rage-shaking so intense. "Fallen?" I hear her hand him the phone. "Yeah?" I know he's got it hooked up so that all our other brothers can listen to the conversation.

"Is Bent's old lady there?" When we couldn't find Evonne, Silver's VP offered to send his wife to look after Teddy. She came with three other girls and a whole host of bodyguards. "Yeah. She's right here. Teddy loves her." I nod, though he can't see me.

"Good, put it on speakerphone so that everyone can hear

me," I tell him, my head falling back on my shoulders. "Go on," he tells me.

"Evonne? I want you to hear this straight from me. I did not marry Vivi because I had to. I married her because I wanted to. I wanted her. I wanted her from the moment she showed up, dusty and beaten. I married her because, God help her, I want a future with her. I want more kids with her. I married her because I love her. I don't know shit about how to love someone, but sure as fuck, I am going to give it my everything. Because she is my everything. I know you thought you were doing the right thing, but you put my wife in danger. You put Dulcie in danger. Did you know that Dulcie is pregnant?" Silence and more sniffling. "You put a pregnant woman and my motherfucking wife in the crosshairs of some crazy fucking people. My daughter was alone for HOURS; they could've taken her too. DID YOU KNOW THAT?" I scream the last few words, and she bursts out in hard sobs.

"Evonne, if you were anyone else, I would have you killed right this minute. Fallen has a gun, and it's pointed right at you as we speak. But I will let you live because you have been loyal, and I know my wife would be upset. You have one hour to get your things packed. Exactly sixty fucking minutes. I don't care if you can't get all your stuff in that time—whatever you leave, I will burn. I am going to have some Princes escort you to the Texas border- you decide what direction. After that, I never want to see or hear from you, ever. You will never enter this state again. If you do, I will kill you myself. If you speak on anything with my family or ranch, I will kill you myself. If you even think about me, I will end you."

"And if you try to contact Dulcie in any way, I will find you. Don't forget who I am, Evonne." Devin's voice comes from behind me. "Fallen?"

"Yeah, Dev?" I turn around to my troubled brother.

"I want her gone in less than an hour. Make it thirty minutes." With that, he walks away and starts his bike, putting on his helmet and easing toward the road.

"I want Mallory found. Start with her mom. I don't care what we have to do to her. Do you get me?" I don't give a shit about anyone but my wife and Dulcie. Everyone else can get fucked.

"Copy, King," Silver drawls.

"Got it."

"Yes." Everyone else chimes in their agreement.

"There's one more thing, Free. Kagan has also up and vanished. I don't think that's a coincidence, either. I'm running a check on all of his people, too. Got a grab on his phone; I'm sending that over, too." Fucking Mallory.

"Do that. We think Mallory somehow contacted Koslov? It's what fits," Devin asks impatiently. He's tapping one foot on the ground, the other holding his bike.

"How, though? Mallory doesn't know anyone in that world?" Kaz asks. I can hear the whoosh of cars, meaning his group is still on the move.

"The how is irrelevant. If we think Koslov has her, we need to move on him. Everyone-route yourselves to Chicago. Fallen, find the best routes for everyone and a convergence point. Gear up if you need to, but make it fast." I click off and start my bike. My team is the closest, so we can recon until everyone else shows up. I push down the sick feeling in my gut. Vivi has been gone too long at this point. I pray to the God I don't believe in to protect my wife.

Hold on, Thief. I'm coming.

CHAPTER 63
VIVI

"We are getting out of here tonight." I'm lying on the floor of our cell, my whole body shuddering in fever and pain.

Last night, Ivan and his goons tied me to the desk in his office and took turns beating me with a freezing-cold belt. The bite from the slaps, combined with the hardness of cracking leather, cut into my skin, making the pain ten times worse. They asked me over and over about Trace and Koslov and I never broke, telling them that I knew nothing, and Dulcie knew even less.

"*Kukla,* I may be starting to believe you, but how can I be sure?" He flicked the belt against my bare back, making sure the buckle clipped my spine. I held back my tears, my lips bloody from biting back screams. The welts were burning roadways onto my skin; the skin they had burned and sliced in the days before.

"I told you, I don't know about your boss. Trace was just a guy I met. I don't know anything." I grit my teeth as the whistle from an incoming blow carves the air. The impact rattles my teeth, and I can feel blood pouring down my body. I close my eyes and try to picture my daughter's face, my husband's laugh—anything to take me away from the agony. I feel the darkness creeping toward my head and pray I don't pass out. The last time I did, I woke to my pants being pulled down my legs. I let out a scream so loud, I swear the windows rattled. Ivan came barreling in, yelling at the man fumbling with my clothes. My jailer came out of nowhere and carried me to my room, and I heard a single gunshot. And I never saw that guy again.

"This is your last chance before we resort to other methods, my little *milyy*. You understand?" He rolled the belt around his fist and gave his assistant a head nod. My hands were untied, and the rope holding my legs down was loosened. I fell directly to the floor and lay there, panting. He squatted down and got as close to my face as he could. I eye him warily, raising an eyebrow, a small spit of defiance.

"I have left your precious little friend alone, yes? If you do not tell me what I want to know, perhaps it's time to let Pyotr play with her. He has taken a liking to her pretty face. And she is pregnant, no? I could make a nice profit on top of it."

Hell. Fucking. No.

I still said nothing; I just balled my fists into my sides and turned away.

"Tsk tsk. Perhaps if I let you watch, it will change your mind, no?" He stands up, and a pair of hands grabs me under my arms and drags me to my feet. I sway, my knees buckling. My hands tighten, and I fight for my balance. He watches in amusement, my stubbornness somehow a turn-on. More than once, I caught him rubbing his crotch while beating me, his arousal obvious. I threw up when I saw a wet patch after one of our sessions. But I know that if I show weakness, it will make everything that much worse. And it's the only way I can protect Dulcie.

"Leave her be," I managed to let out. I will go to my grave before I let them touch her.

He smiled, a cruel, charming smile. "We shall see. I look forward to our night together tomorrow. Take her back." He waved his hand in dismissal. I lurched around and then stopped. "Ivan?"

"Yes, *kukla*?" He'd seemed pleased, which made me want to vomit.

"Do you know who my husband is?" I'd been wondering about his lack of urgency, his imprisonment of us almost... cavalier.

He cocked his head to the side and frowned. "The farmer? What about him?"

The farmer???

"My husband isn't just a rancher, Ivan. You know that, right? Your boss can't save you from him when he comes." I shrugged and stumbled out, glancing over my shoulder, seeing his frown had deepened in confusion. Good. I fell into our room, which unfortunately was spinning, but I had bought us a little more time. I dropped into a fitful sleep, but now it's time to get all three of us home.

"Thank God. That guard touched me weird today, and if you hadn't told me to play dumb, I would've slapped him," she huffed, placing a cold washcloth against my wounds. I tuck my lips behind my teeth and try not to scream as I sit up, my whole body an inferno of pain. "I've got a plan. You'll have to play a part, Dulcie, and I need you to listen to everything I say, alright?" I stretch my legs out and stand up, going to the bathroom. I lift the toilet tank cover off, careful not to make noise, and remove the items I'd been working on the last few nights. I put the cover back, my arms shaking in the effort. I shuffle back and drop them on the bed, covering them with the threadbare blanket.

"What are those?" Dulcie whispers, peeking under the cover.

"I made a directional spigot, a striker, and a lockpick. We only have a few hours. Help me move some stuff." I don't tell her that we've run out of time.

"OKAY, you know what to do? As soon as I've got him, you move out of the way and then take everything out of his pockets. Stay behind the barricade until l come. Don't even peek your head out, got it?" Dulcie nods vigorously, her eyes huge in her head. "I know you're scared, but we have to do this exactly like I said, okay?" I glance at the clock and know that Pyotr will be by in a few minutes to bring us both to Ivan. I double-check that everything is in place and wince at the desk stacked on the bed. It's going to be obvious as soon as he walks into the room, but I have to trust that Dulcie can distract him.

"Vivi?" I open my eyes and smile at my friend. "What's up?" I ask playfully, and like I wanted, she grinned. "When we get out of here, will you be my baby's godmother?" My eyes tear up, but I brush them away. "Of course I will. I'll teach your baby how to hack and everything." She cracks up and then sobers, and both of us silently think the same thing. I lean forward and hug her tightly as a small sob escapes my lips. "I love you, Dulcie."

"I love you too, Peaches," her dimples pop. I swallow down my fear and let stubbornness take over because I'm not losing another sister. I got this.

I hear the jingle of keys, and we both stiffen before scrambling into position. The door opens, and Pyotr comes in, balancing a tray. Dulcie immediately doubles over with a cry, and just as I expected, he drops everything to grab her. Before he can touch her, I use everything I've got and bring the toilet tank cover down over his head, the impact a thick thunk. He drops immediately, blood pooling quickly. "Go, Dulcie!"

I grab my tools and open the door, glancing from right to left. I quickly jam my improvised spigot into one of the antifreeze barrels I first spotted outside the door. I've been stealing paperclips and other shit off of Ivans's desk for days, the idiots never checking my hands or pockets. The first night, I grabbed a handful of stuff while they were playing Rotisserie With Vivi. The spigot is on what I pray is a forty-degree angle, which leads to the north side of the building. I pop another hole leading to the wall in front of us. I glance at the clock again and see we probably only have about four more minutes. I quickly pull my sock out of my pocket and dip it in the fluid, shoving it back and stepping back into the room.

"Dulcie, what did you get?" I whisper, and she answers from behind the shield. "Ummm, a phone— a weird one, a wallet, some gum, a condom, and a set of car keys, but I don't know what kind." A treasure. "Okay, put it all in your pockets and crouch down."

"Ready."

I say a quick prayer and drag one of the matches against the homemade striker. As soon as it lights, I throw it into the trickling liquid. There is a flash, and I dive behind the makeshift barricade, the impact jarring my bones. The whoosh is instant, and the loud boom concusses the whole building. It startles me for a second before I get my wits back.

'Let's go!" I grab Dulcie's hand and pull her through the burning door. As I expected, there is a giant hole in the wall, and I yank her through it. I can hear shouts and yelling from the other side and see nothing in front of us as we run in a straight line. The shouts get louder, and I zig-zag us around the property, trying to get my bearings. I see an old metal tool shed, and we scramble behind it. I peek around the corner and see that we are in the middle of a backyard of sorts. To the left is a bunch of cars parked, and to the right is woods — and not lovely, but dark and deep.

Pass.

"Give me those keys." She gives them to me with a shaking hand, and I grab it and squeeze. "Almost gone, girl." I hold the key fob above my head and point it toward the cars. A car furthest from us flashes its lights. I look at the distance and realize we have no choice but to run for it.

"Dulcie, we have to run toward that car. We can't spend time sneaking. They are going to start looking for us soon. Can you do it?" She scoffs in the dark.

"Girl, I have four older brothers. You think I didn't learn how to run to my mama as fast as I could? Let's do this." We grab hands and break for it. I press the fob again for accuracy and then once more to unlock the doors. We make it just as a few guys spill out and start shouting and pointing at the raging fire. We freeze as they run toward us, but then suddenly angle toward the backyard we were just in. I open the passenger door, and Dulcie slams it behind her. I hurry to the car next to me, a lovely Mercedes, and jam the wet sock into its tailpipe, using my last match and touching it to the dry part. I jump into the driver's seat and stick the fob into the slot, pumping the brake and turning it on. The dashboard lights up, and the CHALLENGER logo flashes at me.

Hot damn.

I push into gear and shoot out of the lot, fishtailing and correcting, following the bumps until the road smoothes into the pavement—a ping clips near us, and another.

"Are they shooting at us?" Dulcie asks, crouching down in her seat.

"Yes, but they don't know who is driving." Thank God for mob tint. I push the gears again and see we're doing eighty. A sudden explosion comes from behind us. Bye, Mr. Mercedes.

"Can you see any signs? I have no idea where we are." She leans forward, looking up. "I can't see anything. It's pitch black."

I nod and see a split in the road, deciding on the right at the last minute. "I've got to get some distance between us. The car explosion should've bought us a little more time. Keep looking behind us and see if you see anyone." The road twists and turns, and I try to control the car; its power is a bit much. I'll never tell Free that, though. "Let's see that phone." She pulls it out and flips it open, pushing the buttons. "It won't let me dial out."

"Let me see." She holds it up to my peripheral, and I grimace. "It's a StarBreak. Okay, I need you to listen to me carefully. Type in these numbers exactly as I tell you. Zero, zero, one, one, seven, zero," I rattle off the code slowly, taking another sharp turn, seeing a sign for a highway with a thirty-mile marker. "Hit the star key and then these numbers." I continue toward the road, glancing in the rearview every so often. "Now the hashtag sign and then this." My hands are still shaking, and a slow pain starts stabbing me in the forehead. From the sweat I'm pouring, I know that the infection I've been hiding is making itself known, but I say nothing to Dulcie.

"It's unlocked!" She squeals, bouncing in her seat.

"Great. Now who's phone number do you know by heart?"

CHAPTER 64

DEVIN

My Bluetooth dings in my ear, and the drive-assist tells me it's from a 'maybe spam' number. Fucking spam calls. The number calls again, and I send it to voicemail out of aggravation. My patience, the trait everyone says is my best, is gone. My worry and fury have stamped it out; I can only focus on Dulcie and our baby. And though no one is saying it, each hour that slips by pushes the girls further and further away.

My phone beeps with multiple voicemails and I ask the drive assist to dial Fallen. "Yo."

"Is there any way you can filter my calls so that the spam shit stays out? I've got some stupid number hitting me up. It says, 'Maybe spam.' Probably some house warranty shit."

"I'll get on it. You holding up, okay?" He's probably gotten less sleep than the rest of us between trying to keep us all connected and looking for any information we ask him to source. I know he lives for this shit, but even he has his limits.

"No. I keep thinking about what they might be doing to

her, to them both. I can't take it, brother. It's been a long time since I've felt this kind of violence." He makes a sympathetic noise but just listens. "If we don't find them, I don't know what I will do. And Free..." I look forward at Free's back, his wild hair blowing in the wind, his back stiff and unyielding.

"I don't know what to say except, keep your head up. Those girls are soldiers." I hear him clicking away, and a phone call beeps in again. "It's the same number. Can you conference us in? And then, can you take down their network or something? This is fucking ridiculous." As far as I'm concerned, all the robocalls and bullshit can go to hell. I hear a click and then silence.

"Hey asshole, what are you trying to sell me now?"

"Devin?" I swerve off the road, pulling my bike across three lanes of traffic. The furious beeping of the outraged cars doesn't even register.

"Dulcie, baby?"

"Yes," she says, sobbing. I've always hated it when she cried. "Baby, are you okay?" My brain is on overdrive, and I see Free jump off his bike and run to me, Nox right behind him. "Honey, you are on speaker with everyone; they can all hear you, okay?"

"Okay. Hi guys." I hear Daze choke up, and I smile. "Dulcie, is Vivi with you?" I hear a murmur and watch as Free falls to his knees. "Yes, but she is driving very fast, so she can't really talk; she's got to concentrate. Wait, just let her say hi." They fumble with the phone a little, and then Free sobs at the sound of his wife.

"Hello. This is Vivi," she says with some tired humor in her voice. "I don't know where we are, but I saw a sign for Highway three fifty-five. I don't know where that is, though. Also, the phone we are on is a StarBreak— you can't trace it." I see Nox pacing on his phone, and I know he is probably on a separate line with Fallen. "Um, can you guys come pick us up from school?" I know she is probably keeping it light for Dulcie, and I swear I will never let this woman want for anything in life.

"Thief?" There is some silence, and Vivi finally answers. "Free, I'm so sorry," she sobs a little, and he shushes her quietly. "No sorrys, baby. Now we are going to meet you, okay? Keep driving, and when you get on that highway, tell us the first sign you see." She sniffles and agrees. "I need to pay attention, though; this car is a lot." I can hear the purr of an engine. "What kind of car is it?"

She snickers. "A Challenger." Free curses and then laughs. "Enjoy it while you can, girl. That pickup truck is waiting for you at home." She hands the phone back to Dulcie, and we mount up. Nox signals at us, and we follow him. "Baby, how much battery do you have left?"

"Ummm, it's at like ninety-eight percent? But Vivi did something, and we can charge it if we need to, like a hot wire or something." Of course she did. For the first time in days, I saw a smile flash across Free's face.

"Okay, we are three miles from the highways. Oh! It says Naperville, fifty miles. Do you know where that is?" I see Nox nod, and we take off, heading west. "Yes, baby. We are headed that way now."

"You are two hundred miles from them," Fallen's voice breaks in. "I'm going to destrand everyone and let Dulcie and Devin talk. That way, I can GPS everyone and not interrupt." The line beeps, and I hear quiet breathing. "Devin?"

"Yeah, baby?" I smile at the sweet sound of her voice. I feel like a thousand-pound anvil has slipped off my soul.

"Did you like my surprise?" I feel a tear burn my eye. "I loved it. And I love you. You are going to be an amazing mama." She sniffles again, and I follow Free as he hits the open highway and flies. "And you're going to marry me as soon as we get home. And I don't want to hear no lip."

"Okay." I can hear the smile in her voice. "Hey, Devin, were the fairy lights still on?"

CHAPTER 65
FREE

"There is a Super WalMart thirty miles from them. It's still open and busy. That should be enough cover just in case." Fallen tells us as Devin stays on with the girls. "You will probably make it there before them."

Vivi expressed intense worry that the car could be tracked or followed. Fallen sent them on some forward and backward routes until we were in striking distance. They had to stop once for gas, which gave her more stress because they had to use the car owner's credit card. Fallen was able to do some stuff so that the card wouldn't be charged until a few days later, giving us cover. They both sounded exhausted, but Vivi worried me because she kept dodging my requests for reassurance that she was okay.

"Cage's group is two hours behind you. Daze is five hours. I made reservations at a motel near the Wal-Mart and booked out an entire floor. Okay, twenty more miles Free." Fallen's voice keeps up a steady chatter, pushing down my nerves. I cannot settle until my wife is in my arms. "I got all the medical stuff Kaz requested being messengered over."

"Patch in Daze and Silver." I hear the beep.

"Yeah?"

"Yup?"

"Is this still Reject territory?" The last time I knew, the area around Chicago was the Stone Reject MC's land. The old President was under featly to me, but he died shortly after we went straight.

"Yeah. Jackson is the President now. You met him once, I think. Why?"

"Because if we are about to go to war on his territory, I want to make sure that he knows it's not personal. Daze, can you get in contact with his Enforcer and tell him what's going on? I'm not asking permission—it's purely a courtesy." The warning is there, and I know Daze will get it across.

"Will do."

"Five miles, Free." I signaled to Devin, who had already told me that Dulcie had fallen asleep, so he was silently keeping my wife company. Nox pulled to my left and surged ahead. Devin did the same on my right and passed Nox. I saw him swerve into a parking lot, and the store's bright lights made the pavement white.

"They will be there soon. I told them to meet you at the back of the building."

Devin is off his bike and pacing like a madman. He's muttering into the phone and walking in circles. I see head-lights barreling down the back alley, going too fast to be safe. The black Challenger turns sharply and stops short of us by about twenty feet. Devin runs toward it before it stops entirely, and the passenger door opens. Dulcie is flying to meet him, stumbling and tripping. She jumps into his arms, wrapping her legs around him. I rush to the driver's side, where the door is still closed, the engine idling. I slow down and approach with caution. The tint is too dark to see, so I breathe before pulling the door open. I blink as the pain in my heart curdles into rage.

"Vivi?" My wife's head rests on the steering wheel, her arms gripping the top. I can see the welts and burns covering every inch, the bruising hiding her beautiful skin. She is facing away from me, her breath shallow.

"Vivienne?" She jumps as if I woke her up, and I ease my arms around her and tug her toward me. Her skin is flaming hot, and she is drenched in sweat. "Nox!" I yell out and pull her quickly to me. Her head lolls back, and I wince at the sight of the bruising on her face, a circle of cigarette burns on her cheek. Her eyes are crusty, and there are even cuts on her neck —my poor, poor baby. Nox pulls up next to me and mutters curses when he sees Vivi. "She is not responding well. Call Daze and tell him the Rejects to have their medic meet me at our hotel. Call Kaz and tell him what's going on. Make sure the medic takes a look at Dulcie too." I move Vivi into the backseat. She looks so thin. "Baby, I'm going to take care of you. Just hold on for me, okay?" I lift her top and see the horror continue. There is a crisscross of black and blue on her torso and an imprint of some kind on her left breast. I pulled her pant leg up, the same pants she wore when she was taken, and saw cuts on her ankle, too.

"Sor-ee." I lean over and look into her eyes, brushing her tangled hair off her face. "We said no sorrys, remember? Baby, who did this to you?" Her eyes roll back in her head before coming back to me.

"I-van." I kiss her nose, and one side of her mouth lifts. "Koslov's guy?" She nods weakly, her hands fluttering. "Milk, not good. I counted."

"Counted what, baby?" Nox returns and slides into the driver's seat, whipping out of the lot. "I counted steps. From garage. Dulcie has them. Free?" I lean closer, bracing my hand next to her head. I can feel the heat without touching her. "Yes, sweetheart?"

"I love you. Tell Teddy I loved her too." With that, my wife passed out.

"IT'S NOT GOOD, MAN." Joe, the Rejects medic, is puffing on a cigarette outside our room. "She's got a nasty fever and a bad infection. I have an IV going into her, but she needs more than I can give her. That with the beatings and the lack of nutrients..." He shrugs. "Your own man an MD?" I nod, the acid from my stomach crawling up my throat. "Hopefully, he'll be able to do more than me. I'm just an old Army medic."

"Thank you, Joe. I'll owe you one. Do you mind sitting with her when I leave? Kaz will be here soon."

"No problem, King." He pats me on the back as I go back into the room. I stripped Vivi of all of her clothes and barely held back my howls when I got a look at her body. There was scarcely an inch of her that didn't have damage, barely an inch they didn't touch. How could this have happened in just a few days? I slipped one of the shirts from my saddlebag onto her, wiping her down with a cool washcloth. She is still unconscious, and I lift her hand, kissing every finger and her palm. Her wedding band is missing.

"Baby, I'll be back soon, alright? Kaz is coming, and he is going to make you all better. You wait for me, okay? I love you, Vivi." My voice cracks as I lean over and kiss her lips. I tuck the sheets around her and walk out the door. Joe is out there, and he nods at me as I head down to Devin and Dulcie's room. I hear bikes roar as Cage, Pallas, and Silver pull in. I signal them to meet me here as I knock on the door. Devin answers it, the grim look on his face gone. "I need to ask her some stuff, Dev."

"Come in Free. I'm still awake." Devin lets me in, and I see Dulcie sitting in bed, her wet hair in a bun. There is an empty salad bowl and a milkshake on the nightstand. "How ya doin', cricket?" The old nickname makes her smile. "How's Vivi?" I sit beside her on the bed, the hotel sheets bunching under me. "She's not great. Joe has her on antibiotics and some fluids. Can you tell me a little of what happened?"

Her eyes tear up, and she nods, her pretty face creased with sadness. "They kept us in a room the whole time, except when they would come and get Vivi. The first night we got there, they burned her with cigarettes." Her breath hitches, and Dev flies to her side and holds her hands. "They didn't feed us much, just bread and water. Vivi wouldn't let us drink the water; she always poured it out and got it from the tap. She... made me eat everything. She said the baby needed it more than she did. But she started looking wrong right away. She thought she may have had a milk fever; she was in a lot of pain. They, um, did all kinds of stuff to her: belts, knives. She'd come back time after time, and they'd done something different. The guy, Ivan, had a thing for her too." I stare at the ground, my hands laced in front of me. "Did they rape her?"

"Hey, no." She pulls my face toward hers. "They didn't, but I think they threatened her with it." I feel a sagging relief and manage to take a deep breath. "Alright, okay." I run a shaking hand down my face. "How did you all get away?"

Dulcie smiles and leans back into the pillows. "We fooled the guard that came and dropped off our food into thinking I was sick. He liked me," she makes a face, "so Vivi hit him with a toilet seat cover when he came to make sure I was okay. My job was to clean out his pockets to see what we could use. We had made a barricade for me to hide behind, and Vivi stole a whole bunch of office supplies and made some kind of rig—she used it to do something with some chemicals. She blew a hole into the wall while I hid, and we ran. The guy we hit was the one with the car and phone."

"Vivi said she'd counted steps? And that you had them?"

"Yes! She reverse-mapped our route so that you could find the way back. You can find it if you start from where we stopped and go backward by direction. We didn't have a pen, so I carved it into the dashboard with a paperclip. So, the last set of numbers is the miles and our direction. The next is the same, etc. When you get to the first set of numbers, it should be the place." Her grin is triumphant, and I chuck her under her chin. "You did good, bug. I'm proud of you." I stand up and pat Devin on the shoulder. "Free?" I turn around, her pale face sad.

"She saved me, you know, Vivi. From the moment they took us, she was doing everything she could to protect me, even when it was hard, and she was hurting." She starts crying, and I leave Devin to console her. The guys are all in the doorway except Pallas. "You heard?"

"Yeah. Pallas went down to the car. Are you ready to roll?" Cage lights up a cigarette, which I raise my eyebrows at. He hasn't smoked in years. "Yeah. I'll call Kaz on the way. Silver, I want you to stay behind and guard my wife. I'm leaving Devin here as well."

"Like hell you are. I'm going." Devin steps out of the room, closing the door behind him. "They took my woman, my pregnant woman." I shake my head. "I know they did. But she needs you more than I do right now. And I need you to back up Silver in case any shit goes down." Pallas comes bounding up the stairs with Fallen on the line.

"I gotta say, Free, your wife impresses me more and more

every day. I was able to work from her 'map' and found it. It used to be a garage years ago. Property records are a whole tangled mess, but Google Earth shows a fire still burning. If y'all take the road on top, it should take you five hours to get there."

"Saddle up."

CHAPTER 66
FREE

"How do we want to do this?" Daze asks, leaning on a tree. We stopped a few miles from the garage, grouping inside several trees. The other brothers caught up to us mid-trip, and Silver had four Princes tag along.

"I don't feel like being sneaky. I just want to roll in and kill them all," I drawl, taking a few puffs from a cigarette I stole from Nox. "I don't feel like mercy, I don't feel like strategy, I just feel like bringing them Death. Y'all alright with that?" I get the nods I'm looking for and check my weapons. Daze unclips his knives, and Pallas pumps his shotgun. Everyone else primes their weapons, and we take off.

A mile in, I can smell the fire. It has a sweet, acrid scent that creeps down your lungs and itches your throat. As we drive closer, I can hear shouts in Russian. The Rejects guy told us that they think the Russians run drugs out of this area—the garage a front. They'd been trying to get them out of their territory for years, but their numbers were too small, and the Russians were legion. We pull up the driveway and see the giant hole Vivi managed to blow on one side of the building. Several cars are burning, and a mess of men are trying to put them out. It takes them all a moment to realize that we are rolling up on them, but by the time they do, we are already off-bike with guns on 'em.

"Which one of you is Ivan?" I ask my Luger in hand. A tall white-blonde man steps out, his size rivaling my own. He's wearing a suit, even with all this mess, and I see the imprint of his gun on his waist.

"Who are you? You are not Rejects?" His eyes squint at my cut, and I see a brief flash of recognition. His hand moves slowly, and as I step closer, Pallas shoots a warning shot at his feet. I'll give the fucker credit—he doesn't even flinch.

"Not Rejects, motherfucker. Name is Free. You know me?" He pauses before nodding slowly. "I was under the impression you were out of the game, no?"

I smirk at him, just staring for a moment. The boys fanned out behind me in formation while Pallas, Riggs and a Prince search the building for stragglers. "I was. But you took something from me. And I don't like that."

"I took nothing from you." He rebalances on his feet, eyes scanning for an opening. If this were just a territory dispute or a deal gone wrong, I would've enjoyed tangling with him a bit. He looks like he'd put up a good fight. But this is about my wife. So this bitch only has a few minutes of life left.

"You took my wife."

His eyes widen, and then he smiles. "Little *kukla* was telling the truth. She warned me that her husband was not the simple farmer that I was told." He claps his hands together in ironic applause. "By you being here, I take it she survived the explosion?"

"She caused the explosion, you cunt. You kidnapped the wrong woman. She was too much for you." Pallas spits out.

Ivan nods slowly. "You know, I admired her. I've never failed so many times at killing a woman. I was sure she was dead in that parking lot, then again at her house. Such a shame I had to hurt her—but she never broke. You trained her well."

"I didn't train her at all; I got her from the factory with all the settings included. Daze?"

Daze steps up to the man closest to him and, in one clean move, slices his head off. It rolls on the ground, stopping near Ivan's snakeskin shoe. His smile never wavers as Pallas cocks his gun and shoots the next guy in the throat- the gurgle of his bloody breaths choking in the air. The Russians don't stand idle; they fight back, which causes a whoop from Nox, who takes out a guy at the knees and then shoots him in the eye. Cage has another one in a chokehold before he twitches and snaps his neck. Daze has a trio of heads gripped in his hand and flicks a blade at another, blubbering in fright. Pallas has knifed one in the heart while shooting another in the groin. My men make quick work of the rest, leaving just Ivan and I in a standoff. We never take our eyes off each other, and he never loses that grin as his men are slaughtered around him. When no one is left, when he stands alone, we surround him, guns cocked and ready.

"Your reputation is earned. Too often, it's smoke and mirrors, but I heard the Apocalypse is unbeatable. Now I see." He turns his hands up and takes a step toward me. "It's my turn, no?" He doesn't even glance at the crew we just eliminated; his lack of care is common in their world. If anyone dared sniff at one of my brothers, I would've eviscerated them. Hell, when Daze was taken, I took out sixteen men by myself. But that's a story for another time.

"It is. But first, I want to know when Koslov was supposed to collect my wife." I'd be more than happy to get rid of his ass too.

"Koslov doesn't collect anyone," he scoffs. "He is too important for that. And I had no intention of turning Vivienne over to him. I wanted to play with her myself." He smiles at me, and a dark rage streaks through me. "She intrigued me; I've never met someone so determined to defy me. All she cared about was that milk-faced girl and her baby. She would have done anything I asked to protect them," he smirks. "I was about to...enjoy my efforts when she escaped." Daze steps forward and makes a slight movement with his knife that causes a cascade of blood to pour from the back of Ivan's neck. "That girl is my sister, you bitch."

"So Koslov doesn't know she's alive?" Daze circles around and snarls at him. Ivan rolls his eyes and grins. "You are not fools. If Koslov wanted her, she would already be with him, probably in his bed. He enjoys feisty women. I had no intention of giving her up. I would've kept her for myself. For a while, anyway. The other girl, well, I had a broker lined up for her. Now, there will be an unsatisfied client. Tsk tsk."

"Daze?" I ask.

"Truth."

"How did you find out that Vivi was alive?" He shrugs. "I have people who whisper to me. I got a tip that she was hiding out down there and sent men to confirm. They met up with someone, a woman, who led them straight to her."

"Who was the woman?" He scoffs and waves his hand. "A bitch I am sure. She fucked one of my men in New York. Got turned on by the violence and thought she was important. He grew tired of her, but this information gave her new life with him. Something boring and American sounding. I do not know."

"Daze?"

"Truth again."

"Good." I pull the trigger and spray the entire clip into him.

His body jerks and shakes with the impact before falling to the ground. I continue shooting until nothing is left and then pull out my Walther and give him all of those bullets. Daze steps up and slices through him, taking off both arms and then his head. We stand there for a moment, both of us panting.

"It's done. Let's finish," Pallas pats me on the back, pulling and stacking bodies. We all help until there is a giant pyre. Cage found a gasoline can and doused the bodies, leading back to the garage. Nox throws his lighter into the pile, and we watch as the flames ignite.

"Let's go home now. Vivi needs her husband." Pallas steps in my line of sight, shaking me from my trance. "Time to put the King back to sleep."

CHAPTER 67

VIVI

Seriously, I am tired of this smell.

It's what's making me swim toward the light, that horrible, antiseptic scent mixed with food and plastic. There's a new smell added. It reminds me of Carnage for some reason. I hate it. And if I'm smelling it, that means I'm in trouble. Again.

"No more trouble, Thief. I promise."

Ohhhh. That voice—sexy, deep, and raspy, with thorns and velvet—I want him to keep talking to me. About anything. Read me the back of a soup can.

"A soup can?" the voice chuckles, sending shivers up my legs. I don't feel pain per se, more of a deep, dark ache, as if I'd been thrown off of a bridge—and bounced—several times.

"Time to wake up, baby. We've got things to do. And Teddy misses her mama." Teddy? A dream of a chubby, bouncy baby with dark curls and dimples. I love her so much.

"Gah! Bwwaahhhhh gah!" My eyes fly open, and I turn my head to the side. A string of drool hits my cheek, and then a wet mouth with slobber starts chewing on me. "Gah!" My hand comes up, and I pat my daughter on her diaper-covered rump. "Hey, stinky." She pulls back and grins at me, her one bottom tooth gleaming. "Where did that come from?"

"It popped up overnight. The second one is on its way, too." I shift and see that Teddy is balanced on his lap and leaning over me. His dark eyes look tired, circles underneath. His normal amount of scruff is tripled, but his smile is wide and bright.

"You look like butt."

He laughs, a glamorous sound, gleaming white teeth, and a flash of his tongue ring. "Baby, I have never felt better, now that you are awake, I've been missing you." He rubs his hand across my forehead and into my hair. "Don't ever do that to me again." He picks Teddy up, who is chewing on her fingers, and bounces her on his knee. "We need you here."

I push up until I sit, letting a brief moment of dizziness pass. "How long have I been out?" I reach for the baby, and he hands her over, a giant grin on her face. Free hands her a pink rubber horse, and she grabs it, gnawing on it like it's a juicy bone.

"You've been out a week. Part of it Kaz put you in to help you heal. The rest was you on your own. You had an infection, likely from the sudden stop of your breastfeeding. Plus, your body needed a timeout with all of your other injuries." I kiss the back of Teddy's messy head and lift my arm. I catalog all of the healing cuts, burns, and bruises and see some sort of salve smeared all over me. I take a whiff and gag. "Ew, what is that?"

"It's the arnica cream we use on the horses," Free's voice trembles with laughter. "Don't wipe it off; it's been working great. Kaz thinks you will have minimal to no scarring." I make a face and snatch Teddy's hand when she goes to touch it. "No, baby. Nasty."

"Where is everyone?" I half expect to see a barrage of

company, but it's just the three of us in our bedroom. I see that Teddy's crib has been pushed in here, along with her paraphernalia.

"They are giving us some space. Plus, I haven't been able to let the two of you out of my sight. Vivi, I don't think I have ever been that afraid. I woke up after one of the best days of my life, into the biggest nightmare of my life. My daughter was hysterical, and the love of my life was gone. We had almost no leads and no way to find you. I felt my life force slipping away, and the darkness was taking over. I had no reason to live, no reason to be human. It was like an animal was taking over, just instinct and rage. When I heard your voice over that phone, I almost died—the relief tripped my heart like a shock. I knew it before but knew it even more right then. I love you more than anything in this world. I can't live without you—you are the muscles that make my heart work. You have given me the life I never imagined and can never give up." His breath is coming out harsh, and I can feel tears in my throat.

"The day you showed up, I felt so many things—anger, annoyance, pride, and love—an instant love. For your courage, your will to live, your fearlessness. I stayed away and tried to distract myself, but nothing worked. All I wanted was you. I didn't take a full breath until the day we got married. My wife. My love. The Thief of my heart. Speaking of," he pulls at his pocket and produces my wedding band.

"How?" That is all I can ask as he slips it on my finger. Teddy abandons her horse and grabs his hand, chewing on that instead. He holds up a matching diamond, the giant rock glittering in the light. He places it over my band, and I tear up.

"Let's just say the boys and I had an extermination party." He kisses the baby as she babbles, flirting in response.

A tingle of fear dances in my head. "Ivan?"

"Gone. All of 'em. He never even told his boss he had you,

baby. You're free." He stands up and lies beside me, Teddy between us. "I'm sorry, baby, I didn't protect you better." His liquid eyes meet mine, and I see a sheen of tears.

"Free.." I rub my hand across his beautiful face and cup his cheek. "You did everything you could. There were just things that we couldn't control. The important thing is that I'm here, with you and our baby, in our home. And I want to be. I finally have what I never knew I needed— a family that accepts me, the love of a man who wants me, and a whole place of my own. No hiding, no secrets. I get to be...me. And I owe that all to you. Now kiss me." I lean forward, and he takes my mouth gently, rubbing his lips against mine, his tongue stroking mine with love. We only stop when the baby screeches from being left out and Free laughs, smacking her little cherry lips, too.

"Is Dulcie okay?"

Free snorts. "Yes. She and Devin got married the day they came home. Her mother was waiting at their house, and Devin got an earful. She's still there, and poor Dev is hiding in the stables. They are talking about knocking down walls and all kinds of stuff. Dulcie won't decide without you, so we need to get you nice and healthy quickly."

I'm silent as I watch him play with the baby. "So it's over?" He looks at me softly.

"Yeah, baby. We still need to make sure of a few things, but you will never be hurt again. I swear to you." I smile at him, my love for him washing over me like a gentle wave. For a brief second, I smell lilacs, Riley's favorite scent. I swallow hard, knowing that my girl is watching over me, happy that I found my place, and hopefully not peeking when my husband is naked.

"Free?"

"Yeah, Thief?"

"Do we have any pizza?"

EPILOGUE- FREE

"So if Phineas thinks it's okay to show some of my work, will that be alright with you?" Vivi's blue eyes shine, and I lean over and kiss her lips softly. We've been going back and forth for a few months about whether her trying to step back into her old life would be a good idea or not. With the Koslov threat a non-issue, it might be easy. But I also worry that the spectacle of her returning from the dead would be too much attention. We came up with a compromise—she would slowly start pushing some of her artwork back out into the world, and Phineas would keep her secret. Maybe a few years down the road, once Koslov is dead or locked up, we can visit her family.

"Of course, baby. I know how happy that makes you. We both win—I get my woman satisfied, and Phineas gets to line his pockets." Vivi cracks up, and I smile at the sound. She told me her agent is a tiny guy— no more than five foot five. I've seen his picture, and he looks about as harmless as a puppy. But what he lacks in height, he makes up in balls—he's a fucking barracuda when it comes to my wife and her commissions. "That sounds about right. Oh! Dulcie sent us some pictures." She leans closer and clicks on the text link from Dulcie. My daughter's chubby face appears on the screen, and I laugh. She sits on Pallas's lap, drooling a huge puddle onto his leg. She's got one fat fist gripping Nox's braid, seated on the floor next to them. The following few are of her getting loved by all of my brothers, with the last being her asleep on top of a blanket, near Carnage's stall.

"I miss her already," she says, her soft lips parting in a grin. "I bet none of y'all ever thought you'd be at the mercy of chubby midget." I shake my head in an answering smirk, but not before I lean in and lick at the seam of her mouth. "Definitely not. But I wouldn't change a thing. Every bad decision I ever made, every atrocity I committed, everything I ever conquered led me to the fucking happiness of my life. You were out there waiting for me to find you." I kiss her again, the smile lighting her face, tightening my chest. I kiss her again and then lean back on the couch. Her agent wanted Vivi to come to Seattle to meet him, but I shot that shit down quickly. They went back and forth and then settled on San Francisco. There were many conventions at the hotel, one of which Vivi wanted to sneak into. This is the first time I've ever been to anything like this; my head is on a swivel.

"What time are you meeting, Phineas?" I tug on her long braid, smoothing my hand down her face.

"In about three minutes. I better get a move on. You sure you don't want to come with me?" She pouts, and I can't help but kiss her again. "Hell no. I'm going to check out the auto show thing on the first floor."

She rolls her eyes and stands up, slinging her portfolio backpack onto her shoulder. "It's just as well. I know my agent, and he would spend the whole time drooling over you. We'd get nothing done." She makes a face, and I smirk. "Don't be jealous, Little Thief." She cracks up, and then a weird look crosses her face. She stares hard at something just over my shoulder, and I turn. "What is it?" She's still looking, a frown knotting her brows. "Vivi?

She physically shakes it off and smiles wanly. "You know that feeling, *deja vu*? It's French for 'already dreamed?' I just had that. I thought I saw someone I knew..." She shrugs, but the frown is still there. "You sure? Maybe I should come with you after all." I stand up and pull her to me. She plucks me in the chest and shakes her head.

"Nope. You are my out-clause. Phineas will have me hemmed up for hours if I let him. He will let me go if I tell him that you are waiting for me. Kiss me, now." She stands on her tiptoes and purses those pink lips. Her eyes close, and I press my mouth to hers, fighting the urge to make it deep, so deep that she feels me in her core. I linger before nibbling on that chin and nipping my way to her ear. She giggles and then skips backward. "Remember to text me in exactly one hour. And don't be surprised if Phineas follows me out—he wants to meet you."

"One hour?"

"Yup. Gotta go. Love you." Her excitement is the sun.

"Not near as much as I love you." She blows me one last kiss as she hurries down the escalator.

I catch it—don't judge me, dammit.

"I'm seriously considering it," I tell Daze, flipping my phone camera around so he can see the deep blue Hellcat on display. "Vivi has been wanting one for a while."

"Brother, I hate to tell you this, but your wife cannot drive that. She is a terror on the road. And is that a stick shift? She'll

break that car, Free. You're crazy. Get her a minivan. Trust me."
I grimace and try to picture my tiny wife toting our kid and
some scrap metal in a minivan. "Maybe an SUV, then. What
time is it? Fuck." I'm about fifteen minutes late texting the SOS
to Vivi. "Talk later." I click off and take the elevator to the fifth
floor where the restaurant Vivi is meeting Phineas.

> Hello. This is your husband. I need you.

There is an arrangement of chairs in front of the restaurant,
and I sit on one facing the entrance. The place looks fancy. I
catch the stares I'm getting. I don't think my black jeans and
tattoos would have matched the dress code.

> Time to wrap it up, baby. I know I'm late.

I wonder how Vivi would feel if I told her I wanted another
kid. Hell, I'd like several more. I know she got on the pill, but I
think I may need to toss those when we get home.

> Vivi, if I have to come in there and get you…

I frown when I realize she hasn't responded. A small cold
fission of worry starts to worm across my shoulders. I tap my
leg, an internal debate raging. I don't want to embarrass her,
but I also don't like that she hasn't answered my messages.
Fuck it.
I start toward the maitre'd when I see a man who looks like
Phineas hurrying out the entrance. I step in his path, and he
jumps, staring at me.
"Phineas? I'm Free. Where is my wife?" His eyes widen, and
he looks me up and down a few times, gulping. "I don't know. I
got an email from her telling me that she was canceling our

meeting. I've been waiting over an hour." I grab his arm and drag him down a corridor.

"What the fuck are you talking about? She left me to meet you. What email?" I shake him, and he squeaks in terror. "Here! Look!" My heart is pounding as I snatch his phone.

"Hey Phin! Sorry it's so late, but I have to cancel our meeting. Something came up. Love Vivi." I click the link where her name is and see it's from her direct email. It was sent about three minutes after she went down the escalator. I blink a few times, my brain on the hunt.

"Are you staying here in the hotel?" When he nods, I drag him toward the elevator bank. "Go to your room and don't move from there unless I tell you to, understand? Don't make me have to find you, Phineas." The doors open, and I throw him in it. "Stay put"

I'm motionless for a full minute. I pull up the Finder app and click on my wife's name. "Unavailable" flashes on the screen, taunting me with its warning. I call her phone, and it goes automatically to voicemail. I push for the elevator and take it to our floor. Other people are in the car with me, but I see nothing. The door opens, and I hurry to our room, carding it open to silence. "Vivi?" Everything is exactly like we left it. The bed is a rumpled mess from where I made love to her up until the minute we had to go. Her brush and perfume are on the dresser. I check the bathroom, and it's clear. I open all the closets and even the drawers. I call her phone again and again. I leave again, taking one last glance behind me. I push for the elevator and tap my phone.

"Daze. Someone took my wife. Again."

"The security chief used to be MC. He's pulling up the videos as we speak," Cage tells me while I pace. "There are over one hundred, so it's going to take him a minute," I say nothing, scrubbing my hands through my hair. He, Pallas, Daze, and Fallen grabbed the first plane to San Francisco and arrived late last night. Nox and Devin stayed behind with Teddy in case this was a coordinated attack. Silver and his men are on the way, riding in from Kansas. I spent the whole night walking every inch of this hotel, every staircase, every room. When my brothers arrived, they walked again with me, except for Fallen, who had been trying to see if Vivi had left any other trace. The first thing he checked for was her ring—which pinged out in the middle of the hotel. Fallen told me about the president of a war-torn country that got one for his wife. When she was kidnapped by insurgents, they used the chip in her ring to locate her. I got one for Vivi immediately. When we tracked it- we found it in the trash of a ladies' room. The cold that had been creeping was now encasing me in a block of ice. I feel nothing but freezing blackness.

"I'm going to go check in with him," Cage mumbles. He leaves, and Daze comes over to me, halting my gait. "What's in your head, brother?" I look at him, but I don't see him.

"So much and nothing at the same time." I can't explain the feeling of emptiness, the sheer terror, and the dark, dark anger that is twining around my heart. It's too much. "I think... I think I'm about to burn the world down." He nods and claps a hand on my shoulder. A quick knock on the door before it opens, and Pallas steps inside. He stands in the doorway, a grim look on his face.

"Free; I think there is someone you need to meet." He moves out of the way, and I see a tall man standing there, his face carved from stone yet etched in grief. His hands are pretzeled into fists, and an arctic blast seeps from his brown eyes. It's like looking at a mirror you wish you could shatter.

"Who the fuck are you?"

YEAH I KNOW

So. Many. Questions. And you are probably mad at me too.

Who took Vivi? Who is the man at the end? Who was it that gave Vivi deja vu? What happened to Pallas' family? Why did the GOTA disband? What happened when Daze got kidnapped?

HOW DOES THIS CONNECT TO CASSIDY?? (If you haven't read Books 1 & 2, this is where you need to catch up.)

Evil laughter Well, that's where Book 4 comes in! "Theirs To Fight For" is where every one of your questions gets answered and where you will FINALLY be satisfied. Trust me—it's worth the wait.

Turn the page for the exclusive blurb. I can't wait for you guys to read it.

If you haven't read Books 1 &2, <u>DO NOT READ THE BLURB! HUGE SPOILERS AHEAD!</u>

Until next time.

JM

NOTE

The story that Vivi tells Trace about the photographer and the woman who is driving the convertible is 100% true. How sweet is that???

...and maybe, just maybe, there REALLY is a BYOB strip club in the middle of a cornfield...

SNEAK PEEK— THEIRS TO FIGHT FOR- THE POSSESSION SERIES BOOK 4

STOP RIGHT NOW!!! IF YOU HAVEN'T READ THE FIRST TWO BOOKS, YOU WILL HATE ME FOR THIS SPOILER! PROCEED WITH CAUTION OR READ THE OTHER TWO AND THEN COME BACK! DON'T SAY I DIDN'T WARN YOU!!!

.... OK I TRIED!

Turn the page and be spoiled!

YOU WERE WARNED

Two women abducted in a stunning act of cold revenge. And two men who will risk it all to rescue them...

Ayden

I've clawed my way back from the unknown to reclaim the love that belongs to me; we've rebuilt a family out of the ashes of my lost memories. Now she's gone, and I will stop at nothing to find her, even if it means my life...

Free

I've danced my way through darkness and danger until an angel landed at my feet. I will destroy anyone and anything that keeps her from me, even if it means going back to the evil that once dominated my soul...

Worlds collide when one of the most powerful men in Europe teams up with the King of the MC's in America, both willing to do whatever it takes to save the women they love.

Hell hath no fury like a man whose wife has been stolen...

Ok guys, here it is! The book you have all been waiting for! You'll finally see where it all connects. Hang on for this ride— It's wild!

THANK YOU!

If you are a new reader of mine, thank you so much for reading my stories. You could've been knitting a sweater, writing a law brief, cooking mashed potatoes, doing surgery or scrubbing the grout, so using your precious time to spend with me is a blessing. If you have two more minutes to spare, please consider leaving a review. They mean more than you can imagine.

If you have been along for the ride since #nickandkenna, know that I love and appreciate you. More goodness is right around the corner, and of course, our faves will make an appearance soon.

Love and Jordans,
   JM

SNEAK PEEK- HIS TO BELONG TO—THE POSSESSION SERIES BOOK I

For those of you reading in a different order—xxoo

The Surrey-Mark Hotel is famous for three things.

One- the opulent appointments of its guest rooms and private clubs. Situated in a hidden nook in the heart of Knightsbridge, the Nash-inspired architecture highlights the ultra-luxe decor, marked by pristine antiques, lush textiles, and warm lighting. Each of its fifty-five suites is filled daily with fresh flowers (personally chosen by each guest), beds made with the highest thread count available, and stocked with the rarest wine and spirits. The top three floors are a combination of privately owned lofts and leased apartments occupied by everything from a tech billionaire to a Middle-Eastern prince.

The second, is the Surrey's stringent promise of absolute discretion. Employees are put through rigorous background checks, social media monitoring, and several non-disclosure agreements. So important is this vow of prudence that some workers don't even tell their families where they work. Guests can be assured that all of their deeds (good and bad) will be studiously ignored, making the hotel a favorite of visiting diplomats and the Hollywood elite.

Lastly is the 'Campus'—a clubby bar with high-backed leather booths and a selective clientele. Billion-dollar deals and noble marriages have been arranged inside of its walls; it's not unusual to hear plans for ending wars or the next electric car being spoken of in hushed tones. It's not a place for the newbie: the Steward closely guards the entrance to the Campus- a position gained only by heredity or decree. In the two-hundred and thirty-five-year history of the hotel, only four families: The Soames, The Westons, The Mayerlys, and the Thackers have held that role- a source of pride and distinction. The current Steward- A Soames/Thacker offspring- is a veritable lion with his entree cocktail- simultaneously rejecting and granting admittance with a ruthless relish.

So you can understand my utter confusion when I overhear the absolute bullshit coming from the two knobs sitting behind me. I'm in the process of nursing my fifty-year scotch and debating on taking home the hot little blonde who's been eye-fucking me the last hour, but I keep getting sidetracked by their nonsense. I've been halfway listening to these two idiots blathering about this and that for the past hour- and I'm tempted to have the Steward kick them straight to the street. I managed to block out most of what they were saying until I unwittingly tuned back in.

"It's her. I would know those lips anywhere," Arsehole Number One says excitedly. He has a flat American accent, along with a sickening tendency to form foamy spitballs at the corner of his mouth. The first time I turned around, he had two large ones sponging his lips together.

"No way, dude. She's supposed to be what-five-ten or eleven? She's a supermodel for chrissakes. This chick is nowhere near that tall," Arsehole Number Two replies. "Plus, what would she be doing here? Chicks like that are like on the Riviera or Ibiza—not in an old ass hotel in London."

Alright, first, he mispronounced Ibiza (as most Americans do), and second, did he call the Surrey-Mark an 'old-ass hotel'? I glance/glare over my shoulder again, but they are both oblivious. Their attention is focused squarely on a booth to the left of all of us. I crane my neck to see who they are talking about, but all I see is the very top of a dark head of hair.

"I'm telling you she is the most beautiful woman I have ever seen. I'm about to go over there and ask for her autograph," Spitty is practically bouncing off of his stool. His top-shelf whiskey sloshing all over the tabletop, and the spitballs have returned. I can feel my top lip curling involuntarily as I take in his ill-fitting suit and sweat-stuck hair. The two fingers that are clutching his rock glass are stubbed with dirty fingernails, and ink stains his palm. His partner is no better, with a shiny bald head and smarmy smirk glued to his face.

"You're drunk, bro. That ain't Melina M, and that chick is nowhere near as hot. Hey, maybe she's an escort? I read an article about how hookers in Europe post up in tony places like this and look for rich men. That whole nerdy thing she has going on is probably just a front. Listen, how much cash do you have on you?" He pulls a pitiful stack of notes mixed with American dollars, and his friend does the same. They whisper loudly, predicting what kind of service their money can buy, while the object of their focus remains blissfully ignorant of the hell about to be unleashed upon her.

I take the last sip of my scotch and sigh deeply. There's no way I can let this poor girl be subject to these two twats. I throw a few fifty-pound notes down and slide out of my chair. I know Melina M personally— she runs in the same fast circles that I do. There's no way she would be caught dead in Campus. It's too quiet, too cerebral for her. She prefers the flashy lights and stormy scenery in Chelsea, *Mahiki* in Mayfair, or Notting Hill. Areshole Number Two is partially correct, at least.

I slip past them to the right and make my way in a full circle, passing acquaintances and the hot blonde who I'm still taking with me. I give her a quick wink and a nod, and she squeals something to her friend. I'll remember to have her repeat that sound when I'm stroking into her later.

Not-Melina's booth is curved into a corner, almost facing the wall. As I round the curved seat, I see that her tousled dark head is bent over a laptop and that she is simultaneously typing and making notes on a ratty pad of paper. She's all dressed in black and utterly unaware of the fact that someone is standing in front of her. I clear my throat loudly and wait.

Nothing.

I clear it again and knock lightly on the table.

Still nothing.

I lean over and see that she has headphones in her ears and can faintly hear the steady beat of a dance track. Her fingers are flying over the keyboard, and she whips a calculator out of nowhere, punching in numbers at a record pace. An accountant, perhaps? A student? I move closer to get a look at the writing on the pad, jostling the table a bit, and her head shoots up in surprise. Her eyes lock onto mine, and her mouth forms a soft "O" in shock.

Fuck me standing. She's gorgeous.

I can see where the resemblance to Melina is causing spasms in the bloke at the bar. Melina is famous for her abundant pout and brilliant blue eyes. I can't tell the exact color behind her thick glasses, but her pillowy and wide lips are the stuff of dreams. Her skin is like heavy cream, and even with the dim light, I can see a flush creep up her cheeks. Her thick dark hair is full of curls and bumps, spilling in wild abandon around her shoulders. I know I'm staring like a fool and mentally shake myself out of my inspection. I glance up and see the Twin Terrors about to make their way to her table.

"I don't have time to explain, but trust me, just follow my lead," I hurry and slide in close to her, draping my arm around her shoulders. She fits perfectly under my arm, and I feel her stiffen. Leaning in, I place my lips close to her lobe. The scent of her- heady vanilla mixed with fresh lavender tickles my nose. "There are two men who are headed this way- and trust me; you do not want to face them alone." Her breath quickens, and she nods once. I keep my face buried in her fragrant hair as she quickly flips over her papers and shuts her laptop. She turns her body toward mine slightly and curls into me.

"Excuse me, are you Melina M?" Arsehole One asks without preamble. His friend is standing slightly behind him, that smarmy expression creasing his mouth. His eyes flit over us and lock onto me. He takes in my tailored suit and zeroes in on my Rolex Daytona watch. His mouth opens slightly, and he takes a little step back. Smart man.

The vision in my arms turns her head slightly and gives the duo a hard look. "Excuse me?" Her voice is a bit raspy but sweet. The biggest surprise- she's American.

"I said, are you Melina M? Ya know, the model. Are you her?" Spitty's voice is grating and loud, and sure enough, a round spector of saliva is growing at the corner of his mouth. I can see her eyes zoom in on it and feel her spine stiffen in disgust.

"No. I'm not." She turns back into my chest with a huff, but the two won't leave.

"Are you sure? I mean, you look just like her," the fool rambles while whipping out an outdated cell phone with a cracked screen, "See?" He shoves the phone close to her face, and I feel a growl crawl up my throat. The blurry picture is one of Melina —and yes, the resemblance is uncanny, but this sod is pissing me off with his rudeness. He's pushing himself into what I consider her personal space, and any minute he's going to be touching her. Fuck this.

"She said no, mate. I suggest you leave before I have you removed, or I will do it myself." I grit out the last bit and lift my hand in a slight gesture. I see the Steward quickly take in the scene and lift his antique phone. After a few words, he nods at me, and I turn my eyes back to the soon-to-be-departed. "That wasn't a request. She's not who you think she is. Now kindly leave." I lock eyes with his friend, and my threat is clear—I'm not one to be messed with. My eyes flit over his shoulder, and I watch as two hulking yet discreet security post themselves at the entrance. All I need to do is lift an eyebrow, and they will be tossed onto the street.

"C'mon Sid. It's not her like I said." Arsehole Two pulls at his friend's arm and whispers something low. Spitty sniffs nastily and shoves his phone back into his pocket. "Nah, you're not her. My bad." His wet lip curls up, and they turn to amble drunkenly toward the exit. The two guards follow them at a distance while I once again meet eyes with the Steward. With a quirk of my mouth, I ensure they will never be allowed back.

"Thank you."

The angel in my arms has pulled back from my tight embrace, peering up at me through her glasses. A thick strand of her hair has fallen over her cheek, and I unconsciously tuck it behind her ear. I take in her unbelievable features from a smooth fore-head, down her slim, straight nose locking onto that mouth. Her lips are upturned with a dark pink color, a slight indent in the middle of the lower one. They look like cotton candy and wet dreams. I can already picture them wrapped around my cock, and it twitches hard with the mental image.

"Are you ok?"

Her rough little voice is puzzled as I shake myself and realize that I've not only been twirling her hair around my finger, but I've also been staring at her from a very short distance. I probably look like a complete lunatic.

"I'm fine, love. How are you? They didn't frighten you too much, did they?" I find that I don't like the idea of her being upset. At all.

She snorts, rather undaintily, and waves a slim hand. Her baggy black jumper slides around, and I see a tattoo of something on the inside of her wrist. "Nope. Guys like that are a dime a dozen back home. Just your normal dudebros. How did you know they were going to come over here?" Her glasses slide a bit down her nose, and she shoves them back up.

"I was sitting at the bar and overheard them. Do you often get mistaken for Melina?" I can't believe that this is the first time. Though we are seated, I can tell that my new friend isn't very tall compared to Melina's stature, but that face... The resemblance is unreal.

She shakes her head, and her glasses slide down again. I reach out and slide them up myself. Her breath catches, and she clears her throat. "I don't even know who that is, so no."

"She's a model—a rather famous one. We have mutual friends, so I can assure you that yes, you do look alike. I'm amazed that this is the first time someone has mistaken you."

Her mouth is slightly open, and her eyes widen. "A model? Me?" A giggle bursts from her lips, and I watch as twin deep dimples pop out of her cheeks. Sweet fuck. This woman is lethal. She needs to put those away before she hurts someone.

"I can barely walk across a room without tripping, let alone down a catwalk. Agh! I'm only five foot two. How can I be a model?" Her laughter is infectious, and I find myself chuckling along. "Well, you are outrageously beautiful. It's not that hard to imagine." I reach out and gently trace one of her dimples with my pinkie. Her smile widens, and her blush is delicious. "Bifid zygomaticus," she blurts out, and I blink. "What?"

"Um, bifid zygomaticus. Dimples. A non-dominant genetic trait." She points at her face; I laugh quietly. "I see. Well, I rather fancy your bifid...things. They only make you more gorgeous."

"I don't know about all of that, but thank you." Her head dips, and she fiddles with the frame of her glasses. Talking about her looks makes her nervous. Interesting. I find that once you start complimenting a woman, she either preens or pretends modesty while transparently seeking more praise. But this quirky little bundle of beauty is genuinely embarrassed. I lift her chin with two of my fingers and meet her gaze. I wish the lighting was better so that I tell the exact color of her eyes; I want to see if they change with desire and pleasure. And I want to be the one to cause it.

"You don't have to thank me for stating the obvious, love." Her lips part and I can feel the little puff of her breath against my mouth. My tongue makes a brief appearance in response, and her breathing quickens. I slide the hand that is propping up her chin down her silky throat and around to the back of her neck. Her thick hair curls around my fingers and I tilt her head intending to devour her.

That is until a rather irate throat-clearing interrupts us.

We jump apart guiltily, both realizing how entwined we had been, and rather publicly. Campus is not the type of place for this level of intimacy, and I'm shocked at my behavior. I just met this woman, and I'm already trying to caveman stomp my way into her knickers.

"Hullo?" The throat clearing belongs to the blonde in the red dress that I had marked for the evening. Up close, she is more on the hard-looking side, but she would have made a suitable throwaway. Her arms are crossed her thin chest, and she is glaring at the woman sitting next to me. Any minute now, she is going to say something that I absolutely do not want her to say, so I head her off.

"Leave your direction with the Steward, sweetheart." She perks up, the anger draining away immediately. I have no doubt she knows who I am, and all she wants is reassurance that she will get her turn. "Go on now."

She bobs in some odd semblance of a curtsy and clatters off to the Stewards station. I can see her gesturing excitedly, while his genetically placid expression never changes. I turn back to the beauty in my arms, who is frowning at me. Fuck.

"Did you need to leave with her? I hope I'm not causing any problems for you?" She begins to nervously pack her computer and that ratty notebook, her face splotchy with what I can only deem as embarrassed anger. Her movements are jerky, and I can see that she is about to bolt. There is no fucking way I am letting her go anywhere.

"I don't know her at all," I tell her calmly. "I didn't buy her a drink; I didn't pay for her meal—I know nothing about her. She mistakenly thought that I was going to approach her, so I did what I thought was necessary to make her leave without causing a scene. Now, are you ready to leave?" I gesture to the coat she now has draped over her arm, and an ancient leather bag slung over her back.

She stares at me, her eyes darting over my face searching for honesty. I never lie to women, ever. I prefer my dalliances brief, true, but I am always brutal with my upfrontness—I find that it lessens the sting when I move on to the next flower. Too, my mum always says that women can sniff out a lie faster than a bloodhound.

"You mean ready to leave with you?" She puts it right out there, so I see no reason to put up any pretense. "Yes."

She blinks at my response, and I can see the wheels turning. "I...don't ...why?" She can't be serious? I was about one minute away from stripping her down in front of everyone in this place.

"Why? Because we need privacy for what I want to do to you." More honesty.

Her pupils dilate, and she gulps. "We just met like fifteen minutes ago."

"True. But I knew in the first minute that I wanted you. And if we hadn't just been interrupted, I'm quite sure everyone in here would have known it as well."

I slide out of the booth and hold my hand out to her. "Come." She stares at my hand, teeth nibbling violently on her bottom lip. She moves to stand without taking my offer, and I move closer. I tug her lip out from her teeth and ghost a kiss over the tortured mound.

"Come, love. Let's go."

I brush another kiss over her cheekbone, eyelid, and forehead. Her breath catches while she nods once. Slipping the surprisingly heavy leather bag from her shoulder, I drape it over my own while lacing her fingers with mine. We pass the Steward, who discreetly avoids eye contact, and slip through a small hallway to a private elevator. I use my left hand and press a keycard against the rosewood panel. The doors slide open, and I board while pulling her behind me. "You live here?"

"Sometimes." I touch the keycard to another console, and it lights up gently with the letter "P." I peek at her from the corner of my eye and see that she is staring at the floor- her bottom lip retaking punishment. I reach over with my free hand and slowly stroke the side of her face. Her head snaps up, and her light-colored eyes focus on mine. We stare at each other in silence, a tight rope of desire-and something else I can't name- tying us together. I barely hear the chime of the lift reaching our floor as the door opens to the spacious flat that I keep here. I flick a switch in the foyer, and the ample open space floods with light. Leading her like a small child, I drop her case onto the antique settee and turn toward her. She is standing still, arms still clutching her overcoat, body language screaming that she wants to run. Her precious face is turned away, eyes taking in the luxurious appointments before finally settling on me. Walking toward her slowly, I unbutton my jacket and reach up to remove her eyeglasses. I place them on the small table beside me and tug the coat off her arm. Cupping her face in my hands, I tilt her head back and get a first look at her eyes. They are an unimaginable blue-green, the color morphing the longer I stare. She is truly a magnificent specimen, and the lust mixed with innocence shining from her warms me rapidly.

"I don't normally do this," she blurts out. "I mean, I don't meet men and then just leave with them. Like never." Her fresh breath dances across my lips, and I can't wait any longer. Pulling her toward me, I nip first her top, then bottom lip, before slipping my tongue in between. Her plump mouth molds under mine and I twist and plunder inside of it, my hands tightening on her cheeks and pushing into her thick black hair. We kiss for long minutes before I pull back and answer her.

"You didn't need to tell me that, love. I already knew."

ALSO BY JM BLAKE

The Power Series: (*Nick and Kenna*)

Impelled

Compelled

Inflamed

Embraced

Entwined

Masen (Coming 2025)

The Possession Series

His To Belong To

Hers To Belong To

Free

Theirs To Fight For

Stande

Their Love, Best Love (Coming 2025)

The Persuasion Park Series

Most Beautiful

Most Reckless (Coming Soon)

Dear Tequila,

A New Monthly Serial

About the Author

JM Blake has a few thoughts about life:

-Wine and coffee are a must, daily
-I talk through every movie and TV show-
you have to get used to it if you want to be my friend
-Cats beat dogs, hands down
-Nerds run the world
-Nothing beats a good sex scene
-Chocolate is the food of the gods
-"The Talisman" is history's most perfect book

Chat me up:

Instagram: @authorjmblake
Twitter: @authorjmblake
BookBub: JM_Blake
Verve Romance: JM Blake
GoodReads: JM Blake
Website: www.authorjmblake.com
Facebook: @jmblakewriter
TikTok: http://bit.ly/3nKYNvh